The Last Of Their Race

By

Annie S. Swan

Double 9
BOOKS

The Last of Their Race
by Annie S. Swan

ISBN: 978-93-63055-78-0

Published by

DOUBLE 9 BOOKS

2/13-B, Ansari Road
Daryaganj, New Delhi – 110002
info@double9books.com
www.double9books.com
Tel. 011-40042856

ABOUT THE AUTHOR

Annie S. Swan, a prolific Scottish author, penned "The Last of Their Race," a poignant masterpiece that delves into themes of heritage, resilience, and the passage of time. Swan, known for her compassionate storytelling and keen observation of human nature, crafts a compelling narrative that follows the dwindling clan of the Macdonalds, the last remnants of a once-proud lineage. Set against the backdrop of the Scottish Highlands, Swan's novel intricately weaves together elements of family saga, historical fiction, and social commentary. Through vivid prose and rich character development, Swan transports readers to a bygone era, inviting them to witness the struggles and triumphs of a proud people facing the inexorable march of modernity. With meticulous attention to detail and a deep reverence for her subject matter, Swan paints a portrait of a community grappling with its past, present, and uncertain future. "The Last of Their Race" stands as a testament to Swan's literary prowess and her ability to evoke emotion, provoke thought, and leave a lasting impact on readers long after they turn the final page.

CONTENTS

CHAPTER I
THE INDIAN MAIL

Isla Mackinnon came out from the narrow doorway of the Castle of Achree, and stood for a moment on the broad step, worn by the feet of generations, while she thoughtfully drew on a pair of shabby, old leather gloves with gauntlets which came well up her slender arms. Hers were small, fine, capable hands, in which at that moment, though she knew it not, lay the whole destiny of Achree. Its very existence was to be threatened that cool, clear March day, and there was none but Isla to step into the breach.

She did not look incompetent; nay, about her there was a fine strength and courage, in her wide grey-blue eyes an undaunted spirit.

It was a spirit that had had much to try its quality in her six-and-twenty years of life, for half of which, at least, she had been the chief buttress and hope of the house of her fathers.

She looked her age, though her figure was very slender and straight. The years that had brought her womanhood had left her the heart of a child. It looked out from the clear eyes under the delicate lashes, it was in the slightly downward curves of the small sensitive mouth that had not had sufficient occasion for smiles to bring out all its sweetness.

Her hair, under the small tweed hat turned up at the brim with a pheasant's wing, was a clear brown, with here and there a touch of the sun inclining it to ruddy gold. She wore a short skirt of Harris tweed, leather-bound, and a woollen coat of her own knitting, a pair of brown brogues well fitted to her shapely feet, and under her arm she had a shepherd's crook with a whistle at the end of it.

Presently, when its clear, low call broke the stillness of the morning, three dogs came bounding from some region beyond the house, betraying a wild excitement which even her remonstrance could not keep in check.

"Down, Murdo boy, and don't nip Bruce's ear again, or back you go to the stable. Janet, you silly old woman, at your time of life you ought to have more sense. Well then, off you go!"

The big deer-hound, the fat, glossy, sable collie, and the small, wiry Aberdeen lady who rejoiced in the sober name of Janet, thus admonished, bounded before her down the drive between the laurel and the pine trees, barking joyously as was their wont.

About fifty yards from the house the carriage-way took a sharp turn, so that the next few steps hid all except the cold slate roof and the pinnacles of the little round towers which mark that particular style of architecture called the Scottish baronial.

The old Castle of Achree was considered one of the best examples of it in the country, and it certainly was picturesque, if a little "ill-convenient," as the country-folk had it. It was a large mansion of sorts, but totally unsuited to the needs of a family and almost completely devoid of all those modern conveniences which, in these days, every artisan has at his command.

It was so cut up by winding stairs and queer little passages that there was scarcely a room of decent dimensions within its walls. It was full of legend, of tragic memories, and did not even lack the ghost, a mailed and headless warrior who haunted the dungeon-room where he had been done to death.

It was whitewashed or harled, but looked sadly in need of the washer's brush. The rains of many a year had soddened and discoloured it, while, here and there, at angles specially exposed, there were green patches where the moss and lichen clung.

Yet it made a picture of indescribable beauty, not untouched with pathos, as the cradle of every great race must be, its history woven in with its very stones. People came from far and near to see it, and many artists had lingered enchanted over its picturesque detail. It stood on a small, green plateau facing south, sheltered at the back by the pine-clad hill of Creagh, which stood, like a sentinel, guarding the great moor of Creagh that stretched away in the distance till it joined the lands of Breadalbane towards Loch Tay.

With the moor of Creagh the Mackinnon property ended on that side, but it was still a goodly-sized estate, with shooting of some value, though it had been cut down to as narrow dimensions as the extravagance of some of the Mackinnons had dared to cut it. But never, never had Achree been in such dire straits as now.

When Isla left the gateway beside the little lodge and turned down the beautiful road, she lifted her head and took a long deep breath. For the morning air was good, though there was a nip of frost in it, and the red sun lay warm and kindly on the clear summit of Ben Voirlich, of which, at that point, an exquisite view could be obtained, though it was in the next few steps lost again. The ruddy glow was reflected in the clear waters of Loch Earn, and altogether the scene was one of incomparable beauty, and it was knit into the very fibre of Isla Mackinnon's being. It was her home, and the people were her own. She had known none other.

A few rare trips to London when her cousins, the richer Barras Mackinnons, had had a house for the season, with occasional visits to them at their home in one of the islands of the western seas, comprised her whole knowledge of the world outside her own glen. But beyond that she had neither asked nor desired anything else. The things she most passionately desired and prayed for--peace for Achree and decent comfort in which to live--were denied her. She lived in hope, however; but this day was to see its utter quenching, so far as any earthly intelligence could predict.

The dogs, gambolling in front, knew their destination--the Earn village; that is, if they did not meet David Bain with the post-gig on the road.

For more than a year now it had been Isla's custom to meet the postman for the purpose of intercepting any letters which it might not be wise to let her father see. In this simple act a great part of the tragedy of Achree may be apprehended. For even such innocent deception was foreign to the soul and heart of Isla Mackinnon, which was as clear and true as the waters of her own loch.

She saw the fat, white pony presently, standing before the dry-stone dyke that shut in the garden of Darrach farm-house from the road, and she quickened her steps in order that she might reach it before he started out again, and might thus save him another stop on the steep ascent. That act was natural to her, if you like; for if at any time by her thought or speech or act she could help another, then she was happy indeed.

But David of the grim face and the silent tongue had got into the gig again, and the fat pony had ambled off before she could stop him. Presently they met where a little water-course merrily crossed the gravelly road, seeking its way to the Glenogle burn.

"Good-morning, David. I hope you are quite well. You had letters for Mrs. Maclure. Surely you are earlier than usual."

"It wass only a post-cairt from her niece, Jeanie Maclure, from the school at Govan sayin' she would come for the week-end maype," answered David, as if the matter were of moment to the whole glen. "Yes--there pe lots an' lots of letters. I hope yourself an' the General are fery well this mornin'."

"Thank you, we are," said Isla as she leaned against the shaft of the old cart, stroking the fat pony's yellow eldes, her eyes a little more bright and eager than usual.

David fingered the letters with outward and visible clumsiness, but he was most careful with them, and in all the years of his service he had never made a mistake with one or failed to deliver it to its proper recipient.

"Thank you, David; this is all I want," said Isla as her fingers closed over the thick letter enclosed in its foreign envelope. "Take the rest up to Achree. My father will be waiting for them."

"Yes, Miss Isla. That I will do, and hope it will pe good news from Maister Malcolm in foreign parts, an' that he will pe fery well."

"Thank you, David. He is sure to be well," said Isla, trying to speak lightly, but her fingers were nervously closing over the letter, and into her eyes there crept a strange shadow.

She had sometimes said that she had the gift of second sight which was so common among the Mackinnons. Certainly she knew before she opened that letter, about a hundred yards lower down the road, that it contained bad news. It was too thick to be of no consequence, for her brother Malcolm was no great letterwriter when times were easy and his credit good.

She nodded good-bye to David Bain and passed on, hastening more quickly than usual past the farm-house of Darrach, though there lived one of her best and most faithful friends in the whole glen--one Elspeth Mackay married to Donald Maclure, the big crofter who was respected in the glen, from end to end of it, as a man of his word.

But Elspeth's tongue was long and her eyes were very keen, and Isla was not ready for them yet. Therefore she hastened past the gate of Darrach, not even smiling as the rich, fine smell of Elspeth's baking was borne out through the open door. Down the hill a little way she came to the old brig that crossed the Darrach burn; and there she paused, for there was no one in sight and the slope hid her from view of Elspeth's windows.

She could never afterwards recall that half-hour by the Darrach Brig without an inward shudder.

Thus did Malcolm Mackinnon, the ne'er-do-weel, write airily and lightly, telling the miserable story that well nigh broke his sister's heart:--

"DEAR ISLA,--Last time you wrote me you hoped I would have better news to send next time. I'm sorry I can't comply. I seem to have the devil's own luck here in this beastly country. In fact, I may as well say at once that it's all up with me and that I'm coming home.

"I've never been very happy in the Thirty-fifth nor got on well with old Martindale. He's a beast, if ever there was one, a regular martinet, and unless you practise the whole art of sucking up to him you may as well give up the ghost, as far as any chance of promotion or even of fair play is concerned. Of course, no Mackinnon can suck up to anybody--we've got too much beastly pride. Anyway, I haven't been able to soft-sawder Martindale enough, and I have been in his black books ever since I joined. But it's got a lot worse in the last nine months.

"When I wrote the governor last year, asking him to use his influence to get me shifted, I was quite in earnest, and if he'd done it all this row might have been prevented. We've been up country a goodish bit since I wrote last, and there again I didn't get fair play or a bit of a chance. We've had several brushes with a hostile tribe, but the other chaps got their innings every time and nothing but the dirty work was left to me. We had such a lot of beastly, unnecessary fag on our marches that most of the chaps were on the verge of mutiny; but I was the only one with the courage to speak up. Whatever garbled version of the story may get home, you may take it from me, old girl, that is the bottom truth of it. Anyhow, I've got to send in my papers--that's the long and the short of it. All the chaps, except the few that suck up to Martindale, think I've been treated most beastly badly, and unjustly besides. But of course nobody listens to a poor subaltern's defence or excuse.

"By the time you get this I shall have started for home. I'm coming by the 'Jumna,' a rotten slow boat, but I think it better for many reasons-- chiefly those of economy. I shall be pleased to see the old place again, and I hope the governor won't cut up too rough. Try and get the worst over for me before I come, because naturally I'm raw enough about the whole bally thing, and couldn't stand much more. Fact is, it's all right in a crack regiment for the chaps who have big allowances. There's only one word to fit the case of poor, hard-up beggars like me, and that one I mustn't use. Poverty opens the door to all sorts of mischief and misery that a girl who never needs any money can't begin to understand.

"I'd better make a clean breast of it while I'm at it, and you'll have time to digest it before I get home. I'm in with the money-lenders both in

London and in Calcutta. I owe about two thousand pounds, and how it's to be paid is keeping me awake at night. Of course, it's been advanced on Achree, so heaven only knows what will be the upshot. I'll have to see that old starched stick Cattanach the minute I get back so that the old man may not be worried.

"If only I had the place in my own hands I'd make things hum a bit. You know, Isla, everything has been shockingly neglected in the last five years, and a perfect horde of pensioners have been kept off the poor old place. The half of them ought to be chucked; it's nothing but pauperizing the glen from end to end. A bit more could be screwed out of the tenants, as most of them have their places dirt-cheap.

"Well, old girl, I'm beastly sorry, for you can't be expected to like this. But suspend your judgment, for really I'm not half so bad as I'm painted, and if I had only half a chance I might prove it to you. I must try and get somebody to introduce me to the Stock Exchange. That seems to be the only way of turning an honest penny nowadays. There are hundreds of military men on it.

"Don't be too downhearted over this. You are such a one for taking things seriously, and there's hardly anything in life worth worrying about, really. You have the best of it, for nobody expects anything of a girl, and she hasn't a chap's temptations.

"Good-bye, old girl. I shall see you soon, if I don't fancy on board the 'Jumna' that the easiest way out would be to drop quietly over the rail some night when nobody's looking.--Your affectionate, but down-on-his-luck,

"MALCOLM."

Just for the space of five minutes or so the world was a dark place to Isla Mackinnon. She had no mother, and for the last ten years she had borne a double burden--had experienced both a mother's anxiety and a sister's shame for the ne'er-do-weel. The history of Malcolm Mackinnon's misdeeds in the glen, and out of it, would fill a book. But such a book would not be worth the writing. Through him evil had fallen on an old and honourable house--its revenues had been scattered, its very existence threatened.

While Malcolm was stationed at home, at Colchester, at Sheerness, and at the Curragh, complaints had been many and his scrapes innumerable, and Isla had welcomed with abundant relief the news that his regiment was ordered to India. That was three years ago. And now the final blow had fallen. He had been dismissed the army, in itself a disgrace so overwhelming that Isla knew there must be some scandalous story behind.

Presently he would be home to loaf about in idleness, to harry the people, to wring her heart and the heart of the old man, in so far as he was able to comprehend. And, with it all, he would smile his wicked and alluring smile and get off scot-free. This was the first time condign punishment had been meted out to him, and he took it lightly and merely remarked that it was injustice. Everything was injustice that sought in any way to hamper the wayward impulses of Malcolm Mackinnon. It had been so from his youth up.

But what was to be done? That half-hour of anguish did its work on the face of Isla Mackinnon. It ploughed a few more lines on it and took away the last remnant of its girlish curve. She had a woman's work in front of her, and a man's combined, for the intellect of the old General was clouded now, and his bodily health frail. There was no one to act for Achree save her alone.

And she would act. Presently she threw her head up, and the pride of her race crept back to sustain her, and her eye even flashed with the swift strength of her new resolve.

The dogs, hovering wistfully about her feet, asking mutely why she lingered and cheated them out of their scamper down the hill, reminded her of the passage of time. She pulled herself together, thrust the letter into her bosom, and, grasping her stick, walked on with feet which faltered only at the first step.

She reached the village, gave her order at the little shop, inquired for a child who was sick in the house above, passed the time of day with all whom she met, and even listened patiently to a tinker's tale, told with the persuasive guile of her tribe. She felt herself a dual person that day. Never had the brain of the inner self been so active. Her swift planning was so intense as to make her head ache.

All her small commissions done, she breasted the hill again and so came to the gate of Darrach farm-house, where Elspeth Maclure was looking out for her.

Now it must be explained that Elspeth had been a nurse-girl at Achree and had had Isla in her absolute care for the first seven years of her life. Then she had married honest Donald Maclure and had flitted to the house of Darrach, whose chief recommendation, in her eyes, was that it stood straight on the main road and that, from its windows, she could see all who passed to and fro between the village and the old Castle.

The private life of its inmates was not hid from Elspeth. She, too, remembered and took anxious note of the Indian mail-day. As she came down the path, wiping the flour of her baking from her hands on the snow-white of her apron, her deep, dark eyes scanned the beloved face of her darling with all a mother's solicitude.

Elspeth was now considerably over forty--a comely, motherly woman with a clear, rosy face and abundant black hair, a model wife and mother, and the staunchest friend of Isla Mackinnon's whole life.

When she opened the little gate, she saw that Isla could not speak, and that her face was wan and dark under the eyes. She took her by the two hands and drew her towards the door of the house.

"It is pad news, whatefer, my lamb. I knew it wass comin' at twelve o'clock last night when that thrawn prute of a cock wouldna stop his crawin'. I wass for Donald gettin' up to thraw hiss ill neck, only he wouldna."

Isla did not speak, and, quite suddenly, when they got within the house, where the baby, in a queer little cage of Donald's making, was crowing in the middle of the floor, she threw herself into Elspeth'e arms and burst into a storm of weeping.

Now, this was the most terrifying thing that had ever happened in Elspeth's experience, and it seemed to presage such woe as she had not dreamed of.

For the Mackinnons were a proud and self-contained race, and to make parade of their feelings was impossible for them. It may be that they, as a family, had erred in repressing them too much. There had been but three in the family--the third being an elder sister who had married young and died in childbed. Her death was the first sorrow that had helped to take the spring out of the old man's heart. He had never, perhaps, been quite just to Isla, because he had loved his first-born best.

"There, there, my lammie! God forpid that you should cry your heart oot like that. Put there--it will do ye good! Oh, the man that invented the post hass a heap to answer for. In the old days the trouble had plown ower, whatefer, afore we got wind of it, especially when it happened in foreign parts. What is he sayin' till it the day, my dear? It is not impident curiosity that pids me ask, put I canna pear to see ye like this."

It was all spoken in a crooning voice which had the effect of soothing the overcharged heart of the girl. That outburst of natural tears was the very best thing which could have happened to her. Thus relieved, her heart quickly recovered its strength. She drew back, smiling weakly, begged to be forgiven for such an exhibition, and fumbled inside her blouse for the missive that had wrought such woe.

She smoothed it out and, for the moment, she thought to pass it over to her faithful friend, who, though no scholar, would have had no difficulty in reading that big, sprawling, crude schoolboy writing. But again the shame of it overcame the girl, and sitting down on the edge of a chair, she lifted her wet eyes to Elspeth's face and said mournfully:--

"It's the deluge, Eppie. I've always said it would come, and it is here."

"What hass happened? Pe pleased to tell it quickly, Miss Isla, for I nefer wass a good hand at waitin'."

"Malcolm has been dismissed from the Army, and he is coming home. He has sailed by now," she added, referring to the second page of the letter, "and his ship, the 'Jumna,' will arrive in about three weeks. It's a slow boat, but inside a month he'll be at Achree."

Elspeth bit her lip, and her hands worked nervously in front of her apron.

"For the good God's sake, Miss Isla, what are we to do with him here?"

"That's what I want to know. It will kill my father. He must never know that Malcolm has been sent home. He must just think that it is an ordinary leave of absence. Poor dear, it is not so hard to bamboozle him now as it once was! If he grasped the fact that Malcolm had been cashiered it would simply kill him. Now I shall be hard put to it, watching for other letters from India or from the War Office. Oh, Elspeth, I'm so tired of playing watch-dog! It's killing me. Sometimes I think I shall get up quite early one morning and go down to the little loch and just walk in, where it is all silvery with the dawn. Then everything would be over, and I should be at peace!"

"God forpid, my lamb, since ye are the one hope and salvation of Achree," said Elspeth Maclure fervently.

Isla shook her head.

"There is little hope for Achree now, and, so far as I can see, nothing can save it. My brother owes so much money, that, to get him clear, we ought to sell it. It is what he will do himself, without doubt, whenever he gets it into his own hands."

Elspeth Maclure stood, thunderstruck and horrified, staring vaguely in front of her.

"Sell Achree what hass peen the place of the Mackinnons for efer and efer!" she repeated slowly. "God forpid. He would nefer let it come to pass. Oh, Miss Isla, the laws made py men are not good laws. I'm only a plain woman, put this I see that, when a man iss like what Maister Malcolm iss, without the fear of God or man in hiss heart, he should not haf the power. I suppose he hass porrowed the money on the place, put it iss not him that will haf to pey," she added fiercely.

"No," repeated Isla, with a hard, far-away look on her face, "it is not he who will have to pay."

CHAPTER II
THE OLD HOME

Isla rose to her feet, and, suddenly, observing the baby clutching with his chubby hands at the side of his cage and smiling engagingly into her face, she stretched out her hands to him.

"Oh, you darling! Did Isla forget him, then? What a shame!"

She lifted him out, and his small chubby hands met tightly round her neck, and his cheek was laid against hers with a coo of delight. Elspeth stood smiling by, thinking of the wonder and gift of the child that can charm grief away.

"If only you had a good man of your own, Miss Isla, and a heap of little pairns, like me, things would pe easier," she said quaintly. "It's not for me to say, put I whiles think that if there had peen ither laddies in Achree, Maister Malcolm wouldna haf had it all his own wey, which would haf peen a good thing for him."

"Yes, Elspeth, what you say is true; but I shall never have a man or any little bairns," she said with a sigh. "My life-work is cut out plainly enough--and has been from the beginning. I have to save Achree somehow--and I will."

"That would be a fery good thing, no doubt, put the ither would pe petter, my lamb," said Elspeth with such yearning in her eyes that Isla, feeling her composure shaking again, hastily kissed the child and put him back in his little enclosure.

"Donald must positively patent this, Eppie--he would make money by it. It's the cleverest thing I've ever seen," she said lightly.

"It does the turn, and I'm not sayin' put that Donald is clever--clever with hiss hands. It makes up for the gift of the gab which he hass not got. I never saw a man speak less. I whiles ask him if his tongue pe not tired with too little wark."

"Ah, but his heart is of gold, Eppie. Don't you ever miscall Donald to me, for I won't listen."

"Wha's misca'in him, whatefer?" asked Elspeth with a small laugh which hid a tear. "Good-bye, Miss Isla, my ponnie dear, and may the good God go wi' ye and help ye ower this steep pit of the road."

Isla nodded and sped away, not daring to trust herself to further speech.

Left alone, Eppie Maclure sat down and incontinently began to cry. She came from one of the islands of the western seas, owned by kinsfolk of the Achree Mackinnons, and her heart was as soft as her speech, which had the roll of the western seas in its tone.

There were no tears in Isla's eyes as she breasted the hill bravely, brain and heart so busy that the good mile seemed but a stone's throw. It was half-past twelve when she stopped at the low doorway of the house, and with a wave of the hand dismissed the dogs, who went off with hanging heads, as if they were conscious of having missed something in their walk. They knew--for there are few people wiser than the dumb creatures that love us--that, though the body of their mistress had accompanied them down the familiar way, her heart was clean away from them and from all the little homely happenings that can make a country walk so pleasant.

She lifted the sneck softly and went in, closing the door behind her. It was rather a wide low hall, with a flagged stone floor washed as clean as hands and soft rain water could make it. A few deer-skins were scattered on it, some of them rather worn and bare, as it was a long time since a Mackinnon had stalked a deer in the forest of Achree. Some fine antlered heads stood out upon the wall between the stout wooden beams that supported it and were now black with age and shining with the peatreek. A fire of peat was burning now in the wide fireplace, in which there was no grate. On the oak mantelpiece there were queer, carved wooden pots, full of stag's moss and heather that had lost its bloom.

It was a bare, cold place, with very little beauty to arrest the eye, yet it had a dignity difficult to explain or to describe. The stair went up, wide and steep, from one end of the hall for a few steps, and then it became a winding one leading to all sorts of nooks and crannies having small and unexpected landings, with doors opening abruptly off them--a bewildering house, and very "ill-convenient" to quote once more the language of the glen. But Isla Mackinnon loved every stone and beam of it, and the heart of her was heavy, because she saw in the very near future the day approaching when the Mackinnons would be out of it, root and branch.

"But not before I've done my best to save it, please God," she said under her breath, as she cast her coat aside and went to look for her father.

An old serving-man in a shabby kilt emerged from the faded red-baize door that shut off the servants' quarters, bearing a tray with glasses in his hand.

"I suppose it is just on lunch time, Diarmid?" she said. "Where is the General?"

"I have just put him comfortable with the paper by the library fire, Miss Isla," said the man, as he scanned her face almost wistfully.

He, too, knew the day of the Indian mail. She motioned him to the dining-room, a long, narrow room furnished in what the irreverent called spindle-shanks, but what was in reality genuine and valuable furniture of the Chippendale period. Many old and very discoloured family portraits covered the walls, and the carpet, once a warm crimson but now almost threadbare, gave the only touch of colour to the place. The table was beautifully set, and the silver on it was fit for a king's table.

The Mackinnons were very poor, but there were certain dignities of life which they never ignored or made light of. Whatever the fare might be--and on most occasions it was simple enough--the table was always so laid that the best in the land could have been welcomed to it without shame. The damask was darned, but yet it had a sheen like satin on it such as they do not achieve on the looms of the present day.

Isla closed the door and, steadying herself against it, spoke to the old man who had served them as boy and man for five-and-forty years.

"There is a letter from Mr. Malcolm, Diarmid. He is on his way home."

Diarmid set down his tray rather suddenly, so that the glasses rang as they touched one another.

"Yes--Miss Isla?" he said almost feverishly. "But why will he come home? Is it leave he is having already so soon?"

"No, Diarmid. He is leaving the Army for good. I am telling you, because you love us all so much and understand everything. This news must be kept from the General."

"Yes, Miss Isla--but how? If Mr. Malcolm comes home he comes home, and the General will see him."

"Oh, yes, but he must think only that he is home on furlough. We must make up something that will satisfy him--for a time, at least."

"Yes, Miss Isla, and if Mr. Malcolm is to come home what will he do here in the glen, for sure he is a great big, strong gentleman--glory be to God--and it is not thinkable that he can be here doing nothing?"

"I haven't got so far as that, Diarmid," said Isla, wearily. "My head aches and aches with thinking. I sometimes wish I could fall asleep at night and never waken any more."

"Yes, Miss Isla, but then the sun would go down upon the glen for efer and efer," said the old man with twitching lips.

He had carried her as a baby in his arms, he had set her almost before she could toddle upon the back of the old sheltie that now lived, a fat pensioner, in the paddock behind the house; he had watched her grow from sweet girlhood to womanhood, and his heart had rebelled against the hardness of her destiny. She had never had her due. Other girls in her position had married well, had happy homes and devoted husbands, and little children about their knees, while she, the flower of them all, remained unplucked.

Diarmid, a religious man--as befitted one who had lived such an uneventful and happy life--was sometimes tempted to ask whether the God whom he worshipped had fallen asleep over the affairs of Achree. Of late, his rebellion had become acute. In the silence of his dingy pantry he had even been known to shake his fist over the silver he was polishing and to utter words not becoming on the lips of so circumspect a servant.

"Say nothing to the others, Diarmid. Let them think that Mr. Malcolm is only home on furlough," she pursued. "I must make it right with my father somehow. I'll go to him now and tell him about the letter."

"Yes, Miss Isla. And Mr. Malcolm, he is quite well, I hope?"

"Oh, yes, he is always well. Perhaps, if he were not--but there, I must guard my tongue. The days are very dark over Achree, Diarmid, and it may be that its sun will soon set for ever."

"God forbid! He will nefer let that happen--no, nor anypody else, forby," he said vaguely. "Keep up your brave heart, Miss Isla. I haf seen it fery dark over the loch of a morning, and again, by midday, it would clear and the sun come out. It will be like that now, nefer fear."

But though brave words were on the old man's tongue, black despair was in his heart. He was only a servingman, but he could read between the lines, and he knew that this sudden and unexpected home-coming of the ne'er-do-weel meant something dire for Achree. His hands trembled very much as he proceeded with his table duties, while his young mistress made her way across the hall again to the library, a queer little octagon room on the south side of the house, with no view to speak of from its high, narrow windows that looked out on the rising slope of a heather hill which made the beginning of the moor of Creagh. It was, however, the snuggest room in the whole house, for which reason it was used almost entirely by the General as a living place.

He was frail now, going to bed early and rising late, and seldom caring to ascend the winding stairs to his bedroom after he had once left it.

Isla entered softly, and his dull ear failed to apprise him of the opening of the door. She was thus able to look at him before he was aware of her presence. Once a very tall man, standing six feet two in his stockings in his prime, his fine figure was now sadly shrunk. He sat in a straight, high-backed chair--principally because there were very few of the other sort in the old Castle of Achree, and because there was no money to buy them with, but she could see the droop of the shoulders as they rested against the small cushion that she had filled with down to give him a little ease. He wore a velvet skullcap, from the edge of which there showed a fringe of beautiful silvery hair. His feet, in the big loose slippers of the old man, were raised on a hassock and he was holding the newspaper high before his eyes. Isla observed, from its continuous flutter, that his hands were a little more shaky than usual.

His face was very fine. In his youth Mackinnon of Achree had been the handsomest man in West Perthshire, and he was reported to have broken his full complement of hearts. Even now the classic outline of his face was plainly discernible, and he reminded one of some old war-horse that was past service, but that retained to the end all the noble characteristics that had distinguished him in the heyday of his glory.

"What news to-day, father?" asked Isla's fresh, clear voice.

When he heard it he rose to his feet with that fine courtesy towards women which had never failed him.

She laid a hand in gentle reprimand on his arm.

"Now, how often have I told you, old dear, that you are not to be so ceremonious with me? You can keep your fine manners for the great ladies who never, never now come to Achree. Your little Isla knows that they are there, and she doesn't need ocular demonstration of their presence."

He smiled and patted her cheek. He was an old man, now in his seventy-fifth year. He had been so long on foreign service that he had not married till late in life, and he had then made a marriage which had been the one mistake of his life, and into which he had been led by the softness of his own heart. Yet in battle, and in the affairs of men, he had been a terrific person, to be avoided by those who had offended him.

The fruits of that marriage, unfortunately, had come out in the son and heir in whose veins ran the wild blood of the woman who had broken Mackinnon's heart. There was no fight in the General now. He was a broken old man--very gentle, not altogether comprehending, a mere cypher in his own house, though his honour and his prestige were more jealously guarded by his household than they had ever been when he could guard them himself.

His health was frail, but he suffered apparently from no disease. The doctor from Comrie who paid a weekly visit often assured Isla that, with care, there was no reason why her father should not live for other ten years. Only he mustn't have any shock. He so often insisted upon this that Isla would ask herself after he had gone how, as circumstances were with them now, shock could be avoided. Apprehension was in the very air, and when Malcolm came home shock would most certainly be the order of the day.

"Where have you been, Isla?"

"Down to Lochearn, and I stopped at Darrach to speak to Eppie. You know how her tongue wags. Sit down, dear, and let me tell you something. Have you had any interesting letters?"

"I don't know," he said vaguely. "I looked at some of them. There is one from Cattanach, but I don't understand it. You'll explain it to me, Isla, and write what is necessary."

Cattanach was the family lawyer, the head of a big legal firm in Glasgow that had administered the affairs of Achree for many years.

Isla seized upon his letter jealously, and read it even with a feeling of foreboding. But as her eyes quickly covered the typewritten words, lo! a great relief was hers. The thing she had dreaded now manifested itself as a blessing--perhaps even as a way out.

"Father, have you read this letter?" she asked, drawing her chair to his side and still holding it in her hand.

"I read it--yes, but I don't think I understand. He says something about strange folks coming to Achree. You can write to him, Isla, and tell him that we are not in a position to entertain, as we used to be. We have not the folk about us to make guests comfortable--nor perhaps have we the heart."

"No, no; but that is not quite what he means, darling," said Isla eagerly. "Let me read it over to you quite slowly, then perhaps you will understand."

"ST. VINCENT PLACE,

"GLASGOW, March.

"DEAR GENERAL MACKINNON,--I hardly like to approach you on the subject of this letter, but a client of mine is so insistent that I don't seem to have any alternative.

"I write on behalf of Mr. Hylton Rosmead, an American gentleman who is looking for a place in your neighbourhood to rent for the season. He wants it for six months at least--from Easter to October, with the option of stopping on if agreeable to both parties.

"It seems odd that, with the whole of Scotland to choose from, he and his family should hit upon Achree which, as I told him, is not in the market. They saw it in course of a motor tour last autumn, and were so struck with it, it seems, that it is the only place they would have in the whole of Scotland.

"I may say two things that may help you to a decision. They are Americans of the best type, and he would pay a fancy price for the place.

"I have no alternative but to lay the offer before you and may I remind you that the letting of places to people of this type has become so common among the old families that it is the exception not to let them at some time or other.

"I shall be glad to hear from you at your very earliest convenience as Mr. Rosmead is anxious to get settled. Hoping you feel yourself better with the approach of spring, and that Miss Mackinnon is quite well,--I am, dear General, yours faithfully,

"ALEXANDER CATTANACH."

Long before Isla had reached the close of this letter the old man's attention had wandered and, though his eyes had not fixed themselves on the paper again, Isla saw that he was not in the smallest degree either interested or comprehending.

"You don't understand, dear, that some one wants to take Achree from us for a few months and to pay a high rent--a very high rent--for it. Why shouldn't we let it? Look how often Uncle Tom has let Barras. He has told us he couldn't get on without letting it."

"Oh, no, of course not. Read this account of affairs in Rhodesia, Isla. It's the aftermath of the war. Heavens, we'll never get to the end of that precious muddle! I said so at the time."

Isla laid down the letter quietly, intending to return to it later. It was part of the difficulty of her life, part of the hopelessness of the present acuter stage in it, that she could not get her father to comprehend facts and details which were of the utmost importance. Either he could not or he would not understand--there were times when she was at a loss to say which.

As she laid Cattanach's letter down she drew her brother's from the bosom of her blouse.

"Did you remember that this is mail-day, father? You know you can't read Malcolm's scrawl, which seems to grow more illegible with every letter. Shall I read it out to you?"

"No. Tell me what he says. His letters weary me. They are full of words I don't understand and have no use for," he said with a sudden touch of querulousness. "I can't understand why a boy that has been at Glenalmond and at Sandhurst wants to fill his letters with unintelligible jargon. How is he?"

"He's quite well. He is coming home, father. He will be here very shortly."

"Coming home! Leave again! Far too much leave in the service now. They have no time to lick them into shape. Seventeen years I served in Northern India without a break--and never a murmur; and I've known men who served thirty. Now it's leave every third or fourth year. It doesn't look like five since he was last here, but I suppose it is. Well, when is he coming?"

"In about a month."

"A bad time of year, too--nothing to kill but a stray rabbit. I think I'll write to them at the War Office and stir them up about this perpetual leave business. It's bad for the men, bad for the officers, bad for the service all through, and accounts for its unpopularity and inefficiency. In my day the Army was a man's business--the serious business of his life. Now it's his play. How can a country be kept together on these lines?"

Isla betrayed no weariness, though she knew that he had started on his interminable theme. It was the only one in which he retained any active interest, for Mackinnon had been born a soldier, and the medals he had won could not be pinned all at one time on his breast. But his failing powers prevented him from being able to adjust his mind to the new conditions of things. In his estimation, the old style of warfare was best, and all the new methods were fit only to be criticized and partly abolished.

"He doesn't say anything about the duration of his leave. I, too, am rather sorry he is coming home just now, father, for, as you say, there is nothing to kill and Malcolm isn't a man of resource. I think I'll go and see Cattanach and ask his advice."

"Cattanach? Oh, yes. What did he write about, did you say? Anything to sign? Or was he writing only for his own amusement to earn six-and-eightpence? Terrible fellows these lawyers--even the best of them are worth watching."

He laughed gently but quite mirthlessly, and his eyes glued themselves again to his paper, in which he at once became completely absorbed.

Isla, knitting her brows slightly, turned away to the table to glance through her father's letters, which he had not so much as touched.

Everything was in her hands. Something whispered that she, and she alone, must be the saviour of Achree.

CHAPTER III
ISLA TAKES ACTION

Isla, already dressed for a journey, took in her father's breakfast-tray next morning.

"You are surely early afield, my dear?" he said, looking at the trim figure with quick approbation.

"Yes, dear. I am going to Glasgow to see Mr. Cattanach, because I found when I started out to answer his letter that I couldn't say half I wanted."

"His letter wasn't very clear, I thought. Ask him why he doesn't learn to express himself better. I thought that was a lawyer's business. But it seems a long way to go to Glasgow to say that to him. When do you get your train?"

"Nine-thirty, and Jamie Forbes has come up from the hotel to drive me to Balquhidder. So good-bye, dear. Diarmid will look after you till I come back, and you may expect me about tea-time."

He did not ask any other question. His mind was now curiously detached from all immediate happenings, and he lived more and more in the past. Even his reading of the newspapers was coloured by the tendency to retrospect.

Isla got away with a considerable sense of relief, and when she mounted to the side of Jamie Forbes in the hotel dogcart her eyes even sparkled. There was now no horse of any kind, nor was there any carriage in the stableyard of Achree, though the old people, even Diarmid himself, could sadly recall the time when it had been full.

Isla was glad to be doing something. She had all the restlessness of an active nature that could not endure a policy of drift. They had been drifting so long with the ebb tide at Achree that she welcomed the crisis which made it necessary to take an immediate step.

She went ostensibly to ask the lawyer's advice, but her own mind was made up as to the best course to pursue. Her judgment was singularly clear, and she was not now in the smallest doubt as to the right--nay, the only-- thing to be done in the circumstances.

At Balquhidder Station a few passengers were waiting for the Oban train, and, slightly to Isla's chagrin, directly she appeared on the platform a tall young man in a tweed suit and a covert coat came forward, with evident signs of satisfaction, to greet her.

"Good morning, Isla. This is an uncommon bit of luck. Are you going to town?"

"To Glasgow," she unwillingly admitted. "And you?"

"Glasgow too," he answered joyfully. "I was cursing my luck as I drove over the hill from Garrion, but if I had known, I should have driven with a lighter heart."

Isla scarcely smiled. She liked Neil Drummond very well as a friend, for they had known each other since their childhood. But in the last three years he had spoiled that friendship by periodically asking her to marry him. The expression in his eyes now indicated that very little provocation would make him ask her again on the spot, for he was very much in earnest. He was two years younger than Isla, and she always treated him like a young and very inexperienced brother, which incensed him a good deal.

He had just come into the property from his uncle, and wanted nothing but a wife to make Garrion complete. He was a finely-built, good-looking young fellow, with an honest, kindly face, with not a very high type of intellect perhaps, but with sufficient common sense and sound judgment to fill admirably the position to which he had been called.

He and his sister Kitty, being orphans, had been brought up by their uncle at Garrion, and had known no other home. Kitty and Isla were friends, of course, though there was not so very much in common between that dashing, high-spirited, happy-go-lucky girl and the more staid and placid Isla.

"How's Kitty? We haven't seen her for a long time," she said as they began to pace to and fro on the platform--objects of much interest of a significant kind to those who knew them.

"Kitty's alone, but when are you coming to Garrion? Aunt Betty is always asking why you don't come."

"That's easily answered. It's five miles to Garrion, and I haven't either a horse or a bicycle; but tell Lady Betty I'll walk over one of these days."

"You needn't do that, Isla--and very well you know it. All you have to do is to say the word, and the best bit of horse-flesh in Garrion stables is at your command."

"I haven't much time," she said rather quickly. "Father seems to need me more of late, and----"

She hesitated, and then came to a stop, deciding that she would not just yet mention a word about Malcolm's coming home. It was not that she could not trust Neil Drummond, but the shame of that home-coming held her back from speaking of it even to a friend of such long standing.

"It is very unusual for you to go to Glasgow, isn't it?" said Neil, looking down with a slightly rueful expression at the bonnie, winsome face by his side.

"It is very unusual. Last night father had a letter from Mr. Cattanach, which we found rather difficult to answer, so I came to the conclusion that it might save further complications if I went up and had a talk with him about it."

"Well, if that's all, you can come and lunch with me, can't you? St. Enoch's Hotel, one sharp. I'm only after a horse. It won't take me more than an hour."

Isla hesitated, but finally promised.

"I must get the two-ten train, and if anything happens to prevent me from keeping the appointment, don't wait. I'll be there at one if I'm coming."

"All right," said Drummond joyfully. "This is a red-letter day--and no mistake. Shows that a fellow never knows when his next bit of good luck is going to turn up."

He looked so young and boyish at the moment that Isla suddenly smiled upon him.

"What a boy you are, Neil! I don't believe anything will ever make you grow up. Even being Laird of Garrion hasn't had the smallest effect. Here's the train. Now I warn you I won't speak to you on the journey, because I have heaps and heaps of things to arrange in my mind. Remember, I'm going to a lawyer's office, and nobody goes there unprepared."

"All right. So long as I am sitting next to you, and preventing anybody else from speaking to you, I shan't grumble," said Neil calmly as he helped her into a corner of the third-class carriage.

He had a first-class ticket himself, which he carefully hid from her. Had he dared he would have paid the difference for the privilege of having a compartment to themselves, but Isla would not have permitted that.

Shortly after eleven o'clock they arrived at Glasgow and, saying that it was necessary for him to have a cab to take him to his destination at the south-side, he put Isla in and drove her the short distance to the lawyer's door. Then with the prospect of meeting her at lunch in little more than an hour's time, he departed in the seventh heaven of delight.

Miss Mackinnon, sending in her name, was not kept waiting an unnecessary moment. Indeed, so much was she respected in the office that Cattanach turned over a rather important client to his junior partner and at once went to see Miss Mackinnon, escorting her to his private room.

"I came in consequence of your letter to papa yesterday, Mr. Cattanach," said Isla as they shook hands. "It was of such importance that I thought I would come and have a talk with you about it."

Cattanach was not an old man, and he bore his fifty years lightly. He had a somewhat heavy yet keen face, was a little stern in repose. But, when his genial smile irradiated his face, the sternness was forgotten. His reputation in the city was that of being one of the first lawyers of the day, and business simply flowed in upon his firm.

His father had been at the helm of Achree affairs when they were in a more prosperous state, and he had been a life-long friend and admirer of the General. He had managed to communicate his sincere and sympathetic interest to his son, who had done much more for the Mackinnons than they could have had the right to expect from their man of business or than could ever be repaid. He had indeed helped young Mackinnon out of several scrapes for his father's and his sister's sake, though doing that had been a service very ill to his liking. An interview with Isla herself, however, was a pure pleasure, which, on this occasion, was all the keener that it was wholly unexpected.

"Yes, thank you, I am quite well and father too, though he is failing, I think," she said rather sadly. "I came in answer to your letter and in order to show you this."

She had a small bag of curiously-wrought Moorish leather on her arm, from which she produced the letter that had come yesterday by the Indian mail. She did not immediately pass it over, however, or read any extract from it, but, leaning slightly forward in her chair, she fixed her clear, grave eyes on the lawyer's face as he stood in quite characteristic attitude in front of his desk, leaning one hand slightly on the table.

"Won't you sit down, Mr. Cattanach? I'm afraid I must take up quite a lot of your time this morning--an hour perhaps. I have to lunch at the St. Enoch's Hotel at one."

"Then I shall not have the pleasure of taking you to lunch myself."

"Not to-day, thank you," said Isla, and he imagined her colour rose slightly. "It is about your letter I first want to speak. My father did not comprehend it, I am afraid. He sent the message to you," she added with a faint, wandering smile, "that he was surprised that a lawyer did not express himself better. But of course to me what you said was perfectly clear. Tell me about this man who wishes to take poor old Achree. Is he--is he at all a possible person?"

There was just the slightest suggestion of hauteur in the question, which, at another time, might have amused Cattanach hugely. Out in the hard world of men and business things were called by their right names, and there would have been small sympathy expressed for the Mackinnon pride.

But he understood. This fine creature, product of an ancient race and embodiment in her own personality of all that was best in it, appealed to him beyond any power of his to express. He was prepared to meet her and to help her, not only to the best of his ability but even beyond what his prudence and his better judgment would have permitted. And it would not be the first time in the record of his transactions with Achree that service had been rendered by Alexander Cattanach from purely disinterested motives--service that had never found its way into the columns of any ledger.

"He is a very possible person indeed, Miss Mackinnon, quite the best type of educated American--and the type is very good."

"Is it?" asked Isla with a little shiver. "I have never encountered it. The few specimens that come to the glen are not--are not what one would call the best type. And the people who had Edinard for two seasons running!--shall one ever forget them? Their flying motors with screaming hooters, their impossible costumes, their disregard for our quiet Sabbaths, their noise--all were indescribable. I should not like such people as they at Achree. But, indeed, I don't suppose such people would so much as look at it. Lady Eden told me that the first year it cost her half the rent to put into the house what her tenants wanted. They were so mean in regard to trifles that they would not buy the simplest thing."

Cattanach smiled understandingly. He also had some acquaintance with that type.

"I don't think you would find the Rosmeads like that. I should say myself that they are simple gentlefolks and that, this summer at least, they would be certain to live quietly. They wish the place for retirement on account of Mrs. Rosmead, who is recovering from a long illness, and for their elder daughter, who has just had an unpleasant experience in the Divorce Court--one of those curious matrimonial entanglements of which America seems to be full. She was here on Tuesday with her brother. She is one of the most beautiful women I have ever seen."

"Poor thing--and had she a bad husband?"

"I understand so, but, of course, the subject was not mentioned. There is a younger daughter called Sadie, and there is also a boy at Yale or Harvard, who would spend only his summer here. I think you would like the family, and they would be willing to pay three hundred for the house, and five with the shooting."

"Five hundred!" murmured Isla, and her eyes had a sort of hungry look.

Money for its own sake did not exist for her. She was naturally of a generous, even of a prodigal mind, and she was certainly made for the gracious dispensation of great wealth. But she had had to count the pence so long that she had arrived, by many painful processes, at full appreciation of their market value.

"We could certainly live at Creagh on three hundred; then two could be laid by, couldn't they, Mr. Cattanach?"

He turned swiftly away, for there was something in the eager question, almost childishly put, which gripped him by the throat.

"Yes, of course. In the country life is simple," he said at last. "I gather from what you say that you would be willing at least to consider the offer of Mr. Hylton P. Rosmead."

"I haven't any alternative now," she said, as she pulled the strings of the leather bag again and produced her brother's letter. "Please to read that, Mr. Cattanach."

She passed over the thin, and now crumpled sheet covered with Malcolm's sprawling undignified handwriting, which the lawyer's eyes quickly scanned. The expression of his face as its full significance dawned upon him quite changed and perceptibly hardened. When he refolded it again it was a moment before the suitable word came to him. He knew that words of pity or condolence would be quite out of place, if spoken to Isla Mackinnon, and that the truest kindness he could show her would be to accept the situation as a matter of course and do his utmost to help, as he had opportunity, or could make it where he had it in his power.

"This makes acceptance of Rosmead's offer imperative, as you say, Miss Mackinnon. Perhaps the best thing I can do is to send him to Achree to see you. He is in the city this week. He has many friends here connected with the engineering profession. I believe that in his own country he is a distinguished engineer, and he certainly is a very gentlemanly, well-informed man."

He praised the American of a set purpose, deeming it best to direct Miss Mackinnon's thoughts to the pleasant side of the inevitable.

"Do you think they would wish a great deal of money spent on the house? It is very bare, really, and rather dilapidated. But if he wanted even a tithe of the things that Lady Eden's tenants asked for I'm afraid the bargain would have to be off. I could not owe money myself, even to let Achree."

"I don't think there will be any difficulty. They are without doubt very wealthy people, and, further, they are so anxious for the place that they will take it at your terms. You spoke of the Lodge of Creagh a moment ago. You would go there to live in the interval?"

"Yes. It happens to be empty since Mrs. Macdonald died last autumn, and if it were well fired and aired we could be quite comfortable there. Of course, it is small, but I would give up the dining-room to my father, and, so long as he is comfortable and does not suffer by the change, nothing else matters much."

"It is very remote," suggested Cattanach, "and the road across the moor is nothing to boast of, if I remember it rightly."

"Of course it is only a shooting-lodge--and a small one at that; but its remoteness won't matter to me, and, as for my brother, perhaps it would be a very good thing for him to be shut off by the moor of Creagh."

Cattanach nodded gravely.

Then she put another question to him of a more disconcerting kind.

"Mr. Cattanach, why are men usually dismissed from the Army? What are the offences, I mean? They must be grave, of course, because it is so serious a thing to cut short a man's career at the very commencement."

"It is a serious thing, and it is not done on trifling grounds," he answered quietly, not dreaming of evading her question. "What your brother says about injustice is, of course, nonsense. It exists in small things in the Army, as elsewhere, but it would never reach the length of, as you say, cutting short a man's career."

She sighed a little as she rose to her feet. He had not specified, but she was answered.

"It is all very dreadful, and it would certainly kill my father if he knew. Happily--how strange it is that I can use the word in relation to what has been such a sorrow to me, but happily--his failing faculties don't permit him to grasp the affairs of life. He understands that Malcolm is coming home, and he is full of wrath at the amount of leave allowed in the service in these days. It will thus be all right for a little while, but if Malcolm is to live on as a loafer," she said with a sad inflexion of scorn in her voice, "he will be troubled about it. Oh, Mr. Cattanach, what is to be done with Malcolm?"

Her brave voice shook, and again there was in her eyes that agony of appeal which a far less kind-hearted man than Cattanach could not have resisted.

"Dear Miss Mackinnon, the trouble is very real and awful, but it is not on us just yet. Let us get the question of the tenancy of Achree settled, and then we shall have time to tackle the other. The Rosmeads wish to get settled in the place before Easter. Would that be possible?"

"I shall make it so, and I want to be at Creagh before Malcolm arrives. He would create all sorts of difficulties, and it will be far better to get the people into Achree before then."

"And your father?"

"Ah, that will be difficult, but I have never been beaten yet, Mr. Cattanach, though sometimes I have been very near it. Yesterday I thought I was, but to-day, when I woke up, I felt quite strong and able, and now, after your kindness, I am sure we shall get through."

"I shall help to the very best of my ability. I can come down to Achree if you think I can be of any use to you in persuading the General."

"Thank you. I shall write if I think it necessary for you to come. But he is so like a child! He will be quite pleased to go to Creagh, I believe, and he will not understand why we have to leave Achree. I am glad that it is so now. If he had been his old self it would have been so difficult for him."

"Undoubtedly it would."

"And Malcolm's affair too! He must not be allowed to idle about indefinitely in the glen, or I shall never have a moment's peace. I'm going to talk very straightly to him when he comes. He has always got off too easily. But this money--how is it to be found? If they begin to press for it would they take Achree?"

"We shall prevent that. You must leave this in my hands, Miss Mackinnon. The best thing your brother could do would be to emigrate to one of the new countries--to Canada, or the Cape, or even the Argentine. As you say, it will not be possible to allow him to loaf about the glen."

"But he is so difficult, because, you see, he thinks nothing matters, and his only desire is to have what he calls a good time. Even if he has it at other people's expense he will have it. About this money he owes? I will do my utmost to save for it out of the money the Americans will pay. They will not do anything drastic about it, I hope--seize upon Achree or any part of it," she repeated wistfully, as if yet unconvinced.

"I can deal with them, Miss Mackinnon. You must leave that part of the business for your brother and me to settle between us. You may trust me to do what will be absolutely for the good of yourself and your brother."

"Oh, I know," she said with eloquent eyes. "Thank you so much. You are always so kind. Things seem easier when one has seen you. Good-bye, then. And you will send the American man to view the land soon? I hope I shall be able to please him."

A clock on the mantelshelf struck, and she made haste to the door.

"I have to lunch with Mr. Neil Drummond of Garrion at one. I must run," she said.

The lawyer himself escorted her to the street door, put her into a cab, and, as he returned slowly up the stairs, rubbed his hands together meditatively.

"Drummond of Garrion! Well, well, perhaps it might be the best thing she could do. Poor, poor girl, but game to the innermost fibre of her being! Where would our old families be but for such as she--but for the fine fibre of their women? Garrion! Garrion! By Gad, I must look into it and see whether it would be worth her while."

CHAPTER IV
THE AMERICANS

"Did you ever see such a shabby room, Peter? It positively reeks of poverty."

Thus did Sadie Rosmead deliver herself to her brother after the drawing-room door had been shut upon them at Achree, and Diarmid had gone to seek his mistress.

On the Monday following Isla's visit to Glasgow, and, in consequence of a letter from Cattanach, the Rosmeads had made a hurried journey out to Glenogle for the purpose of making acquaintance with the interior of the house that they so much admired, and, if possible, of coming to terms with its owners.

They were a handsome pair. Rosmead himself, a man of about thirty-five, well, but quietly, dressed, and carrying his firmly-knit figure with conscious ease and strength, had a strong, fine face, lit by pleasant grey eyes that gave a very fair index to his character. He was a man who, by his own effort, by the sheer force of his ability, which, in his own domain amounted to genius, had achieved a distinction and a success manifest in his very bearing.

Once seen, Peter Rosmead would not be readily forgotten. He was a man who could not be in any company without leaving the mark of his personality upon it.

His sister was small, but elegant; dressed with conspicuous plainness, but in a style which has to be paid for with considerable cheques. The feature of her costume was undoubtedly her veil, which, when worn by a really elegant American woman such as Sadie Rosmead certainly was, becomes a thing of distinction. It was only a long width of blue chiffon attached to a small felt hat of the same hue, but it made a most becoming setting to her dark, piquant face.

"Yes--it positively reeks of poverty. Look at the darn in the carpet, Peter!" she said severely. "This is a house of makeshifts, but it's decent poverty, and I've never seen anything so clean in the whole of my life. It would charm mother. How I wish she could have come to-day!"

Still Peter did not answer. There was something about the room which pained him, but he could not have explained what it was. It seemed to him indecent that two strangers, such as they were, should have come to view the poverty of the land. Cattanach had told Rosmead several things that he had not mentioned to any of his women folks; therefore, he was very eager and interested to see Miss Mackinnon.

Sadie babbled on.

"If it were not so clean it would be impossible. But there are some awfully pretty things. Look at that bit of tapestry on the end wall and at that coat of arms worked on the banner screen. It's just too sweet for anything. Now, what are you looking at, Peter?--oh, the miniatures! Anything good?"

There was a small collection on the mantelpiece, framed in ebony and standing on little brass tripods--very exquisite things in their way, and part of the few remaining treasures of Achree. Rosmead was studying them intently, and his sister was examining with interest the various bits of old needlework in the room, when the door was opened by rather a quick, nervous hand, and some one came in.

Rosmead turned back from the mantelpiece, and Sadie dropped the cushion with the peacock sewn upon its cover, and turned with a charming smile.

"Don't be angry, Miss Mackinnon. We are not sampling anything, but we are Americans--don't you know--and everything in this lovely old house appeals to us. You are Miss Mackinnon, aren't you? I'm Sadie Rosmead, and this is my brother Peter."

It was charmingly done, and it brought a slight smile, in spite of herself, to Isla's parted lips. She had been walking very fast, and the colour was high in her cheek. Her jacket was thrown back to show the neat flannel shirt belted trimly to her waist, and the black tie held in its place by the silver brooch, curiously wrought and displaying the arms of the Mackinnons, the same design being repeated in the buckle of her belt.

"I am so sorry you have been kept waiting. I was at the other side of the wood, seeing a sick woman. How-do-you-do?"

She shook hands with Sadie, but it was at the brother that she looked.

And she was well pleased with what she saw. She was not concerned at all about the impression she might be making on them. The only thing that mattered was that the people who were coming to Achree should not be objectionable.

Just for a moment she had been a trifle dismayed by Miss Rosmead's very obvious nationality--by the twang in her voice and by the familiarity of her manner. Isla's own manner inclined to hauteur. She fought against it, for the person who has goods to sell cannot afford to be too high and mighty in procedure. Yet she carried herself, in spite of her efforts to the contrary, like one who had a favour to bestow.

An intensely good-natured person, overflowing with the milk of human kindness, Sadie Rosmead did not even notice this characteristic manner, but not a shade of it was lost on Rosmead himself. It did not, however, either irritate or repel him. He had an immense gift of understanding, and he knew what this interview meant to the girl before them, whose face, now that the little flush of excitement had died from it, was pale, and even a little haggard.

"I am sorry you did not let me know, so that you could have been met at the station and could have come to luncheon. Have you had any?"

"Oh, yes," answered Sadie, "a very good snack at the station buffet at Glasgow, hadn't we, Peter? We should like a cup of tea perhaps, by and by, after we have seen the house. I have heard of your Scotch scones and butter and honey. They have very good imitations of them at the hotels, but we've been told--haven't we, Hylton?--that they don't begin to taste like the real thing."

Isla noticed the change of name, and she decided that the more dignified one suited the brother better. "Peter" was certainly ridiculous, and yet it had a kindly human sound and she preferred to think of him as kindly to thinking of him as dignified at the moment. Achree so much needed kindness, and she--poor girl!--more than all, though she was hardly conscious of her own need.

Rosmead was fully conscious of it. He had never in the whole course of his experience met with anything that touched or appealed to him more than the sight of this tall, slight girl upon whose shoulders rested what made her life a burden--the whole responsibility of the house of her fathers. Cattanach, a discerning man, had told him just sufficient to arouse his compassionate interest. Though he spoke so little, Isla felt comforted by his presence. The thing that had been a nightmare resolved itself, under his kindly touch, into something that might not only be possible, but might also prove good.

This man, of alien race though he was, would never harry Achree, nor would he bring to it strange new ways of life and thought. He looked strong, generous, and simple--as the truly strong always are.

While this subtle bond was being established between these two thus so strangely brought together, Sadie did the talking.

"Yes, we would like to see the house--every bit of it--but not to poke. Only, however, if it is convenient and only what you are willing to show-- eh, Peter? We don't want to rush Miss Mackinnon, and we can easily come out another day and bring Vivien."

"Vivien is your sister?" said Isla inquiringly, as she laid her jacket down on the end of the high-backed old sofa.

Sadie nodded.

"She had a headache. She is not so very strong, and she can't stand racket. I'm the untirable, uncrushable, wholly inextinguishable member of the family. But not a bad sort--eh, Peter?"

Peter indulgently smiled.

"I hope General Mackinnon is quite well?" he inquired. "I have heard from Mr. Cattanach that his health has not been good of late."

"No--he is not very strong. To-day, because it felt really like spring, he has gone for a little walk. I was with him. But, yes--he is quite all right. One of the men is coming back with him. If you don't mind, will you come and see the library before he returns? It is the room he sits in chiefly, and I am afraid it will be a little difficult for him to understand what you are doing in it if he should see you there. We can come back here, of course, for tea."

She led the way down the winding stair and across the flagged hall, which Sadie mutely pointed out to her brother as they silently followed their guide. All the windows in the library were open, and the cool, fresh air met them on the threshold. Again the same note of shabbiness and painful care was evident, but the room was well-furnished with books, which completely lined the walls.

"I suppose they are centuries old," said Sadie in an awe-struck whisper. "There--Peter, surely now you will be able to read your fill."

"Some of them are very old, I believe, and there are first editions among them," answered Isla, in a matter-of-fact tone, as if unaware that she talked of treasures which could be exchanged for gold. "You see this is quite a good room, and everyone likes the shape of it. It is so warm in winter, and so cool in summer."

It was duly admired, and they made their way from it again to the dining-room. They also took a quick glance at the servants' premises, where Sadie's sharp eyes took in most of the details.

"Now--upstairs," said Isla with evident relief. "And on the first landing, where the little door opens, just here is the dungeon-room. It has a trap-door and a stair going right down from it."

Sadie's eyes grew positively wide with excitement.

"A dungeon-room," she repeated again, in an awe-stricken whisper. "And where does this stair lead to? Can anyone go down?"

"Oh, yes. It leads to the dungeon, and there used to be--about the fourteenth century--a passage from it going both ways, one to Killin and down to the Earn, but it has not been opened for hundreds of years."

"Do you hear that, Hylton Rosmead? The fourteenth century! Where were we then? How do you see down?"

"If Mr. Rosmead will be so kind----"

She stooped to pull back the faded strip of home-made carpet, and so revealed the rusty hinges set level with the floor.

Rosmead stooped also and, with one swing of his strong arm, he raised the heavy door, so that they could look into the depths beneath. A curious odour met them, and Sadie, her imagination now wrought to a high pitch, fancied she heard mysterious sounds ascending from below.

"I should love to go down, but we can explore later when we come to live here. Fancy a place like this right in the middle of one's house and stairs and passages leading all over the country! It's positively creepy, but most fascinating. And a room with a bed in it too! I wonder whether I should get any sleep in it if I took it for my own?"

"It is rather small, isn't it?" said Isla with a smile. "It was used as a sentinel's or guard's room chiefly in the old days, I fancy. Now, will you come up and see the bedrooms?"

"I'll take a turn outside if I may," said Rosmead. "My sister will accompany you, Miss Mackinnon. I'm perfectly satisfied with what I have seen."

"Can you find your way? There are two staircases, but you can get out by either," said Isla, and they stood just a moment on the narrow landing till Rosmead had found his way out.

He passed out into the mellow sunshine of the afternoon with a sense of relief. The old house saddened him. It seemed to be peopled with dead hopes and with old memories and to have no kinship with the warm and happy life of men.

As he stepped on the gravel the sound of wheels broke the stillness, and a dogcart, in which was a beautiful, high-stepping chestnut horse, was rapidly driven up to the door. It contained two persons--a man and a woman, both young--who had evidently come to pay a call at Achree.

Raising his hat slightly, he turned aside to walk round by the gable-end of the house in order to see it from the back.

Just beyond the rolled gravel he came upon another pathetic sight--the old General in his Inverness cloak and with his bonnet on his thin white hair, leaning heavily on his stick and watching the antics of a little brown dog in front of a rabbit-hole. He was quite alone; and Rosmead, in whom reverence for the old was a passion as well as a virtue, involuntarily took off his hat.

"Come back, you little vixen!" the old man called with a little chuckle to the brown dog.

And, just at the moment, Janet, conscious of the approach of a stranger, gave a short, sharp bark and ran back.

The General looked round and, seeing the stranger, took his bonnet from his head. Rosmead had then no alternative but to introduce himself.

"My name is Rosmead, sir. I am here owing to correspondence with Mr. Cattanach."

"Cattanach? Oh, yes--very decent fellow, Cattanach, but not a good writer. Have you seen my daughter, and has your horse been put up?" he said with all the fine dignity of the hospitable old laird, always ready to welcome the stranger within his gates.

"We have only a hired trap, and it is waiting in the stable-yard. We have to get back to catch the four-thirty train."

"Oh, yes. Well, you will see my daughter, and you will at least have some tea before you go away. Can I direct you back to the house? I was taking my walk in the sun. I am not so strong as I was, and I have to choose my days. That is what we have to come to, sir,--we choose our days, when they are not chosen for us. Well, if you can find your way back to the house, I shall continue my walk."

He touched his bonnet and turned away, as if he had dismissed the man and the incident from his mental vision.

Rosmead immediately grasped the whole facts. He saw that the old man was wholly detached from the affairs of life, and more and more his heart ached with compassion for Isla Mackinnon. He walked right round the house, admiring its outline, even the huddled little towers touching his fancy, and he made up his mind on the spot that this should be his future dwelling-place. No matter what should be the price, he would pay it, because something told him that here was a place in which his money could be of use.

There was something deeper, however--the conviction that destiny had willed it that his life was somehow to be bound up with this old house and its inmates. The idea appealed to him and gave him a quickened interest in the place.

When he returned to the drawing-room in about ten minutes' time he found that it now contained four persons--his sister and their hostess and the two who had arrived to call.

"This is Mr. Rosmead, Kitty," said Isla, in whose face the pink spot of excitement burned again. "Miss Drummond, Mr. Neil Drummond, Mr. Rosmead."

Rosmead gravely saluted, but though Kitty beamed upon the handsome stranger, Neil was hostile. His face positively gloomed, and he had hardly a word to say.

His manners did not show to advantage that day. He seemed a boor beside the smooth, polished man of the world that Rosmead, by contrast, appeared. When tea was brought, it was Rosmead who established himself by the table, leaving his sister to chatter to the Drummonds. He did this of a set purpose, because he wished to say a word in Isla's private ear, and there did not seem to be any opportunity--unless he made one--of saying it.

"Miss Mackinnon, Mr. Cattanach has told you that we are anxious to get settled soon on account of my mother's health. Do you think you could give me a definite answer as to what you intend to do regarding the letting of the house to-day?"

"Yes, easily. If you care for it, now you have seen it, please take it," she answered without looking up.

The tone of her voice slightly disconcerted him, because he knew that her depth of feeling must be occasioning her the greatest pain.

"We would not hurry you--or seem to embarrass you in any way. My mother is the kindest and most reasonable of women, and I hope that you will permit her to know you if she comes to Achree. Are you likely to stay in the neighbourhood?"

"Yes," she answered, and her breath came a little faster. "We are going to the lodge at Creagh, at the other side of the moor."

The information seemed to please him.

"Then, perhaps you will write to Mr. Cattanach when your arrangements are made."

"Yes, I will do so, but there is something I must say first. I tried to say it to your sister, but somehow I could not," she said, still hurriedly and with her eyes on her tray. "I am sure that you will find that the house needs many things. We have been so poor that it has not been replenished, as it would have been in different circumstances. That must be taken into consideration in settling the question of the rent to be paid. I will tell Mr. Cattanach so. I hope I make myself plain?" she said, lifting her eyes to his face when he gave her no answer. "I am saying, Mr. Rosmead, that we can't spend any money on the house, and that whatever you find it lacks you will supply for yourselves."

"I quite understand that. Pray, don't speak of it--it is not worth mentioning. I understand that it is a sacrifice for you to let us have the house at all. I wish I did not realize that so keenly."

She looked at him again, and the expression in her eyes wholly changed. The child-look came back--the look of trust, of ingenuousness, of innocent sweetness, and it moved Rosmead profoundly. A very reticent, self-contained, observant man, he was interested and drawn by the tragedy, the unfathomable sadness of this girl's life. To possess Achree, and thus to come within sight and possible touch of Isla Mackinnon, had suddenly become to him a matter of personal moment.

But it was not so with Isla; she liked him; she was grateful to him for his reticence and his consideration, but to her he was simply the man who wanted Achree, and for whom they must leave it.

"You are very kind, but in a matter of this kind business must be the basis," she said presently, with a sudden return of her original hauteur. "I shall write to Mr. Cattanach to-night, and ask him to arrange things. Our removal to Creagh is only a matter of two or three days for the gathering together of our few personal belongings--that is all. I hope there will not be any difficulties in the way, and that you will be able to come to Achree, for your mother's sake, at the time you wish."

His next words arrested her attention, in spite of herself.

"If there are difficulties I shall do my best to overcome them. That has been the business of my life up till now."

"How do you mean?" she asked with an involuntary interest.

"I am a builder of bridges," he answered.

At this moment the Laird of Garrion, glowering like his own moor in a snell winter day, came stalking across the room, his step and his manner indicating that he considered that the stranger had already presumed too much.

Rosmead, in no way perturbed, drew out his watch.

"Sadie, it's time we went if we are to catch that train," he said to his sister, who, deep in girlish talk with Kitty Drummond, rose reluctantly.

The good-byes were quickly made, and, though her more kindly impulses prompted Isla to go down and speed the parting guests, she bade them good-bye at the drawing-room door with the slightest suggestion of stiffness, and left Diarmid to show them out.

"Who are these people, Isla?" asked Drummond impetuously the moment the door closed. "He's insufferable. Whence these airs of his? Who is he?"

"A rich American, and they are likely to take Achree for six months, or perhaps a year," answered Isla quietly, realizing that the thing could not be any longer hid.

Kitty gave a little exclamation of dismay, but on Drummond's face the scowl rose again.

"Let Achree! Heaven forbid! Isla, you won't do it. It's unthinkable--it's--it's, I want to say it, only I mustn't. Kitty, go down and find the General. I must speak to Isla alone."

CHAPTER V
THE BRIDGE BUILDERS

Kitty did not look so surprised as might have been expected. She walked with alacrity to the door in spite of Isla's rather eager protest.

"It's my belief, Isla, that you shut up the poor old General to prevent people from seeing him. I should not be at all surprised to find him in the dungeon-room," she said saucily over her shoulder as she disappeared round the sharp turning of the stair.

Isla reluctantly re-entered the drawing-room, fully aware of what was coming.

"Don't, Neil," she said, lifting a deprecating hand. "It has got to be done, so there isn't any use of talking about it."

"But, Isla!" he groaned, "it can't be done. Why, it will kill the General! Does he know what is in contemplation?"

"I have tried to tell him, but he can't understand," said Isla pitifully.

"He'll understand quickly enough when it comes to the bit--when you take him away from the old house. Why, it's the house he was born in, and he can't leave it now when he is old and frail. It's worth any sacrifice to let him have his last days in peace."

"It is; but I have made all the sacrifices possible, and have reached the end of my tether. If somebody could awaken the sense of sacrifice in Malcolm it would be different."

"Malcolm will be furious! Have you written and asked him, for after all he's the heir, you know, and a step--a big, drastic, horrible step like letting a property--can't be, or at least ought not to be, taken without consulting the heir."

Isla smiled drearily as she dropped into a chair.

Her old friend's anger was quite understandable and natural; but, oh, if people only knew how futile it all was!

"Listen, Neil. I thought of telling you the other day when we went to Glasgow together, but it was too new and raw then. Of course, that was the business I had to see Cattanach about. It is Malcolm who has caused this--who has wrought the red ruin of Achree."

Drummond was silent before the poignancy of her tone. Nor could he say that he was altogether astonished, since he knew Malcolm Mackinnon, and was fully aware of part at least of his unspeakable folly and misdoing.

"I may as well tell you now," went on Isla hotly. "Soon it will be the common property of the glen. Malcolm has had to send in his papers."

"My God, Isla, you don't say so!" said Drummond, and his fresh, kindly face grew a little white under the shock.

She nodded.

"Yes--and he owes over two thousand pounds to money-lenders, and our account is over-drawn at the bank. So now you know why the Americans must come to Achree."

She leaned back, and a small, very dismal smile just hovered about the corners of her sad, proud mouth.

Neil Drummond could scarcely have looked more thunderstruck and overwhelmed had the disaster come to his own Garrion, nor could he have felt it more acutely. He took a turn across the floor, and then he came and stood in front of her, his broad shoulders squared, a sudden look of strength and determination upon his kindly face.

"Why didn't you let us know before things got to this stage, Isla? What are friends for--that's what I'd like to know? Your silence just shows what a poor place, after all, any of us have in your estimation."

"No, no, Neil. But don't you see it was such a big, desperate, hopeless thing that nobody could give any help in the matter? And the dearer the friends are, the more impossible it would be to take money from them. You must understand that. You do understand it--only it pleases you to be denser than I have ever known you in the whole course of our acquaintance."

"The whole course of our acquaintance!" he repeated, half-eagerly, half-wistfully. "It's been spread over a pretty long period of years now, hasn't it, Isla?"

"Yes, but it looks like centuries. To-day I feel a century old myself."

"What you're needing, my dear, is somebody to take care of you," he said with a great gentleness. "I must speak again, though I promised to be silent till you gave me leave to speak. Won't you let me step into the breach, Isla? Marry me, and I'll do my best to smooth things over, and the General shall certainly not leave Achree. Garrion coffers are not so very full just at present, but I think there might be enough raised to prevent that unthinkable catastrophe."

She shook her head.

"I can't, Neil, I can't! Don't say another word about it."

"I'm not asking anything," he said with the humbleness born of a really unselfish love--"only the right to take care of you and shield you and, if need be, fight for you. Malcolm is your brother, Isla, but I'd like to get into grips with him just once to punish him for all these lines that have come on your dear face through him. And if he comes back to the glen I'll tell him what I think of him, even if it should be the last word I speak in this world!"

"It is easier to have one's men folk killed in wars, Neil," she said in a low voice. "Last week Lady Eden was bewailing Archie's death, even though she had his little V.C. on the table beside her. I could have cried out to her to go down on her knees and thank God because he is safe from all hurt and evil. She does not begin to know the meaning of sorrow, as we know it here. I have only one consolation--that my father will never now be able to grasp the real meaning of what has happened. You'll have to help me to keep it from him--to talk and to act as if nothing out of the common had occurred; and you must promise to come and to bring Kitty to see us at Creagh."

"At Creagh!" cried Drummond aghast. "You don't mean to say that you are going to bury yourselves in that God-forsaken hole? Oh, my dear, Garrion may be bad, but at least it is get-at-able. Shut up in Creagh, with the General and with Malcolm when he comes home!--it will be the death of you, Isla."

"No, no, I take a lot of killing. Do be a bit more cheerful, Neil. I'm sure you must have thought the Americans quite nice people. He is charming, I think. He builds bridges in America, and Cattanach says that he is a man of genius."

"He may build what he likes, but if he comes to Achree, whatever the price he pays, he commits the unpardonable sin," he said sourly. "Don't let us talk about him. I'm waiting for an answer to my question. It isn't much I ask, Isla. I promise not to molest you or to beg for your love, though I'll do my best to win it. Why is it that you won't believe in me?"

"Oh, I do, Neil. It is because I like you so much that I won't marry you," she answered frankly, but a little wearily. "You deserve something so much better than a half-hearted wife."

"I'd rather have the half or the quarter of you than the whole of any other woman," he made answer in the reckless way of the lover. "At least, promise me that if you should change your mind, that if things should get desperate, you'll come to me? A word will be enough, Isla--even a look. I'll fly to your bidding on the wings of the wind."

"Oh, Neil, I wish that all this eloquence and this devotion could be given to a better woman----"

"She doesn't exist," put in the lover stoutly. "Now, tell me about Malcolm. What is the meaning of this horrible thing that has happened, and who told you?"

"He told me himself in last week's letter. Oh, yes--he minds, of course, but he thinks he has been unjustly treated. Somebody is always treating Malcolm unjustly, you know; and, whatever happens, it is always another person's fault."

"But it must be very serious, my dear. Has there been any other communication--anything from his Colonel, or the War Office for the General?"

"No--nothing; and when anything comes I shall intercept it," she replied without the smallest hesitation. "What is concerning me most is that, in about three weeks' time, Malcolm will be at home, loafing about idle in the glen, and I shall never know a moment's ease of mind. That's the redeeming feature of Creagh--it's at least five miles from everywhere. But, of course, he can't be permitted to loaf about. He must find some occupation. I wonder----"

She stopped there, however, and Neil was left to conjecture what it was that she wondered. He would not have been so well pleased had he known that her thoughts had flown with a curious sense of restfulness and hope to the man who had just left them. The hated man had said that the business of his life was to demolish difficulties and to build bridges where none had been before. Could he--or would he--undertake the problem of Malcolm's life?

Kitty returned while that question was still lingering in Isla's mind, and, after a little more desultory talk, the brother and sister took their departure.

"Tell Kitty on the way home, Neil," whispered Isla as she bade him good-bye, her fingers aching under his strong, almost painful, pressure which was intended to convey all the thoughts of which his heart was full.

"Give Aunt Betty my love, and tell her that I will pay her a visit before I go to Creagh," she added. "Yes, of course, tell her about Malcolm too, but don't say too much about it, and, of course, outside Garrion----"

She laid a significant finger on her lip.

Neil nodded, and, with gloom sitting on his brow, ascended to his high perch on the dogcart and tucked the rug about his sister's knees.

The next three weeks passed in a whirl of business for Isla Mackinnon.

The very next morning after the visit of the Americans to Achree she had Jimmy Forbes up from Lochearn to drive her to Creagh. The sun was shining so brightly and the air was so soft and balmy that all of a sudden she decided that the drive might do her father good.

He had only just come down from his bedroom and was standing in the doorway, enjoying the air, when the trap drove up, and Isla came down the stairs.

"Where are you for this morning, my dear?"

"I'm going to Creagh. Will you go with me, dear? I have some particular business to do at Creagh this morning, and it's so deliciously sunny and warm and I think the drive would do you good."

"Yes, I'd like to go," said the old man with the wistful pleasure of the child, at the same time taking a critical look at the stout roan cob that had come up from the hotel stable, well and fit for the rough road over Creagh moor.

It did not take Isla and Diarmid long to wrap the General up, and off they went through the pleasant spring sunshine, mounting slowly all the time until they reached the broad plateau of the moor of Creagh, which was the one valuable asset of Achree and constituted its only claim to the dignity of being a sporting estate.

The Lodge stood at the far angle of the moor, about a mile across from the road--a small, bare, ugly house which made no pretence to being anything more than a shelter for sportsmen. It was well protected by a clump of sturdy fir trees, and it had even a fertile bit of garden ground behind, with a small glass-house, and excellent stables. It was furnished throughout, and it was in the care of Margaret Maclaren, an old pensioner of Achree and widow of a former keeper.

She was a faithful servant who attended well to her duties whether her employers were there to see her or not, and she was not at all put out by the unexpected arrival of the trap from Achree.

Bathed in the glorious noon sunshine, the place looked its best, and even the interior did not seem at all amiss. All the windows were open to the sun, and Isla's sharp eyes noted the complete absence of damp, which was her chief enemy at Achree.

"Father, isn't it pretty here?" she asked the General as they stood for a moment in the porch before entering the house. "I should like to come up and live the whole summer here."

"It would not be amiss in the summer, child. Many a happy day have I spent in Creagh and many a jolly night."

She led him into the dining-room--a goodly-sized square room, not unhandsomely furnished in oak, the carpet rolled up in the middle of the floor, and faded chintz covers over the leather chairs.

The open casement windows commanded a splendid and uninterrupted view of the whole moor which, even in its bareness and in the wildness of the winter, had a certain rugged beauty of its own. A low hill rose immediately behind the house, from which a glorious prospect of the whole valley of the Earn could be seen, with Ben Voirlich rising like a buttress behind all the lesser hills in the valley below.

The air was like wine, and Isla's spirits rose as she grasped the possibilities of the simpler life there, in that remote lodge in a wilderness.

She quickly interviewed Margaret Maclaren, and in her company she made a rapid survey of the dismantled house, the result of which showed her that a very few days would suffice to put it in order for their reception.

"We have let Achree for the season, Margaret," she said in the most matter-of-fact voice she could command, "and the new tenants want to come in at Easter. You will thoroughly air and fire all the house, but more especially my father's room above the dining-room. These two rooms will be most exclusively his. We shall eat in the little room at the back, while he has this for his library and sitting-room."

"Yes, Miss Isla, and hoo mony will come up from Achree--of the servants, I mean?"

"Only Diarmid, Margaret. You and he must just manage. I will help all I can. If we find it too much, your niece, Annie Chisholm, could be got. Perhaps this will be necessary when we have Mr. Malcolm at home. Yes--he is coming soon, and he will be here with us for a few weeks at least."

Whatever secret wonder may have been in the soul of Margaret Maclaren, she suffered none of it to be expressed on her face.

Isla was much pleased with her visit and with the possibilities of the house, part of which she had forgotten. She saw that her father, too, was pleased. He enjoyed his walk about the place and constantly spoke of the beautiful view from the front of the house across the moor and down to Glenogle.

"I'll take the reins down, Jamie," said Isla to the hotel groom.

When they were fairly out on the road she turned rather anxiously to her father, talking to him in a low voice which there was no possible chance of Jamie overhearing as he was rather deaf at the best of times, and was almost entirely devoid of curiosity--a trait in his character worth mentioning.

"Father, I want to tell you something. Will you mind very much if we come up to Creagh soon for the whole summer?"

"No, I think I should like it," he answered, unexpectedly. "But you would find it very dull, wouldn't you?"

"I'm never dull anywhere. You saw the folk who came yesterday--the Americans, didn't you? I saw Mr. Rosmead talking to you at the shrubbery."

"I saw them--yes. Who were they and what brought them to Achree? I don't remember having seen him before."

"You haven't seen him before. He's a stranger--a rich American, and I have let Achree to him for six months."

Her hand trembled a little on the reins, and she half-expected either a petulant outburst or some other demonstration of feeling that would vex and alarm her soul and would harm the old man. But when, made anxious by his silence, she turned to look at him, his face only wore the perplexed expression of a child's.

"I don't know for what reason you want to let the place, Isla, or why anybody should wish to take it. But have it your own way. I dare say we could be very comfortable in Creagh unless, indeed, we have a wet summer. Then we would get very sick of it. I suppose the new folk would be willing to go out if we found it not possible to live up here."

"They would be perfectly reasonable, I'm sure, father," said Isla.

Her relief was so great that her features visibly relaxed, and her eyes began to shine. She was getting on famously. If only the latter part of the sad and sorry business should prove as easy to arrange as the first had been--why, then, perhaps she had been torturing herself needlessly. She had scarcely had a good night's rest since the arrival of the Indian mail, and the strain was beginning to tell on her.

"Well, I think I'll get you settled in Creagh comfortably with Diarmid as soon as possible. Then, after you are feeling quite at home, I think I shall go to Plymouth to meet Malcolm's boat. I haven't had a holiday for four years, father, and in the letter I had from Aunt Jean the other day she said they were all going up from Barras this week to Belgrave Square. So I'll take a few days of London dissipation before I meet Malcolm."

The old man made no demur. So great were his faith and his trust in Isla that he seldom questioned any of her doings.

During that week the bargain was concluded with the Rosmeads by Mr. Cattanach, after which a small correspondence began between Isla and Rosmead concerning certain minor repairs in the Castle that he wished to execute at his own expense.

A few days before they removed to Creagh he came down himself, ostensibly for the purpose of explaining to her that what he wished to effect was only a few small improvements with a view to making the home more comfortable for his mother.

Isla at first had resented the idea. Her Highland pride even got the length of tempting her to write and tell the man that he could either take the house as it was or leave it. But she could not afford to do that, so she relieved her feelings by writing the letter and then consigning it to the fire.

It was, however, a rather subdued and coldly aggressive Isla who met him on the occasion of his coming to pay his second call. But when she saw him, she was ashamed that she had written that letter and was glad that she had had the sense to burn it.

"I thought that I had better come instead of writing in reply to your last letter, Miss Mackinnon," he said presently. "We were getting adrift from the main issue. I want to explain that I don't propose to make any structural alterations on the house. The stove that I wrote about is an American invention for the heating of unsatisfactory country houses where, for some reason or other, the ordinary heating is difficult to arrange. It will greatly add to my mother's comfort while she is here, and it can be taken away when we leave. It will not harm the house but, on the contrary, will benefit it by drying it up. I think you mentioned to my sister that it was a little damp."

"It is very damp in parts," said Isla stoutly. "I am not seeking to deny it. I am sorry I wrote like that about the stove. You see," she added with her wandering smile which to him was wholly pathetic, "I am new to the business of house-letting, and you must be patient with me."

Her brief anger and irritation vanished under his clear, kind gaze, and the immensity of comfort and strength that seemed to be created by his very presence.

"You may trust me to do nothing which would alter the house out of your recognition," he said gently. "My mother is an old lady, and her chest is weak. It is absolutely necessary that she be kept warm and that no damp should be allowed to come near her. We are charmed with the house and with the kindness which you showed to us that day we came. My sister has never ceased to talk about it, and my mother is looking forward very much to making your acquaintance."

"Thank you, but at the moor of Creagh we shall be very much out of the way," said Isla softly.

"A quick and strong car annihilates distance," he reminded her.

But she made a quick little gesture of dissent.

"I think the moor of silence would beat it," she answered. "Well, I am taking my father up to Creagh next Monday, and when I have settled him in it I am going to London for a few days. The house will be quite empty and ready for you from next Monday, and I hope that you will not find it disappointing. At least I haven't embroidered any of the facts."

"You are going to London?" he said, as if surprised.

"Yes, I have to meet my brother's boat at Plymouth. He is returning from India."

"A soldier?" he ventured to ask, remembering the General's rank and wondering at the dull flush that rose to her face.

"Yes. But I think he may leave the Army for good. My father's health is so very frail. Nothing can be settled, however, till my brother comes home," she answered, hating herself for the prevarication that her clear conscience told her was nothing short of a lie.

But the pride in her burned high, and she would not demean herself to this man who, with all his pleasant ways and curious suggestion of power and strength, was only a rich, new-made American, who could never be expected to understand any of the feelings that lay deep in the heart of a Mackinnon of Achree.

As for Rosmead, he only smiled inwardly, attracted by her moods, which were as changeful as the face of Loch Earn. He was a builder of bridges, and the conquering of obstacles was, as he had told her, his business.

He could bide his time.

CHAPTER VI
THE HOPE OF ACHREE

When the "Jumna," an old troopship which had been fitted out for second-rate traffic from India, slowly approached her mooring in Plymouth Dock, Malcolm Mackinnon, smoking at the rail, ran his eyes along the waiting queue of expectant people at the landing-stage without the remotest expectation of seeing anybody belonging to him there. He knew the limitations of life in Glenogle, and how very little journeying to and fro on the face of the earth fell to the inmates of Achree.

He did not resemble the Mackinnons in appearance. He was short and thick-set, with his head set squarely on his shoulders, and he had a ruddy, sun-burned face, a pair of light blue eyes, a shifty mouth, and hair with more than a touch of red in it. He was very like his mother who had wrought confusion in Achree.

Isla, of course, did not know the full tragedy of her father's sad married life. Only she did know that she had been often impressed with the feeling and conviction that Malcolm was alien to Achree.

He might have been a changeling, so much did he differ in everything from any Mackinnon among them. Yet he had looks of a kind and a certain way with him which won people and made them, even against their better judgment, forgive him. This is a dangerous possession for a man who is not endowed with a very high sense of responsibility. It may at once be said that on more than one occasion Malcolm Mackinnon had traded on this happy-go-lucky, winning way of his.

When he saw Isla waving to him he gave a great start of surprise, which was almost chagrin. He had made several appointments in London, where he had intended to spend a few pleasant days before his liberty should be curtailed at Achree. His sister's presence would make these days difficult, if not impossible. Then the wild thought flashed through him that perhaps it meant that something had happened to his father. A month is a long time in a frail old man's life, and no one knew what a day might bring forth.

But Isla was not in mourning, and her face was as serene as usual. It would be unjust to say that he wished for his father's death, but certainly had he arrived in Scotland to find himself Laird of Achree, instead of merely heir to it, it would have made a material difference to his immediate comfort as well as to his prospects. For his affairs were in a tangle from which he did not know how he was going to extricate himself.

But now he had to meet the first stage in the coming of the inevitable Nemesis in the shape of Isla, whose frank tongue he knew of yore. He was fond of her in a way, and admired her greatly. He even wondered what all the men were thinking of that she remained unmarried at twenty-five. When he got nearer to her he saw that she had aged but little, while he himself had grown fat and gross, as will a man of his build who is fond of drink and of good living.

"Isla, how awfully good of you to do this! I never expected to see you or any of our ilk here," he exclaimed in greeting. "How on earth did you manage it, and how is the old man?"

"Father is very well. I thought I had better come to meet you, because there are heaps of things to explain; and besides, I felt that I wanted just a few days' change. I'm at Belgrave Square."

His face immediately fell. He did not like his Barras cousins, nor did they like him. Nay, they highly disapproved of him and all his works, and it was, he felt, positively cruel of Isla to have laid him open to the cross-questioning of the whole clan at the very moment of his arrival in England.

"In the circumstances you might have spared me that lot, Isla," he said with the gloom on his face that she remembered so well. "I won't go to Belgrave Square--so there!" he added positively. "There is a small cheap hotel off the Strand will do me--that is, if I don't go up north to-night."

"I haven't told them anything," said Isla quietly. "They only know that you are coming home, and, fortunately for me, they don't seem a bit curious. Aunt Jean was the only one who remarked about your getting leave so soon again. You can please yourself about going to the little hotel to sleep, but I promised that you should dine at Belgrave Square to-night."

"Oh, well, if they don't know anything and won't ask awkward questions," he said with a breath of relief, "I don't mind going."

"I had some difficulty in preventing Marjorie and Sheila from coming down. If they hadn't had a fitting for a Court frock they would have insisted on it. Sheila is going to be presented at the next drawing-room--on 7 May."

"Oh!" said Malcolm, but his interest was of languid order. "Well, I'd better see about my stuff. I haven't much. I sold out all I could before I left. There are always hard-up beggars in the regiment willing to buy, and I knew I shouldn't want much in the glen."

Again he spoke with airy inconsequence, as if nothing was of any great importance. Isla was quite conscious of a vivid and growing resentment. As she watched his strong, well-knit figure busy among the few traps which he was instructing one of the porters to collect, she wondered how he dared to be so regardless as he was. A grown man with a man's strength and ability of a kind--yet nothing but a burden and a care to other folks, to frail folks like an old man and a young woman. The inequality and injustice of it imparted a most unusual hardness to her face. She was hardly disappointed, however, because Malcolm had always held his sins of omission and commission lightly and feared only their consequences.

But in his heart of hearts he did feel his latest disgrace. A certain dogged dourness, however, would not permit him to show it.

After his meagre baggage had been collected there was still no sign of the boat-train leaving, so they paced the platform from end to end, talking together in low, eager tones, indicative of the deep interest of the subject under discussion.

"How long do you intend to stop in London?" he asked.

"I only came down to meet you. I thought we might go home on Friday."

"Oh well, if you like," he said, but she saw his face fall.

"I don't like to leave father any longer. He was very good about my coming, and Kitty Drummond was to go over to Creagh every day while I am away."

"To Creagh, you say! Who's there now, then?"

"We are. I have let Achree to some rich Americans, and they went into residence yesterday, I believe, or at least partly. They are doing a lot to the house, but their tenancy dates from Easter."

Malcolm stood still on the wooden pavement and stared at her in genuine dismay.

"You've let Achree, you say! In Heaven's name what for, and who gave you leave?"

"Nobody gave me leave. I took it; and you are the last person who ought to ask why," she made answer rather passionately.

"But--but--" he stuttered, "whatever did the governor say?"

"He said very little one way or other. I'm not even sure if he grasped the fact. But at least he was quite pleased to go to Creagh."

"To Creagh--to that little one-horse place! Do you mean to say that you propose to live there, then?"

"We are living there," she answered steadily.

"And you did this on your own, Isla? Well, I think you had a jolly good cheek. The decent thing would have been to wait till I came home at least. You won't deny, surely, that I have a say in it."

"I don't know about the say. What I did know was that if you came home the bargain would probably never have been concluded."

"But what was it for, anyway?"

She turned her small proud head to him, and her clear eyes flashed.

"Malcolm, I do really wonder what you are made of."

"Flesh and blood like other folks, and I can't get away from this. How much are they paying?"

"Five hundred a year with the shooting, and we propose to live on three and to lay bye the other two to help to pay off those terrible obligations you spoke of in your letter, which has kept me awake more or less since ever it came."

He laughed airily.

"Now that's just like a woman--to imagine that the practice of small and most beastly uncomfortable economies could do any good! Have you reckoned out that it will take ten years at the rate you speak of to get me clear? Most of us will be dead by that time."

"The train is going, thank God," said Isla in a high, clear, outraged voice. "Let us get in. I don't want to talk any more to you, Malcolm--either now or at any other time. You--you are outside the pale."

"Now take it easy, old girl. I made a clean breast of it all just to show you that I was really penitent; and of course I wasn't to blame for getting chucked. Any fool in the Thirty-fifth will tell you that. But this little attempt to pull the financial wires does strike a chap as rather comical. What did old Cattanach say? I suppose he's still at the helm--worse luck for me."

"Yes, he is. I gave him your letter, Malcolm."

"The deuce you did! Then you shouldn't have done it. He's a fossil--knows nothing about life. But there--don't let us quarrel about such things.

I am jolly glad to see you, old girl. And now I'll relieve you of all these beastly sordid cares. But Creagh, good Lord!--and not a bit of horse-flesh on the premises, I could bet my bottom dollar! I think I must try and rake up a motor-bike before I leave town; otherwise it will be like being buried alive."

The guard was calling London passengers to take their seats, and they made haste into the nearest compartment, which quickly filled up so that no further talk of a private nature was possible. Isla was glad of it. She had had enough.

As she sat opposite to her brother who, immediately the train started, composed himself in his corner for a sleep, she had ample time to study his face. That study filled her with a great and growing sadness. He was just over thirty, and in all these years there were few well-spent days. As a boy he had been a care and trouble to his people and to his schoolmasters, and, in these respects, the boy had been father to the man.

She thought again with a little, faint, passing sight of envy of the gallant boy whom the Edens had given to their country, who had died a hero's death upon the field. She told herself that had such a fate been Malcolm's she could have thanked God for it. Then she drew herself up with a little shudder, remembering sharply certain Bible words which had no uncertain sound--"Whoso hateth his brother is a murderer."

She did not hate him--only her heart was very tired and full of fear for the future.

That night, at the hospitable table of his uncle in Belgrave Square, Malcolm shone with the best of them. He was on his mettle, and he exerted himself to please, showing a nice deference to his stately aunt as well as to his jolly uncle, and he made himself perfectly adorable to his cousins.

Isla felt herself quite put in the background, but she did not mind. It was even a relief not to think, but just to sit still and let Malcolm's false light shine. Soon enough they would have to know what had happened, and then she knew that her Aunt Jean would never forgive him.

She came into Isla's room that night when the girl was brushing her hair, and, touched by the expression on her face, put a kindly question.

"What is it, dear child? Don't you feel very well? You haven't looked like yourself all day."

"I'm all right, Aunt Jean," Isla answered, but she did not meet her aunt's eyes.

"Malcolm is simply splendid! How improved he is! What charming manners! After all, the Army is the place for boys like Malcolm. Do you remember what an anxiety he used to be to your father in the old days? How proud of him he must be now!"

Isla did not answer--she simply could not. She felt as if she must scream out loud.

"Your uncle is delighted. They've been having a long talk in the smoking-room. Must you really hurry away on Friday, dear? We should simply love to have you and Malcolm for another week. I could get up a little dance for Malcolm. That sort of impromptu affair is often most enjoyable and it really seems a shame to go and bury him in Achree, or rather in Creagh, for so long."

"I can't stop, Aunt Jean. You know how father is. He is really quite frail, and I should not have an easy mind after Friday, but Malcolm can stop if he likes."

"I must ask him. How long has he, do you know?"

"You can ask him that, too, Aunt Jean," answered Ida very low.

"He isn't at all pleased about the letting of Achree. From his point of view, it does seem a little hard. Why did you do it, Isla, when you knew he was coming home this year? Surely it could have waited at least till the autumn."

"It couldn't wait. We had no money to go on with, Aunt Jean," answered Isla.

"Oh but, my dear, your uncle or I would have come to the rescue. What are folk for if they can't be made use of in that direction?" asked Lady Mackinnon almost playfully.

"It didn't matter about the letting, auntie. Everybody does it, and as for Malcolm, he is the very last person who ought to complain."

The voice was so hard that it slightly wounded the woman who heard it. She stepped forward and lifted the girl's chin in her hand and looked down into her face.

"Don't get hard, Isla. It is so unbecoming to a woman. I know that you have had a lot to think of, but now that Malcolm has come home roll it off on to his broad shoulders. It is what broad shoulders are given to our menfolk for. And, above all, don't get thinking that nobody can do things except yourself. Don't you think you're just a wee bit inclined that way, Isla?"

"Yes, I am all that way," answered Isla stolidly. "I fully admit it. But don't imagine I like it, Aunt Jean. The thing that I most want in this world is peace, and I can't get it. Good night, auntie. I'm sorry that I'm so disappointing."

Lady Mackinnon kissed her fondly, yet with a little regret.

"Isla's getting hard, Tom," she said to her husband when he came up a little later. "It's very bad for a girl to lose her mother, though in Isla's case, of course, it would have been worse if her mother had been spared. Don't you notice how hard and dull she has got to be of late? What a pity she couldn't marry! She used to be quite pretty."

"Used to be, Jean! What are you talking about?" asked Sir Tom rather irritably. "She's pretty yet, with the sort of beauty that a man doesn't tire of, and she's clever too. Depend on it, if Isla's hard she has had something to make her so. Malcolm's charming, of course, and much improved, but just once or twice to-night I felt that he didn't ring true."

"Nonsense, Tom. We have been out of the world too long and haven't marched with the times. I should like them to stop for a week or two, but Isla won't hear of it. She says she must go on Friday."

"Let Isla alone. She knows her own business best. As for Malcolm, please yourself, but I haven't got at the bottom of the meaning of this leave of his yet. It's unusual. I shouldn't wonder to hear that there is something behind it."

Lady Mackinnon did not take her husband's words at all seriously. She had no son, and her heart warmed to Malcolm, and she fell asleep, thinking how blessed she would have been among women had he been hers. Another of the mistakes this into which poor humanity, seeing through a glass darkly, is so liable to fall!

Next morning Isla left the house about eleven o'clock to go to an obscure street on the other side of Bayswater for the purpose of calling on an old servant at Achree, who had married a butler, and who now conducted a small boarding-house off the Edgeware Road.

It was a lovely spring morning, and she said she would prefer to walk across the Park. She greatly enjoyed that walk. The wide spaces of the Park, the enchanting glimpses through the trees which, though still bare, were beautiful with the sun upon their delicate tracery of branch and bough, seemed to fill her soul.

She did not greatly care for London life, and she often wondered a little at her cousins' enthusiasm over balls and routs, and all the treadmill of fashionable society. They were so excited over their Court frocks that their dreams were haunted by chiffons and festoons of lace and Court trains hung from slender shoulders.

Isla indeed was far too grave for her years. She had been cheated of her youth. Even she herself did not know what possibilities for frivolity and fun her nature held, nor how gay she could have been had not care, like a gaunt spectre, walked so long by her side.

Her discomfort about Malcolm was keen this morning. Even the gracious influence of the sun could not altogether banish it. But it helped, and her face looked very sweet under the brim of her simple hat, and more than one pair of eyes filled with admiration as she passed.

She left the park at the Marble Arch, crossed the road, and made her way along the Edgeware Road to Cromar Street, where Mrs. Fraser lived. It was not her first visit, and Agnes having been apprised of her coming, was on the doorstep to welcome her.

"There ye are, Miss Isla--a sight for sair een! I have been so put about wi' joy all this morning that I have not been able to do my work. How are you, and how is all at dear Achree?"

"So, so, Agnes," answered Isla with a smile as she grasped the faithful servant's hand and passed across her hospitable threshold. "You look wonderfully well. I hope that Fraser is too, and the children, and that everything is going right with you?"

Isla possessed to the full the faculty of binding those who served her to her with hooks of steel, she was so sweetly kind and interested in everything concerning them. Yet she held their respect, and no servant, even the least satisfactory, had ever been known to presume in the smallest degree upon any kindness shown.

She sat down in Agnes Fraser's ugly, heavy dining-room, which reeked of stale tobacco smoke, but which represented the greater part of her living, being let, with bedroom accommodation, to two permanencies who paid her well. And there Isla listened to the whole recital of the good woman's affairs. It occurred to Agnes only after Isla had gone, at the end of an hour's time, that she had really heard very little about Achree.

As Isla had risen to depart, she had said with a smile: "If you are coming to the glen this summer, Agnes, you will have a longer walk to get to us.

We have gone to live at Creagh for the season, and Achree is let to some Americans."

Agnes looked the dismay she felt, but abstained from comment and only remarked that she hoped they had made Creagh comfortable, and that they would not find it too dull.

But after the door was shut upon her visitor she wept tears of sorrow because the glory was departed from Achree.

Her last duty done, Isla's thoughts as she left the house began to revert with persistent longing to the glen. She had neither part nor lot in cities, and she could not understand the craze that people had for this great, overgrown London, where folk were always in a hurry and falling over one another in their haste.

Mrs. Fraser's house was well up the street, and Isla, walking quite fast and wrapped up in her own thoughts, had no eyes for any of those who passed her. But presently she came to the corner house of a little street near the Marble Arch end of the road. The door opened as she passed, and two persons came out, so close upon her that she could not but notice them.

Then her heart gave a sickly bound, and she sped on without once looking back.

It was Malcolm who came out of that house, and there was with him a woman, an impossible woman--that was the impression Isla carried away--a large, tall person, with an abundance of yellow hair and an enormous black hat perched upon it. Handsome in a way she might be, and her smile as she had made some jesting remark to her companion had been dazzling.

But it did not dazzle Isla. She grew cold all over, and, without waiting on her better judgment, which might have urged some quite simple explanation, she jumped to the conclusion that Malcolm had some entanglement which was at the bottom of his downfall.

CHAPTER VII
THE HOME-COMING

Having been made free of his aunt's house, Malcolm arrived at Belgrave Square that afternoon in time for tea. The room seemed quite full of people, for the young Mackinnons were a gay crowd, never happier than when surrounded by their friends. Somebody had said that the London season was to be Scottish that year, and there were heaps of their own immediate friends already settled in town.

Isla was greatly in request, and it was about twenty minutes before Malcolm got a chance of having a word with her. He came up to her jauntily with an air of the utmost unconcern, and, as he might have expressed it, took the bull by the horns.

"Why were you in such a hurry this morning, Isla, and what were you doing in the purlieus of the Edgeware Road? Don't you know that's the wrong side of the Park altogether?" he said teasingly.

"I might say the same to you," she answered a trifle tartly, and her eyes, which seemed to have acquired a distaste for his face, did not meet his gaze.

"I was doing my duty--and a beastly fagging bit of duty it was too, a little commission for a pal in India--and, as I'd made up my mind to go north with you to-morrow if you really are bent on going, this was my only opportunity."

It sounded a perfectly plausible explanation, and Isla suffered her somewhat unwilling eyes to dwell for a moment on his smiling face. Never did man look more innocent and ingenuous. There was not the flicker of a lid or a tinge of colour to condemn him. Knowing perfectly well that her scrutiny was judicial, he met it without flinching.

"I did not like the look of the woman, Malcolm," was all she said. "But please, I don't want to hear any more about it."

It can hardly be said that she was convinced, but only that she realized the utter futility of trying to get to the bottom of Malcolm's mind or of ever reaching his real self. What that self would be like when she reached it she did not ask.

But a little later, watching his matchless manner with his aunt's guests and the way in which he held his little court of admiring womenkind about him, she marvelled at his powers. So long as he possessed such faculties of pleasing and could attract those with whom he came into contact, nobody need wonder at his gay aplomb. Nothing could greatly matter, for whoever might suffer or go under, it would not be Malcolm. He would sail--a little unsteadily perhaps, but still successfully--on the crest of the wave, and only those who knew him intimately and who had suffered through him would ever probe the depths of his colossal selfishness.

This was the estimate of her brother at which Isla had now arrived. The trials and hardships of the last three years had wrought a great change in her outlook upon men and things and had made her judgment a little merciless. In fact this was a very critical moment in the history of Isla Mackinnon, and but for the timely introduction of some fresh forces into her life she might have become a really hard woman.

Malcolm airily declined his aunt's rather pressing invitation to stay a week.

"I'll return, dearest aunt, a little later, when the Glen begins to pall," he whispered with that little air of personal devotion and interest which even old women found so charming. "Behold the gloom on Isla's face! She represents my duty. I shall take her home to-morrow, Pay my humble respects to the old man, and syne, if you will have me, I'll be only too glad to come back."

Lady Mackinnon nodded, well pleased.

"Come up in time for the Court. Marjorie and Sheila will never be satisfied till you see them in all their bravery. And we'll give a ball for you if you do come!"

"All right, my lady," said Malcolm with extreme satisfaction. "Fix the date and I'll come."

"I'm so sorry about Isla. I keep telling her not to take life so seriously," said Lady Mackinnon, her kind eyes wandering in the direction of her niece. "As I told her last night, it is you who ought to bear the burden of Achree. It's robbing her of her youth. She has changed greatly in the last year, don't you think?"

"Yes, and gone off decidedly, but there----"

He gave his shoulders a little shrug which expressed much that he did not say.

He dined at Belgrave Square that night and showed another side of him--the grave, quiet, attentive side, which pleased his relatives equally, if not even more.

"Why am I distrait?" he asked, when Marjorie twitted him with his quietude. "Well, the windbag was pricked last night. I couldn't sleep in my hard hotel bed for thinking of all the gas I had let out. It was pure exuberance of joy at again finding myself in such an atmosphere after hard service and a month on that beastly boat. Here's to our next merry meeting! Uncle Tom, Aunt Jean--the best of luck and nothing short of coronets for these fair heads."

Then they all laughed, and the last memory of the evening was as pleasant as possible. Next morning the whole family were at Euston to see the brother and sister off, and they duly departed in the full odour of family farewells.

"Well, that's over, thank goodness," said Malcolm as he dropped into his corner. A judicious word and a tip from Uncle Tom had secured them a compartment to themselves, in which they could talk of their private affairs. "Now, it'll be the tug-of-war--eh, Isla? Don't look so glum, old girl. Believe me, there isn't anything in life worth it."

"I don't want to be glum, but I have felt rather mean these two days, Malcolm. Perhaps we ought to have told Uncle Tom and Aunt Jean. Didn't you feel that we were there under false pretences? They would have felt differently, I mean, if they had known that you had sent in your papers."

He shrugged his shoulders, tossed his cap to the rack, and took out his cigarette case.

"Do you mind if I take a whiff? I suppose it would have made a difference, but why intrude unpleasant topics until one can't avoid them? That's a pretty good and safe philosophy of life, Isla--to lie low and keep dark about what can't be helped."

"They will know before you go back to London again, that is, if you were serious about going to them in May."

"Anything may happen between now and the month of May. The thing is to grease the ropes. Now, what earthly good would it have done to have told them the real state of affairs? It would only have depressed them and made us all most beastly uncomfortable. By the by, as we are on the subject, may I inquire how many people in the Glen you have told?"

"Only Neil Drummond."

"That young, unlicked cub! And why, in Heaven's name, should you have told him? Are you engaged to him--or what? There must be some reason why he should be taken into the family's most private counsels."

"I had to tell somebody, and it was in a manner forced on me," she said rather coldly. "But you need not be afraid of Neil telling anyone. He feels it too much."

"Very kind of him, I'm sure. Well now, tell me something about this American chap. Is he a bounder, like the rest of them?"

"No, he's a gentleman, Malcolm."

"It's an elastic term. Do you mean that he wears good clothes and that sort of thing?"

"No. I don't mean that."

"Then, he's a thorough good chap that a fellow might know?"

Isla, with a vision of Rosmead's calm, strong, fine face in front of her, sat back suddenly and began to laugh.

"What's the joke?" asked Malcolm, mildly surprised.

But she did not give him any satisfaction. She felt tempted to say that very probably had Rosmead known the facts of the case he might have declined the honour of Malcolm's acquaintance. She told herself, however, that she must try not to break the bruised reed. Yet there was not much of the appearance of the bruised reed about the airy Malcolm, who looked as if he had not a care in the world.

He was very kind and amusing on the journey, telling her lots of stories of his Indian experiences. More than once she felt herself almost completely succumbing to his spell and inclined to accept without reservation his own estimate of himself.

It was dark when they reached the station at Lochearnhead, where the wagonette from the hotel was waiting for them.

Malcolm elected to sit on the driver's seat and to take the reins from Jamie Forbes, and so Isla was left to her own contemplations in the roomy space behind. She was not sorry that it was so. Once more back in the

Glen, she experienced a return of all her cares, accentuated, because the biggest one, embodied in the flesh, was in front, carrying on an animated conversation with Jamie, from whom, in a few minutes' time, he wrested the whole gossip of the Glen.

He learned that the hotel business was flourishing exceedingly, now that the making of the new railway line was coming near the head of the Loch. It had been started only a year when Malcolm last went away, and now they were at work on the viaduct, which had just escaped being built on Achree land.

"If only we'd been a mile lower down the Glen, Isla!" he looked round to say. "We might have had a haul off the Railway Companies, but that's just our luck all through. We miss it every time by the skin of our teeth. Do you mind if I just stop at the hotel and pass the time of day with Miss Macdougall?"

"Don't stop long, then, Malcolm. I want to get home to father as quickly as possible."

She sat with what patience she might for ten minutes while he was inside the hotel getting a drink, and soon after he had resumed his seat they began the gradual ascent of Glenogle. She was conscious of a quickened heart-beat as they came near to Achree; and presently the blaze of its lights could be seen through the trees.

"By Jove, Isla--no stint there!" he called over his shoulder. "Achree has never been illuminated like that within the memory of man. What are they saying about the new folk in the Glen, Jamie?"

"They like them not that pad, sir. They are fery civil-spoken and kind, forpy peing likely to spend a heap of money. They are fery anxious that whoefer hass things to sell in the Glen shall pring them to Achree. There are not many like that come now to the Glen, Maister Malcolm. The most of them do nothing put send for big boxes to come from the store. They will pe well likit, I'm thinking."

"Oh, yes, it sounds idyllic," said Malcolm drily, the meaning of which adjective Jamie did not grasp.

"It seems a shame to pass by the old place. I'm down to-morrow if I'm a living man, Americans or no Americans," said Malcolm to Isla. "Has he any women-folk?"

"I'll tell you about them later," she answered, and her voice shook a little, for she too felt a qualm as they passed by the gate and the little lodge.

It was a long cold climb to the Moor of Creagh, and she was heartily sick of it before they drew up at the unpretentious white gate from which a straight, short drive led up to the house.

Diarmid was in the porch to meet and welcome them, and, though there was an odd shrinking in the old man's eyes as they travelled with a look of anxious reproach to the young Laird's face, Malcolm himself seemed quite unaware of it. He grasped the old man's hand cordially, asked for his welfare, and then passed in to where the old General, holding himself rather erect and proudly, though leaning hard on his stick, was peering through the dim light for sight of his son.

There can be no man who is wholly bad, and the sight of big father-- that pathetic and yet noble figure, a brave soldier who had spent himself for his country, shook Malcolm Mackinnon as his sister's appealing eyes had altogether failed to do. He now realized that if his father was ever able to grasp the fact of his dismissal from the Army it would kill him. He should never know, Malcolm swore to himself, as he bent low and ashamed over the outstretched hand and saw the quiver of the thin, pale face.

"How are you, sir?" faltered Malcolm.

And Isla, seeing his expression and noting the tremor in his voice, placed that bit of genuine feeling to his credit and wiped something off the slate.

"Glad to see you home, my boy, though this is a queer little house you are come to. Ask Isla about that. She's the culprit, but it's a very comfortable place, and I like it well. We'll have some happy days here, my son. Welcome home."

"Glad to see you well, father," answered Malcolm, though in truth he did not think the old man looked long for this world.

Then there was a greeting of sheer affection for Isla, and a look passed between father and daughter which told of a most perfect understanding.

Malcolm had a sniff of scorn for the cramped little house and, when presently, with the grime of his journey washed off and his dinner-jacket on, he came to the queer little room for the evening meal, he looked round rather grimly until his significant gaze rested on his sister's face.

"You'll never be able to stick it, Isla," he said in his most aggressive tones. "There isn't room in it to swing a cat."

The old man was in good form. The coming of his son seemed to awaken him for a little space to a fresh interest in life.

"Was there anything brought up from Achree cellar, Diarmid?" he asked as the old servant passed the plates.

"Yes, sir," answered Diarmid, not daring to say how very low the cellar at Achree had fallen and how its precious store had been diminished without the smallest hope of replenishment.

They were very abstemious folks at Achree, and the General, being forbidden all stimulants except a little whisky when he needed it, had hitherto asked no questions.

"A bottle of Pommery, then, to drink Mr. Malcolm's health," he said, with the air of old times, when there had been big parties round the table at Achree and when the wine had flowed at his bidding.

Diarmid looked desperately--imploringly at his young mistress, who rose, smiling slightly.

The Pommery had long since disappeared; but, in anticipation of this reunion, she had laid in one bottle of champagne in order that her father might not be disappointed. So it was brought and duly drawn by Diarmid, who filled the glasses and then helped his master to his feet.

"Welcome home, my son. Long life, good health, and honourable prosperity to you and to Achree. God bless you and make you a blessing. Isla, my dear, your best health."

Isla's eyes suddenly swam in tears, and Malcolm had the good feeling to bend his head in honest shame. The General did little more than taste from his glass and then set it down with a little sigh of disappointment.

"It is bad for good wine to be shifted," he said. "Never mind, Malcolm. When we go back to Achree you shall have your pick of the cellar."

The wine was good. The change was in his palate, which had lost its verve. He was very tired after dinner, and his rambling thoughts could not be kept in check. He babbled a good deal of old days, for which indeed Isla was thankful, since it kept him from asking questions about the present ones.

She had dreaded what might happen on the night of the home-coming, but she now clearly saw that her father was less and less likely to disturb himself about any untoward happenings. He accepted everything--a circumstance which certainly considerably relieved the strain.

"He looks jolly bad, poor old chap," said Malcolm, when Isla came down about ten o'clock from seeing him safely in bed. "He can't last long. It was a pity that you didn't let him see it out at Achree."

"He has not got any worse in the last six months that I can see. Of course the excitement to-night wore him out. He will be brighter in the morning."

"I still think it was a beastly shame to bring him up here. There isn't even decent comfort. This is the only room worth mentioning."

"Well, he has it. He is quite comfortable," said Isla, stoutly. "We must take what is left."

"In wet weather, of which Glenogle has its full share, we shall fight like Kilkenny cats," said Malcolm with a grimace.

Isla passed over the vulgarity of the remark in silence, and, after a moment, said quite straightly. "But surely you won't stop long in the Glen, Malcolm. You'll try to get an appointment of some kind."

"I'd be glad if you'd mention the sort of appointment I'd be likely to get," he answered carelessly. "I must say it's very cold cheer you have for a chap, Isla, after three years' absence. If I weren't the most unsuspicious of men I might suspect you of having underhand motives."

Isla, staring hard into the crackling embers of the peat-fire, answered nothing.

"It strikes me from all I can gather that the place wants a good deal of looking into. I'll make that my first business. I thought them all slack when I was home before, and Heaven only knows what they'll be like now. Then, I must be on the spot on account of the way the old man is. I shouldn't like to be out of the way if anything should happen."

Isla rose to her feet and bade him good night. She had had just about as much as her tired body and strained mind could stand.

"Dead men's shoes" were the words that beat upon her brain through the hours of a restless night.

CHAPTER VIII
MALCOLM'S PROSPECTS

It is the mission of the morning to clear the air, and next morning things looked brighter. The sun shone out gloriously, and the air was soft and balmy as a child's kiss.

Isla slept late and rather heavily after a restless night, and she was horrified when she awakened with a start to find that it was nine o'clock. She sprang up, threw her window open to the sun, and leaned over it for a moment to inhale the delicious breath of the morning. She had taken one of the attic rooms for her own, Margaret Maclaren occupying the other one, while Diarmid had made shift with a bed in his pantry.

The attics had storm-windows on the roof, from which you could see across the angle of the Moor and get a glimpse of Glenogle. Also from that high coign of vantage there was a fascinating view of Ben Voirlich, on whose peak still rested the cap of morning mist. But all the little hills huddled around and below were clear, and the day gave promise of being fine.

Margaret, who had been up twice to the door, now appeared with her hot water.

"So glad you had a good rest, Miss Isla. I thought you looked terrible tired last night. The General is still sleeping. Diarmid says he has hardly moved all night."

"Oh, I am glad of that--and Mr. Malcolm?"

"Been out since the back of six and had his porridge with Diarmid and me," answered Margaret proudly. "Now he is asking for his breakfast and inquiring when you are coming down."

"Serve the breakfast. I'll be as quick as I can," said Isla.

She plunged into her dressing with a will. When she got down to the dining-room she found Malcolm in a tweed knicker-bocker suit, discussing the Loch trout that had been sent up from the hotel with Miss Macdougall's compliments.

"I'm surprised at you, Isla. I thought you would have been down at six anyway, giving us all points," he said gaily. "I've been up for two hours and a half and had a tramp across the Moor. It was glorious. Seen father?"

"Yes, he's just waking up after a good night"

"He doesn't come down to breakfast?"

"No. Diarmid is taking it to him now."

She passed round to her place at the tray, and Malcolm admired her trim figure with its slender, well-belted waist, the poise of her head, the glint of her hair, and the clear red-and-white of her complexion.

"You look better here than you did in London, Isla. London doesn't suit you, and that old black frock you had on at Aunt Jean's in the evening was an unbecoming rag, if you'll excuse me for saying it. You could wear vivid colours. I'd like to see you in emerald green--shimmery soft stuff, don't you know?--with trailing draperies round you?"

Isla laughed outright.

"I'm afraid the chances of that are small. The old black rag has been my only evening frock since you went away, and I believe I've had it on only about half a dozen times."

"Poor old girl, what a shame that it can't get pretty clothes! Now, if I were you I'd have them. By Jove, I would, and let pay who will."

"Yes, I know," she answered quietly. "But I've got into the habit of paying for my clothes before I wear them. Well, what are you going to do to-day?"

"Well, the first thing undoubtedly is to rig up a horse and trap of some kind. I'll go down to Lochearn presently--on my feet, that haven't done much walking of late, you bet, and see whether Miss Macdougall can fix me up. It's quite obvious that Creagh isn't livable in unless one is provided with some means of escape from it. What about the post? Do the old primitive arrangements still hold good?--half the day gone before the bag comes in?"

"It's half-past twelve before the postman gets here. I generally walk as far as Little Shuan to meet him."

"I'll get farther than that this morning--probably all the way," he said. "What are you to be about? I suppose you have things to see to in the house after having been away?"

"Yes," said Isla. "I want you to be careful about the letters while you are here, Malcolm. There are only some my father cares to see, and even these do not always interest him. But he has gleams of comprehension and of most disconcerting clearness of vision. Dr. Blair says it is most imperative that he should not have a shock of any kind, however small, and in the last year I have been keeping almost everything back from him. He grasps one bit of a thing, you see, and confuses the rest, and so might very easily work himself up into a state about nothing."

"I understand," said Malcolm. "So, between us, we have to keep him in the dark. That's what it amounts to, I suppose."

Isla nodded. "I hate to see it, but it does amount to that."

"I'll make a note of it. But, now that I'm home, the chief cause of anxiety may perhaps be removed," he said airily. "Well, I'll go, and don't keep my luncheon for me. If I want anything I'll drop in at the hotel. It's possible that I may call at Achree as I come up. Of course it is necessary that I meet this American chap and have a talk with him."

"I suppose so, but you can't do anything, Malcolm, even if you see things you don't like at Achree. He has paid the half of his money."

"And where is it."

"In the Bank at Callander, in my name."

Malcolm whistled.

"Rather high-handed, isn't it, Isla?"

"There wasn't anything else to be done. Father can sign cheques, of course, but I banked Mr. Rosmead's money in my name on Mr. Cattanach's advice."

"But surely now you'll let me take over the business part of the show, Isla?"

He pushed back his chair and took out his cigarette case as he put the question.

Isla looked uncomfortable, and her face even paled a little. She hated the position in which she was placed, but past experience had shown her the folly of trusting Malcolm in money matters. He had certainly not the money-sense nor yet the sense of honour where money was concerned.

"I don't think I can do that, Malcolm. Remember, it is all the money that we have to live on until the rents become due again at Martinmas."

"Don't any of them pay now?"

"One or two--Roderick Duncan and the farmer at Little Shuan. But these are crofts, their rent amounting to only a few pounds."

Having lit his cigarette, Malcolm proceeded to turn out his pockets.

"A few coppers, some Indian coins, and two half-sovereigns!" he said ruefully. "I'm stonybroke, Isla. Have I to come to you for the few pence that I shall need in the Glen? By Gad I can't do that! I must speak to the governor about it."

Isla's face reddened where it had been pale before.

"It's a horrible situation," she said almost passionately. "But don't you see I can't help it? It isn't my doing. Since you left we have lived on next to nothing at Achree. We haven't bought any butcher's meat hardly, but have had rabbits and fowls and game of our own killing and the everlasting trout. I never get any new clothes, as you have already observed and remarked upon."

"But now that the American has paid you should be a little rougher."

"I'm going to save that money to pay off the mortgage and the--the other money you owe," she said quite quietly, and he had no idea what fires blazed beneath that calm exterior. "You'll have to find something to do, Malcolm, and that soon. You must see that for yourself."

"I see that I'm to have a jolly rotten time here," he said gloomily. "I must write to Cattanach and tell him to look out an agent's place of some kind for me."

"But you don't know anything about land or estate management, Malcolm."

"I know as much as some of the fellows of my acquaintance who fill fat billets. Meanwhile, I simply must have a fiver, Isla. I shan't spend it, but a fellow can't go about with empty pockets."

She rose and, unlocking the old bureau, counted out five sovereigns from the little cash-box in the secret drawer. He took them without shame and even with a twinkle in his eye.

"Pay Saturday! Well, good-bye, old girl. I'll go out on the hunt and see whether I have any luck. I don't mind telling you I'm rather building on this American chap. If he's a millionaire I must try and coax him to disburse a little in this direction. I'll ask him quite frankly whether he doesn't want a handyman about the place. I could take on that job and fill it to a T."

Isla did not demur, but her pride rose again in revolt at the thought of what Malcolm might do. She thought she did not wish to see anything more of the Americans. She would keep strictly to the letter of their bargain and leave them at Achree in peace. But if her observation was to any purpose she told herself that Malcolm would not make very much of Peter Rosmead, who was far too hard-headed a man to be taken in by his specious ways.

She had a good many uncomfortable moments during the day, however, while contemplating possible interviews between Malcolm and Rosmead, all of which fell short of the actual happening.

Malcolm went up to spend half an hour by his father's bedside, making himself so charming that the old man was full of it when Isla came to see how he was getting on.

Then he left the house and set off with a long swinging step to cover the distance between Creagh and Lochearn. He did not keep to the road. There was not a hill-path or a sheep-track in the district with which he had not been familiar since his boyhood. He came out just below Achree, deciding that he would go on to meet the post first and take it as he returned. About a quarter of a mile from the Lodge he met Donald Maclure driving some black-faced ewes in front of him, and he stopped to pass the time of day.

Donald was a large, slow man, with a stolid face and a shock of red hair sticking out from under his broad bonnet, and he presented a sharp contrast to his trig and sonsy wife. Indeed, many had wondered how Elspeth had ever come to marry him and, above all, who had done the courting, Donald being the most silent man in the whole of the glens.

"Hallo, Donald, how is the world using you?" cried Malcolm cheerily.

"No sae pad, Maister Malcolm," Donald was forced to answer. "I heard ye gae by last nicht--at least Elspeth did. She wass oot wavin' her hand."

"I must go in and give her a kiss for that--eh, Donald? Where are you taking that nice-looking herd to?"

"The other side of the little hill," answered Donald briefly.

"Coining money off the sheep--eh, Donald? It's you farmers who haul in the shekels in these days. What with taxes and reduced rents and what not, there's little left for the poor landlord. You needn't shake your head, my man. We'll thrash it out another day, however. But you can't get away from the fact that we can't afford to live in our own house."

Donald pulled his forelock and passed on with a mysterious Gaelic direction to the sheep-dog, which was attended with magical results. He was neither convinced nor deceived by Malcolm's small hints. He knew him of yore; also Elspeth, having the most perfect faith in her big, silent husband, had not failed to confide to him the true story of the Americans' coming to Achree.

A few steps further on Malcolm saw in the distance two ladies, walking together, with shepherds' crooks in their bare hands and with no hats upon their heads.

Their bearing and carriage at once riveted his keen interest. Wherever there was a petticoat Malcolm Mackinnon was interested, and these ladies were evidently strangers to the Glen.

One was very tall and slender, the other short in stature but neatly built, and both wore most workman-like country attire with a grace that he had never seen excelled.

As he came nearer the face of the taller of the two attracted him still more. It was exquisitely beautiful, being chiselled on pure classical lines, and the skin was soft and clear, the colour so pale and delicate, without giving the smallest suggestion of ill-health, that he had never seen anything like it. The abundant dark hair, slightly waved in front and worn simply parted over her ears, gave a look of Madonna-like simplicity to the face, which, to Malcolm's eyes, seemed most alluring.

The other was more ordinary, though her face had a certain piquant charm. He wondered who they were and whether he dared make any remark as they passed, but they solved the difficulty by bidding him a pleasant good morning.

Instantly his cap was in his hand, and he would have stopped, but they immediately passed on, evidently slightly surprised at his intention to detain them. He waited only until they were over the brow of the next little hill, and then he deliberately entered Donald Maclure's pasture and crept back after them in shadow of the few scanty trees and shrubs that lined the road--and all just to watch where they would go!

From the next hillock he could see the gate of Achree in the hollow, and, having waited sufficiently long, smoking another cigarette the while, he had the satisfaction of seeing them turn in at the Lodge. Then did an immense content steal over Malcolm Mackinnon. With two such charming inmates at Achree, life which had promised to be like a desert, suddenly began to blossom like the rose.

He hastened on without stopping at the farm-house to pass the time of day with Elspeth Maclure, and presently his attention was diverted by the sight of the new railway track which had gradually crept up the side of the Loch, and which was about to culminate in a big viaduct over the burn at the lower end of Glenogle. He had not a very keen sense of beauty, but, somehow, he did not like the ugly scars on the hill-sides and all the unsightly paraphernalia of the work, though he knew very well what a boon it would be to them when all was finished.

He was still contemplating it when the post-gig drove up, and then there was another stop and an exchange of greetings with David, while the letters were handed over. He glanced at them with a sort of careless keenness, and, deciding that there was nothing affecting him, he handed them back and told David to deliver them at Creagh.

Finally he landed in the Hotel, where he spent a good hour at the bar, hearing all the gossip of the Glen and, incidentally, a good deal that he wished to know about the new folk at Achree.

"I think I met them, Miss Macdougall. Have they passed by this morning?"

"Yes. They have been in here, sir--the two young ladies, but they do say that the big tall one is a married woman that has divorced her husband. I don't know the story rightly, but that's what they say. She is very quiet and seems sad-like. The other speaks most of the time and is very lively. The old lady I have never seen, but they do say that they are a most superior kind of folk and not like some of them we get in the Glen in the shooting season."

"Do you happen to know whether Mr. Rosmead himself is in the Glen to-day?"

"No, he iss not, sir, for the motor went by with him for the nine o'clock train and syne came back empty."

"Well, I'm not supposed to know, so I think I'll call at the place as I go up. I have a good enough excuse anyhow, as I have been away so long."

And thus it came about that this bit of information did not deter Malcolm from doing that which he had in his mind.

About half-past twelve he passed through the familiar gateway to Achree and made his way to the house. His pulses scarcely stirred as he did so. The place of his fathers made no appeal to him. It was merely stone and lime, and if it had been in his power he would have sold it for hard cash to any purchaser. In fact, the thought uppermost in his mind as he approached the door was that, having once caught the millionaire, he might find it worth while to keep him. He determined to make himself, somehow, master of the law of entail in order to discover whether there was any loophole of escape from the disability to sell it. Not in his father's lifetime, of course. But when Isla and he should be left, of what use would this great, rambling, uncomfortable old house and its attendant acres of hungry moor and hill be? Far better convert it into the money with which they could enjoy life, making choice in the whole wide world of a place of abode.

A woman-servant opened the door to him, and in answer to his inquiry, informed him that Mr. Rosmead was not at home. Malcolm's sharp eyes noted in the hall beyond the flutter of a petticoat, and as he turned to go he purposely raised his voice.

"I am sorry that I've not a card on me. Will you be so kind as to tell him that Mr. Malcolm Mackinnon from Creagh called to see him and that he will call another day?"

"Yes, sir," said the girl.

But at that moment the figure within came towards the door. It was Sadie, who, having heard the name, advanced with an insatiable curiosity. She extended a very frank hand.

"So you are Mr. Mackinnon that was expected home from India," she said, showing her dazzling teeth in her smile. "Won't you come in and have a bit of lunch with my sister and me? We shall be alone, as my mother does not yet come down."

"Thank you, Miss Rosmead. But that would be presuming on a very slight acquaintance--in fact, none at all, wouldn't it?"

"Oh, but we know your sister and that perfectly dear old father of yours, and, anyway, this is your house and you must want to have a look at the old place after having been away so long. I've no doubt you are hating us for being here. Come in. Oh, Vivien, do come here! It was Mr. Mackinnon whom we met on the road, and I am asking him to lunch."

Malcolm passed into the house, hat in hand, and was duly introduced to Mrs. Rodney Payne. Seen at closer quarters, she was even more beautiful than he had thought. The still repose of her manner contrasted strongly with her sister's vivacity and seemed from the first to cast a sort of spell over Mackinnon.

"We shall be happy if you will stay to luncheon, Mr. Mackinnon," she said, obeying the instructions from Sadie's eyes. "My brother will be very sorry to have missed you. He has gone to the Forth Bridge to-day to meet the contractors there and have a talk with them. It seems it is the annual inspection--or something. Anyway, Peter had an invitation to go. He won't get back till quite late, perhaps not even until to-morrow."

Malcolm Mackinnon did not care. He was in no hurry to meet Mr. Hylton P. Rosmead so long as there was such a charming substitute to take his place. He wouldn't have hesitated about making this glib compliment to another woman, but there was something about Vivien Rosmead which repelled any attempt at even the slightest familiarity. She held herself aloof, and her mouth, made for sweetness, seemed as if it were chiselled in marble. Malcolm wondered what the experience had been that had given her that petrified expression, and he longed to be the man to melt her heart.

Sadie, as usual, did the talking and proved herself an admirable hostess. But while he answered her gay badinage it was Vivien who had his whole admiration. He noticed how little she ate and that her eyes had in them a far-away look which seemed to detach her from the common things of life. Yet she was not dull. A word now and then indicated that she was not by any means dead to the possibilities of life or to the interests of everyday.

"We like your sister so much, Mr. Mackinnon," she said with a sudden warm flash of interest when Sadie left a moment's breathing space. "We hope that she is going to allow us to be friendly with her."

"Oh, yes, of course. Why not? She will be only too pleased, I'm sure," murmured Malcolm eagerly.

"She was so kind about letting us come here in a hurry that we can never forget it. And it is so lovely to see her with your father."

As she spoke of the old General, Vivien's eyes grew large and pitiful, more and more like those of the Madonna.

"It's even more lovely to find how adored she is in the Glen, in all the glens," said Sadie the irrepressible. "Everywhere you hear nothing but her praises. Don't you find it a little hard, Mr. Mackinnon," she added with just a little malicious flash, "to live up to such a sister?"

"Sadie, Sadie, do be careful!" said Vivien softly. "That is not quite kind."

"It's true, Vivien, and I see from Mr. Mackinnon's face that he admits it. You and I must be pals, Mr. Mackinnon, for I'm just like that with my sister. She's so frightfully good that she ought to have a halo, and she makes all common folks who approach her feel worship in the air."

"I am sure of that," said Malcolm with a queer little bow in the direction of Vivien who, though she laughed, was a little vexed.

"Mr. Mackinnon will think us very frivolous, Sadie. Suppose we change the subject and ask him to tell us something about India. Your British rule in India is so splendid! It stands, just like a great rock, immune from the assaults of criticism. I'm sure all this talk about sedition and unrest means nothing. Perhaps you can tell us about it."

Very little did Malcolm Mackinnon know about British rule in India--as little indeed as any Tommy in the ranks.

"Well, you see," he said with rather an awkward laugh. "I was only a bit of the system--don't you know?--a small--very small spoke in the big wheel. My part was to make forced marches in the night and keep an open eye after stray bullets, and to be all ready when occasion rose."

Sadie's eyes positively glowed with excited interest. She loved the Army, investing it with colour and romance, and in Malcolm Mackinnon she pictured to herself a heroic figure--a replica of the fine old father, of whose valour the Glen had many tales to tell.

But Vivien, the more discriminating of the two, had already decided in her own clear and quiet mind that the son of Achree occupied a lower moral plane than the daughter. Her instinct was very swift and fine, and the feeling of distrust born of that first meeting was never afterwards wholly dispelled.

Sadie, with her elbows on the table, wagged her unconventional tongue and asked so many questions about their guest's life in India that he gave her a very highly coloured version of the same, playing up to her for all he was worth and deepening her impression of the soldiery who had upheld Britain's prestige all over the world.

In the midst of this fascinating talk which proceeded almost entirely between Malcolm and Sadie, Vivien merely listening with an odd air of cool detachment which was almost critical, a servant entered the room with a message which she delivered to Sadie. Since Vivien's return to her mother's house she had taken a secondary place, and, though she resumed her own name, it was Sadie to whom were accorded the privileges of the elder daughter.

"Please, Miss Sadie, Mrs. Rosmead would like very much to see Mr. Mackinnon before he goes if he will come to her room."

Malcolm would have declined if he had had any excuse, but Sadie jumped up immediately, saying that she would show him the way.

Vivien did not accompany them, and when, after a brief interview with the beautiful, white-haired old lady who had Vivien's eyes, Sadie and he returned to the hall-place, she was nowhere to be seen.

"Must you go, Mr. Mackinnon? I don't know where Vivien is. She's like that, poor dear. Her troubles have quite taken the life out of her. You'll come again, won't you? In the name of the whole Rosmead folks I make you free of your own house."

She was so frankly kind and her eyes so beamed on him that Malcolm would not have been Malcolm had he not made quick response.

He bent low over her white, outstretched hand and murmured certain words which somewhat heightened Sadie's colour and brought an odd softness to her eyes.

"I like that man, Vivien. He's perfectly lovely, I think, and all the things they say about him in the Glen are lies. Don't you think so?"

But Vivien, whom sad experience had made wise, answered not at all.

CHAPTER IX
THE MESSENGER

As Malcolm strode up the Glenogle road a little later, well pleased with his day's achievement, he was overtaken by a smart drag and a pair of swift roan horses handled by Drummond of Garrion, whose sister Kitty was by his side.

Neil drew up of course, and there was an odd look on his face as the greeting passed. Malcolm's manner was perfectly cool, even a little defiant. It would certainly have been better had Isla held her tongue, but he was not going to eat humble pie before that big, sheep-faced boy who had nothing but his money to recommend him.

He took off his cap to Kitty, however, who smiled sweetly upon him.

"We're going to Creagh--no, not to call on you, Malcolm, so don't think it. We only wanted to know whether Isla had come back."

"We returned last night," he answered. "Well I'll see you later."

"Nonsense. You'll get up, Mackinnon," said Drummond so shortly that Kitty turned reproachful eyes on him.

There were heaps of stories about Malcolm in the glens, but after all, nothing had been proved against him. And, anyhow, it was not the province of friendship to turn a cold shoulder.

"I'd walk, Malcolm, if I were you. Wait a moment, and I'll get down to convoy you."

"No you don't, my lass," said Drummond firmly. "Get up, Mackinnon. The brutes won't stand--you see how fresh they are."

Malcolm did not hesitate longer. It was three good miles to Creagh yet, and a man doesn't walk so easily after a good meal as before it. He swung himself to the back seat and settled himself so that he could talk to both, but chiefly into the ear of Kitty, whose looks, he decided, had improved.

"Neil's manners, as I dare say you have observed, have not improved of late," said Kitty airily. "He has been such a bear to-day that I am forced to the conclusion that he must have something on his conscience."

Malcolm laughed.

"If it comes to that we've all got something on our consciences--more or less," he answered gaily. "Don't let it put you down on your luck too much, old chap. It's good policy to wait till the clouds roll by."

As to what Neil thought of him Malcolm did not care a fig, but he wished to stand well with Kitty, having proved that women were generally a man's best friends and would champion him, often against their better judgment. It was a favourite jest with him that he would prefer a court martial of women to anything in this world, and that he would never despair of getting off.

Drummond had told his sister only a judicious amount about Achree affairs, and it is to his credit that he had kept the fact of Malcolm's dismissal from the Army entirely to himself even when sometimes tempted to tell what he knew.

It was for Isla's sake that he had kept silence--Isla, whom he loved with a dog-like fidelity that was capable of any sacrifice and any suffering in order to make her happy.

Malcolm was unaware of Drummond's sentiments towards his sister, and if he had known them they would only have amused him. He despised Neil as a man of the world might despise and belittle a boy who had seen nothing of life. Neil, on his part, had the heartiest contempt for Malcolm Mackinnon, and cherished such an honest rage against him that it would have relieved him to have given him a good thrashing.

"You won't like Creagh, Malcolm," said Kitty sympathetically. "I can't help thinking that Isla was in too big a hurry to rush the Americans in. They were so frightfully keen on Achree that they would have waited your time."

"That's what I think, but I don't grumble," said Malcolm. "I've been to lunch with them to-day, and they're quite decent--upon my word they are."

"Been to lunch already, have you, Malcolm? You don't let the grass grow under your feet. And what do you think of them? I really think we must call, Neil. Why not this afternoon when we go down?"

"No," answered Neil shortly, "I'm not needing any truck with such folks. If they must swarm into Scotland, then, let them, but they'll get no encouragement from me."

"Touch me if ye daur," whispered Malcolm with his eyes full of laughter.

Kitty laughed out loud.

On the way down she took the opportunity of asking Neil what had made him so disagreeable to Malcolm all the afternoon.

"I'm sure he's very nice and has greatly improved. His manner to his father is beautiful, I think--such a nice mixture of deference and devotion."

"Fiddlesticks, Kitty!" said Drummond in his grumpiest tones. "You don't know what you're talking about."

"Do you?" she asked saucily.

"It takes a man to know a man like Malcolm Mackinnon. I wonder how he can bear to loaf about idle--great big hulking fellow that he is!"

"Loaf about? But he's on leave, Neil, and he has had a hard year of skirmishing. You should hear him tell about it."

"Don't want to--shouldn't believe it if I did," said Neil, biting his lip and conscious that he had very nearly let the cat out of the bag.

He had not had an opportunity of private speech with Isla at Creagh, because he and his sister had found the Edens in the little drawing-room and had left them still there when they went away. The whole afternoon had been a disappointment, and when, as they neared the gate of Achree, Kitty had again ventured to suggest that they should pay a call he refused point-blank.

It seemed as likely as not that Malcolm was to become a bone of contention in the Glen and that very soon there would be two factions--one that believed in him and another that discredited him in everything.

Malcolm himself was the least concerned of them all.

The weather continuing beautiful and spring-like, he went out early and stayed out late, and they saw very little indeed of him at Creagh.

Isla now heard less of the news of the Glen, for it was a long walk down to Lochearn and her father seemed more than ever reluctant to let her out of his sight. These were rather trying days for Isla, because her father talked almost incessantly about Malcolm, praising him to the skies and predicting a glorious future for him.

As the days went by and no letter or communication of any kind came from India or from the War Office, and as no intimation regarding Malcolm's withdrawal from the Army had been seen in any of the newspapers, Isla began to cherish the hope that they had heard the last of it. Of course Malcolm might have intercepted any that had been sent, but if he had done so he did not tell her. They saw little of each other and there was not much brotherly or sisterly confidence between them. They were indeed working at cross-purposes and, without knowing it, each was jealous of the other.

Nobody would have been more surprised and indignant than Isla had anyone told her that she was jealous of Malcolm's frequent visits to Achree: yet that was the truth. Also, she was keenly disappointed that Rosmead, after all his considerate kindness at the beginning, had never made the smallest effort to see her again. She would not go to Achree unless she was specially invited. So she remained at Creagh, living out the dull and narrow days, her heart full of vague discontent and unrest and forebodings which she could not have put into words.

Four weeks passed away--certainly the longest four weeks of Isla's life. She did not like Creagh though nothing on earth would have induced her to admit it. She missed all the cheery, pleasant gossip of the Glen and the little village, the daily intercourse with her own folk, the give and take of a social life which, if limited, was at least very sincere. Achree and Creagh were evidently two different places in the estimation of her circle, for nobody but the Edens and the Drummonds took the trouble to look her up, and even they did not come often. All the fun and all the social life apparently fell to Malcolm's share.

She was thinking of all this one morning as she sauntered down to the gate to meet the post-gig. She was a little late, she found by the watch-bracelet on her arm, and wondered as she glanced down the long white line of the road, on which there was not a single moving object visible, whether she had missed David Bain.

She had been over at the keeper's house about half a mile distant, inquiring after a woman who had had a new baby and, meeting the doctor from Comrie there, had stopped a little to talk with him. She had assured him that he need not call at Creagh, unless indeed he particularly wanted to see her father--as he had not been so well for years as he had been since they came up to live on the Moor.

Presently she saw something in the distance--a man on horseback, rather a rare spectacle on the moorland road at that season of the year. She thought at first that it must be Neil Drummond, who was the only horseman that ever came to Creagh. But a nearer glance assured her that the figure was a heavier one than Neil's, and, besides, she did not recognize the horse, though she could see that it was a good one.

She waited a few minutes longer, and as the horseman drew rapidly nearer she recognized the figure as that of Rosmead. This surprised her very much. Somehow, she had never imagined that an American man, though even a distinguished builder of bridges, would ride a horse and look so well on it.

Having no doubt that he was coming to Creagh, she opened the gate and stood by the white post until he came up. She admired the ease with which he sat, proving thereby that he was no novice on a horse's back. He looked uncommonly well-pleased to see her, and before he reached the gate he saluted her and threw himself to the ground.

Catching the reins over his arm, he took off his hat and kept it under his arm until she had given him her hand.

"It's a case of Mahomet coming to the mountain, Miss Mackinnon. I am here to-day on my mother's behalf and with a message from her."

"Yes?" said Isla, and her smile was bright and very sweet.

She had felt left out in the cold, and that feeling of neglect accounted for the little glow at her heart which had been kindled by the sincere cordiality of Rosmead's greeting.

"Do you know that she feels quite aggrieved," said he, "to think that she has been a month in Achree and that you have never called once to inquire or to make her acquaintance."

"I am very sorry. I did not think--" replied Isla a little confusedly. "And since, as I understand, my brother has paid many calls at Achree I did not think it necessary that I should call. Besides, I am very much tied here on account of my father's health----"

"I understand that," he said gently.

"And it is a long way to Achree," she continued, "and we have no horse or trap of any kind. But I will come one day very soon and make my apologies. I hope that you are pretty comfortable in the house, and that your mother likes it."

"She loves it. She has settled down, and from present signs I don't see that we shall ever get her out of it again," he answered with a laugh, watching at the game time the mobile face beside him.

He thought it the sweetest face that he had ever seen and--almost he could have said--the dearest. Yet Hylton Rosmead had seen many fair women, among whom he might without doubt have made his choice.

"I am so glad," said Isla a little wistfully. "And your sisters--do they, too, like it?"

"They do. Glenogle and Lochearn in such a spring as this leave little, I think, to be desired in the way of winsomeness. I myself feel as if I belonged here, which, I dare say, you consider great presumption on my part."

"Indeed no," said Isla, with a swift, kind glance. "I feel very glad to know that that is how you regard Achree."

"I came with a message from my mother and also, I must confess, on my own account to tell you that I have to leave Scotland for a few months."

"Oh!" said Isla, and her face unaccountably fell.

But Rosmead was not yet sufficiently acquainted with the play of its expression to understand that his news had disappointed her. Neither was he vain enough to imagine that her expression had altered because of his announcement of his impending departure.

"Where are you going?" she asked a moment later.

"Back to America. The object for which I came to this country is accomplished, and I really have no excuse for remaining longer here."

"Oh!" said Isla again, a little dully. "Somehow I imagined that you were going to settle in Scotland, though of course that was a very absurd supposition on my part."

"Not so very absurd. It is what I should like to do--what I hope to do one day. But, in the meantime, I must not forget that I am a partner in an American business and that I am expected to go back with my report."

"What report?"

"You have forgotten, of course, that I told you I was a bridge-builder. Why should you remember it?" he asked lightly. "I came over to meet the engineers and the contractors who have to do with your splendid bridges here, and in the fall I shall have to go down south, where my firm has undertaken to build one of the biggest cantilever bridges in the world."

"Oh!" said Isla a third time. "And you will not come back?"

"I hope that I shall return later in the year--probably to spend Christmas with my mother and sisters."

"They will remain here, then? You wish to extend the term of your tenancy of Achree? Do you remember it was to be for six months?"

"With the option of remaining for a year. That was made very clear, I think, at the beginning, and, as I said, my mother will not be easily ousted from Achree. She is of Scottish parentage, you know. Her mother was a Farquharson, so she imagines that she has a special claim on Scotland. Happily your brother does not mind the extension."

A sort of chill fell on Isla at mention of Malcolm's name, though why she could not have told. She had no fear that he had not made himself pleasant or agreeable at Achree; but, somehow, disaster seemed to associate itself with his name. She feared to pursue the subject. But Rosmead, quite unaware of her feeling in the matter, none of the gossip of the Glen having reached his ears, went on quietly.

"We've had several long talks about it, and practically it is arranged that we take the place on a two years' lease."

"You have arranged that with Malcolm!" she said a little faintly.

"Yes," said Rosmead. "He has been most kind about it. He tells me he has resigned his commission on account of his father's health but that he intends and hopes to get some estate management. I appreciate his kindness to us all the more on that account."

Isla, who heard all this for the first time, felt a natural thrill of indignation because she had been kept in the dark.

"I don't see that there is so very much kindness," she said quickly. "You pay very handsomely for the house."

"It is worth it," he said heartily. "The old Rosmead place in Virginia my mother has lent to her youngest sister, lately made a widow. She is looking after all the servants, and we have not the smallest anxiety about it, so you see, things have arranged themselves very nicely for us."

"Your home is in Virginia, then?" said Isla in tones of deep interest, which flattered Rosmead not a little.

"Yes. My grandfather was a big planter there, and had many slaves. Of course the war changed all that, but the place remains the same. I should like you to see Virginia, Miss Mackinnon, and my old home. It is a beautiful place."

"It seems odd that you should be so willing to leave it!"

"It had sad associations for my mother and also for my sister Vivien, who was married in the neighbourhood and was--and was--not very happy. But there--I have all this time been talking about myself, and not at all about you. Your father, I hear, is very well. I dare say, your brother's return has helped him greatly."

"Yes, I think it has," said Isla, trying to be cordial as well as loyal. "And Creagh suits him. It is very high and clear up there, and he is able to potter about just as he likes. You will come in and see him? Even his mind is much stronger. Certainly he now grasps the fact of your residence at Achree, and, I am sure, he would like to make your acquaintance properly."

"I should like to come in and see him, if I may," said Rosmead. "But before we go in will you promise to go sometimes to see my mother when I am gone? I don't know why I should ask this, but I do."

"I shall be sure to go, Mr. Rosmead. But when do you leave Scotland?"

"Next Thursday. My boat sails from Liverpool on Saturday afternoon, and I have some business in London on the Friday."

"I shall come before then, of course, and I am very sorry I have been so rude and unneighbourly," said Isla, and she meant what she said. "Do you mind walking round with me to the stable and putting your horse in? The accommodation is quite good, but there is no groom," she added with a small, pitiful smile which touched him inexpressibly.

Her whole personality appealed to him. The grave, unimpressionable Hylton P. Rosmead, accounted by his colleagues one of the hardest-headed men of his time, was so moved by this woman, whom he had seen so few times, that he could have taken her in his arms there and then, and asked nothing better than to keep her for the rest of his life and hers.

She was so sweetly natural and womanly, so altogether devoid of pretension that she appealed to every fibre in his being. He hated the artificiality of the women of his set--the smart women whom he had met in New York society and who were ready to make much of the "Bridge-builder," as they called him--and to pour the incense of their flattery upon him. But the atmosphere had always impressed him as being insincere, and he had often told his mother that if he ever married it would be in some very unexpected place. He knew now that he had found the place and the woman.

All unconscious of what was passing in his mind, Isla led the way to the stables, stood by while he tied up his horse, and then walked back with him, pointing out the beauty of the situation and the incomparable view from the little plateau on which the house was built.

"Now I wonder whether David Bain has ever come. I suppose you saw nothing of him on the road, Mr. Rosmead?"

"Nothing. He was ahead of me, I am sure, because he is the most punctual person I have ever heard tell of. I have heard that in Glenogle they set their clocks by David."

Isla passed into the house with a smile on her lips and, crossing the narrow hall, opened the door of the dining-room which her father used as a library and sitting-room.

And there she stood just a moment as if frozen upon the threshold. Her father was not in his accustomed chair, but lay on the hearthrug, where he had evidently fallen with the page of an open letter grasped tightly in his hand.

CHAPTER X
THE HOUSE OF WOE

Isla sprang forward and knelt down in a silence that could be felt. The old man lay slightly on his side, and Rosmead, as he too knelt down, saw at once that all was over.

Isla's white face and terrified eyes turned to him in swift appeal.

"Will you take your horse and ride quickly for Dr. Blair? I left him at the keeper's house at Rofallion. Any of them here will tell you where it is. And even if he is gone from there the people will know what direction he took."

Rosmead rose to his feet, and on his face was a great and sad gentleness.

"I will go if you wish, my dear, but it is useless. He is dead."

Isla sprang up, and her eyes flashed.

"Dead! How dare you say that? He can't be dead--it is impossible. He was quite well this morning--better than he has been for years. I told Dr. Blair so when he wished to come and see him this very morning. Oh, if only I had let him come!"

Her hand on the shabby old bell-pull sent a hundred echoes through the house and brought Diarmid, shaking and apprehensive, to the door.

Isla turned to him sharply.

"Come, Diarmid. The General has had a fit--or something. Help to lift him up, and carry him to his room. Will you, Mr. Rosmead? Oh, thank you very much. Then if you will ride for the doctor it will be the greatest service you can render."

As they would have addressed themselves to their task she stooped and tried to release the sheet of paper from the fingers that held it like a vice. But the effort was useless. As she knelt there she was able to read the address on the one side, and, on the other, which she turned with a shaking finger, the signature of Colonel Martindale.

Then she knew what had happened.

She left the room and flew up the stairs to see that the bed was ready, and, as she heard Margaret Maclaren clucking to her handful of poultry at the kitchen door, she wondered how all the work and business of their little world could go on as before, while her life was over.

The bed was straight and the fair linen sheet turned back when Rosmead and the serving-man appeared with their burden. Even then Isla noted the extreme gentleness and power displayed by Rosmead, and from that moment he seemed, as it were, to take over her case and to legislate for her.

They laid the poor old General on his bed, and Rosmead very gently drew the lids over the staring eyes that seemed to have a great horror in them.

"Oh, go for the doctor--go quickly, for God's sake!" cried Isla--"or it will be too late."

"It is too late now," he said.

And, stepping to the toilet-table, he lifted the General's small shaving-glass that had been carried through many a campaign and laid it against his lips. There was not the faintest sign of a misty breath on it.

"It is the infallible sign, my dear. God help and comfort you! I will send your woman to you and then go after the doctor. It will be well that he should be here even if he can do nothing."

Isla, now almost convinced that her father was indeed dead, did not cry. But Rosmead never forgot the despair of her face. She bent over the prostrate figure and once more essayed to remove the letter from the gripping fingers.

Rosmead stepped forward to help her and, after a small effort, he succeeded in releasing it. She smoothed it out, folded it, and put it inside the bosom of her gown. Her face seemed to harden then till it became set like marble.

"I will never forgive Malcolm Mackinnon this!" she said under her breath, "never while I live."

Rosmead, guessing some tragedy beneath, decently turned away and went down to get his horse from the stable. As he left the house the keeper appeared, having been instructed by Isla to call for some soup for his wife.

"The doctor, sir? Yess, he iss at my hoose whatefer. At least his bicycle iss there, and he iss calling at another hoose not far away. I can bring him?-

-yess, inside of ten minutes. I hope there iss nothing wrong at Creagh whatefer?"

"General Mackinnon has had a seizure of some kind," answered Rosmead. "Can you go as quickly on your feet as I on my horse?"

"Quicker. Forby, there iss no need," answered the man, and he was off like lightning across the moor.

But in less than ten minutes' time he was back to say that the doctor had gone and that nobody knew the way he had taken.

Then Rosmead ascended the stairs once more, to find that they were standing about helplessly, wringing their hands, while Isla, with the desolation of death on her face, was looking out of the window.

He motioned the servants from the room, and went up to her, gently touching her arm.

"My dear," he said, and she did not even notice how he once more addressed her. "I am afraid we have missed the doctor. I will get him for you soon, but meanwhile I want you to grasp the fact that, even if he were here at this moment, there is nothing to be done. I have some knowledge of such things, and I have seen many die. It is all over, and, save for the pain to you, we ought to be glad that he suffers no more."

"Suffer!" she cried shrilly. "You don't know--no one will ever know what he suffered just then."

Unconsciously her hand touched the fold of her blouse where the letter lay. "He had a shock--yes, and it was the one thing to avoid. Oh, I have watched him all these years so that nothing came near him! But I was powerless against this evil thing that killed him at the last!"

Rosmead made no answer, understanding that she was distraught and spoke freely of that which her normal self would not have so much as mentioned in his presence.

His one concern was to get her out of the room, so that the last sad offices might be done and Mackinnon of Achree composed in the dignity of his last sleep. He managed it at last, for even with all his gentleness he was masterful. Then with his own hands he helped, guiding the tearful, but anxious and willing servants so that in a short time the death-chamber was prepared, the fair linen ready, and all done decently as it ought to be.

When he got down to the library Isla was sitting by the table, with her elbows on it, staring into space. The expression on her face hurt him. It was not woebegone, nor yet was it grief-stricken. It was only hard like the nether millstone. He understood that he had come within touch of the tragedy of these broken lives, but not an atom of curiosity stirred in him. His only concern was for her.

She looked round with a little shivering breath, and her lips essayed to move.

"I too seem to be stricken! I wish only one thing at this moment, Mr. Rosmead--that I could be lying dead beside my father."

"Yes, yes, I understand. I was only fifteen when my father died--through a gun accident that might have been averted, and I remember the horror of it yet. But yours was an old man and full of years and honours. You should see him now! He reminds me of the shock of corn fully ripe. You must think of how he was beloved in all the glens, and how, after his long service, he has received his crown from the King."

He spoke quite simply, and the hardness on Isla's face slightly relaxed.

"How kind you are! I shall never forget it!"

"I have done nothing that the merest stranger might not have done better," he made answer. "What I feel now is that I dare not leave you here alone. If you could send some one down to Lochearn--or if you know where your brother is I will find him for you. It is imperative that you should not be left here alone."

"I don't know where he is, and he shall not come in here!" she cried a little wildly. "You don't understand! Nobody understands except me, but he must not come in here."

Rosmead did not know what to say, for tragedy was in the air.

"Come," he said gently, laying a slightly compelling hand on her arm. "Let me take you upstairs. It will do you good. He looks so beautiful and so gloriously at rest. If only you will let your mind dwell on that, half the bitterness will be gone--on that and on the fact of your long and beautiful devotion to him, which has been the wonder of all the glens."

Rosmead hardly knew himself, and certainly those who knew only one side of Peter Rosmead would have been amazed to hear him now.

Isla obeyed him without the smallest demur, and when she entered the room with the drawn blinds, and looked at the still figure on the bed with the majesty of death on the noble face her tears began to flow. And for that Rosmead thanked God.

She was like a little child in his hands then, begging him not to leave her; and his tenderness, his forethought, his encompassing care were like those of a kind elder brother.

But that came to an end with the sudden, swift arrival of some fresh person at the door and with the sound of Malcolm's loud--somewhat aggressive--voice, calling his sister by name.

Rosmead stood aside while she walked steadily from the room, and he very heartily wished that it were possible for him to escape by some back staircase. He had no desire to witness what he felt must come.

Isla sped swiftly down the stairs, and on the downmost step she paused and pointed an accusing finger at her brother.

"Murderer!" she said. "Don't come a step farther. You have no right in this house, which you have destroyed!"

Malcolm looked thunder-struck, and the sight of Rosmead a few steps higher up the stair did not help to lessen the mystery.

"Why, what has happened, and why is Mr. Rosmead here? What is it?" he demanded peremptorily.

Rosmead hastened past them and went out by the door without a word. He knew that the time had come for him to go--that with what now passed in the Lodge of Creagh between the brother and sister no stranger might intermeddle. But he left the woman whom he had learned to love--left her with a pang.

Rosmead was no fool, and he guessed that the letter that had been in the General's dead hand must, in some way, have concerned his son, and that, whatever news it contained, it was the shock of it that had killed him.

This also Isla knew, and Malcolm would have to answer to his sister, to his own conscience, and to his Maker for his sin.

Rosmead's heart was heavy as he took his horse from the queer little stable of Creagh, and, mounting, rode slowly down Glenogle. The mystery of life, its awful suffering--so much of it preventible--oppressed his healthy mind like a nightmare. And always it was the innocent and the good who had to bear the full brunt.

As he rode through the clear beauty of the summer morning he took a vow that he would do what he could to make up to Isla Mackinnon--that if she would permit him he would devote his whole life to making her happy, to effacing the memory of the bitterness that her young life had known.

Only he must not be in too much haste, because the quick pride of her would resent any assumption of right on his part. Isla must be slowly and laboriously wooed. But how well worth the winning! Rosmead's outlook upon life had undergone a swift change, and now it was bounded east, west, north, and south, by the deep quiet eyes and the beautiful face of one woman.

The love that had come to him late would be the great passion of his life--a passion such as few men know. He had kept himself singularly pure and wholly detached from women. His capacity for affection had never been dissipated by lighter loves. He brought a virgin heart to lay at the feet of the woman he loved. And, in spite of the sorrow and the woe to which he had been a witness, life promised fair to Peter Rosmead that summer morning as he rode through Glenogle and watched the sheen of the sun upon hill and water and heard the birds singing their heart out in the crystal clearness of the upper air.

He would go to America and attend with a single mind to his business there, leaving the dear woman in peace. Then, when he returned at Christmas, he would see. His heart would tell him then whether it was time to speak. Few misgivings were his. He believed that Isla Mackinnon was the woman that God had given to him and that she had been kept for him through all the years of his strenuous young manhood, and that for her dear sake he had been able to live without blame and without reproach.

For that, above all else, he gave God thanks in his heart.

Meanwhile, in the Lodge on the edge of the Moor of Creagh the storm rose and raged. Malcolm, a little stupefied, kept demanding what had happened.

"He is dead!" cried Isla, in the shrill, hard tone that had no kinship with that of her usually sweet low voice. "And the thing that killed him was the letter from India--Colonel Martindale's version of the story."

"Give it to me!" said Malcolm, with an air almost of menace as he stepped to her side.

"No, I will not," she answered clearly. "It is not yours. It was father's, and now it is mine. To think that after all our watching, it should have fallen into his hands at last!"

Malcolm, very white and haggard now, moved with a step that was very unsteady into the library, Isla following, for it suddenly dawned upon her that it was unseemly to wrangle there within a step of the chamber of death.

"Tell me what has happened," he said hoarsely. "Surely you will not deny me the right to know."

"There it very little to tell," said Isla drearily. "I went out early, and before going to meet David Bain, I went to the keeper's house at Rofallion to ask for Mrs. Dugid. Then while I was waiting at the gate for David Mr. Rosmead came up."

"And David had delivered the letters, I suppose, while you were at Rofallion?"

"Yes, of course, and father opened that one, and, though he might have looked at a dozen others without comprehending their meaning, he knew the meaning of that one at once," she said.

And her face set again like the nether millstone.

She had no pity for Malcolm, she did not even in that moment of awful bitterness give him credit for one spark of decent feeling. She hardly observed that he was trembling like an aspen and that his face had grown haggard about the mouth, like that of an old man.

"Isla, I want that letter. I must have it," he said in a low voice.

She heard him as she heard him not, and his tone became more desperate.

"Did you read it, Isla?"

"No."

"Will you read it?"

"No."

"Then give it to me."

"Oh, what does it matter? The fire is the place for it--the very heart of it, where it will be consumed quickly, now that it has done its deadly work," she said drearily "Do you understand what has happened, Malcolm? Our father is dead, and it is you who have killed him, just as surely as if you had put a bullet into him."

"For God's sake, hold your tongue, Isla! You would drive a man to the edge of despair."

"What about me?" she cried in a kind of frenzy, throwing her self-control to the winds. "It is all of self you speak. Don't you understand that it is a martyrdom and nothing else that I have suffered in the last five-- no, in the last ten years, ever since I was able to know the meaning of the things that happened? Through you our souls, our hearts, and sometimes our bodies have been starved in Achree, and the old place has been suffered to sink into the dust, and has finally passed into the hands of strangers. All this would not have mattered if only you had been good and brave and a little like what you ought to have been. We could have borne poverty with a smile. But it was your misdeeds, your squandering of Achree that poisoned existence for him until slowly his mind gave way. And I had to stand by and see it and be glad of it, because in that way he suffered less. But I suffered more. If there is a God in heaven He must judge this day between you and me, Malcolm Mackinnon."

"For God's sake Isla, hold your tongue!" he repeated, but his voice sounded weak and almost faint.

He was no coward in some directions, but the look on his sister's face was awful to see and her words seared themselves upon his brain. He had no idea until now of the red-hot fires of passion glowing beneath her quiet exterior. But now he knew, and the revelation never afterwards passed from his remembrance.

"I must speak just this once, for we are going to part, Malcolm; now the last bond between us is snapped. I will never forgive you. You broke my father's heart, and mine is in the dust, where it will lie till the end. I hope that you are very proud of your work."

He turned away with a deep groan and covered his face with his hands.

"Now you are the Laird of Achree," she continued, "and there is none to hinder you from making its devastation complete. As for me, I will pass away from Glenogle and never come near it any more."

He turned to her then, and his eyes looked for a moment as hers sometimes had done, full of a most wistful appeal.

"Hold hard, Isla! Don't you think I've had enough? I don't want to justify myself. I admit that the letter gave the shock, and that is punishment enough for me. Don't rub it in. Far less has sent a man to the lower-most hell."

She did not seem to comprehend the words--or even to hear them.

She appeared suddenly to be possessed by a new idea, and, undoing the pearl button of her blouse, she drew forth the letter and held it out.

"Take it. There is no use for me to keep it. I don't want to read it. It is yours."

She opened the door, passed him by, and went, bare-headed, into the drowsy sunshine, and a lark in the clear blue of the sky seemed suddenly to mock her with his wealth of full-throated song. She walked blindly, yet her feet guided her away to the great spaces of the Moor of Creagh, where she could be alone under the clear canopy of heaven and where the messengers of the Unseen were free to comfort her.

Malcolm, still shaky and trembling, looked about with the air of a man who does not know which way to turn. Then he sat him down and braced himself for the effort of reading the letter which had fallen like the crack of doom upon the old man's heart.

It was such a letter as one true friend might write to another, carefully worded so that it would not inflict any unnecessary pain. It was a letter which had cost its writer several sleepless nights--a letter of duty and friendship for a man whom he had never met, but whose name was still honoured in the service that he had adorned.

Had the Colonel known of the old man's state of health that letter would never have been written. But it told the truth--the whole truth, without varnish or embroidery, in the simple language which is all that a soldier has at his command.

Malcolm Mackinnon set his teeth as he read it, and surely in that awful moment he expiated part at least of his many sins.

After what seemed a long, long time he picked himself up heavily, crushed the letter in his hand, and threw it into the fire, where he watched it caught by a greedy flame and consumed to the uttermost edge.

Then he left the room, passed by, unseeing, the doddering Diarmid in the hall, and slowly mounted the narrow stairs.

He did not pause or falter at the door of the chamber of death, but opened it swiftly, closed it again, and walked to the side of the bed. There, for a moment, he stood in silence. Then Diarmid, listening below, heard a cry which he never forgot. It was that of a soul in an anguish which cannot be uttered.

"Forgive!" was the only word that fell brokenly from his lips as he knelt, sobbing by the bed, and laid his aching and throbbing head on the snow-white gloss of the coverlet.

The dead answered not, nor made any sign. But the peace upon the beautiful old face was that of one who has passed over, and who understands.

CHAPTER XI
VIVIEN

It was three o'clock of the afternoon before Rosmead got back to Achree, and he had not eaten any lunch. In the stable-yard he met his sister Vivien, who had gone round to look at some Aberdeen puppies, arrived that very morning.

"We have been wondering about your absence, Peter," she said with her quiet smile. "Have you had any lunch?"

"None. I have been up at the Lodge of Creagh. The old General is dead. Come back to the house, and I will tell you about it."

A groom came forward to take the horse, and Rosmead, linking his arm in his sister's, walked her away. They were devotedly attached to each other, and the wreckage of his dear and beautiful sister's life at the hands of an unprincipled man had cast a deep cloud over Rosmead which could never wholly be lifted. For every time he looked at her face, every time he thought of the possibilities of her kind nature and of the long years of loneliness in front of her his soul was filled with a holy rage. On such occasions he would have killed his brother-in-law, and thought this no sin.

Vivien Rosmead, made for love, uniting in her sweet nature all that is best in womanhood, all that makes for the precious things of life, had been cheated on its very threshold. But why had she been so blind, you ask? Why had not her finer sense warned her of the risk she ran? The answer is the one which has come from the lips of a vast army of sad women who have believed that their love could win and keep a man from his evil ways. In this some few have succeeded but a multitude have failed. Vivien had failed, and the irony and the misery of it had embittered Peter Rosmead beyond all telling.

"The old General dead!" echoed Vivien in astonishment. "But he was not even ill. His son has been here this morning and said he was very well."

"He had a shock, and he died on the spot. Heart failure, I suppose. You are needed up there, Vivien. I want you to go to-day."

Vivien looked at him questioningly, and seemed to shrink.

"But I don't know Miss Mackinnon, Peter. I've never even seen her. She has shown us very plainly that she does not wish to know us."

"That is of no consequence. This sorrow lifts the things above all such considerations. She is a woman in need--a woman suffering acutely and terribly, and she is almost utterly alone. If mother were able she would go--you know that. You must take her place. May I go back now and order a trap."

"There is plenty of time, Peter," she said, visibly shrinking yet. "It is never quite dark in these long, delightful days. Tell me what happened. Were you there with her when her father died?"

Rosmead briefly explained how the death had occurred.

"And she thinks that it was the letter that killed him? How strange and sad! Did she give you no inkling as to what it contained?"

"No. But I have my own opinion--or rather suspicions. It has something to do with her brother. As I left the house and he entered it I heard her call him a murderer."

"Oh, how dreadful and how unlikely!" cried Vivien in deepening bewilderment. "Malcolm Mackinnon does not strike one at all as that sort of person. He is so transparent--just like a big, jolly schoolboy. I like him so much."

Rosmead was not surprised to hear it. Malcolm Mackinnon had paid many visits to Achree, where he had shown the very best and most lovable side of him. He had jested with the gay Sadie, had been serious and kindly and responsible when talking to Vivien, and had sat like an attentive son by Mrs. Rosmead's invalid couch. To Rosmead himself he had been simply a good comrade, and, on the whole, the American had no fault to find with him. Yet, somehow, these words, falling from Vivien's lips, disquieted him not a little.

"I'm afraid there's something behind it all. Probably Mackinnon has sowed his wild oats, and this is the aftermath. Anyway, the old man is dead, and she is in a dreadful state. Her eyes haunt me. It is a woman she needs--mothering, in fact, and if you could bring her right down here to mother it would be a Christian act. Where's Sadie?"

"Miss Drummond came to lunch and has taken her away to Balquhidder to show her Rob Roy's grave. Then they are going to Garrion to tea. What a bright creature she is! She kept us laughing right through lunch."

"I'm rather glad, on the whole, that Sadie is not about. Well, dear, while you are getting ready I will see mother. I took a message from her to Creagh. Would you like me to go up with you, to drive you and wait outside, perhaps?"

"Just as you like. But perhaps, as you've only just come down, I had better go alone. We don't want to overwhelm her with Rosmeads."

He nodded understandingly, and they parted on the stairs, Rosmead proceeding up one of the winding ways to his mother's room.

They had not altered the interior of the old house in any way. They had only spent money to make it comfortable, covered bare stairs and passages with rich carpets of neutral tints, and gathered about them all the comforts and refinements which are at the command of wealth.

Mrs. Rosmead occupied the General's chamber, which had a large dressing-room adjoining, and from its quaint little windows she could see the Loch and the hills beyond.

She was a gentle, frail old lady, very small and delicately built, but her sweet face in its frame of snow-white hair had great strength.

It was from her undoubtedly that Rosmead had inherited his decision of character, his deeply-rooted principles, his inflexible will. He was very like her physically, and he worshipped her. Up till now no woman had ousted her from the shrine of his heart. The relation between them was indeed idyllic and did much to keep the softer side of Rosmead in the foreground.

Her keen, fine black eyes, so like his own, lifted themselves inquiringly to his face as he entered.

"Well, as you have taken such a long time to carry out my behest, I take it that you were well received, my son."

"Yes, I was, but that is not what delayed me," he answered as he bent to kiss her.

Then in a few words he made her acquainted with the tragedy of the morning. As she listened, full of grief and sympathy, she, unconsciously to herself, watched her son keenly. She saw that he was moved far beyond his wont, that his voice, when he spoke of Isla Mackinnon, vibrated with an entirely new note. And she wondered, and her desire to see the girl was quickened.

"She is the most desolate creature on God's earth, mother, and if only I could wrap you up in my arms and carry you to Creagh you could heal her with a touch, as you have so often healed your other children."

The expression "your other children" impressed her. Could it be possible that already Peter's thoughts and longings had flown as far as the day when he should give another daughter to her heart?

"You must bring her to me, dear. It is the only way."

"Vivien is going up. Next to you, she will be the best to help her. It is a woman that she needs. All her life long apparently she has been fighting side by side with men."

"Fighting!" repeated Mrs. Rosmead with a slight wonderment in her tone.

"Well, you know, she has had to do everything for and to be everything to the old man."

"But how? He has a dear son, Peter. You must not be unjust to young Mackinnon. Oh, I have heard that they say things here in the Glen about him, but when he comes here and sits by me, I believe none of them. He only needs a little guiding, and I think I have gathered from him that his sister has been a little hard on him at times."

Rosmead with Isla's most bitter cry in his ears, remained wholly unconvinced.

"The ins and outs of the story we don't know, mother. Perhaps we shall never know them. But of this I am sure--that Isla Mackinnon would be hard on no man without a cause. She is a splendid creature, and----"

"Peter, come here."

The sweet voice was peremptory, the swift, humorous black eyes were compelling. He came obediently, as of old, to her side.

"Look straight at me--no, not like that!--very straight, Peter Rosmead. Is this to be the woman?"

"Yes, mother," he answered, with the simplicity of a big child. "Please God, it is."

"Then bring her to me quickly, my son, that I may get to know and love her--ay, and to learn whether she is worthy of Peter Rosmead. I have never yet seen the woman who is."

Peter laughed, in no way uplifted by her loving pride. His nature indeed was singularly unspoiled.

"It can't be done in such a desperate hurry. She is cold and fine, and, like her own hills, she is difficult of approach. I shall have to walk warily and win her slowly. But win her I shall or go unmarried to my grave."

Thus did Peter Rosmead quite quietly dispose of the biggest thing that had come into his life. And his mother, watching the firm set of his square chin, the invincible light in his eyes, gloried in his strength, and had not the smallest doubt that he would attain the desire of his heart.

Was any pang of disappointment hers? To every mother the moment when her son takes another woman to his heart is one of supreme pain. This is as inevitable as the law of life.

But Mrs. Rosmead desired her son to marry, and she had kept him at her side a long time.

"So Vivien will go up? Is she getting ready now?"

"I think so."

"Well, bring my writing-block and pencil, and I will write a message for Miss Mackinnon."

He obeyed her, but she did not show him what she wrote. Nor was he curious to see it. He had never in all his life known her to do the wrong thing or speak the wrong word.

She was a woman in whom grace was developed to a very high degree.

Vivien came in presently, her slender, graceful figure enveloped in its capacious coat of Harris tweed, and a small neat toque of green velvet crowning her beautiful head.

"Peter has been telling you, mother. Do you think it is the right thing for me to do--to go to Creagh, I mean? I confess to a little hesitation. I am so afraid of intruding on her. Even the pride of old Virginia must pale before that of Glenogle."

"Your heart will dictate the fitting word, my child. Give this to the poor girl, and if she will come to us here to rest awhile in the house where she was born we shall try not to make her feel that we have taken her home from her."

Rosmead tucked his sister in, and, just as the horse was about to start, he spoke again.

"You won't be discouraged if it is a little difficult at first, Vivien? Try to think only of her desperate need."

"Poor old Peter," she said whimsically. "I never saw him so much in earnest about anything. I do believe he would like nothing better than to be going back himself."

Their eyes met in a smile, and she drove off, waving her hand.

He drifted about the place all the afternoon, conscious of a growing restlessness that he could not shake off, his thoughts all the while following Vivien to the Moor of Creagh.

When she arrived at the small plain house, which she now saw for the first time, a vast pity filled her heart. Creagh had beautiful surroundings, but nothing could make it a home. It was bare and uninviting--a mere shelter; and Vivien, who loved beautiful places, and who had the whole art of the Home Beautiful at her finger-ends, wondered how Isla could have borne to exchange the old-world charm of Achree for this.

She had not heard the whole story of the transaction. Rosmead had preserved a singular reticence regarding the terms of his tenancy of Achree, and Vivien merely thought that the Mackinnons either wanted the money badly or had some other family reason for letting their ancestral home.

The blinds were all down, but, as she directed the man to stop outside the gate, she could see the open door at the end of the short avenue.

"Wait here, Farquhar. I will not disturb them by driving up to the door."

She left her heavy coat on the seat, and in her neat, plain suit of blue serge walked up the short approach to the open door, where Diarmid, who had heard the rumble of wheels, stood waiting to receive her.

"Not at home," were the words ready on his lips, but something in Vivien's face arrested his attention.

"I am Mrs. Rodney Payne, Mr. Rosmead's sister, and I have come at my brother's request to see Miss Mackinnon. Do you think she would see me for a few minutes?"

Diarmid hesitated for a moment. Then he was wholly vanquished by the light in the strange lady's eyes.

"Ma'am, if you'll step inside, I'll see," he said respectfully. "She's sittin' up there in the room with him, and we can do naught with her. Maype, if she would see you, it might be better for her."

"Where is her brother?"

Diarmid shook his head.

"He hass been out of the house for 'oors, ma'am, and we are all to pieces here in Creagh, and there's nothing but dool and woe upon my folk."

Vivien's eyes became moist at this expressive phrase which, falling pathetically from the old servant's lips, adequately summed up the whole affairs of the Mackinnons.

"I am afraid," she said very gently, "that if you take my name to Miss Mackinnon she will not see me. I am going to take a great deal upon myself. If you will just show me the way I will go to her without announcement. She can only send me away."

"Yes, sure, an' that is so, but I do not think, seeing you, ma'am, that she will do that," said Diarmid earnestly, and he held open the door for her to pass in as if she had been a queen.

They trod the narrow stairs very softly. On the half-landing Diarmid paused and stood aside while he pointed with finger that trembled slightly to the closed door of the room where Mackinnon slept his last sleep.

Vivien braced herself, for the thing she was about to do was not only unusual, but might very easily be misconstrued. She took a little quick breath as her fingers closed upon the handle of the door. The next moment she turned it, slipped in, and closed it behind her again.

The blinds of the front window only were down, but the sun, now veering westward, shone in at the window in the gable-end and lay in a soft yellow flood upon the quiet room. A shaft of sunshine even lay athwart the bed, touching as it passed Isla's motionless figure, where she sat upon a chair by the bed-side, her hands lightly clasped on her lap, her eyes staring straight in front of her, unseeing, uncomprehending, a look of almost hopeless misery upon her face. At sight of a strange woman in the doorway, however, she sprang up, quivering with indignation. She would have pointed to the door, to which she tried to hasten, but something in Vivien's beautiful face--some unimagined quality of rarest sympathy deterred her. She stopped with the very words of dismissal frozen on her lips.

Vivien approached quickly, laid a tender hand on her shrinking shoulder and spoke.

"My dear, my dear! I am Vivien Rosmead, I too have suffered. Come out into the sunshine and let us talk. If even we do not talk we can cry together, and that will help us both."

Isla was powerless to be angry. Her brief indignation at the intrusion of a stranger upon her most sacred privacy passed as a tale that is told.

"It is very kind of you, but--but--I hardly know you, and there is nothing to be said or done. Everything is over--that is all."

"I too have thought so, dear," said Vivien softly. "Come, my poor darling. He does not need you any more. Come, and let us talk and think of those who do."

Isla suffered herself to be led away.

Afterwards, looking back upon that incident, she was amazed at herself, at the quiet compelling power which Vivien, in common with all the Rosmeads, seemed to possess, and against which ordinary folk could not stand for a moment.

Vivien's arm was about her slender body as they descended the stairs. She it was who guided her out into the flood of the sunshine which, meeting them at the door, seemed to envelop them in a quiet radiance.

Isla, as if dazzled, put up her hands to ward it off.

"It is cruel," she said in a low, difficult voice. "How can there be any brightness when I am like this? It is very cruel."

"Where shall we go?" asked Vivien softly. "Shall we go to some spot where we shall be very, very quiet and undisturbed? I should like you to forget who I am, even what has brought me, and just to be as if I did not exist. If you feel like talking, then talk. But if you want to be quiet, I can be quiet too. Oh, my dear, I can be very, very quiet. I have been through the deeps, where there is nothing possible but dumb silence."

Isla then remembered the tragedy of Vivien Rosmead's life, and her own pity and sympathy which in times past had never failed any in need, awoke to newness of life. The frozen springs of her being leaped again with life, and, with an almost unconscious desire to help, she slipped her hand through Vivien's arm.

"Why is it that life is so full of hideous suffering for women?" she asked with a vague passion. "I used to believe in God--in all things beautiful and good. Now I believe nothing."

"Your faith will come back. Even I say that," said Vivien softly. "I don't want to belittle your suffering, dear, but it is of an impersonal kind. The woman who cannot be blamed if she loses faith is the one who has been cheated in her own self, whose womanhood has been flouted and scorned, whose love has been trampled on and despised. That is where the silent deeps are. May I say just what I will?"

"Surely," answered Isla, lifted clean out of herself by something tragic and mysterious in that other woman's face.

"Your father was an old man, full of years and honour. His life had become a little burdensome to him, and though I never saw him, I know that his fine spirit must have fretted at his forced inactivity. What you must do now is to dwell upon his rejuvenation. He has gone where there is no death, where his powers will be restored, where once more all things are possible."

Isla's hungry eyes never for a moment left the speaking face of the woman at her side.

All the time they were moving slowly, but surely, away from the house up to the wide spaces of the great moor where the great silence dwelt.

"Tell me more," was the mute question of Isla's eyes and lips.

CHAPTER XII
THE HAND IN THE DARK

"It is all true--what you say," said Isla with a little shiver. "But what is to become of me? He was my life, my work, my all. I have nothing further to do in the whole wide world. My life is over."

"There is your brother," Vivien ventured to say.

She immediately saw that she had made a mistake--that here undoubtedly lay the sting and the crux of the whole sad situation.

Isla impatiently shook herself, almost as a dog might shake from him the element of water he dislikes. She made no remark, however, except to move her head in impatient dissent.

"I have no money, no prospects, no friends, I shall have to go out into the world and earn my bread. But how? That is the curse of people in our position--we are taught nothing, we are trained to take for granted that the world exists for us, that we are in some sense a privileged class. Then there is a crash, and if we go under is it to be wondered at or are we to be blamed?"

Vivien listened in the sheerest wonder. She had no idea that things were at such a low ebb with the Mackinnons. Remembering Malcolm's airy inconsequence and his jokes about his hard-up state, which seemed to sit lightly enough upon him, she was even inclined to think Isla must be exaggerating.

It was not easy for Vivien Rosmead to realize poverty. She had been reared in a luxurious home, and had married a millionaire, and, though she had never lacked in sympathy or benevolence towards the poor, she had not known one ungratified whim. She knew that poverty existed, but it was impossible to associate its more sordid aspects with Isla Mackinnon.

"But, surely out of the estate there must be ample provision for so small a family?" she ventured to say. "Achree is not a small place. The rent of it alone----"

"It is mortgaged to the hilt," interrupted Isla with a sort of dull scorn. "I could not and would not take a penny from it."

"But surely you have relatives. Is not Sir Thomas Mackinnon of Barras a relative of yours? Some friends of ours had Barras for two seasons running."

"He is my uncle, but I couldn't be dependent on him. He is not rich, and he has his own family to provide for."

"He cannot be poor. I saw the account of his daughters' presentation frocks in the fashion papers last week," said Vivien with a slight smile.

"Oh, that means nothing! They got the loan of a house for the season, and a very clever maid of Aunt Jean's, married in London, made their frocks. You are so rich in America that you haven't an idea of the makeshifts some of us have to practise here," said Isla, waxing amazingly eloquent and convincing for Vivien's enlightenment.

Vivien did not care what the theme, so long as it roused even a passing interest in the girl's mind.

"Well, I am sure that something will happen to provide a way," she said hopefully. "It is impossible to imagine Glenogle or any of the glens without you. Have you any idea, I wonder, just how they regard you? I do not go about very much, but my sister Sadie, who has made friends for miles round, is always bringing home some fresh tales about the devotion of the people to their dear Miss Isla. Only yesterday she said quite dolefully, 'We may as well give up the ghost, Vivien. If angels and archangels came to bless Lochearn and Glenogle, they would have to walk behind Isla Mackinnon.'"

In spite of herself, Isla smiled.

"It does not mean so very much--only that I have lived all my life among them."

"It means everything," said Vivien clearly. "It means that you are in their hearts, that none of them could bear hurt or sorrow to come near you."

"Oh, but that is the hurt of it all!" cried Isla most pitifully. "The more we love people the more it hurts us to know that we are powerless to keep suffering or sorrow away from them. I would have laid down my life for my father, but I could not prevent Mal----I could not prevent others from breaking his heart."

"You did what you could, though," said Vivien, again struck by the bitter allusion to Malcolm. "Now I want to give you a message from my mother. She wishes very much to see you. If only she had been able she would have come to-day instead of me. What she wishes to say is that if you would like to take your dear father down to Achree for the last few days we can go out. It seems an odd thing to say--but we should be glad to go out. We can go to the hotel, or even back to Glasgow for a few days, or even weeks. My mother came down so comfortably in the motor that it would not be a trouble, or even a risk for her to return in it. So, dear, just say the word, and we shall be gone to-morrow so that you and your dear ones may come home to your own place. This is a note from my mother to you in which she proposes this!"

Isla took the note with a murmured word of acknowledgment. She was much moved. She stood still on the green tops of the heather, and something indescribable swept across her face. She stretched out her arms so that they fell on Vivien's shoulders, and when she was drawn into her tender embrace she laid her head down on her breast.

"Oh, now I know what dear people you are! God bless you! I should like to do that if it would not hurt or trouble you. Then all the people he loved and who loved him can come and see him before they take him away to Balquhidder. Oh, thank you, thank you, I want to come and see your dear mother. I will go back with you now if you will take me."

She was like a creature transformed, and while the sight touched Vivien Rosmead inexpressibly it also filled her with a great sadness. For, if this was how Isla Mackinnon regarded the house of her fathers, what must it be to her to see strangers in it and to have before her eyes the prospect of losing it altogether?

"Come, then," said Vivien with alacrity. "The evenings are so long and golden now that we can easily bring you back before dark. My brother will drive you himself."

"I am thinking," said Isla, and as they turned to go, it almost seemed as if the spring had come back to her step, "I am thinking why should you go out? There is plenty of room for us all. If you would only lend us one or two rooms for a few days and let us have the freedom of the house----"

"It would not be the same at all," said Vivien decidedly. "What you want is to shut the door upon the outside world and forget all about us, to have only your own people about you and to have to consider nobody but them. It is only in this way that my mother will arrange it. I am sure that you will find that this is the best arrangement?"

"It is a great thing for you to do," said Isla breathlessly. "I have never heard or known of anybody who would think of a thing so beautiful."

"Oh, nonsense. There are many far more beautiful things done in the world every day, and nobody hears of them. It will cost us nothing, you see. And, moreover, it is the right thing to do. It would be clearly wrong for the Chief of the Mackinnons to be carried to his last rest from this lonely and inaccessible place, beautiful though it is. He ought to be--he must be, borne from the house of his fathers."

"Yes, yes," said Isla, with a little sob in her voice. "To think that you feel like that, that--you understand everything! Now, I'm so very glad that you have Achree."

Her hardness had melted and the desperate hunted look had gone from her eyes. Once more she was alert, full of affairs, thinking of all there was to do and ready for all emergencies.

As she drove down Glenogle beside the smart groom on the front seat of the dogcart her face did not once lose its uplifted look.

Her eyes swam in tears as Vivien and she swept through the familiar gates of Achree.

"Tell me, dear Mrs. Rodney Payne, was it your mother her own self, who thought of this--this beautiful thing?"

"No, my dear," answered Vivien quietly, "it was my brother. He is like that. He thinks always of the thing that will make most people happy and of how to do it in the happiest way."

"I thought he was like that when he was up at Creagh with me to-day," said Isla simply. "What it must be to have a brother like that--a brother who thinks of others first!"

But she paused there, and it was as if she rebuked herself.

Peter Rosmead, from the window of his dressing-room, where he was getting ready for dinner, was thunderstruck by the vision of Isla Mackinnon driving up to the door.

"Bravo, Vivien!" he said to himself, and his pulses quickened as he made haste with his black tie, achieving a bow less pleasing than usual to his fastidious taste.

He had reached the bottom of the stair when his sister and Isla came in by the hall door; and, seeing him for the first time in evening dress, Isla was immediately struck by his air of distinction.

"I have come to see your mother, Mr. Rosmead," she said simply. "I can't say any more. Your sister must explain and say all that is necessary for me. Where shall I find your mother?"

It was Peter who took her to the door of his mother's room, nay, who entered it with her. Isla herself saw no significance in that simple and natural act, but Peter, who intended it to be significant, felt a high courage, an indefinable joy at his heart.

"Mother, this is Miss Mackinnon. Vivien has been so fortunate as to get her to come down."

Isla stood still just inside the door, looking wistfully--even questioningly at the small elegant figure on the couch, at the beautiful, softly-coloured face framed by its white hair, and her eyes had a yearning look.

She had never known her mother and, though Aunt Jean had been passing kind, there was little softness about her. Certainly she had never sought to mother the self-reliant, independent Isla, even when she was only a long-limbed girl, needing guiding and making many mistakes.

Sweetness and love had been the rule of Mrs. Rosmead's life. By these she had won and kept her children so near and close to her that they kept nothing hidden from her.

Her eyes, too, were full of questioning as they travelled to the girl's pale pathetic face. Peter had been no common son to her, and it was to no common woman that she could give him up.

"Come here, my dear. You have no mother. I have room for you in my heart," she said.

And Rosmead, with smarting eyes, went out by the door and closed it very softly behind him.

"God bless her! God bless them both!" he said very softly, under his breath, as he went down to Vivien.

"I am all blown to pieces by the winds of the Moor of Creagh, Peterkin," she said. "If you are very good you can come up and sit in my dressing-room while I make myself decent. Then I can tell you what happened."

This dear intimacy, so precious to them both, had never been more precious than on that night. Half an hour later Isla sat down to eat with them in the old familiar room, and by that time the distress, the strain, the awful hopeless misery had gone from her face. She talked quite rationally and naturally of all the affairs of the Glen, and when she said that she would like to go home as soon after dinner as they could conveniently let her away, Peter asked whether he might have the privilege of driving her.

She thanked him with her eyes.

"Where I have to be grateful for so much there are not any words left," she said simply. "I will say good-bye to your mother, if you please, only until to-morrow."

"You are coming back to Achree to-morrow, then?" said Rosmead, when, with exceeding care and gentleness, he had tucked her into the comfortable cart.

"Yes, to-morrow. May we talk of it as we go up? I don't know how to thank you for so kindly driving me home. When I think of what otherwise it would have been like, I am quite speechless."

"So much the better," he answered with a smile. "Look back, dear Miss Mackinnon. The girls are waving to you."

Isla turned round in her seat and blew a kiss on the wings of the evening breeze.

"Is it Mrs. Hylton P. Rosmead--eh, Vivien?" said Sadie whimsically. "Did you ever see anyone more mightily pleased with himself than our Peterkin?"

Vivien smiled, but said neither yea nor nay.

"What have you arranged with my mother, then?" asked Rosmead.

"We are to come down to-morrow evening, Mr. Rosmead. She says you will take her to Glasgow in the car to-morrow. Are you quite sure it can be done comfortably?"

"Quite. Then, you and your brother will bring him down to Achree to-morrow? I suppose Mr. Mackinnon will make all the necessary arrangements."

Isla was silent, a little chill creeping all over her and causing her to shiver. Her companion bent over her anxiously.

"I had forgotten Malcolm," she said quite frankly. "I have always been used to arrange things for my father, you see."

"I understand. But now your brother is the head of the house," said Rosmead gently. "Probably I shall see him when we get up to Creagh, and can make the final arrangements with him. I should like to tell him that the Achree stables are at his disposal. We shall all go to-morrow by the car, and so you will be perfectly free of the house."

"Thank you very much," said Isla.

But her voice was very low, and the spiritless note had crept into it again. Rosmead found the sudden change difficult to grasp, and it confirmed him in the opinion that there was some serious breach between the brother and sister.

"When do you propose that the burial shall take place, and where will it be?"

"The Mackinnon burying-place is at Balquhidder, of course," she said, as if surprised at the question. "I have not thought about the day, but probably now it must be Monday."

They became silent then, driving in the track of the young moon towards the hills and the moor of the great silence. Isla felt no need of speech. A great sense of peace and comfort was hers as she nestled there by Rosmead's side, the thick frieze of his driving-coat making for her a buttress from the wind. She, who had so long cared for others was fully conscious of the sweetness of being cared for. She was in no haste for the drive to end.

Up at the Lodge of Creagh there was desolation and woe--and there also was the brother between whom and herself there was a great gulf fixed. She had not seen him since she had driven him forth from her presence with hard words, and she had no idea of the dreary vigil he had kept, wrestling with remorse and shame up there on the heather of Creagh.

Rosmead was perfectly happy. He loved this woman with a great and growing love, and her nearness to him filled all his being. To render her the smallest service was such a joy to him that just then he asked for no more. All the chivalry of a singularly chivalrous race, all the fine gallant tenderness of the best in old Virginia was uppermost in Rosmead that night, which for both was a night of remembrance.

"I shall always think of this night," said Isla very low as they drew near to the gate of Creagh. "This afternoon I thought it would close in despair. It is you and your dear people who have lifted me out of it, and God will bless and reward you. I never can."

Rosmead, greatly daring, took the small gloved hand which lay outside the rug and raised it to his lips. But no word did he speak, good nor bad.

Presently Isla made a little exclamation of surprise.

"There is a machine of some kind at the door, Mr. Rosmead. Don't you see the lights?" she said rather excitedly. "I wonder who it can be at this time of night. It must be nearly nine o'clock.'

"Close on it. Probably it is some neighbour calling on your brother."

"It might be Mr. Drummond from Garrion. I know of nobody else who would take the trouble," said Isla.

A minute later she proved her surmise to be right. The high-stepping Garrion roans were champing their bits and pawing the ground in front of the narrow doorway.

Rosmead sprang down and with great tenderness helped Isla to alight.

"You will come in of course, as you wish to see my brother."

"I will come in if you desire it, but I do not forget that older friends may have the prior right, Miss Mackinnon."

"I do desire it. It will be a help to me," she said.

And together they passed over the threshold. Diarmid hastened out to meet them, and behind, from the library, came Malcolm and Neil Drummond.

Rosmead, while apparently observing nothing, took note of two things--the curious, half-shrinking, half-defiant expression on Malcolm Mackinnon's face, and the distinct antagonism that marked the manner of Neil Drummond towards himself.

"So you have come back, Isla?" said Malcolm awkwardly. "Neil and I were just discussing whether we should come to Achree to fetch you."

"Mr. Rosmead was so kind as to bring me up, and I think he wishes to speak to you, Malcolm," said Isla. "Good evening, Neil."

Neil came forward with outstretched hand, his honest eyes full of deepest sympathy and compassion.

"I need not say what I feel about this, Isla. I heard it at Strathyre this evening, at six o'clock, and I couldn't believe it. I was only on my bicycle, so I went home straight and got the horses. My dear, this is a terrible thing."

Isla nodded and, seeing that Malcolm had disappeared into the library with Rosmead, she asked Neil to come to the little dining-room which he and Malcolm had recently left, and where the remains of Malcolm's evening meal still stood on the table.

Drummond closed the door, and Isla sat down, as if very weary. He was surprised to behold her so calm and self-possessed.

"What took you away to Achree, Isla?" he asked jealously. "Malcolm has been frightfully anxious about you."

"He needn't have been. I left a message with Diarmid," she answered listlessly.

"But it seemed odd for you to go there to these new people. They are not your friends, Isla. We have a better right."

"Not my friends!" she said in tones of wonderment. "You say that because you don't understand--because you don't know what they are. I think there cannot be many people like them in the world, Neil. Do you know that they are all turning out of Achree to-morrow--even the frail invalid mother--and going right back to Glasgow on their motor-car in order that we may have Achree to ourselves for the funeral?"

Drummond looked the surprise he felt.

"Are they, though? That is uncommonly good of them," he admitted, though only half-heartedly. "Then, you go back to Achree to-morrow with the poor old General?"

"Yes. Mr. Rosmead is arranging the whole matter with Malcolm now, I expect. I am very tired, Neil. I think I shall have to go to bed soon."

"Yes, of course--poor dear girl, you must be! Kitty sent her love. She would have come over with me, she said, only she was not sure whether you would be able to see people. She will come over to-morrow if you'll give her leave."

"Very kind," murmured Isla, thinking of the woman who had not waited for leave--who had come of her own free will and gathered her to her heart. "I don't think she should come to-morrow, Neil," she said, rousing herself with an effort on perceiving his disappointment. "I shall be busy most of the day, you see. To-morrow night, perhaps--if you don't mind. It will not be so far to come to Achree as up here. Give her my love."

Drummond shifted rather restlessly from one foot to the other.

"Isla, I hate to say it, but it is what I feel. I'm beastly jealous of these American outsiders. You must not let them absorb you. Of course we know that their money can do a lot of things. We can't all afford thousand pound motors for quick transit, but our hearts are in the right place and we'd go down on our knees to serve you--every one of us."

Isla's eyes suddenly filled with tears.

"I know, Neil. Don't trouble about it. They have been very kind. Of course I know that if you had had Achree you would have done just the same thing. Was that Malcolm calling? We had better go out."

Neil opened the door, and they passed into the narrow hall again, where Malcolm and Rosmead stood together.

For just the fraction of a moment nobody spoke.

"Mr. Rosmead has told me of their great, unheard-of kindness, Isla," said Malcolm in a queer strained voice, "and we have arranged it all. To-morrow afternoon--late about six o'clock we shall take him down to Achree. Mr. Rosmead is to run his fast motor to Callander in the morning in order to make the necessary arrangements. I have told him we can't thank him."

"No," answered Isla very low, "we can't."

"That's all right," said Rosmead cheerily. "Good night then, Miss Mackinnon. Go to bed and have a good sleep. Good night, Mr. Drummond."

"Good night," said Neil, and he affected not to see the outstretched hand.

Rosmead took no offence. He was too big-hearted, and perhaps he had an inkling of how it was with the young man.

"I had better go, too, I suppose," said Neil a little stiffly, and Isla bade them both good night.

When Malcolm returned from seeing them off he could not find Isla, and when he went upstairs her door was shut.

He tapped lightly at it, and she opened it just a few inches.

"You'll excuse me to-night, won't you, Malcolm?" she said gently but coldly. "I am very tired. I couldn't discuss anything to-night. To-morrow we can talk things over, but I want just to say that I am sorry I spoke as I did this afternoon. He would not have liked it, I am sure."

Malcolm had not a word to say. He murmured good night and went downstairs to the lonely hearth, where he tried to extract some comfort from his pipe.

But his quiet was disturbed by the low sound of his sister's sobbing from the room above.

CHAPTER XIII
THE PASSING OF MACKINNON

A chamber-maid at the St. Enoch's Hotel in Glasgow brought a sheaf of letters to Rosmead along with shaving-water on Monday morning at half-past seven.

He glanced over them with quick carelessness, and, finding one small, square, black-edged envelope, addressed in a handwriting that he did not know, he quickly broke the seal, which bore an unfamiliar coat of arms. Once more his pulses beat high, for this was the first time Isla Mackinnon had written to him, and over a man in love the handwriting of the woman he loves wields a surprising power.

Thus did Isla write to Rosmead, and the few simple words meant more from her than whole pages of words from most women. She did not possess the gift of expression, but could only write of real things, and when these were done with the letter came to an end:--

"ACHREE, *Saturday night.*

"DEAR MR. ROSMEAD,--I am writing to say that I hope--that we all hope--that you will be able to spare the time to come out to Lochearnhead on Monday to attend my father's funeral.

"It is arranged for twelve o'clock from here, and will arrive at Balquhidder Kirkyard at half-past one, which suits the trains from both the north and the south.

"Perhaps you do not know the customs of our country, but it would please me if you would take one of the cords of the coffin as they lower it into the grave. These are taken by relatives and friends only, and, God knows, you have been a friend. It is arranged that if you are there some one will give you your place.

"My uncle, Sir Thomas Mackinnon, arrived from London to-day. He is my father's only living relative.

"Perhaps you will find it convenient either to come by the train or to drive in your motor straight to Balquhidder, in which case I should not see you.

"Please to tell your mother that by Thursday of this week I shall have gone back to Creagh or shall have gone away somewhere else. What I really mean to say is that Achree will be ready for her return. I cannot say more.

"I am, sincerely yours,

"ISLA MACKINNON."

Rosmead forgot all about his shaving-water until it grew cold, and he had to ring for more.

He had longed with a great longing to go out to the burying of Mackinnon, but he had not contemplated doing so without invitation. And, lo! the invitation had come from Isla herself, couched in warm, friendly terms which no man--least of all Rosmead--could resist.

There was a glow at his heart as he stood before the mirror, attending to the duties of his toilet, noticing for the first time, with a kind of silent rage, the lines on his face and the evidences of middle-age beginning to creep about his mouth and temples. He wanted to be for ever young for her dear sake.

She had, in the midst of her forlorn grief, taken time and thought to write to him to offer him what he understood was a family privilege, and he would go--oh, yes, there was no car fast enough to take him--right to her door, to her very feet!

Away with the train or car that would convey him only to Balquhidder when Isla had expressed even the faintest desire to see him! It would be their last meeting until he could return from America, for on Thursday he must set out upon the journey which never in all his life had he been so loth to take.

He pondered on all the details of the day in front of him, and, by copious use of the telephone in his room, had arranged them all before he went down to breakfast. He did not wait for his sisters. There was nothing to hurry them in the mornings in Glasgow, and generally they breakfasted with their mother in her sitting-room.

At nine o'clock, dressed in full motor garb, he tapped at his mother's door.

"I have had a letter from Miss Mackinnon this morning, asking me to go out to the funeral at Achree, and I'm going now. It will take me quite all my time to get there by noon."

Mrs. Rosmead smiled upon him, well pleased. She did not ask to see the letter. She only bade him take care of himself and give her love to Isla, and to assure her that there was no need to hurry away from Achree. He felt glad that neither of his sisters had yet appeared. He left a message for them and went off to the waiting car, ready for what lay in front of him.

It was not a very pleasant day in the city. There was a light fog hanging over it, through which a fine rain was beginning to filter dismally. But when they got away from the river-bed the rain stopped, and, though the sky remained grey and pensive, it was fair overhead.

No sun shone all the way, and when he came to the hills Rosmead thought it was an ideal day for a burying--just typical of the grief which overshadowed a whole glen. The sky was grey and very soft, and a mist lay upon the hills, while the heaviness of unshed tears was in the soundless air.

About eleven o'clock Rosmead, who had had a splendid run without mishap or stop, swept by the incomparable beauty of Loch Lubnaig, through bonnie Strathyre, and down upon the valley of the Earn.

Long before he reached it he was struck by the signs of activity on the usually quiet and lonely road. All sorts and conditions of vehicles moved towards Glenogle, containing all sorts and conditions of people. At the hotel door there was quite a medley of waiting traps. Rosmead drew up there and went inside to remove his motor garb and to put on the decent mourning, safely stowed at the back of the car.

He looked graver and older in the tall silk hat and dark overcoat with the black band on the arm, and he was respectfully recognized by many.

The story of how of their own accord the Americans had vacated Achree in order that the family might have it to themselves for such a great occasion had got about in the glens. It had filled all who heard it with a sort of personal gratitude and appreciation that was bound to have an aftermath. They did not love the stranger--especially the American stranger--in these remote Highland glens, though his money was sometimes necessary to the comfort of their existence. They accepted him as inevitable, like motor-cars, and new railway lines cutting into their fair hill-sides and ugly viaducts spanning their wimpling burns--all necessary evils which must be endured with fortitude.

Driving very slowly towards Achree, Rosmead was astonished at the increasing number of people both in vehicles and on foot. He was unaware that in Scotland a burying--especially the burying of a great chief--is a public event, in which every man, woman, and child of the district takes a personal interest. Everybody came as a matter of course to see Mackinnon of Achree laid to rest, and all were made welcome, though no invitations, in the ordinary sense, had been sent out.

In some doubt as to whether he should take his car up to the house, Rosmead addressed himself to a policeman--a most unusual spectacle in Glenogle--who was on duty at the gate.

"Mr. Rosmead, sir, I think?" said the man, touching his hat.

"Yes, my man."

"Then you are to go up, please. I had my orders this morning. They are expecting you at the house."

Rosmead gave the order to drive slowly, and presently he came within sight of the house where the cortège stood before the open door. There were two other cars, and the Garrion roans were conspicuous at the bend of the avenue.

Rosmead alighted and walked over to the door where Diarmid was on the look-out.

"Mr. Rosmead, sir. I haf a message from Miss Isla for you, if it pe that she would not see you pefore you leave."

"Yes, my man."

"She says will you please come pack to the house if you can spare the time after you haf peen at Balquhidder, as she would like to speak with you, whatefer."

Rosmead silently nodded. Had the American boat sailed that very afternoon it is safe to say that one passenger at least would have failed to take his berth.

Diarmid, very respectful with a touch of gratitude in his mien, waited upon Rosmead and finally ushered him to the library where a small company were already assembled for the service that was to take place at a quarter to twelve.

Malcolm, very pale and slightly haggard, came forward immediately to greet Rosmead, whom he introduced to his uncle.

"Happy to meet you, sir," said Sir Tom, as his great hand grasped the American's slender one in a grip of iron. "We, as a family, will not readily forget your kindness at this time to the son and daughter of my poor brother. It was a Christian act, sir--a Christian act."

Rosmead asked him not to say more, passing it over as if ashamed that so much should be made of it. Then he stepped back and looked about at the people in the room. Some of them he recognized, but Neil Drummond, sourly resentful of his intimate presence there, unaware, of course, that he came by Isla's special invitation, did not suffer his eyes to alight on his face.

Rosmead was impressed by the circumstance that there were no flowers upon the coffin--only the Union Jack and the old soldier's sword, to the hilt of which was tied a bunch of white heather. All was simple, severe, and impressive. The short service was quickly over. Then a sudden, weird sound broke upon the listening ears--the wailing of the pipes, which filled the soundless air with a melancholy music.

All this time Isla had not appeared, and Rosmead strained his eyes in vain for a sight of her. But it was denied him, and he had not even asked for her welfare.

It was a great burying, the like of which had not been seen in the glens for many a year. As the cortège, half a mile long, slowly defiled through Lochearnhead it was joined by a score or more of vehicles that waited it there. And so it was all the way to the Braes of Balquhidder.

Rosmead, who had left his car at Achree and entered one of the mourning coaches, felt the impressiveness of the whole scene, and was almost moved to tears when they turned away from the grave to the sweet haunting strains of the "Flowers of the Forest".

As the mourners fell away slowly from the grave-side some one touched his arm.

"I shall be glad if you will drive back to Achree with me, Mr. Rosmead," said the voice of Sir Thomas Mackinnon. "I should like to have a little talk with you."

This was noted by the curious, and it was afterwards said that more attention could not have been paid to the American if he had been sib to the Mackinnons. But there was not one who added that the attention was misplaced.

"A sad affair, isn't it, for those who are left?" said Sir Thomas as they drove slowly away, "for my niece especially. You see, her father was her life-work, so to speak, and now that it is taken out of her hands she will feel stranded for a bit."

"Miss Mackinnon is one who will always find something to occupy her heart and her hands," said Rosmead.

Uncle Tom assented.

"They tell me you have Achree on an option, Mr. Rosmead," he said--and it was evident that that was the thing uppermost in his mind. "I hope that you like the place, and feel minded to stop on."

"I should like to, but I have not yet had any conversation about it. I shall have to see Mr. Mackinnon to-day, as I leave Scotland on Thursday."

"You leave Scotland? But I understood that you were here indefinitely."

"No. The business which brought me is concluded, and there is work lying to my hand in America."

"Then, do you leave your ladies here?"

"Yes, for six months. Our tenancy of Achree does not expire till the end of October, and nothing, therefore, need be decided now. But I think that my mother likes the place so well that we might take a lease of it--that is, if Mr. Mackinnon does not wish possession for himself. Will the General's death alter nothing?"

"Nothing. They can't afford to live in Achree--and that's the plain truth of it, Mr. Rosmead. In these days very few of us can afford to live in the place of our fathers. Here am I stranded in a London house, like a bull in a china shop. I loathe the life, but I haven't any choice. A relation of my wife offered the loan of the house for the season: my girls had to come out, and we couldn't afford to refuse. I don't know what's to become of us now, as our mourning will stop all the gaiety. But about the Achree Mackinnons? It is a most unfortunate thing that Malcolm resigned his commission just when he did. Of course, it was on his father's account. The best thing he could do would be to try and get back to the Army. I haven't approached him on the subject--that is, closely. He seems uncommonly touchy about it. So does Isla. But it stands to reason and common sense that he can't loaf about Glenogle."

"No. I can imagine that would be quite impossible. But if he does not return to the Army he will probably seek something else. There is room in the colonies for such as he."

"Is there?" inquired Sir Tom with the doubtful air of a man who would be difficult to convince. "Well, they present a problem. She must come back with me to her aunt in London. I don't see what else is to be done with her. She can't remain eating her heart out in that God-forsaken place up at Creagh. I'll never believe anything but that the change killed my brother Donald."

Rosmead recalled the picture of the General's prostrate figure on the narrow hearthrug at Creagh, the letter clasped like a vice in the poor dead fingers, and he had his own thoughts. Such at least had not been Isla's opinion, but it was certainly no part of his business to stir up strife or sow the seeds of suspicion among the members of the family, who were evidently outside the real issue of the case.

Sir Tom was very friendly and communicative, talking to the strange American as if he had been at least an intimate friend of the family--an attitude which was largely due to what Isla had said about the vacating of Achree.

Just a few of the mourners went back to the house for tea, and perhaps to hear whether there was a will. But, though Cattanach was present, there was no mention of a will, and it was speedily whispered about that the General had left none. It was quite well known that for five years at least he had not been capable of transacting business, and, as he had had practically no money to dispose of, and the estate had to pass in entail to his only son, a will would have been superfluous.

But it was of Isla that most of them were thinking, and when they watched the slender, black-robed figure so quietly dispensing tea in the drawing-room, assisted by Kitty Drummond, they wondered what her future was to be.

Neil Drummond was there also, and had taken up his position close to the tea-table, with the result that Rosmead could not get near for a private word.

But his mind was made up that he would not leave Achree until he had seen Isla by herself to bid her good-bye.

He was in no haste--he never was in any of the affairs of life--having proved that most things come to the man who bides his time. But perhaps just there he made one mistake, arising from ignorance of the quick Celtic temperament, which cannot brook slowness or delay.

Isla's eyes met his just once across the room, and there was quite clearly a message for him in the look. It bade him wait.

When all the tea had been served, and she had answered as composedly as she could the remarks made to her by Neil, she rose and quite deliberately walked across the room to the place where Rosmead stood talking to her Uncle Tom.

"You have a long way to go back to Glasgow, Mr. Rosmead. Are you in haste to leave us?"

"Not in haste to leave you, but I must be going soon. Can I speak with you for a few minutes?"

"Yes, it is why I have come. Will you come down to the library?" she said.

And Neil Drummond, with eyes that had something of the baleful glow of the watch-fires in them, had the chagrin of beholding them leave the room together, as if it were quite a matter of course.

"Don t you think that American bounder has presumed a lot to-day, Malcolm?" he said gruffly to Mackinnon, who happened to pass near him at the moment.

Malcolm looked the surprise he felt.

"I don't think so, Neil. He has been most awfully kind, don't you know? I dare say Isla has some message for his mother about when they can come back to the house."

Neil tried to accept this perfectly feasible explanation, but if he had seen the two talking earnestly together at the library window his mind would undoubtedly have been most seriously disturbed.

"It was so very kind of you to come to-day and take all the trouble for us," said Isla, as the door closed upon them. "Do you still intend to sail away on Thursday?"

"On Friday. My boat sails from Liverpool," he corrected gently. "I go to London on Thursday."

"And when will you come back?"

"Not before Christmas, I am afraid. I've had more than six months' furlough already, you see, and I haven't the ghost of an excuse for stopping on this side any longer."

"Except your mother. You will not like leaving her, I am sure."

"I don't. But she is accustomed to my journeyings to and fro in the earth and up and down in it. I shall be very happy, thinking of her here in this house. She has never felt so much at home since she left Virginia. I have had a talk with your brother, and it is practically settled that we take a two years' lease of Achree. I was fortunate in finding Cattanach here to-day also, and so the thing can be put on a proper basis without delay."

"Yes," said Isla, and her tone had a singularly spiritless note in it.

He looked steadily into her face, wondering just how much he might say, or whether he might say anything at all. But she was not looking at him. She was thinking how strange it would be to realize that this man had gone away clean out of the Glen, and that soon the ocean would roll between him and her. She had never felt so in her life about any human being outside of her family circle, and she was disturbed.

"I hope that you will not think I presume if I ask what is going to become of you in the immediate future," said Rosmead presently. "Will you go back to London with your uncle, as he seems to expect?"

"No, I shall simply go back to Creagh," she answered steadily.

Rosmead was silent for a moment, trying to picture the life she would lead there, alone and without occupation, in the company of her brother from whom her heart was estranged.

"To Creagh? It seems impossible! I can't bear to think of you there. It is unthinkable!"

"Oh, no--nothing is unthinkable, or even impossible. People can do anything in this world--anything," she answered. "I have proved it."

"Then, shall I find you at Creagh when I come back?" he asked with an odd persistence, his eyes cleaving to her face.

A tremor ran over it, and had he but known it the opportunity was his. Her heart turned--nay, cried out to him. Had he spoken the word then she would have gone away with him without a question or a doubt.

But he blundered on, longing for her mightily, yet wholly afraid, believing that he dared not begin to woo her until he had given her heart time to recover from its present shock.

Some one tapped lightly at the door.

"It is au revoir, then, not good-bye," he said with an effort, and held out his hand.

She gave hers to his warm, kindly clasp, and her eyes, over which the veil had already fallen, uplifted themselves to his.

"I hope it is, but six months is a long time in life. So many things can happen. I hope you will have a safe journey and a successful issue to all your affairs, and--and that the difficulties you spoke of will all be swept from your path."

"Some of them are big enough. But when I come back I will address myself to the biggest undertaking of my life, and the dearest."

The door was opened, and Malcolm's voice announced that the motor was waiting outside.

Rosmead raised her hand to his lips and turned away, scarcely master of himself.

Isla spoke no more. But, for once in his life, Peter Rosmead had erred on the side of caution. The incomparable chance had been his, and he had passed it by.

When the door had closed upon them Isla leaned her head against the black oak of the window shutters, and a little sobbing breath that was almost a cry, broke from her lips.

Her last prop had gone, but none knew--least of all the man whose one desire on earth was to take her to his heart.

CHAPTER XIV
FAMILY COUNSELS

"And now," said Sir Tom with a large and partially reproachful cheerfulness, "we had better address ourselves to the future of you two children and try to find out just where we are."

He was neither unfeeling nor unsympathetic, but his opinion was that grief and the lassitude which treads close upon it should in due season have an end. The affairs of life cannot stand still, even when death intervenes. They can only be held in abeyance for a little space.

Now that Mackinnon, full of years and honour and followed by the lamentations and the love of all his people, rich and poor, had been carried to his last rest, he must become a tender memory to those who were left.

They had dined together quite alone, and now they sat in the library, where pipe and tobacco and cigars were on the table, as yet, however, untouched.

Sir Tom was getting his pipe ready a trifle absently, his eyes fixed on his niece's face. He was troubled about her. Her white face and her deep, grief-haunted eyes, which no man could fathom, disconcerted and disturbed him. He loved her dearly, but he did not always understand her. Malcolm's apparently simpler nature was better within his grasp and ken.

It was assuredly Malcolm's place, as the head of the house, to make some suggestion or statement, but silence lay upon him heavily, and he seemed ill at ease.

"Has neither of you anything to say? I must be going back to London to-morrow, if I have to go alone. I'll wait till Wednesday, if I am to take Isla. What do you say, my dear?"

Isla, a slim, black figure with white, nervous hands interlaced upon her lap, lifted her eyes to his face from where she sat at the other side of the fireplace.

"No, thank you, Uncle Tom, I will not go to London just now."

"But, my dear, your aunt will scold me no end if I don't bring you. Her last words were that I was to bring you back with me. If she had been well enough nothing would have kept her from Achree just now--and you know it. But I left her in bed, and the doctor forbade the journey. It is nothing serious, only requiring a little care. Fact is, these monkeys have been running her off her feet lately. Three or four o'clock every morning before she got to her bed after their dancing and nonsense. The life of a chaperon in the London season is not a happy one."

"Give Aunt Jean my love, and tell her I can't come just now. Later, perhaps----"

"Later! Heaven only knows where we may be later. Your aunt talks of some seaside place on the Brittany or Normandy coast--some God-forsaken hole, where a man can't get a decent meal of meat. Gad, what it is to be hard-up! Well, and if you won't come to us may I ask without impertinence where you do propose to go?"

"Back to the Lodge at Creagh for a few days at least."

"And after the few days--eh, what?" asked Sir Tom, leaning forward a little, with serious concern in his big, kindly, rather innocent blue eyes.

She made no answer, though Malcolm from where he stood leaning against the fireplace seemed to wait a little eagerly for what she might say.

"Speak to her, Malcolm! She has aye been a high-handed miss, doing that which seemed right in her own eyes. You are the head of the house now. Can't you put your foot down and bid her come with me to your aunt and your cousins? It's where she ought to be in these days, among a lot of kindly, busy women-folk."

"It's what I think, Uncle Tom," said Malcolm in a low voice. "But, as you say, nobody can dictate to Isla. She will go her own way."

"Then, may I ask what you propose to do?" asked Uncle Tom, suddenly directing his attention to his nephew. "Of course, for a few days or weeks there will be things to see to. But, with Cattanach at your back, they should not take very long to wind up. And with the American folk coming back to Achree there's nothing for you to do here. I don't suppose you'll be long content, hanging about the Lodge and the Moor of Creagh."

Malcolm had no answer for a moment, and the silence seemed to grow.

"Why can't you speak--one of you?" asked Uncle Tom a trifle testily. "I like folks to show some common-sense, and you have both seen this coming for long enough. It's not to be thought that you haven't had plans for the future."

"I haven't any plans," Malcolm admitted.

This answer incensed the old man extremely. He looked at the strong, well-knit figure of his nephew in the full prime and strength of his young manhood with critical displeasure.

"Then the sooner you get some, my man, the better it will be for you. It is a thousand pities that you resigned your commission when you did, and since it is somebody to make a proposition that you seem to need, mine is that you apply to the proper authorities and get back to the army as soon as possible. It's undoubtedly the very best thing you can do."

The silence deepened. It was broken by the falling of a glowing log from the bars to the hearth, and, under pretence of restoring it to the grate, Isla moved and bent towards it.

"I never approved of what you did," went on Sir Tom, "and if anybody's advice had been asked it would never have been permitted. I don't like back-draughts, but I can't help saying now, as we're discussing family business, that I'm sure that your father would have been the very last man to have sanctioned your sending in your papers--that is to say, if he'd been in his full mind and faculties. And I think that the best tribute of respect you can show to his memory is to get back to the army as soon as possible and try to follow in the steps of the finest fellow and the bravest soldier that ever earned a sword."

It was a long speech for Sir Tom to make, and at the end he cleared his throat and dashed something from his eyes. He was glad to have got this off his chest--as he might have expressed it. It had lain heavily there for some time; in fact, ever since he had been able to grasp the full significance of his nephew's action. To him it seemed disastrous, unnecessary, and foolish in the extreme. For if a man cannot afford to live on his estate, or if it does not offer him sufficient occupation, surely it were infinitely better for him to take up some honourable calling in which he would have a chance to rise and to distinguish himself.

The Mackinnons, at least the handful that was left, had all been proud of the gallant old General, and, now that it was open to his son to carry on the fine traditions of the race, it seemed incredible and discreditable that he should not be willing and eager to do it.

"I can't do that, Uncle Tom," said Malcolm, shifting uneasily from one foot to another. "I've left the army for good."

"But that's no reason why you shouldn't go back. If representations to the proper quarter were made, I can't see any insuperable obstacles in the way. Can you, Isla?"

She made no answer, and he went on.

"I'll do what I can. I'll go to the Commander-in-Chief myself, if you're such a baby over it, Malcolm, and lay the whole facts of the case before him. No reasonable man would refuse to make an open door somewhere for you, and I don't believe he would--eh, Malcolm?"

"I can't go back, Uncle Tom. Please, say no more about it."

"I'd like to hear a word from Isla on the subject," said Uncle Tom. "I can't make you out, lassie. I have never thought of you as a person without opinions. You have an opinion about this, of course, and a pretty strong one, I could take my affidavit. Let us hear it. Now's the time, for if you won't travel with me to London, I must go south to-morrow."

"It is a matter for Malcolm entirely, Uncle Tom," she said, rising with a sudden sweep to her feet. "Do you mind if I say good-night? I am very tired, and last night I had no sleep. I'll be up bright and early for you to-morrow morning, though, of course, it will only be the two o'clock train you want to catch at Stirling. It will set you down in London before eleven."

"That will do. You're in a hurry, however--and my last night, too! But certainly you look tired, lass," said the old man, and he kissed her with a very real tenderness.

She nodded to Malcolm, said good-night briefly, and went to the door, which her uncle opened for her.

When he had closed it he turned full face to Malcolm.

"There's something the matter with the bairn, Malcolm. What is there between her and you? Have you quarrelled about anything?"

"Nothing special--only we don't hit it off, Uncle Tom," said Malcolm, turning round with evident relief and reaching for the cigars.

"Then the sooner you begin to hit it off the better," said Sir Tom severely. "It's not decent to behave as you are doing. How do you propose to live together in the Lodge of Creagh, even for a little while, if you feel like that?"

"Give it up!" said Malcolm.

And it was as if his whole body and spirit had relaxed now that some strain was removed.

"There was a dryness between us about the letting of Achree," resumed Malcolm, seeing that the old man was still staring intently at him, as if waiting to be enlightened. "Of course, I didn't like it. After all, it was my business, wasn't it, Uncle Tom? And Isla took it all upon herself. See how it has complicated things just now!"

"Yes, but the American money is very good," said Uncle Tom drily. "Barras would be a howling wilderness without it."

"I daresay that Isla and I would have pulled through without it, and I could have occupied myself in looking after the place. It wants a lot of pulling together, Uncle Tom. Everything is slack, and the tenants don't pay what they might--not one of them."

"You can't take the breeks off a Hielandman, lad," was the dry response. "But it's about Isla I'm chiefly concerned. You can very well fend for yourself. You'll have to make proper provision for her, Malcolm. Whoever suffers, she must have enough to live upon. She isn't one who requires much, but providing for her must be your first duty. I don't doubt that you will do it."

"I'll do the fair thing, of course. We'll have to have a talk, I suppose. I do wish she would go with you to London, if it were only for a few days. I could come to fetch her later. It would clear the air."

"She won't--you can see that in the eyes of her. There's something back of it all--God knows what--and I suppose you'll have to fight it out your two selves. But you'll be very gentle with her, Malcolm, for to-night she looks the most forlorn creature on the face of God's earth."

He blew his nose as he said this, and he begged Malcolm to bring him a peg of whisky. They waxed more confidential over their drink, of which, however, Malcolm partook very abstemiously. Drink had never been his besetting sin.

About eleven Sir Tom went off to bed, a little reassured concerning the affairs of the Achree Mackinnons and having no doubt whatever but that Malcolm would do his duty.

Malcolm certainly at this moment wished to do it, if only he knew how. He didn't want to leave Glenogle, still less did he want to live under one roof with his sister. If she refused to leave the Glen he would have no alternative but to go, and what would be the upshot of it all?

Near to midnight he was still pondering this mighty and seemingly insoluble problem when the library door was silently pushed open and Isla in a white dressing-gown, with her long hair tied lightly back and hanging loosely on her shoulders, came in. Her face looked ghastly pale against the whiteness of her wrap, and her eyes were shining like stars.

"I heard Uncle Tom go up to bed, Malcolm, and I thought I'd better come down."

"The fire has gone low," he said, as he sprang up to vacate the most comfortable chair. "Here's a log. We'll get a blaze in a minute. Sit down here."

She sat down on the extreme edge of the chair and watched him a little wistfully while he attended to the fire.

"I thought, perhaps, we had better have a little talk about what we are going to do," she said a trifle unsteadily. "There is nothing but Creagh. The question is--Can it hold us both?"

"Don't speak like that, Isla," he said almost pleadingly. "But really Uncle Tom's plan is the best, considering all things. Couldn't you make up your mind even yet to go to London with him, if it were only for a few days?"

Isla shook her head.

"I couldn't, Malcolm. Aunt Jean and the girls would drive me crazy just now. Don't even mention it again. I--I just want to ask you whether it wouldn't be better to tell Uncle Tom the truth about how you left the army before he goes to-morrow? You know how impulsive he is. He will think nothing of going straight to the War Office or to the Commander-in-Chief, if he can find him, the moment he gets back to London."

Malcolm's face fell.

"By Jove, so he might! I never thought of that. But, hang it all, Isla, I can't tell him."

"Let me do it, then. Don't you see anything would be better in the circumstances than that he should make a fuss? It would make you look such a fool, and it would certainly result in newspaper paragraphs which, through the great kindness of Colonel Martindale, have never appeared."

"I'll see in the morning. I'll be driving him to the station. Anyhow, I'll impress on him that the matter must on no account be opened up again--

that nothing would induce me to go back to the army," said Malcolm, whose policy all through life had ever been to find the easiest way out.

Isla dropped the subject. For the first time since her father's death she had schooled herself to try to speak of it naturally.

"As you let Achree to the Rosmeads for the longer term, what are you going to do? It's impossible that you can live at Creagh for an indefinite time and without an object."

"I want a little while in which to look round, Isla. I must have at least six months to inquire into things. I'm going up to Glasgow on Monday to go over everything with Cattanach. I must see whether the profits of the place cannot be increased in some directions. I can be busy enough for the next six months at least in getting the whole thing into shape. After that I must try to get a berth of some kind. Rosmead was recommending the Argentine. By the time he comes back I shall be in a position to go thoroughly into the prospects there."

"And in the meantime, then, you will live at Creagh?"

"I thought of doing so. I am sorry for your sake that it isn't Achree. But I had no hand in that. You shut yourself out, so to speak."

She leaned her elbow on her knee, dropped her chin, which had become sadly sharpened of late, on her hand, and looked across the space of the fireplace at him with the same wistful expression in her eyes.

"Malcolm, you'll try and pay off that money? When father was able to understand things it worried him most frightfully whenever he thought about the mortgage. For his sake, promise me that you will try to pay it off."

"Why, of course I will--the whole of the Rosmead money will go to that," he answered lightly. "It won't take much to keep me at Creagh--or both of us, for the matter of that. But, of course, a bachelor establishment could be run more cheaply."

"There couldn't be anything much cheaper than Creagh with Margaret Maclaren and Diarmid to do the work," said Isla drily. "But I won't remain long there to be a burden on you, Malcolm. I must go out and find something to do for myself."

"Oh, nonsense," he said loftily. "The only condition on which I should let you leave Creagh would be that you go either to Barras or abroad with them. So don't let us talk any more about that. And, really, Isla, if only you'll be a bit reasonable and not too hard on a fellow, we might have a fairly good time even at Creagh. The Rosmeads are more than inclined to be kind, and there isn't any reason why we shouldn't avail ourselves of what they offer. Then, of course, there are the Drummonds. What ails Neil at Rosmead? He was positively savage about him this afternoon when you went out of the drawing-room with him."

Isla did not smile.

"Neil is rather silly about some things," she answered, and there was a vague regret in her eyes.

She did not forget that, in a moment of keen loneliness and desperation, she had told Neil Drummond the truth about Malcolm's home-coming, and it stood to reason that Neil would not forget it either.

Her one desire was that that shameful truth should never come to the ears of the Rosmeads. She thought of them in the plural number, but it was Rosmead himself she meant. She already knew that his standard was very high, and that he might harshly judge a man like Malcolm if he knew him as he really was.

Isla sat very still, looking rather intently at the open, ruddy face with the smiling eyes and the weak, mobile mouth, and she wondered whether there was any ultimate hope of his complete redemption. He had evidently been able to forget or to put behind him entirely the horror and the tragedy of that frightful day at Creagh and the word with which her accusing voice had smitten his ears. His volatile nature took things so easily and lightly that, in his estimation, practically nothing but the immediate moment mattered.

Well perhaps, after all, she told herself, his policy was best. She had borne the burden and heat of the day, had lain awake at nights, pondering the problem of existence, had worn herself to a shadow for the honour of Achree and of the name she bore, and where was she left?

Stranded, she told herself, and practically without a friend. She had proved to the hilt the truism that the world has neither time nor room for the long face or the tale of woe, and that he who smiles, even if his heart be shallow or false, will win through at least cost--ay, and will grasp most of the good things of life as he floats airily by.

Isla was fast becoming cynical and inclined to accept the creed of the fatalist who says "What is to be will be".

"Well, then, if Uncle Tom leaves to-morrow," she said as she rose to her feet, "we had better go back to Creagh on Wednesday. I'd rather be gone before the Rosmeads come back, and I said Thursday to him."

"Oh, do be sociable, Isla! It would only be the kind thing to stop to welcome them decently and thank them for what they've done. It's the very least thing we can do, if you ask me."

Isla, whom the Rosmeads had surprised out of her usual reserve, in the first overwhelming horror of her grief, felt inclined to creep back into her shell again, but she saw the reasonableness of her brother's words.

"Well, then, I must leave it to you to arrange, I suppose. I mustn't forget that you are the head of the house. I'll be ready to go up to Creagh when you like, and as long as I remain there I'll try to make you comfortable and happy."

She said good-night to him immediately and glided away. But long after her departure Malcolm sat pondering on the future, by no means elated at the prospect of a *tête-à-tête* existence with the sister who knew so much. He would have been a happier and a more easy-minded man had Isla been getting ready to accompany her Uncle Tom to London.

CHAPTER XV
SETTLING DOWN

Having, in pursuance of a partially concerted plan of existence, thus held out the olive branch to her brother, Isla found the rest easy.

Next morning the breakfast-table was unclouded, and Sir Tom departed to London, more comfortable in his mind about his kinsfolk than at any moment since he had arrived in the Glen.

"I'm glad that you have come to some sort of understanding with your brother, my dear," he said, as Isla helped him on with his big travelling-coat in the hall, while Rosmead's horses were waiting at the door. "Just one thing more. Malcolm can't loaf about here longer than is necessary. Your duty now, having been so faithfully ended where your dear father is concerned, is to put a bit of your own smeddum into your brother. What I'd like--what we'd all like--is to get him back to his regiment. It's the only honourable way out of a big difficulty."

Isla busied herself with smoothing the creases in the back of the coat and made no answer at all.

"What about his Colonel--Martindale, isn't it? Your aunt is intimate with his sister, Lady Chester. We can get at him in that way, though I still think that a straight application from Malcolm couldn't possibly fail of its purpose. Eh--what?"

"Don't do anything, Uncle Tom," pleaded Isla, "please, don't. There are reasons--other reasons--why it would be better not, and Malcolm is quite determined. Anyone can see that."

"Well, well. It doesn't seem the right thing, but I don't want to be officious, and you at least have shown yourself capable of managing your own affairs up to now. Take Malcolm in hand now. The best of us need the mothering that a good woman can give. But I hope, my dear, that my next visit to Achree will be a happier one--namely, to give you away perhaps to some gallant bridegroom. Eh--what?"

He smiled his big, enveloping smile as he lifted her chin in his hand and kissed her face.

"That isn't likely to happen. But thank you all the same, dear Uncle Tom," said Isla gratefully.

"And, if we really are to be buried in the sand dunes over there and have to subsist on anæmic omelettes and the everlasting poulet roti, mind you come to us. And Barras in the winter is a very good place. It had a Riviera temperature up to March this year. In November, thank God, we'll make tracks for Barras again."

Again Isla thanked him, and, Malcolm appearing on the scene, she said no more. But she was sensible of relief as she saw them drive away. So long as Uncle Tom remained at Achree anything might happen. His big, kindly, blundering feet would stray into all sorts of forbidden paths.

She spent the morning in the house, going slowly and with a sort of lingering tenderness over every bit of it. The smart servants of the Rosmeads had managed to efface themselves in a very wonderful way, and the magnificent simplicity of the funeral of Mackinnon had left its deep impression on their minds.

Isla thanked each one of them individually in that way of hers that could draw out all that was best in a human being. She offered nothing, because she had naught to give, and would not mock them with pretence. Malcolm, less delicately conscientious, scattered silver among them--the silver that had come out of Isla's hoard in the bureau at Creagh.

Malcolm returned to announce that he had engaged Jamie Forbes to come up from the hotel to drive them to Creagh at three o'clock of the afternoon.

"I want to go to Darrach first, Malcolm, to see Elspeth Maclure. Everything is ready to lift, and I shall get up by tea-time."

"But how will you get up?"

"Walk, of course--that is nothing."

"But I can make Jamie wait till you are ready. He can stop here till four, by which time surely you could be done with that wind-bag, Elspeth Maclure."

"No, I shall stop to tea with her and come when I'm ready, Malcolm. I've neglected her of late, and I have lots of things to tell her."

Malcolm gave his shoulders a shrug.

"I've never understood your fondness for Elspeth Maclure, Isla. Her tongue is a yard long and none too kindly. She was as nearly as possible impertinent to me one day when I stopped at Darrach."

Isla looked unbelieving and wholly unconvinced.

"I can't conceive of Elspeth being impertinent. You must have said something to offend her."

"I gave her the truth about Donald and the croft, if you like. Darrach is a bit of the best land on Achree, and if it were joined to Tully and let to a responsible and capable man it would bring in a good rent. Maclure's lazy, and greedy besides. I'd like to chuck him from Darrach, and I mean to tell Cattanach that when I go up to Glasgow to-morrow."

Isla said nothing, though she thought much. The Maclures had been in Darrach in direct descent for four generations, and Donald naturally regarded the place as his own. To turn him out and join up the crofts into bigger holdings would revolutionize the whole life of the glens and take the bread out of many mouths.

But this was not the time to argue that question. Above all things, she must try to live at peace with Malcolm, and find some quiet, persuasive method of getting him to let well alone.

Isla was a curious mixture. Her temperament was active, her judgment quick and shrewd, but she was bound by the immemorial traditions of her race and ought to have been born in feudal times. She looked upon all the tenants of Achree as the children of the estate, having as good a right to the land as the Mackinnons themselves. The fact that they paid small, in some cases inadequate, rents for their holdings, thereby keeping the coffers of Achree sadly empty, altered nothing. She would rather have starved herself--and that cheerfully--than ask them for more. Besides, she knew the hunger of the land, the late and scanty harvests, the long winters, and the difficulty of wresting a living from the bare hill-sides and the swampy breadths that lay to the Loch-side.

She knew it to the uttermost. She had seen the blackened stocks sodden with November rains and touched with December snows to such an extent that the corn was hardly worth the trouble of carrying to the barn. She had felt the dank smell of the potatoes rotting with disease in the furrows when the autumn was wet, and she knew the poverty of the homes where she was ever a welcome, and never an intruding, guest.

Malcolm knew none of these things. He had no practical acquaintance with the long fight between man and nature in these high latitudes, and he had exaggerated ideas of the profits of farming. Already he was full of ill-considered and half-digested plans for the entire regeneration of Achree. Now that all was over, he was making all the haste he could to let bygones be bygones. He was going to begin afresh a new life, which, he promised himself, might be as interesting and far less strenuous than the old.

His father's death had altered the whole situation, and, from his point of view, had occurred at the psychological moment. Now, as Laird of Achree and head of his clan, he occupied a very different niche in the scheme of things.

Isla left Achree for the second time without any bitter pang. Nay, it pleased and comforted her to think that Peter Rosmead and his folk had it for a home. That thought somehow seemed to bring him nearer to her. In the months to come it would lessen the breadth and depth of that vast dividing sea. Yet how she would have been startled had her own thoughts been mirrored before her, who had never before taken such interest in a man!

She thought of him as she walked down the dry, crisp road to Darrach, and she wondered where he would be at that moment and whether the telegram she had dispatched to them at the St. Enoch's Hotel, announcing their departure to Creagh, would bring him back to Glenogle before he finally set out on his long journey. She did not admit even to herself her secret hope that he would, but it was of him she thought as she approached Elspeth's hospitable gate, of his deep and encompassing tenderness, his continuous thought for her, his earnest eyes looking into hers and assuring her of his devotion to her cause.

She lingered on these thoughts, fully conscious of their comforting sweetness and wholly unaware that they heralded the dawn of love.

She found Elspeth working at her baking board with a downcast face. The baby was asleep in the box-bed by the side of the fire-place, and the rest of the children were at school, even little Colin, aged three and a half, having been admitted to the infant room.

"There you are at last, Miss Isla--a sicht for sair een. I said to Donald this morning that if it should be that you didna come the day, then I must go and seek for ye either at Achree or at Creagh. Where should I have found you?"

"We are leaving Achree to-day, and it is at Creagh that you will find me, Elspeth," said Isla as she took the chair that Elspeth set for her by the well-scrubbed table.

"I've come for my tea, Elspeth, and these scones smell as they ought. If the butter is newly churned, too, then I am in luck, and I will forget all about the rich meats that the American cook has been setting before us at Achree."

"But it wass the right thing for you to be there, Miss Isla, and it was fery, fery good of the folk. From end to end of the Glen you'll hear nothing but praise of them for it."

"It was good," said Isla with quiet conviction.

"And they'll be stoppin' on, at least for a while, at Achree, I hope?"

"Yes, they will be stopping on indefinitely at Achree."

"The little one--her they call Miss Sadie--comes here a lot, Miss Isla, and she hass the pairns quite crazy about her. The other day--it wass the day before the Laird died--she wass here drilling them in the yard. It was the funniest thing you ever saw in your life--and her so sweet and winsome wi' them! There be some that are all for the other one, but she seems high and proud-like and hass little to say to the folk."

"She has had a lot of trouble, Elspeth. Yes--I would like my tea now, and you to sit down and drink it with me."

"Yes, Miss Isla. And so you're to be at Creagh, and Mr. Malcolm--I beg hiss pardon, the Laird--is to pe there, too, and to pe fery busy in all the glens."

The dry note in Elspeth's voice did not escape Isla's ear.

"He iss not going back to the army, Donald says, but means to live on the place. And, oh, it will nefer pe the same again! He wass here wan day, and he said a lot of things that I'm not mindin' to say over again to you. But iss it true that he will take away most of the crofts and make big farms and let them to men from the west country and the Lowlands that haf money in their pockets and will pey what we canna?"

"My brother talks a good deal, but when he has been at home a little longer and gets to understand things better he will change his mind about a lot of them," said Isla, trying to comfort Elspeth.

"Look you, Miss Isla, if it should come that my man had to leave Darrach he will nefer lift up hiss head again. He was born in that bed, and his faither and his grandfaither pefore him, and he wants to dee in it, as they did. That is how Donald is feelin' about the place, Miss Isla, and it iss what the Laird will nefer understand. But I said that you would understand and would speak for us."

Isla was silent, for she could find no words.

"And Donald bein' a silent, quate man, things eat intil him, and he will pe wanderin' for efer and efer by hisself, thinkin' on nothing else. But how to pey more rent for the place is peyond him and me baith. We haf nefer a penny over--we just manage to live and to pey oor way. Mr. Malcolm, he talked a lot about breeding stock and such like, but where iss the money to come from to buy the stock at the beginnin'? They haf to be calves and lambs afore they grow to be bullocks and sheep. And that's how it iss wi' us here at Darrach, and we are feart for the day that will come."

She set the cups down on the table with a kind of mournful clatter and brought out the plate of oatcakes and the delicious scones and the cheese kebbuck and then the firm golden butter-pat from the little dairy.

"You will never leave Darrach while I live and can prevent it, Elspeth," said Isla.

And she meant what she said. As she walked up the road again and plunged into the bridle path that would bring her by the short cut to the Moor of Creagh she foresaw that her work was by no means done nor yet the fight ended. For if these were the lines Malcolm intended to pursue with Glenogle folks, then how could she live at peace with him? There was bound to be strife in the Lodge of Creagh.

She felt a little glow of home-like feeling when the small, ugly, square house, with its smoke curling up, straight and lazy, to the summer sky, came within range of her vision.

Margaret Maclaren, with temper considerably ruffled by certain happenings that day, was busy clearing up what she called a "clamjamphrey" in one of the upper rooms when she saw her mistress coming slantwise across the Moor. It was now five o'clock, and she immediately ran down to see whether the kettle was boiling, in case Miss Isla wanted tea.

Margaret had not been down the Glen at all during these last days and had not so much as seen the funeral of the Laird--in itself a serious omission. Then that day she had had a quarrel with Diarmid anent certain household arrangements which they had not been able to adjust to her satisfaction and which were waiting the judgment of Miss Isla.

Diarmid, a little puffed up perhaps with the attention he had received at Achree and the deference the American servants had paid him, had been a little high-handed with Margaret on his return. Hence the explosion on her part.

The truth was that both were too strong-minded and quick tempered, and that both wished to assert their authority, and it was hopeless to think that they would ever get on together at Achree, where most of the servants had been younger than Diarmid, who had lorded it over them all.

But Margaret held him again, as she expressed it, and they had been almost continuously at loggerheads since he had come to Creagh.

When Margaret saw him waiting at the door to receive his mistress she cast her head in the air and went by him with a small snort that spoke volumes. Isla just saw her disappear through the little doorway at the end of the short passage, and, in answer to Diarmid's anxious query whether she wanted any tea, she simply said "No," and asked where her brother was. But Diarmid could not tell her more than the brief fact that he had gone out after tea without saying where he was going.

Isla, with an odd sense of strangeness and detachment from the interior of the house, climbed the stairs and, as she reached the door of her own room, she heard a heavier foot behind her and beheld Margaret, who was of a substantial build, puffing on the uppermost steps of the stairs.

"Well, Margaret?" she said kindly. "We've come back you see, and have to begin again."

"Yes. Miss Isla. Please, can I speak to you for a minute or so? There's things in this house that must be sorted."

"Sorted" was a great word with Margaret. She sorted everything from the fire to the hens that she chased out of the little garden or the keeper's boys whom she hounded back to the Moor. Her temper was quick and her tongue not very reserved, but her heart was of gold towards the house she served.

"Why, surely. Come into my room. What's the matter with you? You look angry."

"I hope it's a righteous anger, Miss Isla. All I want to ken iss--What are the duties of Diarmid an' what are mine in this hoose?"

"Dear me, Margaret, what a fuss! Whatever do you mean? Your duties are just what they have always been. I've never been asked the question before. How has it arisen now?"

"It's that Diarmid. He thinks himsel' as fine as the Laird himsel'. Just come here a minute, Miss Isla, will you?"

Isla followed her wonderingly across the narrow landing to the door of the room in which her father had slept in his lifetime. It was the best room in the house, and Margaret, in no doubt that the new Laird would occupy it on his return, had swept and garnished it. But he had refused point-blank, and all his things lay scattered now upon the floor and on the bed, and the drawers were open, giving the room a most untidy aspect.

"Here haf I toiled an' slaved to get the place ready, an' then Maister Malcolm, he will not sleep in it, he says."

"Well, Mr. Malcolm must please himself, Margaret," said Isla rather quickly. "It does not in the least concern you."

"I'm not sayin' that it does. But what I do want to know, Miss Isla, iss if I'm to wait on him as well as to do the cookin' an' look after the whole house. I brought down all Maister Malcolm's things from the attic an' put them in the drawers; an' all the General's things are in the big kists up the stairs. Then, when Maister Malcolm came in he fell into the most fearful rage an' swore like anything an' turned the drawers out on the floor an' roared to me to put them all back up the stairs again. An' what I want to know iss whether it iss my duty or Diarmid's to do that. I haf nefer been in a hoose where the man-servant did not wait upon the master; forby, I haf not time, and, unless you pid me, I will not lift the things up the stairs again. It is Diarmid that should pe doin' it."

"Surely Diarmid will do it. Where is he? Tell him to come up."

"In a minute, Miss Isla. But what I do want to know iss how it iss to be in Creagh now? For if Diarmid iss to stop, then I canna. I'm not fit to stand his impidence."

The idea of Diarmid's impudence so tickled Isla that she burst out laughing, which did not please Margaret.

"If it's me you're laughin' at, Miss Isla," she began in a highly-offended tone----

Then Isla turned about on her with a quick glance of disapproval.

"Is that a way, Margaret Maclaren, to speak to me this day of all days? If you and Diarmid cannot live peaceably together, then you had better both go. You are a silly woman. What does it matter who puts away Mr.

Malcolm's things? Go away to your kitchen, and I'll do it myself. You ought to be ashamed of yourself at your age, behaving like a great baby."

Margaret did not take the rebuke in very good part. Old and faithful, she was likewise privileged; and undoubtedly all the Mackinnon servants had been more or less spoiled.

"It's the swearin', Miss Isla. I haf not been used to it, an' I will not stand it--not even from Maister Malcolm, an' Diarmid laughin' in the back, like, when I wass ordered to put away the things. Please to tell me who iss to wait on the Laird--iss it to be me or iss it to be Diarmid?"

"And, supposing it should be you, eh, Margaret?" asked Isla, and the smile did not leave her lips. "Go away down and see what there is in the larder, for we shall need something to eat a little later. And then come up and help me to clear this room. If Mr. Malcolm does not want it I'll take it myself, for it would be a shame to let it stand empty."

Margaret, a little ashamed perhaps and glad of the offered opportunity to recover herself, went out of the room.

The smile still lingering on her lips, Isla began to look over the things which had been brought down from the attic room. The squabble between Margaret and Diarmid was quite a timely diversion, for it had taken the edge off what might otherwise have been a painful moment, and she thought how like children the two were in their slight knowledge of real care.

Pondering thus, she pulled open the upper drawers of the tallboys that stood between the windows, and she saw that they were full of small stuff belonging to Malcolm--papers and photographs and books and toilet articles mingled in inextricable confusion.

Margaret had certainly carried the things down, but she had not made the smallest attempt at putting them in order. Isla took out an armful and carried them to the bed, thinking that when Margaret returned the simplest way would be to get her to bring a couple of trays, on which the small things could be laid, ready for carrying up the attic stair.

As she let a little heap fall loosely on the white coverlet a bundle of photographs fell apart, and one looked up at her with an insolent, half-defiant stare. She grew hot all over and then cold, recognizing in the bold, handsome face that of the woman whom she had seen Malcolm with in the street off the Edgeware Road. He had said she was a friend of George Larmer's; if so, why was her photograph here among Malcolm's most treasured possessions?

CHAPTER XVI
THE PURPLE LADY

The little menage on the Moor of Creagh was a mistake from the beginning, and was bound, in the very nature of things, to have a quick and disastrous end.

This, it must be at once said, was not altogether the fault of Malcolm, though Isla thought it was. Her fine nature had been soured by her experiences, and the hard side of her developed by the responsibilities which she had had to shoulder in her young girlhood, when her heart ought to have been at play.

She had acquired the habit of legislating for everybody, and up to a certain point of setting the standard of conduct. Her conscience she would make the universal conscience, forgetting that there were degrees and differences of temperament. By an effort of will she had held out a sort of grudging olive branch to Malcolm. But she had done this simply and solely because she wished to remain in Glenogle and because there was no place for her except under his roof. The injustice of it all ate into her heart. Malcolm, who had done nothing for the Glen, and who, in her estimation, was totally unfitted to have the destinies of so many in his keeping, had the whole power in his hands, and none could say him nay.

The sudden change in his position had made a great difference to Malcolm.

From being a guest on sufferance, disapproved of by Isla, who was mistress of the situation, he had stepped into power, which simply reversed their positions. Isla, so to speak, was now his guest, and, because there had been no will and there was nothing except the land to divide, a pensioner on his bounty.

Love would have laughed at the difficulties with which the situation bristled. But the difficulty of existence in these circumstances became more acute, and, to Isla, every day more unbearable. It was not that Malcolm was rude or actively unkind. Nay, his gay good humour never failed. But he had no use for her advice and he absolutely ignored anything she said as to his conduct of affairs.

Take the case of the Maclures, for instance.

"You'll never put Donald Maclure out of Darrach, Malcolm," she said one day in the autumn, when Martinmas was looming in sight. "I met him yesterday, and he looked like a man under sentence of death. He had heard that you have been in communication with a man in Fife about the croft. Is that true?"

"It might be, and, again, it might not be," he answered, though there was not a word of truth in the report yet.

He had thought of it, but it was characteristic of Malcolm's nature to postpone most of the serious things of life till a more convenient season. And just then his energies and his hopes were elsewhere engaged.

"But, Malcolm," she said, with a touch of passion, "it isn't right to treat the folk like that--to torment them without sense or purpose. They haven't been used to it."

"No--they've been used to nothing but having their own way, to paying when they liked and what they liked," he answered, with a touch of grimness. "But I'm going to alter all that."

They were at breakfast at the moment, and she looked down the narrow table at him with a feeling of strong disgust. There is no bitterness like the bitterness between those of one blood who persistently misunderstand and misjudge each other.

Malcolm Mackinnon was not wholly bad. Nay, at that very time he was honestly striving to do his duty and to establish himself in the esteem of those whose esteem he valued. But among these he did not include his dependants. Towards them he was a bit of a martinet, as his mother--a creature from the nether world dressed in a little brief authority--had been before him.

Isla knew nothing about her mother except that she had been very pretty and that she had died young. Had she known more she would have understood that alien and lawless blood run in Malcolm's veins. But the old General had never spoken of the one irretrievable mistake of his life--a mistake which had left his heart seared and made his life desolate in the summer of his days. Happily perhaps for Isla the brief tragedy had been enacted in India, and General Mackinnon's wife had never beheld the place of her husband's birth and true affection.

"I am sure Mr. Cattanach can't approve of your turning out the folk like that. And what will a few shillings or pounds a year more do for you? It will make so little difference that, looking at it even from the sordid standpoint, it isn't worth while."

Isla spoke thus because she was intensely of opinion that Malcolm had no feelings, and that this was the only appeal that would strike home. He, knowing perfectly well how she regarded him, was pleased to play upon her erroneous conceptions.

"It's worth while, my dear," he said, with his ready and, to her, most aggravating smile, "because these Highland folk want waking up. They are like the Irish--lazy, easy-going, and without independence. You should hear George Larmer on the state of things on his Wicklow place. He says it is due partly to the rain and partly to the whisky, but there is not a man of them who will do a decent day's work."

"We get rain enough here," said Isla with a sigh, for it had been a very wet summer, and the poor harvest was to be very late. "But our people don't drink whisky. Even Donald is a teetotaller and wears a blue ribbon in his buttonhole."

"Which that shrew of his pinned on, doubtless. Poor devil!--I'm sorry for Donald if that's the set of it, and I'll stand him a drink next time I meet him at a handy place."

"Then, what are you going to do about the Maclures? I wish you would be serious for just a minute, Malcolm. I really want to know what's in store for them. I am almost afraid to go past the door of Darrach now or to meet Eppie. She's wearing herself to a shadow over it all."

"There you are, Isla--you've ruined them, neck and crop, by listening to their grumblings and pandering to their lack of independence! Nobody knows just how much money there is in Glenogle--or in any of the glens, for that matter. It strikes me there are a good many fat stocking-feet hidden among the thatch."

"Oh, nonsense, Malcolm! Nobody does that now. They all use the bank when they have anything to put away, but I don't think that is often the case."

He cut the top neatly off his third egg and proceeded to enjoy it. Malcolm had a healthy appetite, and Margaret Maclaren, still more or less in a state of grumbling rebellion, said that he was hard to fill.

"Look here, Isla, I wish you would take a sensible view of things and leave me to manage my own business. You won't deny that the management is mine now, I suppose? Unfortunately for me, you've been Laird of Achree for the last five or six years, and you're difficult to follow. It's just like what happens in a regiment when an easy Colonel is followed by a smart one. Every unit in it jibs, but they all come into line a little later. And that's what the tenants--my tenants--are going to do if you'll let them alone. But you must let them alone, do you understand? I am sick of all this wrangling, and I won't listen to you any more. It isn't decent for you to act as go-between among the tenants. If they have a grievance let them come to me. Next time you see the Maclures you can tell them it will pay them to address themselves to me instead of putting up a poor face to you."

Isla's colour rose, for both the words and the manner of them were offensive.

"It would be better for yourself, too," he added in a gentler tone. "I don't suppose you ever look at yourself in the glass. You've gone off most frightfully of late. It's the worry and the bearing of loads for other folk that they are perfectly able to bear themselves that are to blame for that. Take me, for instance. You'd like to melt me down and drop me into your own mould. But, my dear, it can't be done. Leave me to go my own way. Maybe it's a blundering bad way, but at least give me credit for trying to make the best of things. Once for all, I won't be dictated to or legislated for. There isn't in the whole world a more difficult or impossible person to live with than the woman who wants to run a universal conscience."

There was just sufficient truth in the words to make their sting doubly telling.

"If that is how you feel about me, Malcolm," she said, rising stiffly, "then the sooner I leave Creagh the better."

"A visit to the Barras Mackinnons would do you a power of good, I admit, and would give me time to look round and get my bearings," he said frankly. "The quarters are a bit close here, you know, for us in our present state. Why not go to Wimereaux to them? The sea air would do you good, and they've asked you often enough, in all conscience."

She rolled up her napkin and pushed it all awry into the ring with the Mackinnon crest on it, and her downcast eyes were full of strange fires.

"I don't want to be unjust or hard. Heaven knows I don't, but you won't do anything," continued Malcolm. "At Achree they're always asking why you don't come down, and I must say I think that, after all their kindness, you've treated them shabbily."

"You go so much," she said sullenly. "We can't both live on the American bounty."

It was a speech wholly unworthy of Isla and unjust to the Rosmeads. But it was prompted by jealousy alone and by the distorted view of things prevailing in the mind of the lonely girl whom nobody now seemed to want.

Her only faithful henchman was Neil Drummond, but on the last occasion on which he had come with words of healing and sympathy on his lips she had sent him away, telling him she would not see him again unless he promised to talk of ordinary things.

"You've got into a beastly habit of nagging when you're not curled right up in a hard shell which nobody can open," said Malcolm, enjoying his opportunity now that candour was the order of the day. "You've choked off nearly everybody, and it's your own fault. I find folk very pleasant because I let them alone. I'm not for ever telling them to do this or that. I've enough to do to look after myself. I know you think me a rotter--and all that. But you might do worse than take a leaf out of my book. I've been out in the world, and I've learned two things--that it's ready to laugh with you, but that the moment you show the other side of your face it is bored to extinction. Your long face bores folk, Isla. Nobody has ever told you the truth about yourself before. You've arrogated the rôle of truth-teller to yourself, but that's it----"

Isla walked out of the room with her head held high in air and fire burning fiercely in her eyes. She was so angry that she dared not trust her voice. Now she knew exactly what position she occupied at Creagh--that Malcolm regarded her as an encumbrance and a nuisance, and that she dwelt there merely on sufferance and during his good pleasure. Well, such a situation being intolerable to a woman of spirit, it must be ended, and that without delay.

She ascended the stairs to her own room, and when she was intercepted by Margaret Maclaren with some inquiry about the meals for the day, she simply told her to get what she liked, and passed on.

Margaret, no stranger to wrangling, having had a bout of it that very morning with her arch-enemy Diarmid, understood that there had been a small storm raging in the dining-room, and discreetly retired.

New, strange, dreadful elements had crept into the quiet life on Creagh Moor, and all its sweet harmony was destroyed.

Isla shut the door of her own room, and dropped for a moment into her chair, wringing her hands the while with a sense of utter helplessness. She was at the end of her tether. Nobody wanted her, and the time had come for her to go away. Not a soul in the Glen, she told herself bitterly, would lament her going. She had dropped into obscurity, and even if she were never to come back any more to Glenogle, how many would mourn her absence or long for her return?

The impulse to go there and then was strong upon her. She even opened the door of her wardrobe and her drawers to take a brief inventory of her belongings and consider what she would take away.

If only she could walk out as she was! But travel, even of the simplest sort, is hampered by the multitude of our needs, by the things which complicate life. Then she looked at her little store of money, counting it out with careful fingers. Eighteen pounds in gold and two handfuls of silver-- well, that would keep her until she could earn more for herself.

She was a forlorn creature, without plan or compass, proposing to let herself drift upon an unknown sea. She had not the smallest intention of going to the Barras Mackinnons at Wimereaux. She must get away quite alone, where she could realize herself, and arrive at some conclusion regarding her ultimate fate.

Through the open window she heard Malcolm go off with the dogs, whistling as if he had not a care in the world. The things which daunted her and lay like a nightmare on her white, sensitive soul, had no power over him. Frankly selfish, he lived from day to day, extracting the honey from the hours, and stoically enduring what he could not evade. Perhaps, she said to herself, his was no bad philosophy. She wished somebody had taught it to her sooner; now it was a difficult lesson, baffling her intelligence at every point.

By and by she grew calmer, and her distracted thoughts began to collect themselves. It was not possible to run away in a hurry without telling any one, and her orderly mind shrank from taking such a foolish and unnecessary step. No--whatever she did, she would not forget herself or the dignity of the Mackinnons. She would put no occasion for talk into people's mouths.

In an hour's time she had decided what to do, and, after making a sort of preliminary division of her possessions, she dressed herself and went out. Margaret, having the feeling that Miss Isla wished to be alone, did not intercept her this time.

It was a fine, clear, hard morning in September, with a touch of frost in the air after a night's rain. But the clouds on the far horizon were still watery, and Isla's keen eyes decided that the deluge had not spent itself.

She would, however, get fair weather as far as Lochearnhead, which was her present destination, seeing that she had to give a certain order to Jamie Forbes concerning the morrow.

Of a set purpose, she kept to the sheep tracks on the hills, thus avoiding the vicinity of Achree. She had been there very few times since her father's death, and as Mrs. Rosmead had had a somewhat serious illness in the interval, her daughters had been too much engaged in looking after her to pay distant calls. But Isla knew that Malcolm was constantly there--if not every day, at least several times a week.

About half a mile beyond Achree gates, on the Lochearn side of the Glen, she had to come out on the road again, because the sheep track ended suddenly with Donald Maclure's pasture. The heavy rains had washed every superfluous particle of earth from the roads, and left the gravelled bottom bare, while there were delicious runnels of water here and there, all making swiftly for the burn, which was swollen far beyond its ordinary limits. There had been very little fair weather in Glenogle or in the valley of the Earn since the Lammas floods.

Isla paused for a moment on the Darrach Brig to watch the brown swirl of the water below, which fascinated her. Her eyes and ears were ever quick and keen to note every change in the aspect of the landscape, and she was more weather-wise than most. She had fallen into a kind of brown study, from which she was awakened very suddenly by the sound of a voice speaking a few yards away.

It was a woman's voice, and when Isla swung round upon her with quickly-uplifted head she saw a lady on the road dressed in garments such as were not often seen in Glenogle. She wore a gown which, Isla decided, was more fitted for an afternoon function than a quiet country road. It was of a somewhat vivid purple hue, trimmed profusely about the bodice with string-coloured lace. The skirt was long, but she had it gathered in her hand, and held high enough to show the froth of white, lace-trimmed petticoats and a mauve stocking against the clear, patent leather of the high-heeled shoes. A large black hat, surmounted with feathers and swathed in a veil like a spider's web, through which the vivid colour of the face appeared somewhat softened, completed the costume, which was certainly a startling one in that remote place, though such a common sight in London streets as to excite no remark.

Isla grew hot and cold, and started back with a little gesture of aversion, for she recognized the woman whose face she had seen once in the flesh, and once again in a photograph in her brother's room.

"Good day," said the stranger quite pleasantly. "Could you tell me whether there is a place close by here called Achree?"

She pronounced the last word without the guttural, so that it sounded like Akree.

"I asked about it at the hotel," the lady continued. "and they directed me along this road. But it seems a good bit away. Is it much farther off?"

"The Lodge gates are half a mile farther on," Isla answered. "Then there is the avenue to the house and that is rather long."

"I may as well go on, now I have come so far, but if I'd known how far off it was I would have hired a trap of some kind."

She leaned against the parapet of the bridge in a quite friendly fashion, as if ready to talk; and Isla hating herself intensely for lingering, yet felt impelled to do so, and even to put a question to the stranger concerning her business at Achree.

"I suppose that it is the American tenants you have come to see? They have been in Achree for about six months now."

The lady shook her head.

"No. I don't know that I've come to see anybody in particular, but I'm interested in the place through a friend of mine. I didn't know there were Americans in it. I thought it belonged to a family called Mackinnon."

"They are the owners, but it is let, as most of the big places are in these days."

"I see. And where are the Mackinnons? Mr. Mackinnon chiefly? He is what you call the laird now, isn't he? I read about his father's death in the newspapers, and what a fuss they made about it! Is he here just now?"

"He is not at Achree."

"But he lives in this neighbourhood, surely? He has not left Scotland?" said the stranger with a quick, apprehensive note in her voice.

"No, he lives farther up the Glen--oh, a long way. You could not possibly walk it," said Isla hastily. "Good morning. I must go on."

She was ashamed of herself for having lingered to parley even a moment with this woman, who, she felt sure, by her coming presaged more dool and woe to Achree. How she longed to get clean away from the Glen before the name of Mackinnon was dragged in the mire! This impossible woman must have a hold of some kind on Malcolm, else she never would have dared to come seeking him in his own glen.

As she turned away her soul felt sick within her.

"I'm sorry you are not walking my way," said the stranger easily. "I'll walk on a bit farther and take a look at the place, now I have come so far. What a country! Such hills! And how dull you must all find it! I'm stopping at Strathyre, and when there are not the hills, there's the water to get on your nerves. I don't wonder the Scotch are a melancholy people. Ta-ta!"

She waved her plump, gloved hand in quite friendly fashion, and showed her dazzling teeth in a pleasant smile as she sauntered off.

Isla, with her limbs positively trembling beneath her, hurried over the bridge, and so on to the hotel, where she merely left a message, ordering the trap to fetch her and her luggage from Creagh in the morning.

She had had various plans when she started out. She had thought she might possibly hire Jamie Forbes to take her through Balquhidder to Garrion, or that she might even on the way home pay a call at Achree.

But after what had just happened, she had only one desire--to get away out of Glenogle as fast as the fastest train could take her.

CHAPTER XVII
HER TRUE FRIENDS

Fortune did not favour Isla that day. At any rate her desire for complete isolation was not gratified.

As she came out of the hotel, after having made her arrangement for Jamie Forbes to fetch her from Creagh to Lochearnhead Station in the morning, she encountered Mrs. Rodney Payne, who hailed her with undisguised delight.

"Dear Miss Mackinnon, we really thought we should never, never see you any more! Why is it that you have quite deserted Achree?"

"I don't know," answered Isla rather humbly. "It is a long way, and--and the days go by."

"But it was not kind. And the messages we have sent by your brother!--has he ever delivered them, I wonder?"

"He has often said to me that you would like me to come oftener to Achree."

"Well, and so we would. And what have you to say for yourself?"

Isla looked at her and smiled. It was impossible not to smile at the beautiful creature whose charm could disarm any hostility. Isla was not hostile to Achree. Only there she must be all or nothing. That was the truth, scarcely yet admitted to herself. A very woman, she could brook no rival, and had stayed high and dry upon the Moor of Creagh, because she would not share Achree and the Rosmeads with Malcolm.

"I am a pig," she said with humility, yet with conviction--a speech which made Vivien laugh.

"Since you know yourself best, I will not presume to contradict you, my dear," she said as she thrust a small and confidential hand through Isla's arm. "Now I have you fast I will lead you to confession. What have we done to offend?"

"Oh, nothing to offend!" said Isla quickly. "I am not silly in that way, I hope. But--but----"

"But what? I thought that I had you hard and fast, that day at Creagh and that, hard to win, Isla Mackinnon, once won, could be kept. Why have I made such a disastrous mistake? I ask everybody, I even write to Peter and ask him, but he answers not. It is all a part of this mysterious life of the glens and of the Scottish character, which no man or woman from the outside can ever hope to get to the bottom of."

"Oh, come!" said Isla a little shamefacedly, "we are not so black as all that."

"Black, but comely! But back to Achree I march you to-day, at whatever cost. Do you know that my mother has been five weeks ill in bed and that you have never once called to ask for her?"

"But I have sent messages by Malcolm, and even written myself once----"

"It is not the same," broke in Vivien. "To-day you shall be taken in sackcloth and ashes to beg forgiveness."

"But you have already had too much of the Mackinnons. I would not have you sicken of the name."

"We should never sicken of you, Isla. It is an ungracious thing to say, and the words come most ungraciously from your lips."

"But Malcolm does come every day, doesn't he?"

Isla turned her quick, penetrating eyes full on Vivien's glowing face, and she wondered whether the colour deepened at the question or whether she merely imagined that it did.

"He has been most kind. He does all sorts of 'cute things for us. We have scarcely missed Peter since he went away. You should hear my mother! Your brother has quite won her heart."

"Yes?" said Isla, but her tone was dry.

In the near distance she saw the figure of the stranger lady in the purple frock coming towards them, and she wondered what would happen. Vivien, too, saw it, and the smile deepened in her eyes.

"Who can this extraordinary female be? I met her as I came down, and she put me through a sort of catechism about the Glen, with special reference to Achree and the Mackinnons."

"I also met her," said Isla, "and she likewise catechized me. Some chance tourist staying at the Strathyre Hotel and hard up for something to occupy her time, I suppose."

"It struck me as more than that. And besides, the season for tourists is past," said Vivien shrewdly. "What garments! And what lack of fitness! I wonder now whether she thinks that we are badly dressed and that she could give us points? She has a complacent air, which is at once my despair and my envy."

Isla made no response. Again the chill premonition of coming evil crept about her heart--she felt that the purple-clad stranger was a menace to Achree.

"Now I wonder whether your brother saw her? I am sure she would stop him if she met him!"

"Malcolm!--but he is not down the Glen? I thought he was going to shoot over the Moor this morning. He certainly said something about it at breakfast."

"He was certainly down the Glen, my dear, for I met him on his grey cob. But where he is now I don't know," said Vivien. "It would have interested her, I am sure, to have had speech with the actual Laird of Achree."

"What did she ask you?" asked Isla quickly.

Vivien's colour rose this time without doubt, but she evaded the question.

"She is greatly concerned about the future of Achree, anyhow, so let us give her a civil good morning as we pass."

"We needn't stop--we mustn't stop," said Isla a little nervously.

And as the purple figure approached Vivien felt the arm she touched tremble a little. But the stranger, who now looked tired and bored, passed them with a languid bow and then seemed to hasten her steps towards the hotel.

"I am very glad of this chance of going to Achree to say good-bye," said Isla, "as to-morrow I am going away."

Vivien nodded, as if she had heard a bit of news she fully expected.

"To Wimereaux--to your aunt and uncle? Your brother told us about your going."

In spite of herself, Isla's face hardened. Malcolm, then, discussed her with the Rosmeads, had even planned her going and spoken of her transfer to the Barras Mackinnons as a settled thing. Yet she had not once so much as said that she would like to go!

"Did Malcolm tell you that I was going to-morrow?" she asked in a low voice.

"He said it might happen any day," answered Vivien. "And, though we would have liked to see more of you. we all understand that a change would be the very best thing in the world for you. I've even had it in my mind to propose that you and I should take a little trip to Paris together next month, and that afterwards you might have gone back to Wimereaux. I have not been in Paris since I was a girl at school."

"You were educated in Paris?"

Vivien laughed rather sadly.

"No--I was what they call finished there," she answered drearily. "A woman's education is in the school of life. Mine has been hard enough, heaven knows! I have always hated Paris since, but still I should like to go there with you. I still have an apartment there. If you could let me know about what time you wish to come back I could join you or we could meet on the way, or even in Paris itself."

The idea pleased Isla. If only there had been no obstacles in the way!

"I've never been to Paris. I've seen nothing but Glenogle except--once in a great while--Barras and London."

"Barras is lonely, isn't it? But the Ogden Dresslers liked it."

"It is an island in the Atlantic. But loneliness belongs not so much to places as to persons. I am never lonely--in the sense that you mean. But I think I could be so in a big city."

"How long are you likely to be at Wimereaux?"

"I don't know. I have to get there first."

"Will Sir Thomas and Lady Mackinnon stop there all winter?"

"No. They will go back to Barras at the end of next month, I expect. My uncle is counting the days."

"Ah, I don't wonder at that from what your brother tells me about him! We expected Peter home in November, but his last letter to mother is not very reassuring. They are finding the Delaware Bridge more difficult than they expected. There is something puzzling about the river-bed. Peter seems to be working night and day."

"But he will like that. He is never happier than when fighting obstacles," said Isla with a faint smile of remembrance.

"That is so--at least it used to be so. But we thought from the letter yesterday that he was getting what we call plumb-tired of it. He wants to come back to Scotland--anyone can see that--and, of course, my mother's illness has made us all anxious. But he doesn't say a definite word about coming home."

Isla was interested in these items of information concerning Peter Rosmead and his family. She was naturally sociable. It was only the habit of life forced upon her by circumstances that had fostered her reserve. With Vivien Rosmead, as with Peter, she always felt her heart expand.

There was no reproach in Mrs. Rosmead's eyes as, from her bed, she extended two warm hands of welcome to the desolate girl and drew her down towards her for a kiss.

"My dear, why is it that you have been so long in coming. Your dear brother has made every excuse for you, but we wanted you--we wanted you very much."

Isla's eyes filled with tears. She told herself that she had been wise to stop away, seeing that the sight of this sweet mother of the gentle eyes and heart who, from her invalid couch, ruled her family with an absolute rule, was bad for her and filled her with acute unrest, with a feeling of rebellion against her own motherless state.

"I forgot to tell you," said Vivien cheerfully, "that Sadie has gone to Garrion for the day. She and Kitty are inseparable. What a dear, bright creature Kitty is! And Aunt Betty!--oh, Aunt Betty is a type! I live for the meeting I hope to arrange between her and my mother, though they will need an interpreter. Her Scotch is lovely, but unintelligible."

Again the swift pang of jealousy tore at Isla's heart. While she had been alone at Creagh nobody had been lonely for her sake. Her point of view was wholly unreasonable, and it but serves to show how long brooding on one particular line of thought can distort the mental vision of the healthiest and sanest person in the world. It was more than time that Isla left Glenogle--it would have been disastrous for her to stay much longer.

She remained to luncheon, and thereafter she sat for another half hour with Mrs. Rosmead, who, while she tried to get Isla to talk about herself, incidentally talked a good deal about her children, especially about Peter, for whom her heart was crying out. Isla learned more about Peter Rosmead from that hour's conversation with his mother than she had yet known, and all that she learned was to his credit.

"I hope, my dear," said Mrs. Rosmead, "that you will be back at Christmas at least, for it is our hope that my son may join us then, and we shall keep it as a family here. Your brother has promised to come to us, and if you are here, too, then we shall be happy indeed. It is where you ought to be at Christmas--under your father's roof-tree."

"It is Malcolm's now," said Isla with an effort. "I don't know whether I shall have returned by then. I have no plans. I am a bit of drift-wood on the shore now, liable to be floated away by the tide, dear Mrs. Rosmead. But whether I come or whether I don't I shall think of you, and I shall be glad that you are here in Achree."

"There is something the matter with that child, Vivien," the old lady said to her daughter after Isla had gone--"something that has taken the heart clean out of her. It is something more than her father's death. Let us hope that the change will do her good."

Meanwhile, Isla was nearing home, having been convoyed on her walk part of the way by Vivien, who, on parting, had bidden her a most affectionate farewell.

Vivien was distinctly disappointed in Isla Mackinnon--her persistent coldness had chilled her. She had proved that Highland hearts can be very warm and kindly, and she thought that Isla had not met their advances with corresponding cordiality. But, having herself suffered, she did not judge any man--much less any woman. She knew she must leave Isla to realize herself and to work out her own destiny.

It was tea-time when Isla got back, and Malcolm was about the house.

His face was serene and undisturbed. Isla therefore surmised that he had not encountered the lady of the purple gown. Should she enlighten him? Was it her duty to warn him that the woman, with whom he undoubtedly had some slight acquaintance--even if nothing more--was in the vicinity making inquiries about him? Though he had happened to miss her that day, she was haunting the neighbourhood, and Strathyre was, so to speak, but a stone's throw from Glenogle.

"I've been trysting Jamie Forbes for the morning, Malcolm," she said quietly. "I'm going with the nine-thirty."

"Going where?" he asked with a start.

"To Glasgow, first. I will have just a word with Mr. Cattanach. Then I will take the two o'clock train."

"For London?"

She nodded. There was no reason why she should hide the first step of her journey from him--no reason at all.

"And will you go on to Dieppe by the night boat, then?"

She shook her head.

"There is no need for such haste," she answered. "And I am not a stranger in London. I can find my way about. I'll stop the night at the Euston Hotel."

"Have you money?" he asked, trying hard to hide his relief.

"I have twenty pounds."

"Oh, you are in clover. It is not a dear fare to Wimereaux, even if you travel first class. And, of course, it will cost you nothing while you are there. They seem to be living at heck and manger for next to nothing, but how Uncle Tom does loathe it! I suppose you'll come back with them as far as Glasgow when they come north next month?"

"I suppose so," she answered listlessly.

There was no reason why she should either affirm or deny, because she herself did not know what she might do. Everything would depend. It might even be on the knees of the gods that she would drift to Wimereaux in the end.

"I've been to lunch at Achree," she said suddenly. "I met Miss Rosmead on the road, and she made me go in. Mrs. Rosmead looks very ill, I think."

"Nothing to what she did look. And they are so accustomed to snatching her back from the jaws of death," said Malcolm grimly, "that they are quite satisfied about her."

"Oh!" said Isla. "You go there a great deal, Malcolm. They seem to think you a splendid sort of fellow."

It was a curious speech and did not sound quite kindly. Malcolm, however, took it well, though there was a touch of bitterness in his reply.

"It's the people's way of looking at it, Isla--they are lovely people. They bring out all that is best in a chap and make him hate the worst. I'll tell you what. If I had been thrown with that sort at one time of my life I should have been a different man."

"We did our best," she answered with a wounded air. "Father and I were as good as we knew how, though, of course, we could not hope to reach the Rosmead standard."

"I don't mean that, Isla. Gad, how quick and hard you are on a fellow! Your tongue's like a two-edged sword. I only mean that there's a time in a chap's life--don't you know?--when, if he gets into a good woman's hands, she shapes him for good. If he gets into the hands of the other sort, then God help him!--he hasn't much chance else."

A fleeting pity crossed Isla's face. It was a passionate human appeal. She began dimly to glimpse the fact of the frightful war between good and evil which ravages the souls of some, making life a battle-ground from the cradle to the grave.

She put out a timid hand and touched his arm.

"I'm sorry if I have been hard, Malcolm. I--I didn't understand. But now----"

"Now I mean to win Vivien Rosmead when I'm clean enough to ask her," he answered in a voice that gripped.

Isla remembered the heightened colour in Vivien's cheek, the tones and terms in which Malcolm was spoken of at Achree, and she had no doubt of the issue. But the woman in the purple frock! Something gripped her by the throat. She did not know what she wished or hoped for. She did passionately feel, however, that if Vivien made another venture upon the sea of matrimony she ought to be very sure of the seaworthiness of her barque.

"I suppose she divorced her husband. Have you ever heard anything about the story, Malcolm?"

"Nothing. They never speak of it. Why should they? That sort of thing is best forgotten."

"She will never forget it. I can't forget how she spoke that day she came to me--the day when father died. Her eyes are very wide open, Malcolm. She will take no risks next time."

"But she isn't hard," he said eagerly. "And a woman who has lived--who has seen life--can make allowances for a man. It's that I'm building on."

Isla shook her head and rose to her feet with a heavy sigh.

"Life is a most frightful tangle, Malcolm. Sometimes I get so tired of it!"

"We all do, but we've got to make the best of it. You don't want any money, then," he added cheerfully. "It's just as well, because I have hardly a red cent to bless myself with, and I'm counting the days till the Martinmas audit and till Rosmead sends his cheque. When I get that I'll send you along something to Wimereaux."

"I'll write if I need it or want it," she said quickly.

Then, as if in spite of herself, the other matter would out.

"Malcolm, did you meet anybody on the road this morning, either in going or in coming home?"

"I met different folks--Donald Maclure and Long Sandy and Drummond seeking you. Only he didn't come up when I told him that I thought you were about Lochearn. Did you see him?"

"No. I suppose I was in Achree at the time. This was a lady--an extraordinary person in a purple frock. She spoke to me at the Darrach Bridge, and she had stopped Vivien Rosmead, too, and asked her questions about Achree."

She saw Malcolm's colour change and his eyes shift.

"What did she say to you, Isla? I suppose she was one of these stray visitors at the hotel. Miss Macdougall has had some queer specimens this summer."

"She said she was living at Strathyre, and she asked questions about the Mackinnons and Achree, as if she knew about them."

"And did she say where she came from or what she wanted here?" asked Malcolm, and by this time he had walked away beyond the range of Isla's eyes.

"No. But I knew, Malcolm," said Isla clearly. "I don't know whether I ought to tell you, but perhaps it will be better that you should know. She was the woman I met you with that day in the Edgeware Road--the woman you said you were seeking for Captain Larmer."

CHAPTER XVIII
GOODBYE TO GLENOGLE

Half an hour later, from the window of the room where she was doing her packing, Isla saw Malcolm ride out to the road upon his bicycle. She did not need to watch the turn he took. She knew just as well as if she had been told that he was bound for Strathyre. It was beginning to grow dusk, but the September evenings are long in Glenogle, and it would be a night of full moon.

Isla's thoughts were rather bitter as she made busy with her scanty wardrobe, laying aside every superfluous article, because she did not wish her movements to be hampered with too much baggage.

Busy with purely mechanical things as she was, her thoughts were free to tarry with the affairs of Achree. Had Malcolm been as other men--had there been no shadow on his past, no complications in his present, she could have wished for no better issue out of the tangle of their troubles than to see him win Vivien Rosmead. She was a sweet, gracious woman, a true gentlewoman, beautiful and rich--a combination not easily found in a wife. How Isla would have rejoiced to see her mistress of Achree, rearing bonnie children who would have loved her and called her Auntie Isla.

It was what ought to have been, she said with a little passionate stamp of her foot upon the floor. And now that Malcolm was in deadly earnest she did not doubt for a moment that he desired to be worthy for Vivien's sake, but spectres blocked the way. The most imminent and the most terrifying was the woman in the purple frock.

Could anything on earth ever explain her away?

She contrasted the woman and Vivien as she had seen them together on the Glenogle road, and she conjured up the supreme contempt that would gather in Vivien's eyes were she pitted against her. She would absolutely disdain such humiliation. Isla felt sure that the man who would win Vivien Rosmead from her disillusionment, who aspired to heal her hurts, must have a clean record. How dared Malcolm, with what was behind and before him, aspire to her?

Isla wondered at the audacity of men. Yet her heart was also stirred with pity for him in that he must reap the bitter harvest of his folly and his sin. Her heart was passing weary, the burden had not been lightened with her father's death, but seemed to have waxed heavier. And she must get away. She felt herself a coward in view of what might come. She could not breast anew scandal in the Glen and she must get away. Such weakness and weariness crept over her that she could have laid her head down and slept for ever. She held on bravely with her preparations, however, and when they were finished she rang the bell for Margaret Maclaren.

"The dinner iss ready, Miss Isla. Am I to send it in?" asked that competent domestic with just a touch of aggressiveness in her mien and manner.

"I don't know where Mr. Malcolm is or when he will come back. But, yes--send it in if it will make you any happier, Margaret, and lift that dour cloud from your face," she added hastily. "I know I can trust you to keep something hot for Mr. Malcolm."

"Oh, as to that, it can be done. But I'm gettin' tired of it, Miss Isla. I nefer saw such a man, or such a hoose--beggin' your pardin for my plain speech. He takes less account of times and seasons than anybody I have ever seen or heard tell of. I don't know what he thinks happens in a kitchen, or whether he knows how food is made, but he expects it to be ready when he iss, whatefer the hour of the day. It iss not in my power, Miss Isla. I'm gettin' to be an old woman and not fit for my job."

"Nonsense, Margaret. You never were fitter, and you must warstle through with it a little longer anyhow, because I am going away to-morrow for some weeks, and you must simply look after Creagh till I come back."

"Where are you goin', Miss Isla? To her Ladyship, iss it? Well, it will do you good, and it iss there you ought to haf gone long since. I will stop, then, till you come back. And I hope the change will do you good, for it iss fery thin and white-like you are gettin', my dear, and it iss time something wass done. I will do my best for Maister Malcolm, and if it should pe that we fall out peyond making up while you are away I'll write and let ye know."

Isla had not expected sympathy from Margaret, who, between Diarmid and his master, was now kept in a state of continual agitation which had a very bad effect on a temper that was not placid at the best of times.

Isla thanked her, and, with a mind considerably eased, went down to eat her solitary meal. After dinner she busied herself writing a few notes of farewell--one of them to Kitty Drummond and one to Elspeth Maclure, regarding whom her conscience was troubling her not a little. But she afterwards tore up Elspeth's, deciding that if Jamie Forbes came to Creagh in good time she would make him stop at Darrach on the way down so that she might say good-bye in a proper manner.

The evening wore on--eight, nine, ten o'clock--and still no word of Malcolm. Isla looked out again and again, and once she even walked out to the gate to see whether the twinkling light of the bicycle lamp was visible down the long vista of the road. When it was half-past ten she went to bed, for she had walked many miles that day, and her packing exertions--to say nothing of the strain of things on her mind--had left her very tired.

She was awakened long after by the banging of a door, she thought; but, listening intently, she heard nothing further, and so she fell asleep and did not wake till morning.

Breakfast had been ordered half an hour earlier than usual to give her time to catch the train, and she had nearly finished before Malcolm made his appearance. She looked at him rather keenly as he entered, and was immediately struck by his haggard looks. He appeared like one who had either not slept or had spent the night in some doubtful place.

"Good morning, dear. I owe you an apology, of course. I had a burst tyre other side of Lochearn last night, and it was near midnight when I got home. I hardly expected that you would sit up. At what time do you start?"

"Jamie ought to be here any moment. I trysted him for half-past eight, and it's twenty past now. I hear the wheel, I think. Yes--there he is. Aren't you going to eat anything, Malcolm?"

"No. Isn't there any coffee? Oh, I forgot--she can't make coffee. It's a cup of black coffee I'd like this morning. Is the tea strong? I'm coming down with you, of course, Isla. What else did you think? Don't wait here if you want to go upstairs or to be seeing after your stuff, though we've plenty of time, really."

Isla gladly escaped. She gathered from the general appearance of her brother that care sat heavily upon him. But she had not the smallest desire to question him. Nay, her longing to get away from the increasingly sordid conditions of her life had now become a positive fever in her veins.

Rest was what she craved--rest from haunting thoughts, from phantoms of dread, from the menacing sword which seemed to be suspended over Achree and all bearing the name of Mackinnon.

But she was to prove before another twenty-four hours were over that there are things in this world from which it is impossible to get away--crosses that have to be endured--heroically if possible, but certainly endured.

Malcolm was in the back seat of the dogcart, and did not speak a single word on the way down. They halted at Darrach, where a slight disappointment was Isla's--she did not see Elspeth. Donald himself, who seemed to be minding the house--at any rate, he had the second youngest child in his arms--came out of the gate to explain that his wife had gone to Govan to see their niece Jeanie Maclure, who was down with pneumonia. She had taken the baby with her.

Isla sent many messages to her, and passed on with a little sense of relief.

When they got to Lochearnhead Station the signal was down for the Oban train, which could be seen gliding swiftly round the curve of the hill. At the last moment the drag from Garrion, with the familiar pair of roans in the shafts, drove up rapidly, and Neil Drummond came bounding up to the platform. When he saw Malcolm Mackinnon handing his sister into the train he went forward eagerly, though the man whom he had come to meet--a visitor from Oban--had already alighted, and was on the outlook for him.

"Good day, Isla. Are you travelling?" he asked; and, seeing the dressing-bag, the rug, the strapped articles on the rack, he looked a trifle blank.

"She's going to Aunt Jean and Uncle Tom at Wimereaux," answered Malcolm when Isla said nothing. "Don't you think the change will do her good?"

"Yes. But how long is she to be away?" inquired Neil.

And his tone was so imploring, that Malcolm, understanding perfectly how it was, good-naturedly stepped back to give him a chance.

"Why this sudden journey, Isla?" Neil demanded with an imperious air, which showed how much he cared about the whole affair. "Last time I saw you you said nothing on earth would induce you to go Wimereaux."

"It was Malcolm who said I was going there," said Isla demurely.

The answer puzzled Neil, and filled him with lively forebodings.

"Isla," he said a trifle hoarsely, "you're not going do anything foolish? What has happened? Have you had a quarrel with Malcolm?"

"Not at all. I only want a change, Neil. Don't worry about me. Nothing can possibly happen to a strong young woman, with her head screwed pretty firmly on her shoulders."

Neil swung himself on the footboard of the train, quite heedless of the fact that his guest was looking about for him on the platform in hopeless disappointment.

"Isla, you are going to your uncle and aunt? Unless I am assured on that point, I'll step into the train and go with you."

Isla laughed at that.

"Why should you care, Neil? I'm only going a little journey on my own. I'll probably be back before anyone has had time to miss me."

"That can't happen. It'll be a long day for me till you come back to Glenogle. And, further, I'm not happy in my mind about you. In fact, I'm most unhappy."

"Don't be, then, Neil. I'm not worth it."

"That's my business, my dear," he said, and never had he looked more manly or more attractive. "Somehow, we all seem to have lost you lately. They all say that--Kitty, Aunt Betty, even the Rosmeads. They were speaking of you the other day. You haven't treated us well, Isla, whatever you may think. And now, this beats everything."

"The train is moving, Neil. Get down, or you will be hurt," she cried nervously.

But he still hung persistently to the half-open door.

"You'll write, Isla. Promise at least that you will write either to Kitty or to me?"

"I'll write to Kitty. Give her my love and tell her she'll hear from me without fail in a week or two."

"And if you want a friend, Isla, if there's anything I can do for you, promise you'll send for me or let me know. There isn't anything I won't do. No journey would be too long or too difficult if I had the prospect of serving you at the end of it, and--and well, you know the rest, don't you? I daren't say all I want."

A strong hand behind him took him by the coat-tails and dragged him from the now swiftly moving train, and the last Isla saw of Lochearn was Neil Drummond's face and the appeal in his eyes.

Malcolm was too late for the final good-bye, but Isla, on the whole, was rather glad that she had escaped it. She pulled up the open window-sash and flung herself back in the corner with a quick, heaving sigh.

It was all over, then. The cords had been cut, and she was adrift from Glenogle and all the trammels of the old life. What would the new bring, she wondered? A little sob broke from between her trembling lips as her eyes looked through the window at the wide Glen of Balquhidder to the misty hills beyond, where the glory of the heather was beginning to be dimmed. When should she see it all again, and in what mood?

At Strathyre her eyes were too red to permit her to look out, and happily no passenger sought to disturb her. By the time the train reached Callander she was calm again, and she arrived at Glasgow, quite composed. She left her luggage in the cloak-room and walked, since she had plenty of time, to the lawyer's office in St. Vincent Place.

Mr. Cattanach was able to see her at once, and he received her with his usual kindness of manner. He had thought a good deal about her of late and had wondered how she was getting on at Creagh with Malcolm, with whom he had had several rather stormy interviews.

"I'm on my way to London, Mr. Cattanach, and as I had an hour to spare before my train starts I thought I should like to see you."

"Surely. On your way to London, are you? For a long visit?"

"Yes. I think so."

"Sir Thomas and Lady Mackinnon are still across the Channel, I think. I saw in the News one night lately that they are not expected at Barras till November?"

"That's right, I believe," said Isla.

"Are you joining them?"

"Not just yet."

Cattanach scrutinized her rather closely. He did not know how far she might stand questioning, but he gathered from a certain quiet determination in her manner that she had some quite definite plan in her mind.

"Mr. Cattanach," said Isla clearly, "you have always been kind to me and have understood things right through. I can never forget how kind you were just before my brother came home. I can't go on living at Creagh with him any longer."

"I'm not surprised. I've been expecting to hear this for some time."

"I'm a dependent on his bounty. I ought not to have been left like that, but I don't want to grumble about it. He thinks I'm going to Wimereaux to my aunt and uncle. But I have no such intention."

"Indeed! I hope that you have at least some satisfactory haven in view, Miss Mackinnon," he said, with distinct anxiety in his voice.

"I have several very clear ideas. To-night I shall stay at the Euston Hotel and to-morrow I shall go to an old servant of Achree who is married in the West End of London. She keeps a boarding-house. From her house it is my intention to seek some employment."

Cattanach looked the surprise he felt. His disapproval, he decided, he had better keep to himself.

"I am honoured by this conference, Miss Mackinnon, and since you have told me so much I am encouraged to ask more. What sort of employment, may I ask, does Miss Mackinnon of Achree think she will find in London?"

Her eyes flashed a little mournfully.

"I belong to the great sad army of the partially equipped, Mr. Cattanach, but I know my limitations and I shall keep within them. Also I shall be able to earn my daily bread. I have come to you, because,--for reasons which I don't think I could really explain, even if I tried--I feel that I should like at least one responsible person to know where I am and precisely what I am doing. But I require that, unless circumstances arise which render it absolutely necessary that it should be known, you will not give that information to anybody in Glenogle or at Balquhidder," she added as an after-thought.

"You forget. I have no communication with Glenogle or Balquhidder now except through your brother. He is not likely to ask me your whereabouts. Will you give me your address?"

"I'll send it," she said diplomatically. "I want to get clean away from everything for a while, Mr. Cattanach, for really I don't quite know where I am standing. I even feel as if I were some strange, new sort of person with whom I have to get freshly acquainted. Can you understand that?"

"I understand that life has been very hard for you, my dear," he said involuntarily. "And I have often prayed that your day of brightness would come."

"It won't come," she said with a little nod. "I'm one of those predestined to gloom. Tell me, Mr. Cattanach, before I go," she added with a little touch of wistful tenderness that wholly became her, "how do you think it is with my brother now? You have seen him several times. Is--is he doing well? You wonder perhaps that I should ask. But my judgment, where he is concerned, has become entirely distorted. That is one of the reasons why I want to get away, because I am seeing nothing clearly, fairly, or justly, especially in relation to him."

"I think he means well. But he is not fitted for the life of a country laird. He would have made a better soldier. It is a thousand pities that he had to leave the Army."

"It is. Don't you think," she added after a moment's hesitation, "don't you think it a very wonderful thing that the true story of his leaving the Army has never got about?"

"I think it more than wonderful. There must have been somebody very high in power, manipulating the strings in the background. But it is a very good thing for you that the story was hushed up."

"But I don't think that Malcolm realizes how he has been spared. He is not so grateful as he ought to be," she said.

And then she bit her lip, as if she regretted the condemnatory words and as if she wished to recall them.

"I can take you out to lunch to-day, I hope?" said the lawyer, pulling out his watch. "Unless Mr. Drummond is waiting somewhere round the corner?" he added with a smile.

"No, I am quite alone, and I shall be very pleased to go to lunch with you," said Isla.

She found the next hour quite pleasant. Cattanach took her to the station, transferred her luggage, and secured for her a comfortable seat in the London train. He could not wait until its departure, however, as he had a West-End appointment at two o'clock. They parted cordially and Isla repeated her promise to send him her London address as soon as she herself was quite sure of it.

She spread her things about and then, tucking her rug about her, began to glance over some of the illustrated papers. So far, no one had interfered with her privacy by entering the compartment. She had no expectation, however, that she would be allowed to retain it all the way.

About three minutes before the train started there was a great bustle and talking outside the carriage window, and presently a porter, laden with sundry small packages, most of them rolled up in brown paper, entered the compartment, followed by a large woman in a brown tweed travelling coat of ample dimensions.

Isla looked over the rim of her paper in mild curiosity and then quite suddenly she paled a little and hastily withdrew behind her screen.

It was the lady of the purple gown.

CHAPTER XIX
IN THE LONDON TRAIN

The train had started before Isla's travelling companion caught a glimpse of her face. She rose up with a sudden bang from her seat, with the result that, in spite of herself, Isla lowered her paper a little to see what was going to happen. What she did see was only the purple lady removing her large and unsuitable headgear, which seemed to interfere with her comfort.

"Hats are gettin' worse every day," she said with a pleasant smile as she jabbed two immense pins with imitation moonstone tops into the stuffing of the cushions behind her. "Soon they'll need to get us hat-compartments. Eh--what? Now, where have I seen you before?"

She took some hairpins from her abundant and really pretty hair, and with a back-comb began to do her toilet.

Isla was saved the difficulty of answering by a sudden gleam of recognition wandering across the lady's face.

"Oh, I know--on the road right down there in Glenogle yesterday! Now, ain't you jolly glad to be gettin' away from that God-forsaken hole?"

"Just at the present moment I am," Isla admitted.

She wondered what means she should take to ensure for herself quiet and privacy. She was incapable of any act of studied rudeness, but the prospect of listening to the woman's talk appalled her. Should she call the guard and ask to be given another seat in another compartment, or should she politely inform her fellow-traveller that she did not care to talk.

The lady flopped upon her seat, shook her head to see whether the coils of her hair were firmer, and then settled herself back among the cushions, smoothing out the creases of her cheap blanket-coat with a plump white hand.

She had now a black frock on, but, in contrast with Isla's neat, trim, well-fitting suit of home-spun, it looked badly cut, badly worn, altogether unsuitable for a journey. There were quantities of white net--not too clean--about her neck, and many brooches and a long chain, on which hung a lorgnette, while a double eyeglass was pinned to her bosom. She wore a great many rings of sorts and a wedding one.

Isla's eyes were quick enough to detect that.

"Goin' all the way?" she asked with an engaging smile.

Isla nodded.

"So am I, and jolly glad I'll be to hear the noise and smell the good old smells of the Euston Road. How they live up there! But there--it ain't livin', is it now? Would you call it livin'--eh?"

"Well," said Isla, diverted in spite of herself, and feeling no longer the appalling dread that pursued her in Glenogle regarding this very woman, "it depends on what you call living."

"Just so. Well, I like a bit of fun myself--a night out occasionally and a bit of stir in the daytime. Them hills, and big, dark locks get on my nerves. I was four days at the little hotel at Strathyre, and I had just about enough of it."

"Visiting friends in the neighbourhood?"

"No," snapped the woman. "It was a bit of business I was on, and it was last night before I saw the party I had to see. Not but what I was comfortable there, and they do make good food. Ever stopped there? They tell me they hadn't an empty bed from Easter till now--full up with fishermen and that sort. Can't understand it--don't pretend to. It's the silence--the big empty silence that gets at me. It would drive me crazy in a month, and I'd be gettin' up in my sleep and wanderin' into that water."

"You would get used to Strathyre," said Isla, smiling a little as she raised her paper, and hoping that there might now be a reprieve.

Her passionate hope was that the woman, who had all the unreserve of her class, would not be seized with a sudden desire to confide the nature of her business to her fellow-traveller. She did not want to hear the truth from these lips. If necessary she would have to tell her somehow that she did not wish to go on talking.

"I doubt it very much! I've been about too much and seen too much life to settle down in the country. I may have to, perhaps, later on, when I get older and not so fond of racket. Nothing to hurt--don't you know?--only a night at one of the halls and a good old canter down Regent Street and Oxford Street."

"I never saw anybody riding there," said Isla in a startled voice.

"I don't mean that, of course!" laughed the stranger; "not but what I could do it and make the traffic sit up for me too. When I was in India I had me own horse every mornin' and them grinnin' black men to hold it for me till I was ready to mount. I had a figure then as slim as yours, and they all said I looked better in me habit than in anything else."

"What part of India were you in?" asked Isla, fascinated in spite of herself.

"Pretty well all over, but latterly I was in the north. My husband was in the Fighting Fifth. Ever heard of them?"

"Yes, of course. They were through the Afghan campaign. My father was a soldier, and he used to show us as children their marches on the map."

"Oh, indeed! Then you know something about the service? Any brother in it?"

"I had one," said Isla, and the colour rose hotly in her face.

"I love it. Even when I was a little nipper I always said I'd never marry anybody but a soldier. And I didn't."

"Is your husband alive still?"

"No--dead. Killed in action he was, a-savin' of his Colonel. I've got the little brown cross at home somewhere. These were the days! There never was a braver chap than Joe Bisley ever shouldered a musket. Ah, poor Joe!"

Isla, perceiving that her companion was now in the throes of reminiscence, shrank back nervously in her corner.

"Doesn't it make your head ache to talk in the train?" she asked rather hastily. "There are heaps of papers here if you like to read. You are welcome to any of them. The gentleman who saw me off bought a great many."

"Ah, I don't wonder!" said the other with an admiring glance of approval. "You are just the sort that they would buy everything for if they got the chance. A little standoffish, too--ain't that what they like? Oh, I know them through and through!"

In spite of herself, Isla laughed out loud.

"Oh, it was a very old friend of my family who was seeing me off to-day! My father's lawyer in fact."

"Ah, then, he knew what side his bread was buttered on. And are you goin' to London, may I ask?"

"Yes."

"What particular part?"

"I shall stay the night at the Euston Hotel. I may go abroad. My plans are a little indefinite at present."

"Same as mine. It ain't an easy thing for a lone woman to make up her mind, and, as I told the party I spoke of, last night, I'm gettin' tired of uncertainty. I want to know where I am. That's what for I took that long journey and stopped at that queer little hotel. I wanted to see a party and get my bearings."

"And did you get them?" asked Isla desperately.

"Yes, I think so. But, bless you, you never know where you are with them. They're as slippery as eels. If you weren't so pretty, my dear, I'd warn you to steer clear of them for the rest of your mortal life. But it ain't in reason that you'll be allowed. There must be dozens after you."

Isla shook her head and then pointed suggestively to the illustrated papers, even making a remark about one of the pictures on the cover.

But the lady did not accept the hint.

"I don't read much," she confessed. "And men and women are much more interesting than books. When you've seen a bit of life, as I have, what's written in a book doesn't count for much. It's like a stuffed sawdust man beside a real flesh-and-blood one. Yes, they're a slippery crew, but they makes life--don't they, my dear?"

"They make its dispeace, anyhow," said Isla, surprised into an expression of opinion that she immediately regretted.

Her companion's face brightened, and she sat forward eagerly.

"Fancy you thinkin' that! Well, as you've had reason to say that, I don't mind tellin' you I agree. They're worth watchin', they need watchin' all the time, though most of them are like babies, with no more thought of what's goin' to happen. Now there's me! When I was in India I was pretty and slim as you are, though you wouldn't think it, and I was a toast in the station and could have had me pick after Joe died. There was the Sergeant--a splendid figure of a man with four medals and pay saved. He would have married me right off, and so would the little Corporal, and even one of the subs. that had an Earl for his grandfather; but I passed by them all and took up with one that nobody could be sure of. He's here to-day and gone to-morrow, so to speak, and even his wife couldn't keep him on the string."

Isla jumped up with her colour fluttering and threw down her paper.

"It's very hot in here, isn't it? Excuse me, but I must go out into the corridor for a little fresh air. I can't stand the heat any longer."

"Oh, poor dear, have a drop of brandy! They do have uncommon good spirits at Strathyre, but then, it's the dew of their own mountains, isn't it? Do have a drop, dearie. It'll buck you up at once."

"No, no, thank you!" cried Isla over her shoulder from the corridor. "I never touch spirits. I only want to be quiet and not talk for the rest of the journey."

Mrs. Bisley looked disappointed, but she comforted herself with a drop of the dew of the mountains and then sat down to have a look at the papers.

Once Isla glanced back at her and, in spite of herself, had to admit the prettiness of her face. She looked about thirty-five, and had she been properly dressed she could have been made to look much more attractive. There was something winning about her, too, but--oh, the irony of fate that should have brought them together in that narrow space, from which it was impossible to escape!

Isla's abnormally quick perception had easily filled in the lines of the story. She had no doubt that the party referred to by her fellow-traveller was Malcolm. And that the woman believed that she had a right to him there could be no doubt. He had not admitted her claim, Isla concluded, else surely he could never have been so base as lift his eyes to Vivien Rosmead.

She felt sick as she pressed her throbbing head against the cold glass of the corridor window, enjoying the swish of the wind on her cheek.

Should she never get away from the shadows which had darkened her life? Was it ordained that she should be pursued, far beyond the limits of Glenogle, by the sordid phantoms of Malcolm's past and present? Was fate wholly inexorable--were poor human beings but puppets, liable to be rudely moved hither and thither upon the boards of the stage of life? If it were so she might as well go back and fight it out on the Moor of Creagh.

"Feelin' better, my dear?" said Mrs. Bisley kindly, when she presently turned her head. "The first lunch will be comin' along immediately, and that'll make you feel better."

"I don't take it," said Isla, seeing a probable respite for an hour or so, during which she might either escape or rearrange her plans. "I have a few sandwiches in my dressing-bag and, later, I shall get a cup of tea. I never eat much when I am travelling."

"A mistake, my dear. Take it from me that has travelled a lot both by land and sea. If you don't eat you get so low that you can't bear yourself. Do say two for luncheon when the waiter comes along; then we'll go in together."

Isla shook her head.

"No, thank you."

The attendant came at the moment to inform them that the first luncheon would be served in about twenty minutes. Isla crept back again to her corner under the sympathetic scrutiny of her companion.

"What a colour you have, to be sure! Sorry you don't feel up to luncheon," she said cheerfully. "It's all use. When you've knocked about as much as I have you'll get more experiences. I'm up to all travelling dodges."

Isla had no doubt of it. She opened out another paper and let her eyes fall languidly on it, praying fervidly for the quick passage of the next twenty minutes. At another time she would have most thoroughly enjoyed such a travelling-companion and would undoubtedly have elicited her whole family history. But now her whole desire and aim was to stem the avalanche.

"Queer--wasn't it?--that we should meet like this," pursued her wholly unconscious tormentor. "I took to you that day when I met you on the road far more than to that other one you was with when you came back. She's a haughty piece, if you like. They told me at the hotel at Strathyre that it's expected she'll maybe be Lady of Achree some day, but we don't think!"

"Nobody pays any attention to the gossip of the Glen," said Isla, the desperate look stealing to her face again.

"Well, you may take it from me that that won't come orf," said Mrs. Bisley with cheerful emphasis, at the same time picking up a paper and beginning a languid inspection of the pictures it contained.

For about ten minutes there was a blessed silence, and then the restaurant attendant appeared to ask them to take seats for the first luncheon. Mrs. Bisley, full of pleasurable anticipation, jumped up and proceeded to arrange her hair and pin on her hat at the most becoming angle. Then she grasped her hand-bag and came out into the corridor, nodding delightedly.

"Sure you won't come, Miss? It would do you no end of good. Do be persuaded."

"Oh, no, thank you. I couldn't eat."

"Then, I leave you to keep our seats. Hope we don't have anyone else put in with us at Carlisle. Then we can have a nice chat all the afternoon."

"Heaven forbid!" said Isla in her inmost soul.

A few minutes after her companion had disappeared, and when the corridor was quite empty, she rang the bell. It was a long time before anyone answered it. Then, indeed, it was only the conductor who came. He had not even heard the bell--he merely came through by chance.

"Will you be so kind as to get me another seat at once and have my things moved?" she said, with that single touch of hauteur mingled with appeal which, somehow, always commanded immediate service.

The man touched his hat, looked inquiringly into the compartment, and, seeing no one, put a question.

"The train is rather full, ma'am. Are you not comfortable here? I don't believe there is another compartment in it with only two passengers."

"I don't mind. I want to move," said Isla desperately. "I--I don't care for my fellow-traveller. No--she isn't in the least objectionable, but I want to move right to the other end of the train, if possible, and if there is no other accommodation I'll pay for a first-class seat."

"Very well, Miss. I'll see what I can do," he said obligingly enough as he moved on through the doorway of the corridor.

Isla feverishly began at once to gather her things together, and she had her dressing-bag in her hand and her rug over her arm when, in about eight minutes' time, the guard returned.

"There is one corner seat in the front of the train--two gentlemen and a lady in the compartment. One of them is going out at Crewe. So if you'd care to wait till then----"

"No, thank you. I'll go now," she said.

The man, still further puzzled, made up his mind to come through later and take a look at the other occupant of the compartment, now absent. He gathered up Isla's things and led the way to the front portion of the train. Isla felt that she was not particularly welcome in her new quarters. A woman, eating oranges, glared at her disagreeably, but at least she was left severely alone. She felt weak and limp after the strain of the morning, and all the afternoon every footfall in the corridor made her start, fully expecting to behold in pursuit of her the companion whom she had deserted. But she neither saw nor heard any more of her until they arrived at Euston and rubbed shoulders at the luggage barriers.

Isla did not perceive her at first, and had just called out to the man that Mackinnon was the name on her box.

At the sound of it Mrs. Bisley started back as if she had been shot, her vivid colour paled, and she put her hand to her side as if she felt some spasm.

"Well, I'm blest!" she whispered inly to herself. "So that's it! I might have known. Oh, Winnie Bisley, once more your long tongue has got you into trouble."

She had the delicacy of feeling to wish to efface herself from Isla Mackinnon's eyes, and yet she had a most insatiable desire to find out her destination. Remembering, however, that she had said she would sleep the night at the Euston Hotel she gave up the idea of discovery as impracticable.

As Isla's porter shouldered her trunk and she turned to follow him towards the hotel entrance she saw the woman again, and their eyes met.

Mrs. Bisley did not even smile, but Isla, as she passed by her, paused for the fraction of a second.

"I did not mean to be so rude as you may have thought, but my head ached dreadfully and I felt that I must get away to where it was not necessary to talk."

"I quite understand," replied Mrs. Bisley. "Don't apologize. I don't take offence easily. I'm not that sort. You're Miss Mackinnon, aren't you?"

"Yes."

"It might have saved a lot of talk if you had told me your name at the beginning," she said a trifle drily. "But, after all, perhaps there isn't any great harm done."

"I hope not. You meant to be kind, I'm sure. Good night, Mrs. Bisley."

"Bisley was my name," she said grimly. "Good night, Miss Mackinnon. If it should be that you ever want to see me again--and stranger things have happened--you'll find me at 21 Henrietta Street, off the Edgeware Road--fourth turning on your left from the Marble Arch."

"I'll remember it," said Isla hastily. "Good night."

She was glad once more to escape. She had got much fresh food for thought, and she was at a loss to know how to act in a matter which seemed to concern her, and yet with which she was loth to intermeddle.

On one point, however, her mind was absolutely made up. Malcolm should not win Vivien Rosmead under false pretences. Not for the second time should the peace and happiness of that dear woman be imperilled.

But she did not yet know how she was going to prevent the crowning act of the tragedy of Malcolm's life.

"Tragedy" was the word Isla used to herself as the whole story beat upon her brain where she lay, tossing sleepless in her noisy bedroom, disturbed by the shriek of the trains, the long dull roar of life in the Euston Road, and, above all, by the phantoms of her own sad heart.

How easily, by putting a few adroit questions, could she have wiled the whole story from her fellow-traveller's lips! It was not her pride alone that had prevented her from asking these questions. She was afraid.

She fell asleep with one last haunting thought in her mind--how much happier than she were the Mackinnons who slept their last dreamless sleep on the Braes of Balquhidder.

CHAPTER XX
THE REALITY OF THINGS

Towards the morning Isla fell into a heavy, dreamless sleep, from which she did not awake till half-past ten o'clock.

A sense of confusion and dismay swept over her when she realized how late it was, until she remembered that, in her scheme of things, time just then was of no consequence.

Certainly she had things to do, but the hour of their doing mattered to no man or woman. She was alone, she was free, this day and other days were in front of her to do with what she willed.

She sprang up, rang for hot water, and, pulling up the blind a little way, looked out upon streets bathed in a flood of glorious autumn sunshine. Somehow, it comforted her that London did not weep at her coming. It seemed an augury of good will. She had not known how physically tired she was until she had stretched herself on her bed. And now, her strength fully restored by sleep, her spirit became less craven.

She was still joyous over her escape. Things might happen in the Glen and she would never know. She, whose interest in the smallest event there had ever been of the warm and proprietary kind, had by one drastic step cut herself off from her old life. And for the moment she had room for little else in her mind but a sense of lively relief that she had gotten clean away.

As she dressed leisurely she reviewed the events of yesterday, among which the meeting and conversation with Joe Bisley's widow stood out in odd relief.

Isla was not without a latent sense of humour. In happier circumstances she could have extracted a great deal of amusement from the passing show of life, and she was able to smile at the situation of yesterday. It had been Gilbertian to the last degree, and might have been culled from the pages of the latest comic opera.

What surprised her most was that she had no feeling of indignation or resentment against this woman who had stepped from the unknown into the Mackinnon scheme of things. Nay, she felt kindly towards her--she felt that somewhere, deep down in that undisciplined nature, there was gold. It was not the woman's fault that she had been born in another sphere, that she was so far from comprehending Isla's own points of view.

She had other qualities which are common to the whole of humanity-- good feeling, honesty, kind-heartedness, and sympathy. Isla was womanly enough and just enough to concede the possession of all these to Winifred Bisley. Her own innate goodness convinced her that this woman was not, and could not be, wholly bad. And no doubt--and here her thoughts again became tinged with bitterness--in this case also Malcolm had been to blame.

She preferred to leave the unfinished story, however, to try to banish from her mind the problem of the loose threads which wanted weaving together. As for the day of unravelling, that was hid in the womb of time, but from past experience Isla had no doubt that that day would surely come.

In her mind's eye this morning Glenogle was shadowy, and even her passionate championship of Vivien Rosmead seemed to suffer some chill. She was concerned altogether with herself. And perhaps just then that was no bad thing for Isla Mackinnon, seeing that she had arrogated to herself so long the rôle of general burden-bearer to the community.

She felt fit and strong and hopeful as she belted her trim waist and fastened the Mackinnon badge into her black tie and set her hat firmly on her pretty hair. The memory of the nodding plumes and the moonstone hat-pins evoked a smile as she turned away from the mirror.

With that smile still lingering on her lips she went forth to conquer London!

She was the very last arrival in the breakfast-room, and she apologized for her lateness.

"I was very tired after my long journey," she said to the head waiter. "If it is too late for breakfast I must take something else.

"Too late, madam! It is never too late here for anything," he said magnificently as he directed her gallantly to a small table set comfortably near to the cheerful fire, and placed the menu card before her.

When Isla had made her choice one of the satellites was instructed to fulfil her order with dispatch, and the head waiter stood near in case that the charming lady should desire further speech with him.

"No, I don't think I shall require my room another night," she answered, when he ventured on a polite inquiry. "I have had to come up rather unexpectedly, and, immediately after breakfast, I shall go out and see the friend with whom I expect to stay while I am in London. I may leave my things here, I suppose?"

"Certainly, madam. The room's yours until the evening."

"Thank you. Have you been having good weather in London? It is lovely this morning. And please, can you tell me the best way to get from here to the Edgeware Road?"

"Underground, madam, from King's Cross. It will take you in about ten minutes."

Isla thanked him again, and when he laid the morning paper before her she felt that a hotel could be a very comfortable place. She was glad to hear about the Underground, because her riches were not great, and she must be careful about small expenses.

About noon she sallied forth on foot to find the Metropolitan station at King's Cross. She was an absolute stranger to that part of London. True, she had frequently arrived at the great termini, but on these occasions she had simply got into a cab or carriage and been quickly conveyed westward.

She enjoyed the new experience--she was in the mood at the moment to enjoy everything and to put the best face even on her difficulties.

At the Edgeware Road station she felt confused by the frightful congestion in the streets until, in answer to an inquiry, a friendly policeman told her that the street she wished to find was near the Park end of the wide thoroughfare.

"About ten minutes' walk, Miss," he assured her.

And, though a policeman's ten minutes is an elastic measure, Isla was not unduly tired by the time she reached Agnes Fraser's door.

Before she rang the bell she looked critically up and down Cromer Street, contemplating the fact that for some time to come it would limit her horizon. It was eminently respectable but dull, and some of the houses had a dingy look. Even Mrs. Fraser's, Isla thought, was less bright and cheerful than usual. The brass furnishings on the doors looked as if they had not been polished for several days, and the raindrops had dried upon the "Apartments" plate which, the last time Isla had seen it, had shone like gold.

An exceedingly untidy slip of a girl about sixteen, in response to her ring, opened the door just a few inches. She had a squint in one eye, which perhaps accounted for her cap being set awry on her unkempt hair.

"Is Mrs. Fraser at home?" asked Isla imperiously.

"Yus, Miss, but she ain't well, she's in bed. You can't see her."

This dashed Isla's fine spirits for a moment.

"In bed is she? What is the matter--anything serious?"

"She's 'ad newmonier, been mortial bad, Miss, but she's gettin' better. Only if it's apartments yer after, there ain't any."

She delivered herself of this statement wholly on her own initiative, and in order to get rid as quickly as possible of her questioner.

"Is Mrs. Fraser very ill? Has she been able to see anyone just lately?"

"Yus, Miss, she's bin up at midday since Monday. She's settin' up now in 'er room."

"I'll come inside," said Isla decidedly. "Go upstairs and tell her that Miss Mackinnon from Achree has called and would like very much to see her."

"Yus, Miss," said the girl stolidly, and, opening the door a little more widely, permitted Isla to step into the hall.

"There ain't anywheer but Mr. Carswell's room. The drorin'-room lidy ain't out this mornin'. Yus--yer can sit 'ere if yer likes. But Missis Fraser, she don't like me leavin' folks in the hall since a werry decent-looking man took away three umbrellas and Mister Carswell's best greatcoat."

Isla sat down on one of the rush-bottomed chairs and asked the girl to make haste to convey her message. Very soon she heard the quick shutting of various doors, the rushing about of feet upstairs, and, after about five minutes, the damsel appeared out of breath and with her cap more awry than ever.

"Yer can come up," she said laconically.

Isla proceeded to ascend the somewhat dark staircase, which received all the light it possessed from a dome in the roof three floors up. All these stairs had Isla to ascend, for Mrs. Fraser was fully let, and she had had to retire to one of the attics when she was laid aside.

It was a very bare room, but a bright fire made it fairly cheerful, and Agnes herself in a red flannelette dressing-gown, blushing all over her face, was in the middle of the room to welcome Isla when she reached the door.

"I'm very sorry, dear Miss Isla, to bring you up all this way. But could I help it? Oh, what I have suffered bein' shut up here, an' the hoose at the mercy o' thae rubbitch in the kitchen! Hoo mony times had ye to ring?-- three or fewer, I'll be bound."

"No, only once--and don't worry yourself, dear soul," said Isla, whose joy at sight of Mrs. Fraser's homely and welcoming face could not be dimmed by the recital of sordid details. "I hope you are really getting better."

"Oh ay. I'm to get doon the morn. I'm very sorry I'm no doon the day for ye. If ye had written I wad hae been doon. Noo I canna offer ye onything- -no even a cup o' tea. I wad never be sure hoo it wad come up."

"I don't need anything," said Isla, as she closed the door and put Agnes back in her chair. "I've only just come out from my breakfast at the Euston Hotel."

"You're not stoppin' wi' Lady Mackinnon, then?"

"No. They are still abroad. They will not come back, I think, for about two months yet."

Agnes looked a trifle puzzled, but sat waiting respectfully for further enlightenment.

"Your little maid told me downstairs that you are full up when she supposed I was looking for accommodation," said Isla presently. "I hope she only said that to get rid of me. I want a room here, Agnes."

Mrs. Fraser's face flushed again with the quick nervous flush of the invalid who is not yet quite able to cope with everyday affairs.

"Oh, Miss Isla, this is not the place for you--and very well ye ken it. I can gie ye another address. Ye mind Lady Eden's own maid Martin? She's in Seymour Street, and doin' well. Ye should go and see her. She wad be very prood to get ye, I am sure."

Isla shook her head, drew her chair a little nearer that of Agnes, and looked at her very straightly.

"I can't afford to go to Martin, even if I liked her--which I never did. Things have not been going very well with me lately, Agnes, and--and it became imperative that I should get away. I can't explain it to you this morning, and I know you will never ask questions."

"I hope I ken my place a little better than that, Miss Isla," said Mrs. Fraser.

But her tone was sad.

"I'm not at all well off, and, in fact, I must look about immediately for something to do."

At this strange announcement Mrs. Fraser fell back in her chair, as if overcome.

"Oh, Miss Isla, ye don't say so! It's awful, my dear! You to be seekin' something to do! It's no richt--it canna be richt. Oh, my dear, what is the meanin' o' it?"

Isla dashed away a sudden moisture from her eyes.

"It's difficult to explain. You must have known that things were not going well at Achree for a long time, not even in my father's lifetime. Since he died and my brother has become the Laird affairs have got all muddled, and the outlook is hopeless. Further, we don't get on, Agnes. You knew Malcolm as a boy of seven years. So perhaps I needn't say much more."

"No. But to let you go out into the world like this--it's a cryin' shame! You--a Mackinnon o' Achree! It shouldna be," said Agnes desperately.

"Oh, he did not actually send me out, you know, Agnes. In fact, he thinks I am on my way to France--to my aunt and uncle."

"And surely he is richt. That is where ye should be, Miss Isla. Oh, tak' my advice and go now. London's a cauld, cruel place for them that has to get their livin'. It's me and Fraser that kens that. And for you to be oot in it! It minds me on naething but a lamb that has wandered frae its mither amang the little hills and wi' the snaw comin' doon like to blind it. Ye canna do it, Miss Isla. Tak' it frae me that kens--ye canna do it!"

"I must, Agnes, and if you can't encourage me you must hold your tongue, dear soul," said Isla bravely. "Let us get back to the point. Can you let me have a room? In fact, you must let me have a room--quite cheap, though at its market-value and not a penny less. All I want to make sure of is that I am under your roof. Nothing else matters."

Agnes, still flushed and nervous, gave the matter rapid consideration.

"The drawing-room floor is what ye ocht to hae, Miss Isla."

"But I couldn't pay for it. So, what comes next?"

"There's the floor below this--the back room. It's big and very quiet, but it doesna get much sun. There has been a French artist in it, and he painted things on the doors and on the mantelpiece. Some thinks them very bonnie. He gaed oot only last week awa' back to his ain country, and he was apparently very sorry to leave. He was a very decent man for a Frenchman."

"That sounds more like it," said Isla cheerfully. "How much, Agnes? Honest Indian, now--how much did the Frenchman pay?"

"Twelve shillings a week, and he had his breakfast for that. But it was a French breakfast--naething but coffee and rolls. I would never charge you that, though. Miss Isla; if ye would just tak' the room it's a prood woman I'd be, and as for Fraser, he would be neither to haud nor bind aboot it."

"That I can't do, Agnes, even to see the expansion of Fraser. If you like to give me the room and a French breakfast, with a very occasional egg when they are good and cheap, for twelve shillings a week--why, then, I'll take it gladly and pay a week in advance if I can come in to-day."

"Oh, but, Miss Isla, I am not able yet to see properly to things, and, as I say, I've naething but rubbitch in the kitchen. Even at the very best, my hoose is not what you hae been accustomed to, and I should never hae an easy or a happy mind aboot ye."

"That's sad, for I am going to be very easy and happy about myself, dear soul. So, do say I may come in this very afternoon. My things are all at the Euston Hotel, and, of course, staying there is beyond my means altogether."

Mrs. Fraser sat back in her chair, and her face was troubled.

"Come, of course, and welcome, my dear. But I am wae for ye. And what is it ye think of tryin' to do? Is it to go as a companion to an old leddy--or what? There is so very little a leddy like you can do."

"I read an advertisement in the 'Morning Post' this morning for a young person to take pet dogs for an airing in the Park. My physical powers would be equal to that, I believe, and it would not need much brain power at least."

Agnes hardly even laughed at the suggestion.

"I ken what I'm speakin' aboot, Miss Isla. I have not kept an apartment hoose in London for seven years for naething. The things I hae seen, they would fill a book."

"I have no doubt of it, but I'm not going to add to your tragic reminiscences, Agnes. Fortune is now going to begin to smile on me. Don't let us meet trouble half-way, anyhow. We'll change the subject. Haven't you anything to ask about your old friends and neighbours in the Glen?"

"I dinna hear frae ony o' them noo, Miss Isla. Oot o' sicht oot o' mind. Hoo's Elspeth Maclure, and has she ony mair bairns?"

"None since the last," laughed Isla.

"And is her tongue ony quater? Eh, that lassie! When we were neibours at Achree I tell ye she fair deaved a body. You'll no mind--ye were young at the time--that I had to ask the hoosekeeper to let me sleep in anither room. Naebody could sleep wi' Elspeth. She wud speak even in her sleep. We were a' sorry for Maclure. But, of course, he was a quate man, or there wad hae been ructions."

Isla retailed a few items of Glenogle and Lochearn gossip for Mrs. Fraser's benefit, and finally returned to the subject of the room.

"I can tak' ye doon to see it, Miss Isla. I was as far as the dining-room yesterday."

Isla thanked her, and together they went down one flight of stairs and entered a large, wide room with two long windows looking out upon a microscopic back-yard, in which was a solitary tree. Though it was little more than noon the room was rather gloomy, and Agnes pointed out that it was the projecting portions of the neighbouring houses that darkened the windows.

"If I get employment I shall be out most of the day, and in the evenings I shall have a fire, and then it will be quite cosy. So these are the Frenchman's pictures! Why, some of them are very pretty."

He had done some sketches in water colour on the panels of the door and also on the sides of the mantel-piece; and, though the furniture was a little hopeless and rather suggestive of the cheaper end of the Tottenham Court Road, Isla was thankful to get it.

But Agnes Fraser felt a little despondent about it all the afternoon, and when Fraser, who was steward at a West-End club, came home at tea-time to see how she was, he found that she had been crying.

He also took a gloomy view of Miss Mackinnon's venture into the unknown.

"It's only her fad, Nance. And afore she has had time to get tired o't or even to get a grup o' the rael thing she'll rue it, or some o' them will come and tak' her away. So let her come, and dinna you fash your heid aboot her. Eh, woman, I'm gled to see ye in a frock at last!"

About six o'clock that evening a four-wheeler trundled up to Mrs. Fraser's house in Cromer Street, and Isla with all her belongings was admitted to her new quarters.

She slept soundly that night, secure in the haven found under the roof of an old friend.

But Agnes herself, who knew the hardships of London life and had very special knowledge of the extreme difficulty the indigent gentlewoman experienced in finding employment, never closed an eye.

CHAPTER XXI
THE MARKET PLACE

That evening, over her fire in the room which Andrew Fraser had christened "The Pictur Gallery," Isla took stock of her marketable accomplishments with the advertizing columns of the "Morning Post" and the "Daily Telegraph" spread on the table in front of her.

She had to confess that they were meagre both in quality and quantity. She had been imperfectly educated by a wholly incompetent woman, who had had to combine in one the offices of governess, housekeeper, and chaperon, and over whom for five years of the General's absence in India there had been none to exercise the slightest control.

Aunt Jean had offered to take the child to Barras to bring her up with her own, but she had altogether declined to have Malcolm even in the holidays. This had so angered the General that he had answered in the hot-headed Highland fashion that he would see to the upbringing of both his children himself and would be beholden to none.

That Isla had emerged from the process even as well equipped as she was said a good deal for her intelligence and native common sense. Her gifts of observation and her love of books had helped her to bridge the gaps in her educational training, but of the skilled attainments that fetch money in the market place she possessed none except the power to keep house with a good appearance on very slender means.

She decided, as her eyes wandered restlessly down those weary "Want" columns, that the only post she was fit for was that of a housekeeper, for which there was a limited demand. Many seemed to be in need of skilled and highly-trained governesses at substantial salaries, but against the unskilled all doors seemed to be shut.

Once more she perused the advertisement for a young person to give pet dogs an airing, and she resolved that, out of curiosity and as a preliminary canter into the unknown, she would call at the address given. It was in Westbourne Terrace, which, from inquiry, she learned was in her own neighbourhood and could be reached on foot.

She was a little subdued when she arose next morning to find "The Pictur Gallery" at eight o'clock in a sort of twilight gloom consequent upon the rain and the fog outside. After the glorious airs, the limitless freedom of the Moor of Creagh it was an experience calculated to damp the bravest spirit.

She had to ring three times before receiving the smallest attention from the squint-eyed maid, and Agnes, tired with the unexpected excitement of the previous day, had not felt herself well enough to get up before breakfast, as she had fully intended.

Much ringing of bells, some altercations in the passages, and a variety of odours were the outstanding characteristics of the Cromer Street house in the early morning hours.

At a quarter past nine Isla's French breakfast was brought up on a slatternly tray, and, finding it impossible to drink the coffee, she had to ask--and she did so in quite humble tones--for a fresh pot of tea.

"I ain't 'ad no borders about brekfus for 'The Pitcsher Gallery,' Miss," quoth Arabella in a rather high and mighty voice. "But I'll get the tea. It ain't all beer and skittles 'ere of a mornin', I kin tell yer, wiv hall the bells in the 'ouse a-ringin' at onct, the missus in 'er bed, and ole Flatfeet on the warpath in the kitching."

When the door had closed Isla sat down on the front of her bed and laughed till the tears rolled down her cheeks. The dreariness of the place in which she sat, the dead ashes on the cold hearth, the indescribable lack of the comforts--even of the decencies--of life appalled her.

Yet just in such conditions, and in others infinitely worse, must thousands of Londoners awake to the duty of each new day. She wondered that the multitude had any heart for the day's work.

She could not start to clean her room or light a fire, and she had been reared in the belief that a bed required a thorough airing before it could be made.

After she had partaken of her meagre breakfast therefore she opened the window and, donning her mackintosh and heavy boots, prepared to sally forth. Even the streets would be preferable to her present surroundings.

She decided not to go up to see Agnes, who probably felt the situation more acutely than she herself did. Perhaps, after all, it might be better, if it was not indeed absolutely necessary, that she should find some other lodging in a smaller house, where she could have a sitting-room and a bedroom. The prospect of unlimited hours spent in "The Pictur Gallery" was a little dismaying.

The rain was falling heavily when she left the house, but the clean, sharp patter on the pavements, somehow, cheered her. It was clean, it was wholesome, it would help to wash away some of the impurity from the streets. The rain, rolling in over the hills upon the Moor of Creagh and sweeping down Glenogle--how often had she welcomed its pure sting on her cheek and revelled in it! But here all was depressing, dark, dismal, and soul-crushing.

In such mood did Isla arrive at the address in Westbourne Terrace, which, in conjunction with three others, she had written on a small piece of paper and placed in her purse.

A man-servant, in a blue coat with brass buttons and a striped waistcoat, opened the door and stood, obligingly waiting to take her message.

"I have called in reference to the advertisement in the 'Morning Post' this morning. Please, can I see the lady of the house?"

The man looked doubtful, but said politely in imperfect English with a very German accent that if she would come in and sit down in the hall he would inquire.

At the moment the door of the breakfast-room at the end of the hall was opened and a lady in a very elaborate morning robe much trimmed with lace and with two black-and-white Japanese spaniels in her arms, looked out.

"Who is that, Fritz?" she asked in a high and rather fretful voice.

"Pleas'm, a young lady about the advertisement in the paper."

"Oh, she can come in here."

She re-entered the breakfast-room, and Isla, in some inward amusement, followed. She felt like a person in a play, but it said something for her courage and determination that, on the second morning of her London life, she should seek such an experience.

She closed the door behind her and said good morning to the lady, altogether unconscious that, instead of looking like a suppliant, she had the air of one about to bestow a favour.

Her possible employer was a woman of about her own age, with a kind of artificial prettiness which depended a good deal on art for its preservation. She had a pleasant enough manner, however, and was quite civil to her visitor.

"You have called?" she said inquiringly, with her head on one side like a bird and her cheek against the glossy coat of one of the spaniels.

"I have called in reference to the advertisement in the 'Morning Post,'" said Isla with difficulty, for the reality, instead of being amusing, was distinctly trying. "But I don't think it will be any use. I am sure I would not be suitable."

"Oh, sit down, and let us talk it over now that you are here," said the lady affably. "I am Madame Schultze. Yes--I am English. My husband is a Viennese. He is on the Stock Exchange. He had only just left the house as you entered. Perhaps you saw him?"

Isla said she had not seen anybody resembling Mr. Schultze.

"I am not strong, and almost immediately I am going off with my husband to Schwalbach. It is very late in the year for Schwalbach, but he has not been able to get away before now. It is about my little darlings! Look at them! Aren't they sweet loves? This is Koshimo, and this is Sada, and this is Tito, and the little one, who was born here, is Babs. Did you ever see anything so perfectly sweet?"

Isla was at a loss what to say. She knew nothing of the cult of pet dogs, or of how enslaved an idle woman can become by them, and she thought the adoration visible in Madame Schultze's eyes was rather foolish.

There were four separate baskets lined with padded wool, with little rugs over them, and other comforts such as many a poor baby lacked. To Isla the creatures looked stolid, overfed, unintelligent, and uninteresting. But she could not say so.

"I suppose they are very valuable?" was all she could bring herself to say.

"I should say so. Koshimo, as a puppy, cost a hundred and fifty guineas. My Karl gave him to me on the anniversary of our wedding. We can't take them to Schwalbach with us, and the other person I had to look after them was a wretch. Behind my back she used to pinch Koshimo, and the poor darling's spirit is quite broken."

"Yet you are going to leave them behind in the care of--of the person you engage?"

"That is what I thought of doing. I have no alternative. They don't permit dogs at the Cure Hotel."

"Then would she be required to live in the house?"

"Oh, no--only to come for a half-day every morning. Sundays included, to bathe the darlings, make their toilets, and take them for a walk in the Park. After that they will be in the care of Fritz, the house-boy, who is quite good. Only he has not a woman's delicacy of touch and sympathy. They need sympathy quite as much as a human being does, if not more so."

Isla repressed an almost overpowering desire to laugh aloud, and she politely inquired what would be the remuneration for this occupation.

"Seven-and-sixpence a week and luncheon. I reckoned that by the time you had returned from the Park it would be one or half-past one, and the servants' dinner would be going on, so that your luncheon would never be missed," said Madame Schultze with an engaging frankness. "Of course, the work is not hard, and it is delightful, besides. You don't know what a privilege it is to have the care of such pets. They are so dainty and so very, very human."

Isla thanked her and said that she was afraid the post would not suit her.

"Oh, but why not come for a few days and try it?" said the odd woman, who had taken a fancy to Isla. "You look different from the creatures who usually call when one wants anybody. You look even as if you might have had pet dogs of your own."

Something caught at Isla's throat as she remembered.

"I have had them. But, thank you, I'm sorry I can't come. The--the money is much too small. I shall have to find something to do which will keep me. I am not well off. Good morning, Madame Schultze."

"You won't leave your name? I might find you something. My husband has a large acquaintance on the Stock Exchange, and we move in very good society," said Madame Schultze with a kind of indolent good-humour.

But Isla, with another hasty word of thanks, withdrew. She felt almost hysterical as the door was politely closed upon her by the foreign butler, and she dashed something like a tear from her eye.

"Serves you right, Isla Mackinnon, for all the airs you give yourself! Seven-and-six a week and the servants' luncheon! What would they say at home?"

She said "they," but it was the face of Peter Rosmead that came persistently before her--of Peter the Bridge-builder, with thousands in his pocket that he could not spend! Would Peter, if he met her in the park airing pet dogs for a livelihood, pass by, like a Levite, on the other side?

Her lip curled whimsically at the thought. She did not welcome the memory of Rosmead, which had come unsought. In her secret heart she felt disappointed that he had not written. True, he had not promised to do so, nor had he even asked whether he might. But other men did not wait for permission. Neil Drummond never lost an opportunity of speaking or writing to her, and often she did not trouble to read his letters through.

She was brought back from her reveries sharply by finding herself once more in the Bayswater Road with the rest of the day in front of her.

"I do want a good breakfast," she said to herself dolefully, for a few mouthfuls of the doubtful bread and butter provided by Arabella had more than satisfied her in "The Pictur Gallery".

Looking down the road towards Kensington, she saw that shops seemed to abound, and she proceeded to walk on. At length she came to a tea-shop, which she entered. There she ordered tea and a couple of poached eggs. These she consumed at a small round table drawn invitingly near a bright fire, where she was able to dry her boots and where she passed a very comfortable half-hour.

But it was all unreal. Once more she had the weird feeling that she was a character in a play and that she would soon awaken to the reality of things.

After her experience in Westbourne Terrace she decided that, instead of calling at any more private addresses, she would go to some of the employment agents, who, judging from their advertisements, seemed to possess particulars of every conceivable kind of opening. She would there give a true account of her meagre accomplishments and candidly inquire what was their market value.

She did not shrink from doing this, because all her life long she had been facing things and making the best of untoward circumstances. But, somehow, it was difficult here in London. In Glenogle all was familiar and most dear. Besides, whatever the state of the exchequer, Miss Mackinnon of Achree had an unassailable position.

Her name counted for nothing here, however. Nay, it were better perhaps that she should exchange it for one less pretentious and betraying.

The rain having ceased, she rode on the top of an omnibus the whole length of the Bayswater Road to Oxford Street, where she presented herself in the office of one of the well-known employment agencies that advertise extensively in all the newspapers.

She had to wait some little time among others, and when her turn came she was again in thrall to the odd feeling of unreality which had possessed her for most of the day.

"What kind of post, madam, and what experience?" said the very middle-aged lady who sat, pen in hand, ready to take the particulars.

Isla explained as clearly as possible what she wanted, and she did not fail to observe that while she was speaking the face of her questioner fell. While she was listening she was, however, observing Isla keenly, and she very quickly came to the conclusion that she was not one of the ordinary applicants, but rather was one who had been driven into the ranks of the workers by stress of circumstances.

"Of course, madam," she said kindly but with great brevity and decision, "you are not unaware that you are handicapped? Our books"--here she patted an immense ledger lying on the table beside her--"our books are full of names of ladies requiring employment, and most of these are very thoroughly equipped. But, even with all the resources at our command, we would never be able to supply all their wants, for the very simple reason that the necessary vacancies do not exist."

"There are so many thousands seeking situations, then?" said Isla hesitatingly.

"Thousands. We have no difficulty with our skilled workers. There is always a demand for them, but for the gentlewoman class--to which you evidently belong--for whom the earning of a living has become a sad necessity, we have practically no demand. You are a good housekeeper, you say, but you would not care to take a working-housekeeper's place?"

"I could not. At least, I should not care to do actual housework, and I can only cook theoretically. I could order a lady's house, and order it well. I've been used until quite lately to superintend a fairly large establishment."

"In your father's house?" said the agent with an understanding nod.

"Yes."

"I thought as much. Well, I have only one post on my books at present which would seem to come anywhere near your requirements, and I tell you quite frankly that I have already sent at least half a dozen ladies after it."

"Where is it?" asked Isla interestedly, "and what sort of a place is it?"

"It is to be a sort of companion-housekeeper to a lady who is not strong. The duties, I think, are not very arduous, but I consider it only right to tell you that this is the fourth time in twelve months that this post has become vacant."

"Why has it been like that?"

"I prefer not to enter into reasons. There have always been faults on both sides, of course. I have myself interviewed Mrs. Bodley-Chard here when she was able to drive out. Latterly, I think, she has not been able. I have always liked her. I'm afraid that the trouble is with Mr. Bodley-Chard."

"Oh, I shouldn't mind him," said Isla quietly. "And, after all, his wife's housekeeper need not see much of him."

The agent smiled.

"I can give you the address if you like. You will be the third who has gone to-day. But that, I think, does not matter. Mrs. Chard, I know, intends to be very, very particular this time."

"What is the salary?"

"Twenty-five pounds a year."

"And to live in the house?"

"Why, of course."

"She would not engage a person who wished to lodge outside?"

"My dear madam, picture a companion-housekeeper who arrived with the milk--shall we say?--and left with the last post at night! It's unpractical, to say the least."

Isla smiled and sighed a little as she rose.

"I see that beggars can't be choosers and that one must give up something in order to earn one's living. I wish, however, that it was not one's freedom. May I have the address, if you really think there is the smallest use in my calling?"

"I am sure that it is worth your while calling. I have even a sort of odd feeling that Mrs. Chard's choice might fall on you. You see, you are just a little different from the average run of reduced ladies who come here."

"Thank you," said Isla, not knowing whether to take the words as a compliment or the reverse.

The agent wrote the name and address on one of the office cards and then noted Isla's in her book.

"And what happens if I am engaged?" she asked with a little humorous smile about her mouth. "Is it like a servants' registry office? Do I come back and pay a fee, or do I pay it now?"

"The fee would be half a sovereign in this case--that is if you are engaged. There is no charge otherwise. I hope you will be successful, Miss Mackinnon."

"I don't know whether I hope so or not," answered Isla.

Her ease of manner, so different from the usual bearing of the agent's clients, made a strong impression on her listener.

"I shall be pleased to see you in any case. And perhaps something else may turn up, if you are not successful," she said with a cordiality which surprised even herself.

Usually the seekers after employment were merely units of the system to be dismissed as soon as possible. But this applicant had drawn out her interest and her sympathy in a very strong degree, principally because she had not proffered a single plea for special consideration, and because she had been so candid about her capabilities.

When Isla got outside she stopped on the stairs and read the name and address on the agent's card--Mrs. Bodley-Chard, Hans Crescent, S.W.

A look of satisfaction crossed her face just for a moment, because this locality was within that part of the area of London with which she was perfectly familiar. As Malcolm might have said, it was on the right side of the Park. But again, that had its disadvantages, one of them being that she might be more easily discovered and recognized.

But some instinct made her decide to go, and to go as quickly as possible. She hailed a passing hansom and got in, calculating that she would reach Hans Crescent in time to catch Mrs. Bodley-Chard immediately after luncheon.

CHAPTER XXII
MR. AND MRS. BODLEY-CHARD

Isla was familiar with the outward aspect of the pretty houses in Hans Crescent, and she had on more than one occasion, in the company of her aunt, made acquaintance with the interior of one.

The town house of the Murdoch-Graemes of Baltasound was in Hans Crescent, but they, too, were poor and, until their daughter married a rich financier, had not been able to occupy their London house in the season.

But there is a vast difference between fashionable London in May or June and in October. More than the half of the houses are shut up in the late autumn, and Isla had no fear of meeting anyone who would recognize her.

Her hansom drew up, jingling, at the door of one of the most important houses, beautifully appointed outside, with real lace curtains at the windows and with everything indicating ample means. A sedate, middle-aged manservant of irreproachable mien noiselessly opened the door and stood at attention to hear Isla's message.

"Mrs. Bodley-Chard is at home, Miss, but she only sees callers by appointment," he said civilly, but firmly.

"Please to take my name," said Isla quietly, "and tell her I have come from Madame Vibert in Oxford Street."

The man shook his head.

"There have been three already this morning, and my mistress has told me she will not see any more. She lies down after luncheon. Still, Miss, I can tell her you are here if you will kindly step in."

Isla was grateful, and the respectful manner of the man was like balm to her perturbed spirit. Here she felt at home, and beyond doubt the man knew--for the preceptions of his class are very keen in certain directions-- that she differed in almost every essential from those who had come before her.

He placed a chair for her by the fireplace in the pretty lounge-hall and departed upstairs. Isla glanced round her interestedly. The house was very bright, painted in white with warm crimson walls, and full of pretty things. It was all very modern, however, and a trifle fantastic. A very large brown bear, mounted on a pedestal and standing up with a pole between his forepaws, struck rather a grotesque note. It was neither a useful nor an ornamental object, and it was instantly banned by Isla's simple, correct taste. The pictures, of which there were many, all struck the same bold note of bizarre taste, and the effect was neither restful nor pleasing.

Isla was not kept waiting long.

"Mrs. Bodley-Chard will see you," said the man when he re-appeared.

She followed him up the white and crimson staircase, her feet giving forth no sound in the deep, luxurious tread of the Axminster carpet. The house seemed to widen out on the upper landing and gave an impression of roominess.

The servant opened a door a little way along the corridor and announced Isla by name. She was ushered into a room in semi-darkness--a sort of boudoir, luxuriously furnished, whose atmosphere was laden with perfume and with the heavy odour of many cut flowers.

A smart French maid with a most coquettish cap moved back from the side of a large couch when the door opened, and as she stepped out of the room she took a very keen look at Isla.

A voice came out of the gloom--a somewhat thin, fretful voice.

"Come forward, please, to where I can see you. You have called at a very awkward hour. I expressly wrote to Madame Vibert that I would not see anyone after lunch."

"I can easily go away, madam, and call at a more convenient season," said Isla quietly.

Her eyes, becoming accustomed to the half-light, now discerned quite clearly on the couch the figure of a middle-aged woman, half-sitting, with a silk shawl about her shoulders, and a trifle of lace--a so-called boudoir cap--resting on her elaborately dressed hair.

"Bring a chair forward and sit down. I'm not strong. I am obliged to lie down all the afternoon. Did Madame Vibert tell you what I really required? She keeps sending me the most tiresome and impossible people--fools, in fact. Are you a fool? Come and tell me."

Isla carried over one of the gilt-brocade chairs, thinking at the same time that it was a little service the French maid ought to have rendered to a caller before she left the room.

"I don't see you very well. Will you ring for Fifine to draw up one of the blinds a little?"

"I can do it myself," said Isla promptly, "if you will tell me which one."

Mrs. Bodley-Chard indicated the window at the end of the room, and Isla very quickly caused a little light to shine in the darkness. The trim lines of her figure were silhouetted against the clear glass of the window, and Mrs. Bodley-Chard looked keenly at her face, when she came back, to see whether it corresponded with the distinction of the figure.

"You are different. Sit down and tell me what that viper, Madame Vibert, told you about me."

"She told me very, very little indeed, Mrs. Chard. Only that you wished a sort of companion-housekeeper. I could act as that, I think, though Madame Vibert as good as told me this morning I had no market value."

Isla had no hesitation in making this damaging statement. As yet she was only at play. In her purse she had sixteen pounds of good money, which, she had calculated, would keep her in modest comfort at Agnes Fraser's for at least two months. And surely in the course of two months among all the teeming millions of London she would find something to do.

Mrs. Chard gave a small, hard laugh. She had a large, uninteresting face with the unhealthy colour of the woman who takes very little outdoor exercise, and there was a lassitude about her which seemed to Isla to arise from lack of will-power rather than from lack of physical health.

"It is what I do want--a common-sense woman in the house who can hold her tongue and keep her eyes on two places at once. I'm being robbed on every side. The only decent person in the house is the butler Robbins. Madame Vibert has sent me nothing but fools, who were either afraid of the servants or in league with them. Have you been out before?"

"No."

"Where did you come from?"

"From Scotland. My father died a few months ago, and I have been left without resources."

"What was he?"

"My father?--oh, he was a soldier."

"What rank?"

Isla hesitated a moment.

"He was a General," she said in a low voice then, as if afraid the fact would militate against her chance.

"I'm not surprised. You look as if you might be a General's daughter. Well, then, you don't need to have your duties defined to you. You will have to keep the house--to run it, in fact--pay the servants' wages and prevent them from worrying me. You will write any letters I want, and you will drive out with me when I do go out, but that won't be often now that the winter is coming on. Then, you will have to dine with Mr. Bodley-Chard in the evening and keep him amused when he is in the house."

"Oh!" said Isla with a small gasp, "will you tell me quite what that means?"

"It means just what it says," answered Mrs. Chard with her wandering, somewhat stupid smile. "It is slow for him at home, of course, for I am hardly ever able to be down."

"Have you been out of health a long while?"

"Yes--about two years now. I have got worse in the last six months. Perhaps I shall not live long. I don't mind. I haven't had much happiness. People soon get tired of a dull old woman, don't they?"

"But why be dull?" asked Isla cheerfully. "You have the means of making life pleasant."

"But there is nobody to care, you see."

Isla wondered about Mr. Bodley-Chard, but she did not ask any questions.

She felt sorry for the woman who, in the midst of her luxurious surroundings, looked like a person from whom all the zest for life had departed, leaving her with a withered heart.

One thing interested her--she felt that she would like to see Mr. Bodley-Chard, possibly because in him might be found a partial solution of the problem of the heaviness of his wife's life.

"Well, will you come? No--I don't want to ask any questions. Either you're the right person or the wrong one. All the others I've ever engaged have been the wrong ones, and, somehow, I knew it before they began their duties. I believe you are going to be the right one. Will you take it on?"

"Yes, if you think I can do what you require."

"I'm sure you can. It ought not to be hard. When I was able to be about I had no difficulty in managing my house. But a fool can't manage servants. That's the chief difficulty--to keep them in their place. And you look as if you could do that. Can you come to-day?"

"Not to-day. To-morrow I might. May I ask you another question? It is about dress. I have only one evening frock. It is old and very shabby. Should I be expected to go down to dinner every night in an evening frock? That is the only thing I can't be happy about. If I could only have my evenings free!"

"You'll have a good many of them free, because Mr. Bodley-Chard is a club-man and is fond of the theatre. Most of them have complained of the deadly dulness. I go to sleep early, you see."

"I shall come to-morrow afternoon, then," said Isla, rising.

She did so, for she saw that a drowsiness was creeping over Mrs. Chard and that the heavy white lids were drooping over the dull eyes.

The impression Isla carried away was one of hopelessness, of absolute lack of interest in life on the part of her future employer. She was not attractive physically, yet there was something kindly and pitiful about her.

As she left the room Isla registered a vow that she would do what she could to arouse her and to give her some fresh interest in life. Probably Mrs. Chard had a doctor--that kind of woman always had a fashionable physician in close attendance. Perhaps he and she could consult together and devise some remedial measure. The prospect of grappling with a fresh difficulty exhilarated her.

When she closed the door she was surprised to see Fifine, the French maid, unconcernedly walk away from it as though she had been listening. She turned quite coolly to Isla, and put her head on one side, while her small, pretty hands met in front of her dainty person.

"Have you got ze job, Mees?" she asked pertly.

Isla coloured, looked very straightly and haughtily at her, and passed her by.

An English servant would have fully understood the rebuke, and even Fifine knew that she had been put in her proper place. She shook her small fist after the retreating figure on the stairs, and from that moment Isla had an enemy in the house.

It was about three o'clock in the afternoon when she got back to Cromer Street, where she found Agnes Fraser in some perturbation regarding her long absence.

Agnes was now fully dressed in her neat black frock with the little Puritan collar, and the whole house looked more comfortable and better cared for. Isla forgot the abomination of desolation that had reigned in the morning, and she greeted Agnes with a gay smile as she came out of the dining-room to meet her.

"I'm so glad to see you down, Agnes. Where have I been? Oh, in search of adventure. Where can we sit down till I tell you all about it?"

The Frasers chiefly occupied a very small breakfast-room at the back--a place which seldom got the sun, but which looked cosy enough on a dull afternoon, with a cheerful fire in the grate and a tea-tray on the end of the table.

"Eh, but I'm tired, Miss Isla. I've been in the kitchen since eleven o'clock. What a place! But I've set them to clean up and, now that I'll be up in the mornin's mysel' things will get a' richt. I was fair upset when I heard ye had gane oot so early this mornin' and withoot a proper breakfast. Hae ye had onything to eat since?"

Isla explained so gaily that Agnes concluded that she must have had some good luck. When she heard the story of the morning she uplifted her hands in sheer astonishment.

"The thing that beats me is that ye should hae got something so quick, Miss Isla. I've had them here lookin' for weeks, and weeks, and weeks. It's a sad business, but I hope thae folk wi' the queer name will be a' richt."

"They interest me, and I'm not in the least afraid. No, there aren't any dark mysteries, I'm sure."

"Eh, but London's a michty queer place, Miss Isla, and ye never ken wha's your next-door neibour. But ye can aye--day or nicht--tak' a hansom and come ower to me, if onything gangs wrang. I'll no let 'The Pictur Gallery' the noo. Very likely I'll no hae the chance till after Christmas. So if ye like to leave onything in it ye can."

They had a long cosy chat over their tea. Then Isla retired to "The Pictur Gallery" to make a fresh inventory of her clothes.

She found that the room had been swept and garnished, and a cheerful fire relieved its gloom, with the result that all things, even "The Pictur Gallery," contributed to her hopeful mood. She was promising herself no end of amusement and interest in her new environment.

She felt very much as a child might who is about to be taken to a pantomime for the first time; and certainly she was quite lifted up beyond all the more sordid and disagreeable aspects of her own private life.

But the good Agnes was conscious of sundry misgivings when she bade Isla good-bye about four o'clock next afternoon and saw the cab roll away.

"You'll promise noo, Miss Isla, that if there's onything wrang, or onything even that ye dinna like, that ye'll come richt back. I canna say I'm as comfortable in my mind aboot ye as I micht be. I wakened Andra up in the nicht-time to tell him I wasna."

"Nonsense, Agnes. It's just because you've grown accustomed to thinking of me in different circumstances that you are anxious about me. I'm going to enjoy myself immensely and see a bit of life."

"And you'll write to them, Miss Isla--either to Mr. Malcolm or to Lady Mackinnon? I want them to ken where you are."

"But I don't. I'll write and give them your address, but I forbid you to breathe the name of Hans Crescent. Besides, I should certainly be dismissed if a horde of my folk appeared at Mrs. Bodley-Chard's," she added with a little whimsical smile. "I didn't ask, but I feel sure that no followers would be allowed."

Agnes was left with a smile on her face, but it faded before she had watched the four-wheeler out at the end of the street.

"Puir thing! She disna ken a thing aboot life! I hope the Lord will look after her. Naebody else can."

Isla had no misgivings when she arrived at her destination. She was received with respectful consideration by Robbins, who passed her on to a house-maid who, with a polite but distant air showed her to her room. It was on the third floor, but it was a large and beautiful chamber, with which even the most fastidious person could not have found a single fault.

"Mrs. Bodley-Chard has waited tea for you in the boudoir, Miss," said the girl.

"Thank you; and may I ask your name? We shall probably have to see a good deal of each other, so we may as well be friendly. I am Miss Mackinnon."

"I'm Cecilia Owen. I'm called Owen upstairs and Cissy in the kitchen," answered the girl, surprised into cordiality of tone.

"And which do you prefer?"

"I don't mind. I shall like whatever you call me, Miss."

"Then we shall say Cissy. In the country--where I come from--we don't call our women-servants by their surnames," said Isla pleasantly as she laid her gloves down and poured out some water.

"I'll get you some hot, Miss, and if you like I'll unpack after tea downstairs. I'd like to help you."

So, in spite of much warning, Cissy capitulated to the newcomer's undoubted personal charm, and from that moment she was Isla's faithful ally and friend.

As she descended the stair Isla met the French maid, and wished her a cool good-afternoon.

"They're waiting tea now, mees; please to hurry," she said pertly, and Isla passed on.

She found the door without mistake, tapped lightly, and entered by invitation of Mrs. Bodley-Chard's thin, reedy voice, which seemed very weak to proceed from such a substantial body.

To her chagrin there was some one else in the room--a youngish man, dressed in a lounge suit of blue serge. He had a slim figure, very dark hair and eyes, and a rather florid complexion. A large moustache, very carefully trimmed, was evidently his pride. He was good-looking after his type, but that was a type which Isla did not admire. He had a gardenia in his button-hole, and the impression created was that of a dandy who gave much consideration to his clothes.

She concluded he was some privileged caller who had dropped in, and, without noticing him, she made her way to Mrs. Chard's couch.

"So you have arrived? Glad to see you, Miss Mackinnon. Let me introduce my husband. Gerald, this is Miss Mackinnon."

Isla gave a start of extreme surprise as she hastily turned to receive Mr. Bodley-Chard's greeting. It was a painful surprise, because the man looked almost young enough to be the son of the woman on the sofa, and the disparity between them in almost every respect seemed in her eyes almost insurmountable.

Mr. Bodley-Chard was most affable, even complimentary, and in that first interview Isla conceived a dislike of him, which was destined to increase with every opportunity she had of seeing more of him.

"Miss Mackinnon will pour out the tea, Edgar," said his wife. "She may as well start right now. Come here, and sit by me."

"Right you are, old lady. See how I am kept in leading-strings, Miss Mackinnon," he said, smiling all over his smooth-featured face. "I came home from business an hour earlier than usual this afternoon just on purpose to receive you."

"It was unnecessary," said Isla quite coolly. "Can I get you another cushion, Mrs. Chard? You don't seem to sit very comfortably. I have been used to waiting on an invalid. Do let me help you before I make tea."

Her deft and willing left arm went round Mrs. Chard's shoulders and raised her up a bit. She then shook the cushions, and made her as comfortable as she could, Mr. Chard looking on approvingly the while.

"You're in luck this time, Jenny. Among all the fools you have had there wasn't one who had the art of making you really comfortable--eh?"

Mrs. Chard smiled, and her eyes gratefully followed the girl's slim figure back to the tea-table. The discontented, uneasy expression had died out of her eyes, giving place to one of peace, which imparted an unexpected charm to her face.

Isla, quite unconscious of the favourable impression she was creating, and only wishing with all her heart that Mr. Chard would make himself scarce, busied herself about her new duties, and, when there was likely to be silence, made small talk with an ease that surprised herself.

Mr. Chard was evidently extremely anxious to hear her talk, and it was he who put the questions. But Isla only answered such as she chose, and, at the end of twenty minutes, she left him very much where he was at the beginning.

Her coolness and cleverness piqued him. He had been accustomed to see his wife's companions shrink before him and efface themselves in his presence.

"The old lady doesn't allow me a whiff here, Miss Mackinnon. Hard lines, don't you think? Much as I should like to stop, I must tear myself away. We shall meet at dinner later on, I hope, and resume our interesting conversation."

Isla bowed slightly, and when the door closed she rose and came over to the side of the couch, where Mrs. Chard sat smiling happily.

"You can't think how glad I am that you have come," she said, putting out an impulsive hand. "I woke up this morning wondering what pleasant thing was going to happen, and then I remembered that it was your coming."

"You are very kind to speak like that. I hope I may be going to be of use to you. That is the only excuse for my presence here."

"Well that is a speech! Most of them have come to serve their own ends, and--would you believe it, Miss Mackinnon?--though this is my house, and all that it contains is mine, I have sometimes felt among them all that I hadn't a single friend."

"I shall be your friend while I am here," said Isla quite simply, and without the smallest intention of gushing or flattering.

To her surprise a small sob suddenly broke from the lips of the woman on the couch.

"I don't pray much or often to God, my dear, but I do believe that He has sent you to me this time. There is a clear light about you--it shines in your eyes. I am sure that you are true and good."

"I try to be. But now you must rest a little, and later on I'll come and get you ready to go down to dinner."

"Oh, but, my dear, I don't go down. They haven't laid a place for me for months."

"But they'll lay one for you to-night, or I shall dine here with you," said Isla quite quietly.

She did not add that nothing on earth would induce her to dine *tête-à-tête* with Mr. Bodley-Chard.

CHAPTER XXIII
AT CROSS PURPOSES

Isla did not see her employer till ten o'clock next morning, by which time she had breakfasted *tête-à-tête* with Mr. Bodley-Chard. When she was asked to go to Mrs. Chard's room the expression of her face indicated that she had not had a pleasant morning.

Mrs. Chard was not yet out of her bedroom, which communicated with the boudoir by folding-doors. She was lying down, but her pale face brightened at sight of Isla.

"Good morning, dear. I wanted to see you ever so long ago, but Edgar said you had not time to come."

"Oh," said Isla stiffly, "I did not know you wanted me, or I should have been here sooner. I hope you slept well and feel better this morning?"

"I sleep too much, I think," she said with a weary yawn. "I was asleep by half-past nine last night, and I'm not long awake. Yes--I've had breakfast, all I ever do take. Sit down, and tell me what you have been about. Did you have a comfortable night, and did they get you all you wanted?"

"Everything. My wants are simple, and I can help myself. The housemaid is very kind and attentive."

"And you gave Edgar his breakfast? I hope you enjoyed that. Isn't he charming? And I must tell you a great secret. He is charmed with you. I am so glad, because I've had such trouble with my lady-housekeepers. Either they could not get on with my husband, or they wanted to be with him too much. Women are so tiresome and so catty to one another."

Isla repressed an inordinate desire to laugh.

"Tell me what you talked about, won't you?" Mrs. Chard continued. "It's being kept in the dark in my own house that I hate so much. It isn't fair--do you think it is? For, after all, though I am not strong I do take an interest in things."

"I didn't say much. Mr. Chard talked a good deal--principally about you."

"Oh, indeed; and what did he say? Told you all sorts of naughty things, I suppose?"

The spectacle of this elderly woman waxing coquettish on the subject of her husband filled Isla with a curious mixture of pity and amusement.

"No. He was chiefly trying to impress on me the fact that you are very ill and that you require to be kept quiet and not worried in the least."

"Dear Edgar! he is most considerate! He quite spoils me."

"I was very much surprised to hear that you had no doctor in attendance, Mrs. Bodley-Chard. Wouldn't it be better for you to see some one?"

Mrs. Bodley-Chard uplifted her hands in mute protest.

"Doctors! I've spent fortunes on them, and they've never done me the smallest good. The last one I had--a man from Mount Street, a very new broom who was going to sweep the West End quite clean--quarrelled with Edgar. What do you think? He actually had the audacity to say that there was nothing whatever the matter with me and that, if I were a poor woman who had to get my living, I should be going about quite well."

Isla privately wished she knew that doctor. She felt sure that she should like him.

"But perhaps, though he need not have put it so harshly, there was a grain of truth in what he said, and at least it was an honest expression of opinion."

"Edgar was furious and kicked him out of the house--not actually, you know, but he told him very plainly what he thought of him. They had a frightful row, and he said all sorts of things to Edgar--impertinent, even libellous things. Poor dear, he was very good about it, and, for my sake, took no further steps against Dr. Stephens, because he did not wish me to be worried."

"And since then?"

"Since then I haven't had anybody, and I'm just as well without anybody. Edgar is very clever. He studied medicine for a time before he went on the Stock Exchange, and I believe that it was because Stephens found that he knew a little too much that they quarrelled as they did. Edgar gives me all the medicine I need, which isn't much--chiefly, sleeping-draughts. I used to have such dreadful nights before he took me in hand. Fancy! Dr. Stephens wanted to stop the sleeping-draughts."

"I don't wonder at that," said Isla quickly. "I should like to stop them, too."

"You'd never be so cruel. Nobody would. Why, they are my greatest comfort. I suffer so with my head."

"But it is very dangerous to use them, as you do, without proper medical supervision."

"But, you see, I have medical supervision. My husband quite understands all about them."

"It is very dangerous," asserted Isla firmly, "and I am surprised that Mr. Bodley-Chard does not see it."

"Ah, now you are going to be cross and horrid, just as my first husband used to be. He hated ill-health. He was one of those great big, overpowering sort of men who never have a day's illness in their lives. But he dropped down dead suddenly one day when we were lunching in the city together. Oh, it was dreadful! I can never forget Edgar's kindness at that time. He was Mr. Bodley's chief clerk and understood all his business. So, you see, when I married him it made everything very easy. I have not the smallest trouble about money now."

Isla listened to all this with very mixed feelings, and she tried to be just in her judgment of Mr. Bodley-Chard. But she found that the most difficult of all the tasks set her at Hans Crescent.

She tried to change the subject.

"It's a beautiful morning, Mrs. Chard. Won't you let me help you to dress so that we may get out in the sunshine? Have you a carriage?"

"Not now. We simply job one at Burdett's. But I don't want to go out, thank you. Edgar is so afraid of a chill for me. We are very happy, Miss Mackinnon," she said with a small touch of dull defiance in her heavy eyes. "In spite of the ten years' difference in our ages, I could not have a more devoted husband. Mr. Bodley was so different! He was the sort of man who makes people run about for him, and he used to shout at the servants dreadfully. Not but what he was kind enough and generous enough, too, in his way. But he had not dear Edgar's delicacy of feeling. He is never cross, however put out he may be. He says that a gentleman's first duty is to control his temper."

Isla listened to this eulogy wholly unmoved. She had by this time arrived at the conclusion that Mrs. Bodley-Chard's mental faculties were impaired by bodily weakness and by indulgence in some form of narcotic. She made up her mind very quietly to do what she could to combat the unwholesome forces which surrounded this woman's life, and already she had vague ideas of her plan of campaign. If only she could persuade Mrs. Chard to call in that Mount Street doctor, between them they might manage to bring her back to the plane of active, healthy life.

Isla's practised eye told her that there was no actual disease, but that her hypochondriacal weakness had been so pandered to that she had completely lost her will-power. It was a sad spectacle, and Isla rose with courage to the idea of working some improvement.

She must go warily, however, realizing the fact that she had much prejudice to overcome. With Mr. Bodley-Chard's opinion or attitude in the matter she did not concern herself. She was his wife's servant, and she would do her duty by her.

Isla's introduction to this domestic drama was the very best thing that could have happened to her just then. She threw herself heart and soul into it with all the ardour of her Celtic temperament; only she was liable to err in the haste and impulsiveness with which she desired to act.

"Then you won't go out to-day?" she said coaxingly--"not even after I have been out and reported on the sunshine?"

"Not to-day--another day perhaps, and if Edgar likes the idea we could all have a little drive together. I'm going to sleep again now. Did you ever see such a sleepy-head?"

Isla had her own thoughts as she left the room to interview the cook and to take up her position definitely in the household. That part of her business presented no difficulties whatever. The one thing that filled her with misgiving was the physical and mental condition of Mrs. Bodley-Chard.

Her dislike of the husband had increased after her conversation with him at the breakfast table. He had started by being complimentary and charming, but, finding Isla unresponsive, had then spoken rather disagreeably about her position in the household, warning her quite pointedly that Mrs. Bodley-Chard was in the hands of a capable maid who understood her temperament and who would not brook any interference from outside. Isla listened in silence, and, remembering her impression of Fifine, felt her pity for Mrs. Chard increase.

Having reduced the new inmate of the house to silence and--as he thought--submission, Mr. Bodley-Chard departed airily to the city to forget all about his wife. For the first time, however, since he had become a pensioner on a rich woman's bounty he was to find himself weighed in the balance and found wanting. Isla's eyes had a disconcerting clearness, and her recent experiences had made her suspicious and critical of all mankind.

She found that her duties in the house were by no means heavy.

There was a sufficient staff of servants to do the work properly, though they wanted careful handling. Isla's gift in that direction was a special one. She had that nice mixture of friendliness and hauteur which made its due impression on the women of a household which had never had a proper mistress. When they found that Miss Mackinnon knew her business, and that she intended that they should know theirs, too, they submitted with a very fair grace.

There were five servants in the house besides the French maid. Fifine was Isla's only failure, and before she had been a week in the house she was obliged to conclude that the Frenchwoman was Mr. Bodley-Chard's ally, working with him to keep his wife in a state of bodily helplessness and mental confusion.

On Sunday afternoon she walked across the Park in the cool autumn wind to tell Agnes Fraser some of her experiences. She found that good lady much perturbed by a letter which she had received from Elspeth Maclure.

"Read that, Miss Isla, and tell me what to say when I write back. It's maistly aboot you."

Isla sat down and took out Elspeth's rather badly written sheet, while Agnes critically regarded her and was obliged to admit that she looked better than when she had left her house four days before.

Elspeth wrote without embroidery to her old neighbour of her own concerns and of the things that were happening in the Glen:--

"DARRACH, LOCHEARNHEAD, 18 *October*.

"DEAR NANCE,--It's ages since onybody has heard from you, but I must write, for things are that queer here that you would hardly ken the Glen. I suppose you have heard about the American folk in Achree. There's naething the matter with them, and some of us wish that they were there for good and that we had no other Laird. We were to leave at Martinmas, but Donald has gotten round the Laird to let him stop another year at a higher rent. That will give us time to look about. But, as I said to Miss Isla, my man will never leave Darrach and live. He'll be found in the Loch afore the day comes, or else dee of a broken hert in the bed where he was born. Miss Isla has gone away from the Glen, but maybe you have seen her. She seemed to forget all about us lately, but the poor lassie's head must be near turned with all the trouble of Achree. They're saying in the Glen that her and the Laird had words before she left and even that he doesn't know now where she is. Some say she has gone away to foreign parts to Lady Mackinnon, and then, again, there's some say naebody kens where she is. It's a terible business anyway, and if you have seen or heard tell of her I wish you would write and let us know, for there's a heap of folk in the glens that are not easy in their minds about it. They're saying, to, that the Laird is after one of the Miss Rosmeads--the one that divorced her man in America, but that there's somebody else has a grip of him. There was a woman stopping at the Strathyre Hotel. William Thorn that is the Boots there told Donald about her the other day. And it seems that she talked a lot about the Laird and about what would happen if he sought to marry Mrs. Rodney Payne. Then, quite suddenly--I believe it was the very night before Miss Isla went away--he went to Strathyre and saw her. They went out for a walk together, and the next morning she left with the train. Sic ongauns, Nance--very different from the auld days at Achree when we wass all happy together! Write soon to your auld neibour and say what you think about all this, and mind you tell me if you've see Miss Isla. That's the chief thing. Only don't send a postcard, Nance, for David Bain reads every wan of them and the Glen hass all the news afore a body gets it themselves. Love from your auld neibour,

"ELSPETH MACLURE".

Isla laid down the closely-written sheet, and a little quiver ran across her face.

Agnes Fraser sat forward, her questioning eyes very eager and bright.

"What am I to say, then, Miss Isla?"

"Say, Agnes, that you have seen me and that I am quite well. But I forbid you to give any particulars. Do you understand?"

"I understand, of course, but I dinna see, Miss Isla, how it is possible for ye to live long like this. Some o' your folk will come seekin' ye--that's a sure thing. If Mr. Malcolm believes that ye have gane to Lady Mackinnon he will soon be hearin' frae them that you are not there. It's a dreadfu' business a'thegither, and I hate the idea of where ye are now. It doesn't sound richt at a'. Leave it the morn, Miss Isla, and come back here."

"No, no. I am very comfortable. I am well paid, and I am interested in what's going on in the house. I had no idea that there were such exciting incidents in real life. I feel really as if I were a sort of Sherlock Holmes, and I don't worry half as much as I used to do about my own affairs."

Isla spoke as she felt at the moment, but the time came when she realized that there had been more truth and foresight in Agnes Fraser's point of view than she had admitted.

After four days' close observation in the household of Mrs. Bodley-Chard she arrived at an absolute conviction as to what was actually happening. Mrs. Chard was being kept continuously under the influence of drugs that were gradually destroying her will-power and leaving her ever weaker and weaker and more utterly in the hands of her unscrupulous husband.

That he was unscrupulous Isla had not had the smallest doubt from the moment she entered the house. Also, she had satisfied herself that the French maid carried out all his instructions regarding her mistress, and, as she was in close attendance on her, while Isla was only an occasional visitor to her room, she had everything in her power.

Finding that Isla kept him at arm's length and that she had not the smallest intention of being friendly with him, Mr. Bodley-Chard abandoned all his efforts to attract her and treated her in a very off-hand manner. Without being positively rude, his manner was most offensive.

Isla, however, entrenched herself behind her natural reserve and did not mind. One day she made so bold as to put a very straight question to Mr. Chard.

"Mrs. Chard is very unwell to-day," she said quietly and politely. "She is quite unable to give her mind to any of her ordinary affairs."

"There is no occasion for her to give her mind to anything. People are paid to do the work of the house," he said pointedly.

"That is not what I mean. Her mind seems to wander. May I call in a doctor? It distresses me to see her like that."

A cold, almost baleful light came into his eyes, and his mouth, under the carefully-trimmed moustache, became very ugly.

"You are my wife's housekeeper--not her nurse."

"Pardon. I was engaged as a housekeeper-companion," said Isla quite clearly. "And I can't see her growing worse every day without being troubled about it. Hasn't she any relations or friends who could come and take her in hand, then? It does not seem right to leave her so much in the hands of a flighty French maid."

"Are you aware that your words are offensive and that they cast an imputation upon me? When I think my wife requires other attention or supervision it will be time to get it. She has the most implicit confidence in me--or had until you sought to undermine it."

Isla did not even take the trouble to deny the false charge, but merely left the room, seriously troubled about what was her duty in the matter.

A week later, she left the house one morning to do her ordinary shopping and, in the course of her outing, walked the whole length of Mount Street, looking for the house of Dr. Stephens. When she found it she hesitated a moment or two before she rang the bell. She was only encouraged to take this step by the reflection that a doctor's consulting-room is the grave of many secrets and that nothing she could say there would be used against her.

A motor-car was in waiting, and when the door of the house was opened she saw the doctor coming out to start upon his rounds.

"I am just going out, but I can see you, of course," he said cordially enough, leading the way to his consulting-room.

Isla's first look at him pleased her. He was tall and thin and clean-shaven with a clever, serious face--a man to whom it would be possible to explain the situation in a very few words.

"You don't know me, Dr. Stephens, and I hardly know how to explain my call this morning. I come from the house of Mrs. Bodley-Chard in Hans Crescent."

"Oh, indeed!" he said interestedly. "And how is Mrs. Chard?"

"She is very unwell," said Isla in a low, quick voice. "I am her housekeeper-companion. My name is Mackinnon."

"Yes?" said the doctor still interestedly. "Mrs. Bodley-Chard has had a good many, I think."

"I have been there only three weeks, and I am seriously concerned about her. It is because she told me you were once her medical attendant that I am here to-day."

"Yes. But as I have ceased attendance upon the lady I hardly know why you should have called."

"I simply had to come. Mrs. Chard has no doctor attending her at present. I understand that she has had none since you left. And it is quite time that somebody was on the spot to--to look after her. Otherwise I believe she will die."

"Why do you think that?"

"Because she is being kept almost continuously under the influence of drugs, administered by her husband and her French maid," said Isla quite clearly and unhesitatingly. "I believe myself there is nothing the matter with her except that, and if she were removed from it all she would get quite well."

Dr. Stephens took a turn across the floor, and when he came back to Isla's side his face was even graver than it had been.

"Miss Mackinnon, I don't for a moment doubt the truth of what you are saying. On the contrary, I know it to be perfectly true. But we are quite powerless."

"Oh, how can you say that! It is terrible if two responsible persons know that this wicked thing is going on and take no steps to stop it! I can't be a party to it, and I was in hopes that you would help me."

"I was kicked out of the house by that unspeakable cad, Chard, and I can't go back again. We have no possible way of getting at him, except one-- to lodge a complaint with the police. Are you prepared to do that? Frightful responsibility is incurred by taking that step, of course--to say nothing of the publicity attending it."

Isla sank back.

"Oh, Dr. Stephens, I couldn't do that! But surely you, an influential medical man, knowing the facts, can do something--ought to do something----"

He shook his head.

"I'm not so well up in medical jurisprudence as I used to be," he said with a slight smile. "But I'll take expert opinion to-day. Could you possibly come and see me to-morrow?"

"I could, of course. What I am trying to do is to persuade Mrs. Chard to let you resume personal attendance on her. If she consents will you come?"

"I don't know. It is a very awkward case. Don't forget that Chard put me out of the house because I told him quite plainly--well, just what you have told me to-day."

Isla saw the difficulties of the position and, after a little more conversation with the doctor which strengthened her determination to get him back to the house, she bade him good-morning.

When she reached Hans Crescent it was almost lunch-time, and Robbins, the butler, was waiting for her with a note.

"This has come by hand from the city for you, Miss. It is from Mr. Chard."

Isla turned aside to open the letter, and when she broke the seal she saw a pink slip that looked like a cheque.

Within, there were written a few curt words, dismissing her from her position in the house and requesting that she would leave before four o'clock.

With reddening cheeks she passed up the stairs and tapped lightly at the door of Mrs. Chard's room. There was no answer, and, after repeated knocks, she tried to open the door and found it locked.

At the moment Fifine appeared at the other end of the corridor with a small, satisfied smirk on her lips.

"Mrs. Chard can't see you, Mees. She particularly said I was not to let you in. She's asleep now. She told me to say that she will write to you in the evening if you will be good enough to leave your address."

Isla turned on her heel, her quick Highland temper flashing in her eyes. She was very sorry for the poor woman, but she could not be ordered from her house a second time.

She walked to her own room and began to gather her belongings together.

CHAPTER XXIV
THE CHAMPION

Malcolm Mackinnon, busy with his own concerns, had no qualms about his sister even when the weeks went by, bringing no line or sign from her. The Barras Mackinnons did not write either, but when Malcolm thought of the matter at all he concluded that she was safe with them. Obviously there could be no other explanation of the silence.

Towards the end of November, however, a somewhat disturbing note from Lady Mackinnon arrived at Creagh.

"As Isla has not chosen to answer any of our letters I am writing to ask what is the matter with her. We kept on expecting her at Wimereaux up to the last, and Uncle Tom was much disappointed that she did not come. I am writing to say that we shall be in Glasgow on Thursday night, en route for Barras, and that if you and she will come up for the night to St. Enoch's we can talk things over. If Isla likes to bring her things and go on with us to Barras we shall only be too glad."

Malcolm stood, staring stupidly at the letter, and, for the moment, he was at his wits' end. Isla had not gone to Wimereaux, their folk knew nothing of her!--where, then, was she? Had Malcolm lived in close intimacy with the folk in the Glen, as Isla had done, he would have heard by now from Elspeth Maclure that she had gone no farther than London and was there still.

Truth to tell, he had been so relieved by his sister's departure that he had not troubled his head about her or noticed the quick flight of time. Things were going well with him, and the spectre in the background was giving no unnecessary trouble. He was a great believer in luck, as many ignorant persons are, and he believed that his had turned. His chief business in life just then was the wooing of Vivien Rosmead, and he was now anticipating the day, not far distant, when he intended to ask her to be his wife.

He hoped to arrange the matter quietly when Rosmead returned to Scotland, and to have his marriage an accomplished fact as soon thereafter as possible. Then he could snap his fingers at all the phantoms of the past.

Malcolm, however, did not reckon with certain forces that are stronger than the poor planning of the human brain, and so he marched on unconcernedly to the crisis of his fate.

He received his aunt's letter one day at Lochearn when he was on his way to Glasgow to see Cattanach. At the station he met Neil Drummond, who was going up to Callander to see a man at the Dreadnought Hotel, and, being full of the news that had just come, he blurted it out to Neil, who had seemed of late disposed to be more friendly to him.

"Look here, Drummond. Has your sister ever heard from Isla since she left Glenogle?" he asked as he offered Neil his cigarette-case.

"No, she hasn't, and Kitty has wondered, of course. I suppose she's still with your uncle and aunt at Wimereaux?"

Garrion folks, in common with others, had frequently made inquiries about Isla's welfare, and Malcolm had invariably answered that she was all right. None of them had any doubt but that she had been with the Barras Mackinnons for the last two months.

"They've left the place. They're going back to Barras on Friday, but Isla isn't with them. She never has been."

"Never has been! Then, where is she?" asked Neil blankly.

"Well, old chap, to tell you the truth, I don't know. When she left she certainly said that she was going to them."

"But haven't you had any letters?"

"Not a blessed one."

Neil looked him all over with a sudden, sharp scrutiny that, to another man, would have been, to say the least of it, unpleasant.

"You say you haven't known all this time where she is?"

"I haven't known. I tell you she hasn't written to me. That's why I asked whether your sister had heard."

"And you haven't made the smallest effort to find out?"

"Why should I?" inquired Malcolm coolly. "She's of age, she knows her own mind, she had plenty of money, and she doesn't want to be harried about her private business. You don't know Isla, Neil, though you think you do, and the man who marries her will have a hard row to hoe. I can tell you that."

Drummond crushed back the desire to take Malcolm Mackinnon by the throat. He was not normal where Isla was concerned, and he took a far more serious view of the situation than there was any need to do.

"Do you mean to say that you haven't the shadow of a clue as to where she is or what she is doing? Haven't you any other friends in London to whom she could have gone?"

"None--except an old servant of Achree who lives somewhere about the Edgeware Road," said Malcolm with a sudden flash of remembrance. "Don't wear such a worried look, old chap, and don't forget that Isla is twenty-six years of age and more capable than either of us of looking after herself."

"But, hang it all, she's a woman, Malcolm, and--and your sister ought not to be adrift like that!"

"She isn't adrift," said Malcolm cheerily. "And, anyway, what can we do? If she chooses to hide herself, as she seems to be doing, who is to prevent her? She has her reasons for doing so, no doubt."

Neil Drummond was conscious of a growing indignation, of a swift return of his old rage against Malcolm, and of scorn of that careless, irresponsible being who had made life such a burden to the woman whom Neil himself loved. He withdrew with a snort into his own corner and jumped out at Callander with a very curt good-bye.

He put through his business there very quickly and returned to Lochearnhead by the earliest possible train. During the whole journey he was racking his brains as to how and where he could discover the address of the old servant of whom Malcolm had spoken. He knew Isla's ways, and he was aware that it had always been her delight when in London to look up any of her own folk who were settled there. He ran over in his memory the servants at Achree with whom he had been familiar, but he could not fix his mind on anyone in particular. Diarmid, however, who had been with the Mackinnons for nearly thirty years, would surely be able to help him. He would go to Diarmid.

His bicycle had been left at the station, because the train had offered a quicker way of getting over the heavy roads to Callander. He now took it out and rode swiftly down the hill to Lochearn and up Glenogle towards Creagh.

Neil had all the swift impetuosity of the Celt in his blood, and he did not let the grass grow under his feet.

He was fortunate, however, in obtaining the information he desired about half way up, at the farm-house of Darrach, where he came upon Elspeth Maclure taking her washing down off the lines in the front garden.

He swung himself off his machine, set it against the drystone dyke, and pushed open the little gate.

Elspeth, surprised and pleased by this little attention, hastened to ask him into the house.

He thanked her, but declined.

"I am seeking information, Mrs. Maclure. I was on my way to Creagh to see Diarmid, but perhaps you will do. Do you remember the name of an old servant of the Mackinnons who married in London and settled somewhere in the neighbourhood of the Edgeware Road?"

A curious flicker crossed Elspeth's eager face.

"You mean Agnes Fraser that was under housemaid at Achree when I was upper of three, do ye, Maister Drummond?"

"I suppose I do if the description answers," he said with a laugh. "But I don't know her name."

"She lives at 18 Cromer Street, Edgeware Road, sir," answered Elspeth. "If ye'll just come intil the hoose I'll write it doon."

"Here you are," said Neil, drawing out a notebook and a pencil. "18 Cromer Street, Edgeware Road. Thank you very much. That saves me that stiff pull to Creagh, and the roads are heavy to-day. I was glad to leave my machine at the station and take a handy train to Callander. Maclure and all the young folks well, I hope?"

"Yes, sir, thank you," said Elspeth, but the odd, eager expression did not leave her face as she followed the Laird of Garrion to the gate. "I had a letter from Mrs. Fraser not so long ago, Maister Drummond."

"You had--eh? And what was her news?"

"She said she had had Miss Mackinnon stoppin' at her hoose. That was aboot a month ago."

"Do you think she is there still?" asked Neil with apparent carelessness, though his hand as he stooped to his bicycle trembled a little.

"I'm no sure, but I think, Maister Drummond, that Agnes wass troubled apoot her. I haf been troubled mysel'. For, look you, it iss an awfu' thing for the Glen that Miss Isla should haf peen spirited away like this. It iss not the same at all. And nopody efer speakin' her naame or tryin' to get her pack--that iss the worst thing of all. If you please. Maister Drummond, askin' your pardon for my free speech----"

Drummond sprang to his machine and waved his hand in parting.

"Good-bye, Mrs. Maclure. I'll bring Miss Isla back if it can be done. But keep a quiet tongue in your head--not a word to a soul."

He rode off at break-neck speed and, to the great astonishment of his folk, announced that he had to leave Garrion that very night for London, having business there.

Drummond slept soundly in the train, for he was young and strong, and he had had a tiring and exciting day.

Arrived at Euston, he entered the hotel and made himself fit for his great quest. But after he had finished his toilet and gone through the whole menu of the table d'hote breakfast it was only half-past eight. Even an old friend may not presume to call on a lady at such an unholy hour of the morning.

London had no bright welcome for the Laird of Garrion. One of the worst fogs of a particularly foggy November lay like a thick yellow pall over everything, and through its impenetrable folds weird shapes and shadows loomed, and strange, half-stifled cries troubled the air as if there were some invisible and ghostly warfare waged in the streets.

"How long do you suppose it will take me to get to the Edgeware Road in this--eh?" he asked the big porter in the hall.

"Ten minutes by the underground, sir," he answered. "After that, I don't know!"

Neil took the risks. About half-past ten o'clock he emerged from the underground fastness of the Edgeware Road Station and began to grope his way about for his ultimate destination. But it was a sorry business. He seemed to be wandering round in a circle, and by noon he did not know which end of the Road he was at.

Then a sudden miracle, often seen in the case of a London fog, was wrought by some invisible force in the upper air. The thick veil was drawn back as if by unseen hands, a few feeble rays of wintry sunshine filtered through the gloom, and London became free and visible once more.

Neil then found that he had wandered into Maida Vale, where he was totally stranded. He hailed a passing hansom and, giving the address, sat back comfortably with his cigarette, all unconscious, until he took a peep into the little mirror at the side of the cab, that his face was exceedingly grimy and that there were various smudges on his collar.

Neil was not vain, but a man likes to look his best when he goes to see the girl he loves. He did what he could to remedy the defects, and was fairly satisfied with the results when the cab set him down at his destination.

The jingling cab bells reached Agnes Fraser's ears in the dining-room, where, with a polishing cloth, she was trying to remove the traces of the fog from her furniture.

She herself opened the door and had no doubt when she saw a tall young man alighting from the hansom that he was only some fresh seeker after "accommodation," which is the word used in her business. She had of course, seen the Laird of Garrion when he was a boy but she did not recognize him now.

He paid the man and came smilingly to the door.

"Mrs. Fraser? You don't know me, I can see, though you must have seen me sometimes at Achree--Drummond of Garrion."

Agnes's face flushed warmly.

"Oh, sir, I beg your pardon. I micht hae kent; but there--of course ye are cheenged. Will you come inside, sir? It's a prood woman I am to bid ye to my hoose."

He entered the house, and, with his hat in his hand, put the one straight question on his lips.

"Is Miss Mackinnon here?"

A great light broke over Agnes Fraser's mind. She nodded silently, pointing to the dining-room, and followed him in.

"This is God-sent, Mr. Drummond. I wad hae written to the Glen the day if ye hadna come."

"But what is wrong? I hope Miss Mackinnon is not ill?" he said with eager apprehension.

"Not ill in her body, though she has got very thin. But will you not sit down, and I will tell you? She is not in the hoose at this very meenit, though I think I can tell ye whaur to find her."

Neil took the chair and waited for all that he might hear.

"She has been in this hoose, sir--let me see--ten weeks a'thegither, coontin' frae the time she cam' first. Three weeks of that time she was at that queer hoose in Hans Crescent."

"What queer house?"

Agnes then grasped the fact that nobody in Glenogle or Balquhidder knew aught of Isla's movements since she had come to London, and she proceeded in her own terse and graphic way to describe them.

"Weel, ye see, she cam' here--for why, I dinna ken. Them that's left in the Glen are the wans that should ken that bit of it. But she cam', not intendin' at a' to go to foreign places to Lady Mackinnon, but jist to live by hersel' and get her ain livin'."

Neil started in his chair. The thing was unthinkable--intolerable. It could not be Isla of whom the woman was talking, yet her broad, comely face was so full of honest concern and her voice rang so true that he could not doubt a word.

"I was wae for her, for I ken London through and through, and what a hole it is--bar for them that hae money and heaps o' folk. In the Glen, see, ye can live withoot onybody and no be that ill aff, but London is--is fair hell unless ye hae folk; I'm sayin' that, that kens. I telt her weel, though I was a prood woman to hae her in my hoose, and wad hae dune ony mortal thing for her. But it was not the hoose for her that had been brocht up in the Castle o' Achree wi' servants at her ca'. Her idea was to lodge wi' me and work in the day-time, but she could get naething like that to do."

Agnes paused, breathless, and dashed away something from her eye.

"When I tell ye ye'll maybe lauch, and maybe ye'll greet. It's what I felt mair like. The first place she gaed to was to a woman that wantit somebody to tak' oot her pet dogs for an airin' in the Park. Yes, she went after that-- Miss Mackinnon of Achree!--she did! And that'll show ye far better than I can tell ye what London is for the woman-body that has neither money nor folk."

Drummond was silent, but the veins began to rise on his ruddy forehead, and his kind eyes flashed fire.

"She didna think she wad tak' that at seevin-an'-saxpence a week," pursued Agnes with merciless candour, "and syne she gaed to the Hans Crescent place to be a kind o' companion-hoosekeeper to a leddy. O' a' the traps there is set in London for a woman-body--that's the warst, for, look ye, Maister Drummond, a servant-lass kens what she is and what she has to dae, but when you're that," she said, with a scornful snap of her fingers, "you're neither fish nor flesh nor guid red herrin'. But gang she would. It seems that Mrs. Bodley-Chard--sic a name to begin wi'--but they're a' daft wi' their double-barrelled names here!--was an auld wife married to a young man that had been her first man's clerk. It was her money he was efter, and Miss Isla thocht he was tryin' to get rid o' her wi' some pooshonous drug. Ye ken Miss Isla. Nae joukery-pawkery can live near whaur she is, and she began to fecht the scoondrel quietly-like, daein' what she could for the puir woman. But at the end o' three weeks she was dismissed at a moment's notice, her money flung at her--like. She didna tak' that, and she cam' back here, whaur she's been ever since. And she's got naething to dae sin syne, and her money's near dune, and--and she's--weel, if ye see her, ye'll ken what wey I was gaun to write to the Glen this very day."

Drummond rose up from his chair, and he was like a man ready to fight the whole of London for Isla's sake.

"But what did she mean by it?" he said a little hoarsely. "There was no need----"

"She seemed to think there was. Forby, she was not pu'in' in the same boat wi' Maister Malcolm--the Laird, I mean--and she has never written to him or heard frae him since she cam'. That I do ken."

"Well, and where is she? I must see her and, if possible, take her back with me to the Glen."

"When the fog lifted she gaed oot for a walk in the Park. She hasna been gane twenty minutes or so. Ye can easy follow her. Do ye ken London, sir?"

"Not this part of it, I am afraid."

"But ye canna go wrong. Gang oot into the Edgeware Road, and turn to your left, and gang on till ye come to the Marble Arch. Syne you're in the Park. She's very fond o' walkin' roond by the Serpentine. Ony bobby will tell ye which wey to tak' when you're inside the gates."

Drummond departed without further parley, and Agnes, with a big sigh of relief, returned to her polishing.

She had given the entire story away without ever having paused to inquire whether the Laird of Garrion had the right to hear it. He had certainly assumed some such right, and, anyhow, the time had come when something had to be done.

The desperate look in Isla's eyes that morning had haunted and terrified her. Each week Isla had insisted on scrupulously paying the full amount for "The Picture Gallery" and for such food as she ate in the house, and now her little store was well-nigh exhausted.

It was a very searching and cruel experience for Isla, the memory of which never afterwards wholly faded from her remembrance, though she always said she could never regret the period of "Sturm und Drang" which had given her such insight into the lives of thousands of women battling with adverse circumstances from the cradle to the grave.

Garrion's temper worked itself into fever-heat as his great, swinging stride took him through the swirl of the traffic at the Marble Arch and into the cool, wide spaces of the Park. Against Malcolm Mackinnon his anger burned with an unholy fire. He would never forgive him for this--for his callous indifference to his sister's fate, for his absolute failure to make the smallest inquiry on her behalf. In future she should be removed from her brother's jurisdiction altogether, and he would have to answer to him.

Such was Neil's mighty resolve as he strode along, his restless eyes, sweeping from side to side in search of the dear, slim figure of the woman he loved. There was very little alloy of self in his thoughts that winter morning as he swept round by the windy Serpentine in search of Isla. It was all of her he thought with a vast, encompassing tenderness which equalled Rosmead's, and was less cautious and deliberate in its operations.

He did not doubt in the least that he would find her, but he had to walk a little farther than he expected. At the end of the beautiful sheet of water there is a winding path, and, passing there, he looked up and saw, sitting on one of the seats, a solitary figure which he thought looked like Isla. Only at the distance he could not be quite certain. It did not take him long to cover it. Dashing past the smart nursemaids and the bonnie bairns, whose sweet freshness even London fogs could not dim, he came presently to her side. And Isla, sitting with her head slightly turned away, was not aware of his presence till the gravel crunched under his impetuous foot and her name was spoken in the quick accents of apprehensive love.

She rose up a little wildly, stretched out her hands, essayed to speak, then went white all over, and collapsed, a little heap of unconscious humanity, on the seat.

CHAPTER XXV
THE ARCH-PLOTTERS

Lady Betty Neil, the aunt of the Drummonds, who lived with them at Garrion, was a Highland lady of the old school. She loved the Gaelic and deplored its increasing disuse in the Glen, she had all the lore of the North country at her finger-ends, and was, moreover, gifted with the second-sight.

Certainly, when she received a peremptory telegram from her nephew on the second day after his departure for London, she evinced neither perturbation nor surprise.

"You go to London, Aunt Betty!" cried Kitty, open-mouthed. "What does he mean? How dare he? Let me see the telegram."

Lady Betty, leaning on her ebony stick with her left hand, produced from her reticule the crumpled piece of pink paper bearing the summons.

"I need you in London. Will meet you to-morrow night. Euston, half-past six."

Kitty looked from the telegram to her aunt's face and back again in sheer amaze. Never had Lady Betty looked more like "an ancestor," which was Sadie Rosmead's name for her.

She was a picturesque old lady of great height and commanding mien, her hair and eyes still as black as sloes, her face beautiful still, in spite of its wrinkles--the face that had once been the toast of a county. She was the Drummonds' nearest relative, their mother's sister, in fact, and, though immensely wealthy, she had no fixed habitation of her own, and she had agreed to live at Garrion, at any rate until Neil brought home a wife.

That he had found one now she did not doubt, and she hoped that he had. Isla Mackinnon was a woman after her own heart. Neil had confided to her the nature of the business that had taken him to London, but he had enjoined silence.

"Kitty can't hold her tongue, as you know, Aunt Betty. Besides, she's too thick at Achree at present, and I don't want them to get wind of it. This is a business that has to be done on the quiet."

"Aunt Betty, what took Neil to London?" quoth Kitty with a severe expression on her piquant face. "You and he are keeping me in the dark. It isn't fair."

"Neil has his reasons, my dear, and they are good ones, depend on it."

"But you can't go to London by yourself, auntie! The thing's outrageous! It can't be contemplated for a moment. I must go with you to take care of you."

"No, I'll take Lisbeth, and I must go and arrange matters with her now."

Lady Betty was now seventy-four, but she was as straight and supple as a young birch tree. She carried a stick--not because she needed it, but because it was her whim to do so and because it had been given to her by an old sweetheart for a wager. She had never parted with it. It was her faithful companion by day, and at night it stood in a handy corner by her bed. Lady Betty had never married. But had any married wife a life so full of romance? This is not Lady Betty's story, however.

She sniffed a love story afar off and rose to it with the keen scent of a war-horse for the fray. There she would be in her element--keen, shrewd, sympathetic, and full of common-sense. Neil had made no mistake in sending that telegram. He knew the hour had come, and the woman.

Aunt Betty was as gay as a young girl over her preparations, which were so elaborate that Kitty felt called upon to remonstrate.

"Mind your own business, my dear. I know mine. A lassie like you can afford to rise and run. A woman like me must uphold the dignity of her age and position. Neil has not said what he wants me for. I must be prepared for any emergency."

Kitty was speechless, consumed with curiosity and inordinately jealous. She travelled to Stirling, however, to put her aunt on the London train, and on the way back drove to Achree to acquaint the inmates with the astounding news of Lady Betty's departure for London, that gave her one hour's rare enjoyment and partly consoled her for being left behind.

Lady Betty arrived at Euston as fresh and gay as when she had left Garrion in the raw of the winter morning, driving down Balquhidder in a blast of half-frozen rain.

And Neil was on the platform to greet her, overjoyed at sight of her clever old face.

"You are a brick, Aunt Betty. But I knew you would come. How did you get rid of Kitty?"

"Not easily, my lad. But I did manage it. Lisbeth is here. Where are we going, and where can she ride? We want to talk together in the cab, you and I."

"I have a brougham waiting. It's quite fair, and Lisbeth can go on the box. We are going to Brown's Hotel."

Lady Betty nodded an approval. She was known at Brown's. In the old days, when she had been a figure in London society, she had often spent a season there.

"It's Isla Mackinnon, of course. Where is she?"

"She's with an old servant of Achree living in a place off the Edgeware Road, from which you will fetch her to-morrow," said Neil quietly.

"And do what with her?"

"That's for you to say."

"Tell me about her.--everything you can or will. I must know how I stand, and where. It's not for nothing that an old woman of seventy-four rises and runs at a young man's bidding."

Neil nodded comprehendingly, and in his quickest and most graphic way he put her in possession of the facts.

"It's an unco story," she said, folding her slender hands with an unusual grip on the ebony stick. "It's not a story that Donald Mackinnon would have liked to bear in connexion with his one ewe lamb. I'm glad he's in Balquhidder," she said brusquely. "But the spunk of the lassie! There's grit there Neil Drummond! She'll fight--ay, and starve, but nobody shall know of it. That's the true spirit that has made Scotland great! It's in the women yet, Neil, but it's scarce, very scarce among the men."

Neil had no time for platitudes. His head was a whirl of plans.

"Does Isla know I'm coming?" asked the old lady then.

"Yes. She expects you to-morrow."

"Has she left herself in your hands, then, lad?" asked Lady Betty with a curious straight glance under which Neil reddened.

"So far. She's run down, body and spirit, Aunt Betty. I want you to realize that before you see her. She--she has lost grip. My God, to see

Isla Mackinnon like that! It makes me itch to get with my two hands at Mackinnon's throat!"

"Leave him out of the count, Neil. His Maker will deal with him, I dinna doubt," said the old lady quietly. "Then, she's to be turned over to me to do with what I think fit."

"Yes, and what she will agree to."

"But this is a big thing, Neil. Does it mean that one day she will come to Garrion?"

"Please God, it does mean that. But only a brute would think of himself at such a time. She must first be made well in body and spirit, Auntie Betty. I'll come in later."

"But if she's let you do all this she must like you, Neil. Isla Mackinnon is not the woman to take favours of this kind from frem folk."

"Wait till you see her," he pleaded, and she said no more.

She ate an astonishingly big dinner, insisting on going down to the restaurant, dressed in an elegant gown of rich black satin, with priceless lace on the bodice and a diamond star glistening among its filmy folds. Many looked in the direction of the handsome young man and the still handsomer old lady and wondered who they were.

Aunt Betty slept like a tired child the whole night long and rose at eight o'clock when Lisbeth brought her morning tea, every faculty alert and braced for the day's work.

At half-past ten the brougham came again, and Neil drove with her to the end of the Edgeware Road, where he got down, saying that he would meet her at lunch at Brown's, whither she was to bring Isla if she could persuade her to come.

Agnes Fraser herself joyfully opened the door to Lady Betty Neil. She was graciously recognized, and her welfare was asked for before Isla's name was even mentioned.

"Miss Isla is in her own room, my lady. Will you come up? A very dark mornin', isn't it? I hope you are not very tired wi' your journey."

Lady Betty suitably replied, and, with the aid of the ebony stick, she climbed to "The Pictur Gallery," where Isla was sitting over the fire, very white and spent, but with a more restful look on her face than it had worn for many a day.

She sprang up at the opening of the door.

"Lady Betty, Lady Betty! You came all this way to see me!" she cried breathlessly, holding out both her hands.

"Wheesht, my dear--that's nothing. I loved your father well. I just missed being your mother: and if I had been there would have been none of this gallivanting. Where can I sit?"

Isla drew in the most comfortable chair she could find, and the old lady sat down and assumed her most characteristic attitude, in which the ebony stick played a prominent part.

"We're not going to talk about what's past, Isla, nor even about what's to come. Our concern is with the present moment. Now I have plumed my feathers and flown from Balquhidder, I've no mind to go back until the sun begins to shine again. Will you go with me to-morrow to the south of France? I've not been there for eleven years. We'll go to Monty, my dear, and have a fling with the bravest of them. It stands to reason that I can't go alone. Will ye go?"

Isla sat very still, and from the expression of her face her thoughts could not have been gathered. Perhaps the old lady partly guessed them. The gift of second-sight brings in its train a sort of sixth sense that enables its possessor to be sure about things that other people only wonder about.

"But I have no money, Lady Betty, and it is Kitty that you ought to take."

"Kitty can come by and by. Besides, she has been so many times there that she is not caring about going any more. As for the money, I have plenty, and soon I shall not need it. We don't take it with us when we lie down in Balquhidder, my dear. And to spend a little here and there while we have it--why, that's a big pleasure, and it is one that you ought not to deny an auld wife."

It was delicately done. Isla raised her swimming eyes and capitulated in a moment. The prospect allured her beyond any power of hers to tell, and no feeling of obligation to Lady Betty troubled her. One fine nature responds to another. It was what Isla herself would have done in similar circumstances--what, indeed, she had often done on a small scale in the glens when she had the chance. The kinship of good deeds was between them, and there is none closer.

An immense satisfaction shone in the old lady's eyes at this unexpectedly easy capture of the fort. They positively glowed with her inward triumph, and, without so much as alluding to the odd circumstances that had brought them together, she proceeded to expatiate on what they would do when they got away to the sunshine. This was the crowning touch of the wisdom that comes from the second-sight.

Isla was sick to death of herself and of the sordid problems of her life. What she wanted was to get away from everything that would remind her of them, and, above all, from the people that would talk about them.

"I have no smart clothes for the Riviera, Lady Betty. But take me as your maid."

"Lisbeth is here," was the grim answer. "I can get a maid for the hiring, but companions and friends have to be won. I suppose you have things to cover you, and, if I mind rightly, the shops at Nice were not that bad, though they put it on for the English. But you and me will get the better of them. Come then, my dear, and we'll go back to Brown's to lunch and talk about all our plans."

Then an odd shyness seemed to come over the girl.

"Neil will be there, Lady Betty?"

"Yes, I suppose that he will."

"Then, will you excuse me? I--I haven't got over things yet. Did he tell you how he found me?"

"In a general way he did, but Neil has not his sister's gift of the gab. You have to fill in with him. Of this you may be sure, Isla--that Neil Drummond will not tell to me, or to anybody a thing that would vex or humble you. He has set you up there!" she added with a slight upward inflection of her eyebrows as well as of her voice. "So come, and remember that you and I are not women with a past, but only with a future."

Cackling at her own joke, she carried off Isla, who met Neil in the luncheon-room of the restaurant in a way which commanded Lady Betty's highest admiration. Isla Mackinnon was no fool. She was neither hysterical nor emotional. Lady Betty knew that in what the girl had done her reason had fully justified her, though her method perhaps had been at fault. She guessed that in the sunny days to come she would hear the full story, or at least enough of it to enable her to fill in all the gaps.

Neil's manner was also admirable, and they appeared just like a happy little family party, of which the old lady was the life and soul.

That evening after dinner, over the fire in Lady Betty's sitting-room, she indicated to her nephew his course of action.

"It will not be a good thing for you to come with us just now, Neil. We can make the journey by ourselves and get settled. Then I'll write."

Disappointment immediately wrote itself large upon his face. He had already wired to Garrion for another trunk to be sent and he had looked forward to being the director of the little travelling party to the south.

"I am understanding Isla better than you, my dear, and just at the present moment the sight of you humiliates her just a wee bit. She canna forget how you found her and the weakness she thought she betrayed. She has to get over that, and she will do it all the quicker if you are not on the spot."

"But, hang it all, Aunt Betty, to go back to Garrion--and Christmas without you, too! I won't do it!"

"I didn't lay down the law as to times and seasons. What is at the back of my mind is that you will bring Kitty to Nice, or to Monte Carlo, or to wherever we have settled ourselves, and spend Christmas with us. Then folk will not have any talk about us, because I, of course, can do as I like and nobody dare say a word."

Neil's face brightened as he consulted his pocket-diary.

"This is the fifth, so we shall come inside of three weeks."

"You will come when I bid ye--not a moment sooner or later," she said severely. "Don't forget how you hauled the old wife from the Garrion fastnesses to the gay world again. Now she must have her revenge."

When Neil did not answer she leaned forward on the ebony stick, and her eyes grew soft and luminous.

"Listen, lad. Ye may trust your Aunt Betty. She is not without knowledge of a woman's heart. If Isla is to be won it will take time and some skill. Her heart is asleep, but if I can waken it it shall be done. Do you think I am to be idle in these three weeks? I think ye may safely leave her in my hands. I will be true to your cause, for I would dearly like to see her in the house of Garrion for all our sakes as well as for her own."

It was Neil's turn to capitulate, which he did with all the grace he could muster.

Next day at two o'clock of the afternoon he saw his aunt and Isla off by the boat-train at Charing Cross, and thereafter he got ready for his own return at night to Scotland. There was nothing to keep him in London now, and he had left certain loose ends of his affairs at home which would be none the worse of his handling.

At the station Isla had broken down, trying to thank him with a faint, wavering smile on her pathetic lips.

"Don't, Isla, for God's sake, don't! It's down on my knees I'd go to serve you, and besides, we made the pact--didn't we?--that day long ago when we went to Glasgow together and lunched at St. Enoch's. I've lived on the memory of that day all these months. Don't grudge me what I've been able to do now. Besides, it's nothing but what Highland folk are doing for one another every day."

Lady Betty, observing the emotional moment, frowned upon him warningly from the background, and he tried to restrain himself. When the train fairly moved out Isla leaned out of the window to wave to him, and when she drew back to her seat her eyes were still wet.

"I've a job with that laddie, Isla. He's very thrawn. I'm often thinking I'll wash my hands of him and Kate. What with his dour temper and her tongue, my life is not as peaceful as a woman of my years has the right to expect."

"Neil--a dour temper, Lady Betty!" cried Isla spiritedly. "This is the first I have heard of it, and I don't believe it now!"

"It's there, my dear. And forby, in some things he hasna the sense of a paitrick on the moor. I'm tired of them both, I tell ye, and glad to get away."

Oh, the wily old plotter! Isla would have argued the point with her and was only restrained from doing so by her sense of decency. But this was the line of diplomacy Lady Betty started on--belittling Neil up to a certain point and voicing her relief at being rid of his company until Isla waxed furious and championed him both by spoken word and in her secret thoughts all the way south.

Lady Betty, a real diplomatist in her way, took care, however, not to overact her part. She would throw in at intervals a judicious word which had the odd effect in casting a full glare of sunshine on all that was best of

Neil and so giving unexpected glimpses of his fine young manhood. Then, after a time, she left the subject in order that her words might filter down to the bed-rock of Isla's heart.

Very grey and dour seemed Balquhidder and the Garrion hills when Drummond drove up in the snell winter morning, meeting a bitter wind that seemed to skin his face.

"All right at home, Hamish?" he asked the groom, and, being answered in the affirmative, he spoke no further word until they turned in at the Garrion gate.

"Miss Kitty is at Achree, sir. They came and fetched her away the day you left," observed Hamish stolidly.

"Why didn't you tell me that at the station?" inquired Neil rather hotly, to which question the man answered never a word.

"I took the telegram over last nicht, sir, and she will come back to-day," he said after a moment in the same stolid fashion, wondering what had happened in London to shorten his master's usually placid temper.

Kitty arrived in the Achree motor, alone, about luncheon-time.

"I want to hear all about Isla, Neil," she cried. "I thought I should find her here. What have you done with her and Aunt Betty?"

"They have gone to the South of France."

"Oh!" said Kitty, and her piquant face fell. "I don't call that fair of Aunt Betty. She might have taken me."

"If you're a good girl and don't talk too much between now and Christmas," said Neil provokingly, "I'll take you myself to be there in time for Christmas."

Kitty danced in ecstasy.

"Oh, I shall be glad. It's going to be a frightfully dismal Christmas here this year, and nobody is going to do any entertaining. The Rosmeads are all down in the mouth because their brother can't get away for Christmas, and now it may be Easter, or even later, before they see him. Bridge-building seems to be a very unsatisfactory business, though you make so much money at it. Peter Rosmead has to work like a navvy. He goes down into caissons- -and things in diver's clothes to the bottom of the river. That's where the difficulty is. Things are always happening--silting, and queer things like that. Then the work has to be done all over again. He seems annoyed about it, but he'll keep on at it. He hasn't got that square jaw for nothing," cried Kitty breathlessly. "Well, tell me all about Isla Mackinnon. What has she been doing all this time?"

"Nothing particular. There isn't any romance or tragedy--or anything. She was simply living with an old servant of Achree and getting very sick of it. She would have come home soon, anyway."

"Did she seem glad to see you?"

"Isla doesn't say much at any time. But, yes--I think she was glad. Have you seen anything of Mackinnon at Achree, Kitty?"

"Why, yes. I've seen him every day. He spends the most of his time there, and I think it's going to be a match between him and Vivien."

The colour rose a little in Drummond's cheeks.

"I should have thought that she would have had enough of matrimony after her experience," he observed drily.

"I should have thought so, too, Neil. And at first I was angry at Malcolm, thinking he was only after her money. But now anybody can see that he cares. I wonder how long it will be before we hear the news, and what Isla will say."

Drummond had got fresh food for reflection. Knowing what he did of Malcolm Mackinnon, he wondered just how much or how little the Rosmeads guessed. It was a certain fact that had they known the whole truth about Malcolm Mackinnon he never would have been permitted so much intimacy at Achree.

But the thought uppermost in Neil's mind was an unholy joy that caissons, and silt, and other queer things, as Kitty put it, were keeping Peter Rosmead safely out of the way at the bottom of the Delaware River. He would not have minded much though he had never come up again.

CHAPTER XXVI
THE LURE OF VIVIEN

Six weeks later, on a snowy January day, Neil Drummond rode one of his big roans to the Lodge of Creagh, where he had a luncheon appointment with Malcolm Mackinnon. It was one o'clock when he breasted the last bit of rising ground and beheld in front of him the little house standing sheer on the edge of the Moor of Silence, its bleak outline silhouetted against the clear grey of the sky.

The smell of Margaret Maclaren's baked meats was in his nostrils as he turned in at the gate, whetting the appetite he had gained in his long ride from Garrion.

Neil never looked better than when astride a horse, and he was the best judge of horse-flesh in all the Glen. In fact, that was his one extravagance. He was looking particularly well that day. There was an air of buoyancy about him which would not be repressed. He had whistled and sung all the way from Balquhidder and had given Pride of Garrion her head in a way which that damsel particularly liked and in which she had seldom before been indulged. Her sleek sides were wet with foam as she ran quivering to the door, tossing her pretty head, the breath coming fast in her delicate nostrils, life brimming over in every pore and muscle.

Malcolm, who had been watching, opened the door immediately, bade him good day, and in a word expressed his pleasure at sight of him.

They walked together to the stable, where Neil himself rubbed down his horse, saw that she had a modest drink, covered her up, and then turned, ready to accompany his host back to the house.

"Had a good time abroad--eh?" asked Malcolm with a somewhat covert glance at Neil as they walked.

Neil threw his head up with a joyous air.

"Ripping. It's a bit thick coming back to the grey silence of the glens. It's a white silence with us. We've heavy drifts from Balquhidder up. You're pretty free here."

"It's coming, though," said Malcolm, with an upward glance at the snell skies. "Come inside. The house is small, but it's easily warmed. That's one comfort."

When Neil had washed his hands and brushed his clothes they passed into the little snuggery, where Malcolm sat and smoked of an evening. He had made some little alteration in the arrangement of the house, and the room which the General had used as his library and sitting-room was now converted into a dining-room, which it had originally been. It was a man's house now, the few tokens of Isla's presence having long since disappeared.

Whether Malcolm was able to keep the peace between his two elderly and contentious servants nobody knew. Truth to tell, he never bothered his head about them, and many a storm rose and raged in the kitchen and was followed by many a dead and ominous calm, but of these he seemed to be totally unaware. He had none of those finer shades of feeling which had rendered Isla immediately conscious of any rift in the domestic lute.

Drummond stretched himself in the lounge-chair before the blazing peat with a sigh of content. He was in the mood to be at peace with the whole world and to give every man more than his due. It occurred to him as he looked at Malcolm, on whose face the full light from the window fell where he sat, that he had improved in looks of late. The coarseness had disappeared from his features, and there was an expression of refinement and delicacy which had been at one time wholly absent.

It was such an improvement that Drummond decided that Mackinnon's looks had been underrated. The keen, hard, simple life, in conjunction with the pursuit of a certain lofty ideal, had wrought its saving grace in Malcolm Mackinnon, as it will in any man who gives it fair play.

"Surely you didn't stop away as long as you intended," said Malcolm as he lit up his pipe, while waiting for Diarmid's summons to eat.

"I was there three weeks--long enough to idle about, though I could have stopped three years," said Drummond significantly.

"Your sister didn't come home with you?"

"No. They haven't any plans just yet. Aunt Betty talks about staying over Easter, and if they stop as long of course I'll go back."

"Nice, is it, or Monte Carlo?"

"Their headquarters are at Nice. My aunt has taken a villa. The old lady is going strong, and she is looking younger every day. What a warrior she is! She could give points to most of the girls one sees. She knows how to enjoy life at seventy-five. She had her birthday when I was there, and she had a dinner party of twelve. She has unearthed all sorts of old friends on the Riviera, and more are turning up every day. The latest is a Russian princess, whose mother was a Scotswoman somewhere away back in the dark ages. They're all having the time of their lives."

Neil was making talk, and they both knew it. It was not to rehearse these trivial items that he had come up that day to the Moor of Creagh.

Just then Diarmid made timely diversion by announcing that luncheon was served. His manner was irreproachable and dignified, and it could not have been excelled in the most distinguished establishment.

It was a great day for Diarmid, and he waited behind his young master's chair with a secret pride, for the Laird of Garrion was a guest worthy of honour.

The luncheon, though simple, was excellent, and they both enjoyed it to the full. A modest bottle of claret with the cheese just unloosed their tongues, and when Diarmid had left them Neil looked across the table very earnestly at Mackinnon's face.

"I don't suppose it will come as a very great surprise to you, Malcolm."

"What?" asked Malcolm with a start.

"About Isla."

"What about her? You saw her, of course. I didn't like to harry you with questions, but I suppose she's all right with Lady Betty. She has never written. I have managed, somehow, to commit the unpardonable sin where Isla is concerned. I'm sorry, but there isn't anything I can do now but wait her pleasure. You see it was she who cut the knot, so to speak."

Neil nodded as he crumbled the biscuit on his plate.

"I don't know whether you know, Malcolm, that I have always wanted Isla. I've asked her to marry me on the average about twice a year for the last three or four years. Last year, I believe, I asked her six times."

"Such persistence deserves its reward, and I hope you've got it, old chap," said Malcolm, but his tone lacked warmth.

He could not understand the man who wanted Isla. To him she seemed lacking in most, if not all, of the qualities which make a woman desirable.

"She has said 'Yes' at last, Malcolm, and that's why I am here to-day," said Neil.

And his hand trembled ever so slightly as it rested on the sheer white of the tablecloth.

"Well, and what's going to happen next?" said Malcolm with a curious dry note in his voice. "I'm glad, of course. It--it's a mighty relief to me to hear that anything is likely to anchor Isla or settle her. Though nobody may have given me credit for it, Neil, I've had many a bad hour--ay, and day-- about her up here."

"I suppose you have," said Neil. "But, all the same, I can't help saying that I don't think you ought to have left her as long as you did--in London, I mean. That's all past, however, and there isn't any use of going back on it now. It's the future, thank God, that concerns us. I hope ours is going to be very bright."

"She has agreed to marry you, then? Is it likely to be soon?"

"What I should like, and what I'm hoping for, is that it may take place at Nice. I've had to leave the details to Aunt Betty, and they're safe with her. She's the most ripping General on earth. I owe this happiness to her, I don't doubt. There's a Scotch church there, and we could go south a bit for the honeymoon and get back to Garrion for the summer."

"It sounds all right, and in that way you would escape all the fuss and talk of the glens," said Malcolm musingly.

"I wanted to see you, Malcolm, because you're the head of the house, and I must lay the position before you."

"Oh, but there isn't any need, Neil,--between you and me, I mean. I haven't the right. Isla has always managed her own affairs, and she wouldn't like my interference now, I'm sure. Of course, anything I can do I should like to do if I'm permitted. I'd go out to Nice to give her away if she asked me."

"We'll come to that later. I want to tell you that after I'm married we'll have Garrion to ourselves. My aunt will get a place for herself somewhere and take away Kitty. I'm not a very rich man, and you know what Highland estates are in these times. But--again it's Aunt Betty to the rescue. She says she'll give us ten thousand pounds as a wedding gift and that there will be more to come later on. So you see you needn't have any anxiety about Isla's financial position."

"I couldn't have any in any case if she was in your hands," said Malcolm with difficulty. "Ten thousand pounds and Garrion clear! By Gad, Neil, you're a lucky beggar! Try to put yourself in my place for a moment and see whether you wouldn't have some crumbs of pity for a poor devil who can't make ends meet and who is just as anxious to have a home as you can possibly be."

A something swept over Malcolm's face--a spasm of infinite yearning which oddly moved Neil Drummond. Happiness brings out all that is best in a man. He forgot all his doubts of Malcolm Mackinnon, all his secret and open blame of him, and he was able even to bury his anger against him for his treatment of Isla as he stretched his hand across the table to grasp Malcolm's.

"Never mind, old chap. The luck will turn. It's bound to sooner or later, you know. No man goes through the hards from first to last."

Malcolm shook his head.

"I suppose most men get the luck they deserve," he said a little heavily.

Later, these words recurred with poignancy to Drummond's mind.

They smoked another pipe of peace together in the den afterwards, and about half-past three Drummond took his horse once more and rode through the fine powder of the newly-fallen snow towards the home that was now illumined by so many stars of promise.

A strange restlessness was upon Malcolm Mackinnon when he was left alone, and, after a little deliberation, he took to his horse--the poor common cob that had so often filled Drummond with compassion for the man who had to mount it--and rode slowly down Glenogle.

Though not bred in any of the glens, the cob had learned the way to Achree and needed no guiding when he came to the gate. Achree, with the delicate powder of the snow lying upon it and lightly touching the exquisite tracery of the trees, was a dream-place that looked the fit cradle for a thousand lovely hopes.

Malcolm took his horse to the stables, and when he presented himself at the door asked for Mrs. Rodney Payne.

"She has gone to the village, to the post, sir," the man answered.

This information caused Malcolm to turn about and walk away without another word. What he had to say were perhaps better said in the open, where none could hear and where there would be room to breathe and to think. He had a die to cast that day which would make or mar the rest of his life.

It was below the Darrach Brig he met Vivien walking alone with step a little fleet, the snow sprinkled over her long coat and lightly powdering her beautiful hair. She was pleased to see him, but her colour did not rise, nor were there about her any of the signs the impatient lover can interpret to his own joy.

That was the lure of Vivien. She was so still, like the waters of Loch Earn on the quiet autumn days or in the hush of the early morning when the dawn was waking upon its breast.

"It is not a day for you to be out in. We are going to have a great storm. At Creagh, Diarmid predicts the drift of the year. You must be more careful of yourself."

"Oh, but I love it!" she cried, her eyes lighting up. "There is something ethereal in it all. I should like to walk on and on in it to the limit of the world. Have you been at the house, and is there nobody at home?"

"I asked only for you," he made answer, greatly daring.

But still the clear paleness of her face had no touch of flame upon it.

"I had Drummond to lunch. Perhaps you met him? He went down the Glen in front of me. I didn't ride with him, because I couldn't pit my sorry old hack against his fine bit of horse-flesh."

"He does have lovely horses, and he loves them--and don't they know it!" said Vivien musingly. "Even a horse thrives best in an atmosphere of appreciation and of kindly care."

"And that's a true word, Mrs. Payne. May I tell you about Drummond and what was his business with me to-day? It was a bit of family business, but I hope you will do me the honour to be interested in it."

"Surely, if you care to tell me I shall be interested," she answered without a moment's hesitation.

"You know, of course, that he has just come back from Nice?"

"I knew he had gone anyhow, because Sadie has had budgets from Kitty."

"And you know, too, that my sister is there with Lady Betty Neil?"

"Yes," she answered quietly, "I knew that, too."

"She is going to marry Drummond," said Malcolm then, not looking at her.

It did not occur to him that she could have any acute personal interest in the news. As for Rosmead, in his absence he had in more senses than one dropped out of the count.

"She is going to marry Neil Drummond!" said Vivien after a while, and her voice was a little faint as if the news staggered her. "How very extraordinary and unexpected!"

"Why do you say that?" he asked anxiously.

"Well, because, somehow, one never expected to hear that in this world. Did you?"

"I wasn't surprised. He has been in love with her since they were children. He told me he had asked her six times last year."

"Oh!" said Vivien with a little gasp. "Then one can only hope that they will be very happy," she added, as if recovering herself by an effort of the will.

But her reception of the news was all very half-hearted, and Malcolm was deeply disappointed.

"I thought you would be pleased."

"I am, if you are. I suppose you would like Mr. Drummond for a brother-in-law."

"Drummond is a very good sort. But what chiefly pleases me is that Isla will have a proper home at Garrion and the position she ought to have. It's a fine old place, and Drummond will be a rich man one day when Lady Betty Neil is done with her money. She is to give them ten thousand pounds as a wedding present."

"'The Ancestor' has come up to expectation," said Vivien with a little smile. "Have you heard from your sister? Is she very happy?"

"I haven't heard from her," he answered lamely. "I'll be writing this evening. May I send her a message from you?"

"If you like. But I shall write myself--unless she is coming home soon."

"That is unlikely. Drummond talks of a marriage at the Scotch church at Nice. In that case I, of course, would have to go there. But nothing can be arranged till I have heard from Isla."

"Don't you feel a little sore because she did not write to tell you herself?" asked Vivien straightly and in a puzzled voice.

The relations between Mackinnon and his sister had always puzzled and saddened Vivien, and in her heart of hearts she had sometimes blamed Isla. At other times, recalling the glimpse of the real woman she had obtained on that never-to-be-forgotten day at the Lodge of Creagh, she wondered whether there was not something in the background which, if known, would have explained everything and justified Isla.

"Well, you see, we are not a writing family, and I was so long abroad that we got a little out of touch," said Malcolm lamely again.

Vivien was fully conscious that there was evasion in the answer, but it was not her business to probe into depths with which she had no personal concern.

Quite suddenly Malcolm stood still on the road and looked at her straightly with a kind of dull fire in his eyes.

"Vivien, I must speak! I haven't the right, for there is very little I have to offer you. But I love you as my own soul--no, as some higher thing, for my soul is a poor thing to mate with yours. Will you--will you--be my wife?"

He had often anticipated this hour and had conned in secret the phrases in which he would plead with this woman for his very life.

But all the fine, set phrases fell away from him and left him bare, so that he could only blurt out his immense desire in words that had no grace of diction to commend them. Yet they were warmed by an honest passion, and they reached the heart of the woman to whom they were spoken and awoke some response in her eyes.

But she put up her hand as if she would ward off that which she feared.

"Oh, don't!" she said rather brokenly. "I don't want to hear it. I--I am afraid!"

"Afraid of what?" he asked.

And a new-born tenderness enveloped him and lifted him up from base depths to the full height of the manhood that ought to have been his had he not trailed his heritage in the dust. "Not afraid of me, my--my--darling?" he said, and it was as if the torrent was let loose. "Listen. This once will I speak, and then be silent, if you bid me, for ever. I am not worthy of you. No man could be--but I am less worthy than most. Yet if you would stoop and give the chance to prove what a man might be and could be for your sake I should worship you to the last day of my life and make your happiness, and that only, my chiefest care. For God's sake, don't send me away! At least give me a crumb of comfort. If I had but known there was a woman like you somewhere in the world--my God, if I had only known!"

The anguish of his voice appealed to the very woman in her, and, though her face was very white, she stretched out a trembling hand and touched his arm.

"Don't speak like that. It--it hurts me," she said, and her whole body seemed to quiver as if all the springs of being were stirred. "You have never heard my story. You can't know that I, too, have been down in the depths. I have suffered all, I think, that a woman can suffer. And now, I am afraid! It is--it is so terrible a thing when one is bound and there is no hope."

It was all she could permit herself to say, but the unstudied intensity of her words was more self-revealing than any deliberate account of her unhappy married life could have been.

Malcolm stood awed before it, and knew for the first time in his life what a white thing the soul of a good woman can be, and how great are the sufferings that can rend it.

And in that moment he knew that he had not the right to take her life into his; that there were no floods deep enough to wash him clean enough to mate with this woman who had been down in the depths--and who knew.

"Don't you see I am so afraid! I could not live through it a second time. I don't know you well. And I am afraid! Let us put it away now, and let us be friends, as we have been."

"It can't be," said Malcolm simply. "If that is your final answer, I will go away out of the Glen and never set foot in it again."

"Oh, but that would be terrible! It is I who can go, for what does it matter where I live now? This is your place. These are your people. You can't leave them. You ought to be proud that you were born here and that Achree is yours. It is a place that grows into one's heart. I love it more than any place I have ever seen."

"Then keep it, stay in it! Come to me, Vivien, and bless it and me," he said, moved to an eloquence which amazed even himself. "I make no pretensions. I have not been what a man should be. But there is nothing I would not try to be and to do for your sake."

She shivered slightly, but there was wavering in her eyes.

"I vowed I would never marry again. I have been often asked," she said simply. "But I have always given the same answer. It is a little harder to-day--that is all."

She suffered her eyes to meet his, and the next moment his arms were round about her, and he knew that he had won.

It was a strange wooing, and when Vivien crept back to the house, knowing that she had pledged herself to another venture on the sea of matrimony, her eyes had unfathomed depths in them.

Yet when she went to her mother's side she said never a word about her own story, but with a little accent of sad wonder in her voice asked, "Mother, Isla Mackinnon is going to marry Drummond of Garrion and who is going to tell Peter?"

CHAPTER XXVII
THE CALL

Isla Mackinnon was sitting in the stone balustrade of the loggia in front of Lady Betty's villa at Nice, reading a letter that had been written three days before in the small hours of the morning at the Lodge of Creagh in Glenogle.

The sun was upon her hair and on her face, but her eyes were full of a wide and mute astonishment.

Lady Betty, attending to her own voluminous correspondence at the ormolu desk which stood across the open window of the drawing-room, saw that expression and wondered at it.

It was now a fortnight since Neil Drummond had left Nice, carrying Isla's promise with him, and this was Malcolm's first letter. It had cost him much travail, and as Isla read it through she felt its note of sincerity.

"I dare say you have heard from Drummond about his visit to me the other day. I have tried to write lots of times, but I haven't got the gift of the pen and I found it difficult to get words.

"Of course, I am glad, Isla, for Drummond is a ripping good chap and his prospects are rather splendid. You who are living with Lady Betty know what sort of fairy godmother she is to them. What I like best of all to think of is you as mistress at Garrion with plenty of money at your command. It will suit you down to the ground. There is no doubt that, as a family, we Mackinnons have been cursed through lack of money. It is easy to be good when one has plenty and nothing to worry about.

"I have waited, half hoping you would write first. But as you haven't, will you take this letter as an expression of my affectionate good will? We haven't quite understood each other up till now, but things are going to be better in future.

"I also have a bit of news for you, and I am wondering whether or not it will be a great surprise. Vivien Rosmead has promised to marry me, and we are not going to wait long--only until her brother comes home, which may be any day now. The last letters say that the initial difficulties of his bridge-building have been overcome and that he can be spared--at least for a few weeks.

"I hardly know how or what to write about this, Isla, because it is a thing that a man has a natural diffidence in speaking of. You know what Vivien is--how good, how far above me. I will try honestly to be worthy of her. I think I have convinced her of my sincerity.

"Of course she has a large private fortune, which will lift all the burdens off the old place and make it possible for us to start the new life unencumbered. The luck of the Mackinnons has turned at last and, after all our troubles, we may surely look forward to a little run of prosperity and peace. I hope you'll write to Vivien, even if you don't to me. I'm sure she expects it."

Isla dropped the sheet on her lap, and her eyes swept the blue line of the sea a little wildly. The colour which the soft southern air and the restful life had wooed back to her face receded and left it a little grey. The old terror, the vague, haunting dread crept over her once more, and so insistent was it that she could not push it away.

Had the luck of the Mackinnons really turned? She was pledged to marry Neil Drummond, perhaps in two months' time, and there was not an atom of joyful anticipation in her heart. Malcolm was engaged to Vivien Rosmead, and what would be the end?

In the whole of Malcolm's letter there was not one reference to the past. She knew him too well to hope for a moment that he had laid it bare to Vivien Rosmead--nay, rather was she certain that he had trusted to luck. The purple lady!--the vision of her arose before Isla's eyes and shut out the incomparable view of the terraced garden, the blossoming trees, the wide blue sweep of the southern sea.

A quick tap on the window pane attracted her attention, and, looking up, she beheld Lady Betty beckoning to her sharply. She rose slowly, picked up the letter, and went in through the open window.

"What ails ye, lass?" asked the old lady brusquely. "You look as if ye had the wail of the pibroch in your ears."

"I've had a letter from Malcolm, Lady Betty."

"Well? And is he ill pleased about you and Neil?"

"Oh, no. He tells me he is engaged to Mrs. Rodney Payne. I want to go home, Lady Betty."

Lady Betty sat back in her chair, set her eyeglass more firmly on her aristocratic old nose, and looked Isla straight in the face.

"What for do ye want to go home?"

"If I could tell you I would," she answered simply. "You have the gift, and you know that when the call comes one does not question, but just rises up to obey. That is how it is with me. The Glen is calling me. There is something for me to do at the Lodge of Creagh."

Isla spoke quite quietly, and the old lady neither flouted nor rebuked her.

"It's very unfortunate. Do you know that every day for the next month is filled up? And you have been such a success here and so many wish to know you that we need not have an idle hour."

"I shall have to go," was all that Isla said.

"And what will become of me? What will be the end of it? I have the house till Easter. Will you come back after you have answered the call? Neil could bring you."

"I can't promise anything," answered Isla. "Will you mind very much if I go to-day?"

Lady Betty did mind, but she knew that to throw obstacles in the way was useless. She might delay Isla's departure, but she could not altogether prevent it. Besides, there was the call. When it came clear and swift, as it had done to Isla, everything else had to give way.

"You would travel by yourself? You are not afraid?" she said kindly.

"Oh, I am afraid of nothing, dear Lady Betty, but the forces that work in the dark--the things we can't grapple with."

Lady Betty once or twice slowly inclined her head.

"I understand. Well, then, make your arrangements. The train-de-luxe to-night, I suppose, and London the day after to-morrow? Oh, Isla, ye mind me on nothing but a petrel that has no rest night or day from the storm. God go with ye, my dear, and at the long last give ye peace."

The words were very solemnly, very tenderly spoken, and Isla with a swift movement knelt beside the old lady's chair.

"Dearest Lady Betty! How can I thank you? I won't even try. You know--don't you?--oh, you must know how full my heart is!----"

Lady Betty dropped her fine white hand with its sparkling rings on the girl's bent head.

"I know nothing but good of you, Isla Mackinnon, and I love ye as ye were my own. But, oh, lass, my heart is heavy, and I would fain rise up and away to the hills with ye! My one consolation is that you are going back to Neil. I will wire to him this evening."

"No, don't, dear Lady Betty. It would be certain to bring him to London. I want no one to meet me there. If I have to sleep the night I will go to Agnes Fraser's. I--I would rather be alone."

Then something smote hard and cold on Lady Betty's heart, and she knew by the inward vision of her soul that the thing on which she had built high her pride and her hope would never take place. She did not know what was going to happen to prevent it, but she felt that Neil's cause was lost from that hour!

She suffered no depression to manifest itself, however. She undertook to still Kitty's garrulous questioning, and she herself saw Isla off at the station by the night train. But she did not close an eye all that night, being haunted by a sense of the futility of earthly planning and of the vanity of human hopes.

Isla arrived at Charing Cross Station at five o'clock in the afternoon of one of the loveliest of spring days. By that time she had a quite clear idea of what she wished to do. Speaking of it afterwards, she declared that each step of the way seemed to have been planned out for her, leaving her in no doubt whatever about the next.

She had her luggage transferred to the Charing Cross Hotel, engaged a room for the night, and, having enjoyed a very excellent cup of tea, sallied forth to take an omnibus for the West End.

Those weeks spent under Agnes Fraser's roof, and the long days she had utilized in traversing the length and breadth of London in search of impossible employment, had given her an intimate knowledge of the best and quickest and most economical means of transit.

But on a pleasant spring evening the omnibus was the most enjoyable. She had bought a copy of the "Morning Post" at the station, and she unfolded it in her seat with a view to taking a glance through the pages. There two items of intelligence which were of the deepest interest to her met her eyes. The first was purely personal and occurred a little way down the page, below the Court Circular.

"A marriage has been arranged, and will take place before the end of the season, between Malcolm John Mackinnon, Esq. of Achree and Glenogle, and Mrs. Rodney Payne of Carleton, Virginia, and 31 Avenue Castellare, Champs Elysees, Paris."

Her face flushed as she read these significant words and for the moment she felt as if all her fellow-travellers had read them with her and were aware of their meaning.

She sat a long time pondering, surprised beyond measure at the announcement, which seemed premature. She wondered who was responsible for its appearance, but decided that it was probably Malcolm who had sent it to the newspaper for the purpose of establishing his credit and consolidating his position. As yet Isla was disposed to be hard on him and to credit him with merely sordid motives.

Turning over the page she discovered the second item of intelligence, which riveted her attention immediately and sent her thoughts flying in another direction. It was under the heading of Wills and Bequests, and merely stated that the will of Mrs. Jane Bodley-Chard had been proved at seventy-five thousand pounds, the greater part of which passed to her husband, who was her sole executor.

By the time Isla had come out of the reverie induced by the reading of these paragraphs the omnibus had rolled her to her destination.

She alighted at the Marble Arch, crossed the way, and proceeded quickly along the Edgeware Road until she reached the end of the street where she had first seen Malcolm with the purple lady. She had not made a note of the address, but she remembered it vividly, and she made no mistake about the number.

Her slightly hesitating ring was answered by a person who seemed to be a charwoman, and who, in reply to her inquiry for Mrs. Bisley, shook her head.

"She ain't 'ere, Miss."

"But can't you tell me where she is, or at least how long she has been gone?"

"Oh, she ain't bin gone long--only since this mornin'. Are you a friend of 'ers?" she asked, peering rather inquisitively into Isla's face.

"At least I can claim to know her, and I particularly wished to see her to-day."

"Well, you carn't. She's gone to Scotland. She was orful upset this mornin' by sumfink she saw in the papers, and she went orf all of a 'eap, like, not even takin' proper luggage wiv 'er. Said she didn't know w'en she'd be back."

Isla turned away, so sick at heart that her dismay was visible on her face.

"I don't know nothink, but it's got summat to do wiv that military gent. she knew in India. A toff, 'e was, and she expected to marry 'im, don't you see? And 'e'es given 'er the slip--leastways that's wot I think. But, of course, I don't know nothink for certing, and you needn't say as I said anythink. I didn't hev no call fer to say anythink, reely."

Isla thanked her and turned away.

She was just one day too late. What could she do now? Even if she were to hasten by the night train to Glenogle, what could she do there? A meeting between Vivien and this woman seemed inevitable. At least Malcolm would have to explain his position and, if possible, justify himself.

Just for one brief moment she regretted having acted on the swift impulse to leave the pleasant sanctuary she had found by the Mediterranean Sea. What good had she done, or could she do? She had only once more committed the mistake of thinking that she could arbitrate in the destiny of others--she, who had so sadly mismanaged her own!

She crept dejectedly along the street, still clutching the paper in her hand, and when she reached the wider thoroughfare crossed it in a slanting direction and, as if through force of habit, turned in at Cromer Street and made her way to Agnes Fraser's familiar door.

It was the busiest hour of that good woman's day, because her first floor came in to dinner at half-past seven and it was now half-past six. But when she heard who it was that had asked for her she ran up the kitchen stairs, several steps at a time.

"Oh, Miss Isla, excuse my apron and the flour on my hands. But I couldna wait. I'm terribly busy jist for a meenit or twa. Can you come in and wait till I get the denners fairly on the road? It'll no tak' me mair nor a quarter o' an 'oor."

"I can't wait, dear woman--at least not now. I didn't mean to see you to-night, really, but I had business in this neighbourhood, and I just ran in for a look at you. I shall be in Glenogle to-morrow night."

"Yes," said Agnes breathlessly. "And it is true that ye are going to marry Mr. Drummond? I've aye been expeckin' to hear from yoursel' aboot it. But Elspeth Maclure says that it's quite true and that everybody is pleased I am, I'm sure. I jist sat doon and had a guid greet when Elspeth's letter cam'. And Andra lauched at me and said it wasna a thing to greet ower. But that wass hoo I felt."

Isla nodded, and her proud mouth trembled.

"You're lookin' fine--quite like yersel'," resumed Agnes. "And when is it to be, Miss Isla? Oh, hang their denners! Come in here and let me hear ye speak."

But Isla, laughing a little hysterically, shook her head, and began to move towards the door.

"It was very bad of me not to write, but I've been passing through all sorts of phases, Agnes, and even now I don't know quite where I am. When I get home I'll sit down and write you a very long letter. Have you seen the 'Morning Post' to-day with the announcement of my brother's engagement to Mrs. Rodney Payne?"

"No, but that news was in Elspeth's letter, too, and so Achree is on the mend again, thank God. Are ye awa'? Oh, I am sorry, Miss Isla! I would have liked to keep you for the nicht. Can ye not come back?"

"Not to-night. But probably I shall be in London again soon. Good night, dear soul, and thank you very much. Whatever the future may hold for me, Agnes Fraser will have a warm place in it. I hope that some day I shall be able to thank you properly for all you did for me."

Agnes was able to give only a very divided attention to the cooking when she returned to the gloom of her underground kitchen, while Isla rode back the way she had come, singularly out of love with life.

She had done no good by her impetuous journey--none at all. She was half minded to take the night mail to Calais again and throw herself once more on the tender mercies of Lady Betty. Her uppermost feeling was one of shrinking from Glenogle and all that might happen there.

The dusk was falling when she got down at Trafalgar Square, where she crossed to the hotel entrance at Charing Cross. It is always busy there, arrivals and departures taking place at all hours of the day and night. A four-wheeler, piled high with luggage, stood before the door, and a tall man in a long travelling-coat with a fur collar was directing the hotel porter what he wished to be done with the larger boxes.

He turned his head as Isla was about to pass in, and he found herself face to face with Peter Rosmead.

It was a supreme moment for them both. All Rosmead's heart leaped to his eyes, he dropped his dispatch-case, and grasped both her hands while his gaze covered her with an overmastering and encompassing tenderness.

"This is a bit of God's own luck!" he said, and his voice was thick with the passion of his soul. "How is it you are here?"

"I came from Nice only to-day. I am going home to Glenogle to-morrow," she answered, and her voice had a faint, far-away sound in it, as if she suddenly felt very tired. "And you?"

"Just arrived by the Norddeutscher-Lloyd steamer at Southampton at noon to-day. Are you here alone for the night?"

She inclined her head.

"It's God's own luck," he repeated. "You'll dine with me, then--in half an hour or an hour, or at any time that you choose to name?"

She hesitated just a moment. Should she refuse? But why? In another day it would be all over. Only the present hour was hers. She nodded and sped from him quickly, ascending to her room on the third floor by the lift.

When she entered it she turned the key and looked round a little wildly, working her hands in front of her nervously. Then, with a sob, she threw herself face downwards on the bed and buried her face.

She wanted to weep, but a song was in her heart, because, though she was pledged to marry Neil Drummond and was bound to him by every tie of gratitude and honour, she belonged to Peter Rosmead and he to her, and nothing could alter it. For the moment she, who had had so little of the joy of life, gave herself up to the vision of the might-have-been. And it was so glorious that it transformed the bleak hotel bedroom into a heavenly place.

After a long time, when she had risen and was making her toilet, there came a quick tap at the door. When she opened it a chambermaid stood without, smiling.

"Please, Miss, can I help you? The gentleman is waiting, and dinner is served in eighty-nine."

CHAPTER XXVIII
WITH HASTENING FEET

Because this was her hour and to-morrow all would be over, Isla did not disdain a woman's art. She wished to look beautiful for once in the eyes of the man who loved her, even though she should henceforth disappear from them for ever.

She put on a wonderful frock that had come from the hands of a clever *couturière* at Nice--a simple black thing, fashioned with such consummate art that it seemed moulded to her figure, showing all its grace. As Riviera fashion dictates, it was high to the neck, with a yoke of clear net through which her white skin shone, while a string of pearls about her stately throat made her sole adornment.

"Oh, Miss, you do look nice!" said the chambermaid as she stepped back from fastening the skirt.

Isla smiled into her eyes. Then she asked where she could find eighty-nine. The girl took her down to the next floor and to the door of the room where Rosmead, in evening dress, was waiting.

"Come," he said with a smile.

He drew her in, and the door was shut.

The warmth of the cheerful fire and the fragrance of flowers met her on the threshold of the private room, where Rosmead had ordered the meal to be served. This was no night for them to dine in a public restaurant--they must be immune from prying eyes.

"You don't look so tired now! And to think I was cursing the luck that would keep me here for another twenty-four hours! I have an appointment at the Colonial Office to-morrow and can't go north till Friday. But I never in my wildest dreams anticipated this."

She smiled as she took the chair he offered. Her eyes had a far-away look, her cheeks were softly flushed, she seemed like a dream-woman, and she was so beautiful that Rosmead blamed himself that the vision of her he had carried with him so long had fallen so far short of the reality.

The waiter came in with the soup presently and waited upon them deftly. But Isla ate little. While the small, daintily-appointed, and exquisite meal was being served they talked of commonplace things--of the Riviera in the season, of Rosmead's business in America, of the bridge whose foundations had taken so long to lay.

"But it is accomplished, isn't it?" she asked with her swift glance across the table. "Of course I always knew it would be. I remember that you said that in your estimation difficulties existed only to be demolished."

"That was a very high and mighty utterance," said Rosmead a little shyly. "But this time I thought I was going to get beaten. Do you know that I left the very day after the thing had passed the bar of my own judgment, just five days after the other experts had pronounced it unassailable."

"You always trust yourself last?" she said inquiringly.

"It is I who have to pay the price of failure, and so I leave nothing to chance," he answered. "Will you take nothing to drink? I am a teetotaller myself. Some day I will tell you why. But you are tired, and wine will do you good."

She shook her head.

"No. It is delightful to think that one can dine without it. I do believe that you are the first man I have ever met who could."

"Oh, come!" said Rosmead, laughing. "Where I come from there are many."

Isla laughed a little and shrugged her shoulders. She was feeling so warm and comforted and happy that she wished the hour to last for ever.

"How kind of you to think of this room! As I was dressing I thought how horrid it would be in the restaurant to-night."

"I knew it would be. I grudged it. This was the thing," he said.

And his pulses thrilled as he thought of all the days that were coming when they should dine together alone.

It came to an end at last, and Rosmead showed haste in getting the table cleared and the coffee-tray brought in.

Then he wheeled a big easy chair towards the fire for her, and he himself stood against the end of the mantel-shelf, while an odd silence fell between them.

"I am sure you want to smoke. I should like it," she said a little nervously, fearing what she saw in his eyes.

He shook his head.

"That would be desecration. By and by, perhaps, but not yet. I wonder if you know just what it meant to me to see you to-night downstairs, just what it means to have you here like this, alone?"

She made no answer, and the veil dropped over her eyes, but her lips trembled, and she worked with her fingers in the fringes of the delicate white scarf which had fallen from her shoulders across her arms.

"You must know that I love you," he said. Then in a low voice which vibrated keenly with intense feeling he added, "I have lived for this hour during all these interminable months. I have risen up each new day, thinking it brought me a day nearer to it and to you. I know all you have suffered. Let me try to make you forget. Give your precious life into my keeping, Isla. You are the only woman I have ever cared for. The knowledge that you were waiting somewhere for me has kept me a boy in heart for your sake. Will you give yourself to me?"

There was terror, anguish, hopelessness in her eyes. She gave a small shuddering sigh and buried her face in her hands. Instantly he was on his knees beside her, trying with a very gentle force to take her hands away.

Suddenly she drew back, rose to her feet, and faced him--very pale, very stricken, but wholly calm.

"Oh, please don't say any more. I--I must not listen. It was even wicked of me to come here when I knew--when I knew--and even hoped that you would speak. I--I am not free. I am the promised wife of another man."

Rosmead's face became set like a stone.

"But you are the woman God has given to me," he said quietly. "Who is the man?"

"Neil Drummond," she answered feverishly. "Don't look at me like that! Let me sit down again, and you stand where you were before and I will tell you how it came about. You said that you knew all I have suffered. But you don't. I want to tell you everything. Then you will understand."

He obeyed her to the letter, and with the breadth of the hearth between them she began her recital.

She went back a long way, even to the days of her troubled girlhood, keeping nothing back, telling him in simple language all the story of her life.

All unconscious was she of its complete self-revelation. Peter Rosmead, listening, with only a brief word interjected here and there, was filled with a pity so vast that he did not know how to contain himself. He saw this young woman-creature, at the time when she ought to have been enjoying girlhood, doing not only a woman's work in the world but also forced to act the man's part--to face abnormal difficulties, to solve the problems of existence in loneliness and without help.

And when she came to the end and related simply, yet with a sort of bald power, the story of her London experiences, he could bear no more.

"My God, Isla, you must cease! I tell you I can't hear any more."

"You must," she said clearly, "because this is the part which explains--which explains--why I am not free. You see, I had got so very tired and hopeless, and my money was all done, and I had no more heart left to fight. And just then Neil Drummond came, and he was like a brother to me, and--and he had loved me all my life, and I thought I, too, could care a little, and that we might be happy together."

He put his hand up to his forehead with a sudden gesture and kept it there until he felt the flash of Isla's mournful reproach on his face.

"If only you had written a single line!" she said almost piteously. "If I had ever known or guessed that you remembered my existence I could have held out. But I was so tired, so tired!"

She who had been strong so long, whom trouble had never daunted, gave way before the insistent clamour of her woman's heart. For the moment she could not forgo the real heritage of her womanhood--could not make the final renunciation. For she was not old yet, and life can be very long to the sad.

Rosmead was as one who took swift and decisive counsel with himself.

He lifted a chair to the hearth in front of her and sat down so that he could the better see her face.

"Listen to me, my dear," he said in his quiet, compelling voice. "We must face this thing together, try to grasp exactly what it means, and decide what is to be done. Let us do it quietly, try to deal with it as if we were not the chief actors in it."

Isla sat back and folded her hands on her lap. She was willing to listen--nay, listen she must. And, somehow, she did not seem to care. She had rolled away the stone from the door of her heart. Peter Rosmead knew that she loved him, just as she knew that he loved her. Well, he was strong and good, he would decide and act for her. Hence the peace upon her face, at which Rosmead, himself torn with conflict, wondered.

"It does not mean only a disappointment to me--a lifelong disappointment, the overthrow of everything that I have been waiting for," he began slowly. "It means the shipwreck of three lives. If you don't care for Drummond how can you be a good wife to him or make him happy?"

"There are many women who are married to men they do not care very much for. I have seen them, and they seem to get along," was all she said.

"What other women might do with impunity you couldn't. You are the soul of truth, and, moreover, you cannot hide what you think and feel. If you could have done it better, dear woman, life might perhaps have been a little less hard for you."

"But after a while," she said in a low voice, "it might be possible. I should try very hard. And, after all, it is not happiness we are here for. One has only to look around to see how very little of it there is in this world."

"By heaven, Isla, I can't accept that--no, I can't! God means us to be happy. It is what He has created us for. Only we do wrong things. It is we who make the shipwreck, and I believe that if you go on with this marriage you will ruin three lives."

She only shook her head.

"Is Drummond the man--do you think?--to be contented with what you purpose to give him--wifely duty, without wifely love?"

"He is very good," she said wearily. "His kindness and his patience never fail."

"That may be true. But afterwards would come the crucial test. You can't do it, Isla--you can't! There is--there must be a way out, and we must find it together. Will you leave it to me?"

"I'll leave everything! I am so tired! I can do nothing more. But I will be true to Neil Drummond. I may tell him, but I will keep my promise if he holds me to it, and if you will let me go now I will say good night. It is nearly ten o'clock. I have been travelling for two days, and I feel as if I could not bear any more."

He instantly forgot his own sore disappointment and was concerned only for her with that great and tender concern which belongs to the strong and which the tired woman felt so perilously sweet.

"Just a moment; what about to-morrow? Can't you wait until Friday? If I could get away I would travel with you to-morrow, but it is impossible to do so without giving offence in quarters where it is important not to give offence. Will you wait till Friday? You are not fit to travel alone."

She looked up at him, and her eyes wavered.

"I should like to, but I can't stay here. Let us meet in the morning and decide. At least, I need not travel until the two o'clock train."

He suffered her to go then, merely touching her hand at parting, because of the barrier that was between.

Rosmead had boasted that difficulties in his way existed only for the purpose of being demolished, but he was now in front of one that taxed his boasted powers.

Isla slept the dreamless sleep of complete exhaustion, but he fought with the problem the night through, and in the morning he was no nearer its solution. They did not meet at breakfast, but at ten o'clock she sent him a message that she would see him in the drawing-room.

She met him, tranquil and calm-eyed, a little pale, but without trace of stress or strain. Rosmead himself had a slightly haggard look.

"Good morning," she said quietly. "I think I shall wait until to-morrow. To-day I shall go back to my old quarters in Cromer Street, Bayswater, and I shall meet you to-morrow at the station."

"And am I not to see you to-day at all?" he asked, and his eyes travelled hungrily over her face.

She shook her head.

"I don't think so. If there is any more to be said there will be time to say it to-morrow. You will help me to do the right thing, won't you? It is--it is what I look for in you."

The words were a rebuke to Peter Rosmead, but he took it well.

"I will do the right thing--yes," he answered humbly, "but only until we get back to Glenogle. Then, I warn you, I'm going to fight for you with all the powers I possess. I don't know how it is going to be done, but win you I shall. You have not come into my life only to go out of it again."

She smiled as she turned away, and a strange, deep contentment, gathered in her eyes. She asked no questions, troubled herself not at all about what was coming. So far as she was concerned the fight was over, and the issue lay with Peter Rosmead. Her trust in him was so large and fine a thing that she was content to leave herself and her cause in his strong, tender hands and to let him undertake for her.

They parted then, and they met no more until they entered the train together at Euston next morning. But during the hours of that interminable day there was no sense of distance or of separation between them. The same sky covered them, they breathed the same air, they were within call of each other; it sufficed.

Rosmead went early to the station, and he had made his full arrangements for Isla's comfort by the time she arrived. She smiled when she saw a first-class compartment marked "reserved," but she made neither remark nor demur. She had left him to legislate for her and would not cavil at trifles. That she was happy for the moment there was no need to ask.

Many times that day when Rosmead looked at her dear face he registered a mighty vow that the man did not live who would be able to keep her from him. Drummond must take his defeat like a man. He was young, and there were others to choose from. In all his life Rosmead had not, until now, met a woman who could stir his pulses or make him long to lay his freedom at her feet as a thing for which he had no further use.

The train glided out of the station, and the sunshine was upon their faces and in their hearts. Rosmead, an accomplished traveller, had left nothing undone to secure the comfort of his fellow-traveller, but all his love and care were powerless to save her from the last bomb flung by fate.

She did not care for papers, she said, but she begged him to look at his, while she watched the swift retreat of London roofs before the speeding train.

He unfolded the pages of the "Daily Telegraph," and had Isla happened to glance round at the moment she must have discovered that something fresh and terrible had happened.

On the first page this paragraph confronted Rosmead's eyes under large head-lines:--

"TRAGEDY IN SCOTTISH HIGHLANDS.

"A sad occurrence took place yesterday on Loch Earn in Western Perthshire--one of those deplorable accidents which show what care should be taken in handling small boats on these treacherous inland seas. Full particulars are not to hand, but it seems that late last evening Mr. Malcolm Mackinnon of Achree and Glenogle, who had been in Lochearnhead earlier in the day, left there, ostensibly to go to his home at the Lodge of Creagh, four miles distant. That he had not done so was clearly evidenced by the fact that his body was found by a boatman, washed up on the shores of Loch Earn at a point about two miles from its head. The boat, bottom upwards, was floating near. The day had been one of the very stormiest of the season, with blinding showers and a squally wind. Mr. Mackinnon was a skilled oarsman, but it is supposed that he had been caught by one of the sudden squalls which so frequently rise on these Highland lochs and constitute a danger that it is necessary to guard against. It is not known why Mr. Mackinnon should have gone on the loch late in the afternoon, and he had no fishing gear with him. The occurrence has cast a gloom over the whole Glen, where the family are so well known and so beloved. The tragedy is accentuated by the fact that Mr. Mackinnon had only recently become engaged to Mrs. Rodney Payne, whose family are the present tenants of Achree. We understand that Mr. Mackinnon's only sister is at present abroad. Much sympathy is felt and expressed for her."

Rosmead, with the paper held high in front of him. stared steadily at it, his face very white and set, his lips twitching. It was a full minute before he obtained complete control of himself and dared to glance over the edge of the paper at his companion.

But she apparently had forgotten him. Her chin was resting on her hand, and her eyes were fixed upon the landscape, bathed in sunshine, which was speeding past them. She did not even look round when he carefully folded the paper and put it well under his travelling-rug in the tar corner of the rack. Then he lifted the "Times" and glanced through it, only to find on the second page the same item of intelligence considerably condensed. That also he removed, and took up one of the magazines.

He was totally unaware that he was holding it upside down. He had to find some way out of this awful difficulty--to coin words which would acquaint Isla with what seemed to be the final tragedy of her life. He was scarcely alive to the fact that he now learned for the first time of Mackinnon's engagement to Vivien, the letter informing him of it having only reached America the day after he had left it.

He had concern only for one at the moment, and his sole consideration was how to break the news to her. One moment he thought of giving her the newspaper casually, and thus getting over it; the next he thought he would keep it from her to the last moment. But they were speeding towards Glenogle, where the last act of Malcolm Mackinnon's tragic life had been played.

Presently Isla turned to him with a smile.

"It is very pleasant to be going home, don't you think? I was just counting how many weeks I had been out of Glenogle and thinking how glad I shall be to see it again. When I left it I never thought I should wish to come back any more."

"I am glad you feel like that," he said with an odd note of strain in his voice. "I have ordered the car to meet us at Stirling, so that we shall get home ahead of the train."

Her eyes sparkled with a child-like enjoyment.

"Oh, that will be delightful! I wrote to Malcolm yesterday. He will probably be waiting at Lochearnhead Station. I must wire to him at Crewe."

"I'll see to it," said Rosmead heavily, and his tongue felt as if it were cleaving to the roof of his mouth.

He took her to lunch, and she enjoyed it all, though it concerned her that he ate so little. She was not troubling herself that the other matter seemed to have disappeared into the background, and that he made not the smallest allusion to it. She was grateful to him for his consideration, but she was not surprised. From Peter Rosmead she would expect only the best. He would neither say nor do that which would vex the heart of a woman or increase by a hairsbreadth her perplexities.

Oh, she had made no mistake! she thought as she glanced confidently across at his grave, strong face, when she left him to act for her.

After carefully observing that the papers were out of the way, he got out at Crewe and made his way hastily to the telegraph office to send an explanatory message to his mother. By that time he had arrived at a quite clear estimate of what was in front and at a decision as to the right thing to do.

He would tell Isla after they were in the car, and prepare her as best he might for what she had to meet.

But he was spared the need. All his carefully concerted plan for saving her was rendered unavailing by the shrill tones of a newsboy's voice. The passing of the smallest coin of the realm in exchange for the first edition of an evening paper, and Rosmead got back to the compartment to discover that Isla knew the truth.

CHAPTER XXIX
THE LAST LEAF ON THE TREE

Once more the burying-place of the Mackinnons in Balquhidder kirkyard was opened to receive a Laird of Achree. While a small band of mourners stood by it in the soft spring sunshine Isla sat with her Aunt Jean in the library of the Lodge of Creagh, staring in front of her with a far-away expression on her face. Lady Mackinnon, who had not yet recovered from the effects of the hurried journey from Barras, was talking in subdued tones about the future. But Isla heard her as she heard her not.

"Of course you will just come to Barras, my dear, and we'll do our best. It is a very fortunate thing that the Rosmeads have Achree for another year and more. It will give us time to turn round. Don't look like that, Isla. It is all very terrible, of course, but it is not the end of everything."

At the moment there was a tap at the door, and Diarmid's grey head appeared, his lace looking old and worn, his eyes tired with weeping.

"Please, Miss Isla, it's a leddy. She will not go away, whatefer, and I have putten her in the little pack room till I ask whether you will see her."

"No, of course not. I will," said Lady Mackinnon, bustling up. "A lady! Don't you know her, Diarmid? Hasn't she given you a name?"

"No, my Leddy, I don't ken her. She's frem to Glenogle, and she says Miss Isla would not ken her name, forby."

Isla was already at the door.

"No, Aunt Jean. Thank you very much, but I must see her. I think I know who it is."

Rather disappointed--for anything would have served to break the dreary monotony of this awful house--Lady Mackinnon sank back into her chair, but a moment after, acting on a sudden impulse, she rose and swiftly drew up the blind. She then saw that a hired trap was waiting outside the gate, the man nodding on the box-seat, while the reins lay loosely across the horse's neck.

She knew nothing of the tragedy at the back of Malcolm's life, and, though it had been more than whispered in the Glen that there had been no accident on Loch Earn, but that Mackinnon had gone forth, meaning to take his own life in the way that seemed easiest and would occasion least remark, these rumours had not been permitted to reach Creagh.

But Isla, in her heart, had knowledge and confirmation of these things, though she had not heard of them.

How surprised, then, would Lady Mackinnon have been could she have heard what passed in the little room behind.

Isla entered quietly, closed the door, and faced the woman with whom she had already spoken twice and who, in some strange way, was mixed up with the tragedy of Malcolm's life and death.

"You're not surprised to see me, I can see," she said without preliminary. "Did you know I was in Scotland?"

"Yes," answered Isla clearly. "Please to sit down and tell me all that you wish to tell me and that it is necessary I should hear. But first, let me ask one question--Are you, were you, my brother's wife?"

She shook her head.

"I ought to have been, but I wasn't. That was the beginning and the end of the trouble. I waited for him so long, and he promised me faithful and true that if I would only wait quietly till he got out of his sea of troubles he would marry me."

"I understand," said Isla rather faintly. "Please say no more now, but tell me as quickly as you can what you know about it all."

Neither sat down. Isla stood by the table with her white, frail hand on the red baize of the tablecover, her shadowed eyes looking forth with a strange sad pity on the woman's face.

All her high colour had faded, her eyes were dimmed with weeping, she had forgotten to take a pride in her beautiful hair, she looked what she was--a dishevelled and broken creature on whom even a hard heart must needs have had compassion. And Isla's heart was not hard any more.

"Well, you see, Miss Mackinnon," she said, wiping her eyes with her sodden handkerchief, "you don't want to hear the whole story as to how we got to know each other in India and how fond he was of me and I of him. So I'll hurry on to where I met you first. I came to Scotland then, because he hadn't written to me for such a long time and because, when I learned that his father had died and that he had come into the property, I thought it was time I looked after myself. He spoke very fair then--explained how hard up he was and what a tangle everything was in, and he promised that if only I'd wait other six months he'd make everything straight and right. He told me all that right down by the water at Strathyre that night when he rode down from here to see me--the night before you and I met on the London train. Well, I went back to London, because he asked me to trust him a little longer. But I was not very easy in my mind. I kept quiet, living on my little bit of money and doing a bit of needlework and going out occasionally with a friend, but never forgetting that some day I was to be lady here and wife to the man I loved. Then I saw the thing in the paper--that he was going to marry the American woman, and I think that I went mad for a bit. I don't know quite where I was or what I did. I only know that I rose and went to Scotland straight to the hotel at Lochearnhead, and in the afternoon I walked up to Achree and asked for Mrs. Rodney Payne."

"Oh!" said Isla with a little gasp, and she pressed her hand to her heart.

"You feel for her. Perhaps she's a friend of yours, but it had to be done. You don't know what it is to see another woman get hold of the man you care for and who belongs to you. I like you, and I pray God you may never know what it's like. Well, I told her just the whole story--the story I haven't told you, though you're sharp enough and can fill it all up.

"What did she say?--not much, but I could see that it finished him in that quarter, which was all I cared about.

"Well, then I sent for him. When he came he had seen her. I could tell it by the white despair on his face, and then I knew that it was not her money he wanted at all, but that he cared about her as he had never cared about me, that she was his own kind--the sort that would lift him right up and make the best of him.

"Something seemed to snap inside of me. I believe it was my heart that broke. I didn't reproach him. He did all the reproaching--there, in the dark, by that God-forsaken loch. We seemed to walk for hours, and I don't know where we were when he left me. He said his life was over, but I never thought or believed he would take it away. To tell you the truth, Miss, I didn't believe he had the courage to do it."

"You think he did it, then?" said Isla in a low, tense whisper.

"I know it. He simply went out in that boat, never meaning to come back. You and I know it, but we needn't tell. And anyway, perhaps it's better; only I wish it had been me--I wish it had been me!"

Her voice broke into a little wail, and she covered her face with her hands. Isla went to her side and laid her hand, which trembled very much, on her shoulder.

"I am very sorry for you. If I knew how to help or comfort you I would."

She caught Isla's hand, laid her cheek a moment against it, and then began to walk unsteadily towards the door.

"You're a good woman--one of the best," she said, pausing a moment. "I hope you'll be happy yet. You'll never hear of me again. I'm going away to-night back to my own place. But I thought I'd like to see you before I went and tell you the truth. Good-bye."

But even after Isla's hand was on the door she lingered, as if something still remained unsaid.

"When you see her tell her that I loved him and that I could never have been so hard on him as she was. If he had really cared, tell her, she would have forgiven even me."

"Oh, hush!" cried Isla in distress. "You don't know all she has suffered. But it is no good to talk. Life is an awful thing. Thank you for coming. I shall often think of you, and, though I have no right, for I, too, have been hard, I'll--I'll pray for you."

A kiss passed between them, and they parted--never to meet again in this world.

Isla went through the house and out by the kitchen door to the hill beyond. She was so long gone that when she came back the Garrion carriage was at the door, and Sir Tom with Neil Drummond was in the drawing-room with her aunt.

Isla's face went a little white when she saw Neil, and she stood by the tea table with her back to him for a moment. Even Sir Tom's genial personality could not relieve the great strain. When Isla after a time, in response to a certain question in Drummond's eyes, left the room with him, Sir Tom turned eagerly to his wife.

"We must positively get away in the morning, Jean. Another day in this house would finish me. There seems to be a curse on Achree. Have you spoken to Isla, and is she going back with us?"

"I don't know. She hardly speaks at all, but of course she must go. There isn't anything else to do, and the sooner Neil Drummond follows her and we have a quiet wedding at Barras the better it will be. It is the only solution of the problem of Isla's life. I'm more tired of that problem than of anything else in this world, Tom."

He took a turn across the floor.

"The American chap was at the funeral. There's something uncommon taking about him. He and Drummond were talking together for a good half-hour after we had left the churchyard, and, judging from their faces, I'm sure it was some matter in which they had a life-and-death interest that they were talking about. Then Drummond, looking a little white about the gills, came up to me and said he was coming over to see Isla, and asked if I would drive with him."

"It was quite natural for him to come and see Isla, of course, and probably he was only discussing the situation with Mr. Rosmead. Neil will have to act for Isla now."

Lady Mackinnon had very little imagination, but Sir Tom was not easy in his mind.

Isla went out of doors with Neil Drummond, and they climbed up the slope to the edge of the Moor, and there they stood still. They were very near the house, but nobody could see them, and Isla waited--for what she did not know.

"I've seen Rosmead, Isla. I suppose the thing he has told me is true?"

"What did he tell you?"

"That you and he--that you and he care for each other."

"Yes, that is true. But I will keep my promise to you, Neil. A little suffering more or less--what does it matter? There is nothing else in the world."

He smiled a little hardly.

"I've cared a long time, and a lot, Isla. But I haven't sunk so low----" he made answer. "I give you back your freedom."

"But even if you do, it does not follow that I will marry him."

"If you care about him it is what you must do," he said quietly. "Tell me, Isla--Are you sure about this? If I thought there was any chance I wouldn't give you up. Are you sure?"

She was silent for a moment, her unfathomable eyes following the flight of a wild bird on the wing until it was lost in illimitable distance.

Neil Drummond had no great gifts. He was only a simple, honest soul who did his duty according to his lights, but in that moment he tasted to the full at once the anguish and the high joy of renunciation. Such clear understanding of a woman's heart came to him that for a moment he forgot the intolerable ache of his own.

Isla's gaze came back and fell upon his face as she answered simply, "I am sure. I would follow him to the end of the world without a question or a doubt, and I would not have a wish apart from his will. That is how I care, Neil. If I could feel like that for you I would give the best years of my life. I didn't seek this thing," she went on when he made no answer. "It came to me, and I think when it is like that we----we cannot help ourselves, Neil. It is part of the mystery of life. I am so tired with it all that I would wish to-day that I could lie down in Balquhidder beside them."

"Your life is only beginning," he said slowly and with difficulty. "I will say good-bye, and I will ask you to believe that there is nothing in the world I want so much as your happiness. You have had none, and, though I am not the man who can give it to you, I ask you to take it--and to take it soon--from the man who can."

Thus did Neil Drummond, a commonplace, everyday man such as we meet so often upon the highway, rise to the height of renunciation and prove himself a hero.

Isla's eyes swam in a strange tenderness as she turned to him, trying to thank him. But even while she would have spoken he had left her, and soon she heard the rumble of the wheels on the road--the wheels which took him back to Garrion--never more, in obedience to a lover's quest, to speed across the rough road to the Moor of Creagh.

After a time Isla went back very quietly and soberly to the house to astonish her relatives by another vagary.

"I am ready to go to Barras to-morrow, Aunt Jean, and to stop as long as you like."

"And will Neil come with us or after us, my dear?" asked Lady Mackinnon, her shrewd eyes lighting up cheerfully. "You know there is room and to spare in the house."

"No, Aunt Jean, Neil will not come. I am not going to marry him now-- nor any man," she answered.

And she sped away to make her preparations for the journey which, an hour before, she thought nothing on earth would induce her to undertake.

A strange peace seemed to brood that night upon the Lodge of Creagh and the Moor of Silence. Sleep was very far from Isla's eyes as she sat before her uncurtained window, looking out upon the limitless space on which the white moonlight lay.

The end of all things had come, so far as human judgment could determine. The last Mackinnon of Achree slept with his forefathers, and she, a poor weak woman of no account, was left to tie up the broken threads. Her thoughts of Malcolm were very tender, nor had she any misgiving, thinking of where he might be.

"It is better to fall into the hands of the living God than into the hands of men," she might have said, had she been called upon for an expression of her state of mind.

Upon her knees, with her chin upon the sill of the open window and her eyes upon the great silence where the moonlight lay, she asked to be forgiven for her hardness of heart, for her swift condemnation, for her poor, puny, disastrous efforts to set the world right. She knew now, in that moment of clear vision, that no man or woman is called to so great a task, but that what is asked of us all is merely and only the simple performance of each day's homely duty, by the doing of which, nevertheless, the whole fabric of human life and human achievement is ennobled and perfected.

With her chin resting upon the window-sill and her eyes, uplifted to the kindly, but impenetrable skies, Isla prayed. And then, leaving herself and her destiny for ever in the Hand which alone is capable of unravelling and setting in fair order human affairs, she crept to her bed to sleep off the overwhelming fatigue of the day.

Next morning there were many leave-takings in the Lodge of Creagh, and Diarmid and Margaret, whom the sorrows of their folk had drawn together in a touching unity, stood side by side on the step to watch Isla drive away with her uncle and aunt.

The young, small, frail woman, to whom their fealty was still due and who represented all that was left of the Glenogle Mackinnons, waved to them smilingly, bidding them be of good cheer until she should come back.

And when the last bend of the road was taken and the rumble of the departing wheels had died upon the air, the two old servants looked at each other a little pitifully, while tears rose in Margaret's eyes.

"She nefer will come pack, Diarmid, and you and me maype will grow old man and woman here in Creagh till they come to lay us in Balquhidder."

Diarmid answered never a word, but, later in the day, he delivered himself to Rosmead, who came on the swift feet of impatience to seek Isla.

"She hass gone away, sir, to Barras with Sir Thomas Mackinnon and his leddy, but whether it pe a long time or a short time afore she comes back I am not able to say."

"To Barras!" said Rosmead with musing in his eyes. "Tell me how she is, Diarmid. Did she seem sad?"

"Not so fery sad, considering sir," answered Diarmid, compelled, he knew not why, to lay bare his innermost thought to the man before him. "Me and Marget stood here, watchin' them, and she smiled as she went, and her face seemed to shine. But it iss a fery peetifu' thing, Maister Rosmead, for me and Marget to ken that soon the Mackinnons will be swept from the Glen, root and branch, and their fery name forgot."

"As long as she lives, Diarmid, that can never be," said Rosmead with the conviction of a man who knew. "Good-day, my man. Keep up your heart. There are new days coming for Achree and the name you love."

Before he turned away from the Lodge of Creagh, Rosmead climbed to the edge of the Moor of Silence and stood still for a moment on the very spot, though he knew it not, where Isla had stood with Neil Drummond but yesterday.

From where he stood he commanded a vast view, the Moor behind and beyond, and the winding road down Glenogle, with all the little hills huddling on its flanks, and widening out to the glory of Loch Earn.

Achree he could not see, but his eyes, as they ranged towards it, were filled with that vast tenderness which proclaims that the deeps of being are stirred.

Isla had gone away without message or sign, but that neither grieved nor troubled him. Some day, from out the silence, the sign would come, or he would himself know the day and the hour of her need of him.

And as he turned, with the westering light upon his face, he made his vow that if God should give him a son, Donald Rosmead Mackinnon he should be called, so that the name should not die for ever out of Glenogle and the Moor of Silence.